S.W. YOCHEM

SIMIAN CAUCUS

A NOVEL

"THE MEEK SHALL SAVE THE EARTH"

SIMIAN CAUCUS

"The Meek Shall Save the Earth"

Copyright ©2011 S.W. Yochem

All Rights Reserved

ISBN-13: 978-1466441637

www.simiancaucus.com

HEPHAESTUS PRESS

For Kimberly Mortimer

****

Special Thanks to

Donald Roller Wilson
&
Patricia Altschul

SIMIAN CAUCUS

Chapter 1

June 14, 1989

Mrs. Celine B. Stertevant
c/o Addison, Metz and Diehl
34 West Mesa, Suite Four
Santa Barbara, CA 93102

Dear Mrs. Stertevant,

My name is Roger Caldwell and I live in Santa Barbara near your beautiful estate, Glenwhylden.

I was born and raised here. When I was little my parents would take me to the beach. From there I could see the trees and gardens of Glenwhylden on the hill above. My Dad said there was a mansion at the top, but the owner didn't live there and hadn't even visited for decades. That made me very curious.

I grew up watching your gardens change each season. A few years ago the big cypress tree by the gate blew down in a storm. I was sad, that tree was like an old friend. I rode my bike under it every day going to school.

Well, twenty years later I'm still curious about your house. I checked at the county clerk and got your name and the law firm that represents you here. I called your attorney, Phil Holmbard, to ask if I could be allowed to see the house. He said there's a strict policy of no visitors, but promised to forward this letter anyway.

Mrs. Stertevant, would you please make an exception for me? Just a quick look would be wonderful. I won't tell anyone.

Mr. Holmbard has my address and phone number in case you might grant my request. I thank you most sincerely.

Yours Very Truly,
Roger V. Caldwell

****

True, Roger did have a lifelong fascination with Celine Stertevant's mansion. Yes, he did very much want to visit the place he'd been curious about for so long. But lately there was a new twist. He wanted more than just a peek inside the big old house. Somewhere among the Eden-like gardens, or perhaps standing right on Glenwhylden's grand front steps, he would blow his brains out.

****

"Roger, you're too serious!" Franz Eichthaller gently chided him.

"Guess I'm thinking too much again, boss."

"Well, you should smile more, my boy. You always look worried. Why don't you go see a funny movie or something?"

Eichthaller's shop was nationally famous for restoring vintage Porsches and Mercedes, with an atmosphere more like a club than a garage. As one of Franz's best mechanics, Roger earned good money for his meticulous craftsmanship. His clients were mostly rich, middle-aged men whose devotion to German go-carts verged on religious zealotry. These "car guys" respected their mechanics and didn't nitpick over costs. It made for reasonably low-stress work.

Roger rented a Montecito cottage, the former pool house for a mansion. It was completely private from the main residence, a true bachelor's pad. For lowered rent, he maintained the pool. No one else used it anyway; the elderly owners wouldn't be caught dead in a bathing suit. There were other nice things: the best stereo gear, a big-screen television. He drove a 1988 Porsche Carrera cabriolet, dialed-in all the way. Silver hand-rubbed lacquer with saddle-tan leather and a navy blue top. It was bedraggled when he scored it dirt-cheap at an insurance company auction of recovered stolen vehicles, but over about a year he brought it back to magnificence in every detail. He tweaked the engine and suspension, making it far faster and better-handling than a stock model.

He had a girlfriend, too, Gwynn. She was the blonde head-turner in the thong bikini at the beach volleyball courts. Ditzy, but a lot of fun. In all, just about anyone would view Roger's life as desirable.

Yet lately the poolside pad, perfect car, and even the bombshell babe were bringing him scant joy. A series of personal tragedies had begun about three years earlier; cruel blows, each more crushing than the one before. And now something had happened that promised to be unbearable.

Roger was soft spoken and personable. Not a movie star but not bad looking either. Six feet tall, broad shouldered, with sandy brown hair and grey eyes. As an only child, he was raised by older parents in modest but comfortable surroundings: a spacious apartment in suburban Santa Barbara. His father was a C.P.A., his mother a school nurse.

"You should be a doctor, son," she persuaded him early on. "They're respected, and there's financial security there, Roger. But the best part is that doctors truly help people. They save lives. What's better than that?"

In pre-med at UCLA, Roger played intramural volleyball and read avidly. He worked hard at his studies and was near the top of his class. Unlike most college students, he drank very little and never experimented with drugs. His goal was to become a heart surgeon, a cardiothoracic specialist. He joined a fraternity where his circle of friends included the sons of wealthy families, young men whose comfortable futures seemed assured. Visiting their homes he saw the very different lives they led. "I'll be like them," he thought. "I'll strive, I'll achieve. I'm meant for something important, I know it."

Home for a fall weekend during his senior year, he found his father wearing glasses. He'd never needed them before. "They're not reading glasses," the older man responded soberly to his son's kidding.

The reality was chilling. He'd been diagnosed with Retinitis Pigmentosa, a rare form called Usher's Syndrome. Usually it struck much younger people, but for some unknown reason his father had fallen victim to the disease later in life. His sight and hearing would both be drastically affected. The doctors were blunt; the affliction was progressive and incurable. He would be completely blind and stone-deaf within two years.

Early the next spring, just as Roger was leaving his apartment for class, the phone rang. It took a moment to recognize his father's anguished voice. "I'm at the hospital, son," came the sobbing. "Mom's gone, Roger. Oh God, we've...we've lost her. She was out in the kitchen fixing breakfast. I smelled the oatmeal burning." It was a massive stroke.

During Roger's commencement ceremonies in May, the pale father sat like a bespectacled mannequin in the audience. He'd fallen into a deep hole when he lost his beloved wife, and with his vision and hearing rapidly ebbing, he couldn't climb out of it. His weight dropped and he was on medication for depression. Only sixty, he looked every day of eighty.

After the graduation, they went to lunch, not talking much, both keenly feeling the absence.

Finally, with dessert on the table his father blurted: "You're my son and I'll always love you, Roger. I wish there was something more I could do for you." Magnified by thick lenses, his enormous watery eyes searched the son's startled face. "I wish there was *something*."

Two days later the despondent man hiked alone to an overlook above Santa Barbara. With the sun sinking into the ocean he opened his backpack and placed a framed family portrait on a flat rock, arranging some flowers and a votary candle before it. After carefully pocketing his glasses and hearing aids, he leaned close, then squeezed the trigger of a compact revolver he'd recently purchased.

The note left at the apartment reflected his despair: "Son, I pray that you will understand. I just can't keep going," it said. "It's like I'm already in a coffin and the lid slides shut another inch every day. I see only darkness and silence coming, and without your mother beside me I'm not strong enough for it. This way I won't be a burden to you. It might not seem like it at first, but it's better that I do this. Please forgive me, Roger."

There was a little money put aside, and some furniture and a worn Pontiac to sell. But there were also funeral expenses and other debts. When it was all over and the apartment was cleaned out, there wasn't much left. Even Roger's happy memories of growing up seemed all but lost.

He tried to make a fresh start; he knew he had to. If he was going to attend medical school, he'd have to raise substantial funds. With no one to co-sign, he couldn't qualify for student loans. So he asked a mechanic friend if there was anything available part-time at the shop. Franz Eichthaller hired Roger to clean parts and rebuild carburetors, but he learned other skills quickly. Soon he was a restoration mechanic making top wages. He kept putting off starting medical school, thinking to save enough so he wouldn't have to work and handle a grueling class schedule at the same time. He expected to return to his studies within a year.

And for awhile he was doing fine, really. Restoring cars, saving money, planning for the day when he'd be a successful surgeon. In his off time he hung out with Gwynn, playing volleyball on the beach. It wouldn't be long now, he told himself. The pain was behind him and soon he'd have a whole new life.

Then, he began having trouble focusing on the small parts he was assembling. It seemed that people were mumbling. A battery of tests at the doctor's office confirmed his worst fears. He, too, had Usher's Syndrome; it was hereditary. He was told to expect it to progress rapidly.

On the afternoon he was diagnosed, a light rain was swirling out of a chilly overcast. For awhile Roger sat in his car in the clinic parking lot, watching the drops roll off the windshield. It slammed into him like a rock-slide; blind and deaf, he'd never be a surgeon. What could he be? In a short time, maybe a year or two, he wouldn't be able to watch the raindrops, admire a pretty girl, hear the breeze or music, or even receive the kindness of another human voice. All that would be gone forever.

Numb, he drove to the cemetery. On the wet grass by his parents' graves he sank to his knees and wept bitterly, cursing God, cursing the Devil, cursing whoever else called the order of things. He swore against whatever had brought such disappointment and suffering into his life, when all the while he had strived for nothing but good. As the rain pelted harder, he hugged himself, wishing with all his soul that it could be his mother's arms around him, or his father's. But he had only himself; there was no one, nothing at all to give him any comfort. The whole world seemed as cold as the water-streaked tombstones surrounding him.

When his father committed suicide, Roger's first reaction was anger. It was hard to forgive the man for taking his own life, knowing that he had a son who loved him so much; a son who would be left all alone. But now, with the same specter of silent darkness looming, Roger could understand why he did it. His father had chosen to watch one final sunset and go out on his own terms, before the rest of the world was beyond reach.

Roger kept the pistol his father used. The police had returned it to him after the investigation. He meant to get rid of it, the evil object; smash it with a hammer, throw the pieces off the end of the harbor pier. But it was the last thing his father held in his living hands, so Roger delayed parting with it. It was stuffed into an old sock at the bottom of a drawer.

Now, shivering in the rain-soaked cemetery, he remembered the revolver, seeing it might be of use again. Then he thought of the most beautiful place he knew: the magical estate above the sea that had fostered his childhood daydreams.

There, he resolved. There.

Chapter 2

Glenwhylden is a 35 acre estate covered with exotic trees, fountains and manicured lawns, set on one of the most beautiful promontories on the west coast of the United States. Its existence is well known, but the place has always been cloaked in secrecy, and there are numerous mythical tales about it. The truth outstrips all the gossip.

Approaching from the south on the Ventura freeway, you're whizzing along, glad to be out of the choking smog and traffic of Los Angeles. Just as you enter Santa Barbara, take the exit marked "Beaches".

Now you're on a curving boulevard running toward the ocean. And as you round the bend, suddenly there it is: a long, high wall, a sharply rising hillside beyond, the slope covered with brilliant flowers and curious-looking shrubs you've never seen before.

Massive sandstone pillars and bronze gates front on the street. Your eyes trace the winding brick driveway as it switchbacks upward. Near the top, the towering trees begin, and the driveway disappears into a dark forest that cloisters the crown of the hill.

Some of the smaller structures on the property are partially visible from the road: a gardener's residence, a cedar barn. But the main house, situated over the crest of the hill facing the ocean, is completely invisible from the boulevard below. In fact, there is only one way to get a decent view of the sprawling, monolithic mansion: get in a boat and go out around the point, to a position about a quarter-mile from the beach.

From there you'll see sandstone cliffs rearing forbiddingly from a narrow beach, making a sheer rise of a hundred feet. About ten feet from the top, a course of barbed-wire protrudes out, fending off adventurous climbers. At the cliff-top, a row of hedges gives way to a sloping expanse of lawn. And beyond, commanding it all, the majestic residence: Glenwhylden House.

When viewed on a bright morning with sunlight glowing on the pale grey granite façades, protective towers of cypress and redwood trees looming on each flank, and the ramparts of green mountains behind, Glenwhylden House bespeaks the most inspired application of great wealth and power.

It owes its existence to one man's desire to please and impress his new bride. Glenwhylden was conceived, planned and constructed in the flush of passion, and it is possibly this element, this single quality more than any other, that confers its majesty and magnetism.

Charles Barton Stertevant created Glenwhylden as a surprise honeymoon gift for his beloved. Shrewdness and hard work had provided him the wealth to give his imagination complete freedom in fulfilling his vision.

Stertevant was born in St. Louis, Missouri in 1883. His father was a prosperous lumber broker well-connected with the major railroad companies. The railroads were splendid customers, engaged in vigorous expansion at the time. Charles was given the privilege of a good education, earning a degree in civil engineering from Purdue. After university he returned to St. Louis to begin work with his father's firm. Although his college career had been less than stellar, he succeeded in his studies by sheer determination, putting in the long hours necessary to see a task completed by the deadline. He learned that opportunity appeared more often when one actively sought it. And, he made friends easily; writing letters, keeping in touch, and doing a favor whenever he could. Charles' personal touch brought great returns. Soon he was a partner in tin mining operations outside his family's business. Then, he built his own tin-can manufacturing plant in Columbus, Ohio. A contract with the U.S. Army put him in the big leagues.

To mark his 37th birthday, he planned a small party at the Plaza Hotel in New York. His parents and sister rode the train out from St. Louis. The evening would begin with an opulent supper, followed by a Broadway show. It was Monday, May 17, 1920, and aside from his birthday, Charles had much to celebrate. The mining and can manufacturing businesses were booming. He now maintained homes in both St. Louis and Columbus, and was considered a pillar of both communities. With his success he had shouldered philanthropic duties, funding the expansion of hospitals, libraries and churches.

Yet in order to accomplish all this he'd devoted every available moment to business, leaving his love-life arrantly featureless. In the process of all of the material accumulation, there had not been time to search for a life's partner. He was married to his work, period. The whisper at society parties was that he was impotent or even asexual.

On this warm spring evening in New York City, Charles left his suite on the twelfth floor of the Plaza to join his family in the hotel dining room. He stepped into the elevator and the car began its descent, but paused to answer the buzzer at the tenth floor. The doors parted to reveal a striking young woman.

Without raising her eyes, she entered the car and turned to face forward, whispering to the attendant, "Lobby, please." As the doors closed, Charles became aware that she was wearing the most wonderful perfume. She was also weeping discreetly. This, along with her tall slender frame, strawberry-blond hair, and the trembling of her small hand as she touched a handkerchief to her eyes, caused the normally staid Charles Stertevant to become overwhelmed by feelings and sensations such as he had never before experienced. He vaulted beyond his normal reserve.

"Pardon me, Miss, I don't mean to intrude, but may I be of some assistance?"

She dabbed quickly, embarrassed. "Oh, no thank you, sir. You're most kind."

Yet she could not stop the tears.

"Oh, I *do* beg you to allow me...I am Charles Stertevant, of St. Louis."

There was a brave smile. "I am Celine Bell, from Old Lyme."

"Miss Bell." He grasped her delicate hand. "Truly, you appear so distressed. I would do anything at all."

As they arrived at the lobby, his earnestness must have been clear. Miss Bell was in town for some shopping and to attend the theater. She had been expecting her mother to arrive and join her within the hour.

"But she's just called, you see. Our Cairn terrier, Herkel, has died. He was mother's favorite. And mine." Her beautiful eyes filled once again. "So now mother's not coming, and I must return home in the morning on the early train. I'm going to the desk for my ticket."

Charles could not take his gaze off the young Miss Bell. Such a noble face, with an upturned nose, cornflower-blue eyes, and a spangle of freckles across her high cheekbones. He feared his pounding heart could be heard even above the din of the lobby.

"Now please, see here, Miss Bell," he declared. "It's my birthday, and my family's here to celebrate. It will all be spoiled if you won't join us. Please let us take care of you. I just can't bear to think of you sitting alone up in your room. I'm certain we can cheer you up a little." His mother also loved animals, he told her.

After much protesting that she would be intruding, she finally accepted. The evening was a smashing success. Charles later told friends that he'd been in love from the moment the elevator doors opened on the tenth floor.

Born on New Year's Day, 1900, Celine was twenty when she met Charles. Her father, Gerhardt Bell, was a Swiss immigrant who'd invented a process revolutionizing the mass-production of window glass. He married a great beauty, and they produced two girls. By the time she was twenty, Celine had graduated from Brown and was contemplating which of several suitors should be offered more encouragement. To say the least, she was much in demand socially. Celine's sister, Margrethe, four years her senior, was devoted to the world of art. The contented family lived quietly on the coast in Old Lyme.

Charles courted Celine for fourteen months. During that time, he often cleared his business schedule to repair to Connecticut or New York, and spared no effort or expense in holding her attention. He dreamed up extravagant outings, such as a secluded picnic in the countryside mysteriously intercepted by a twenty piece orchestra playing waltzes as the couple had a basket lunch. They attended tennis matches, the opera, went sailing, and took leisurely horseback rides. With relentless frequency, gifts of flowers and fancy trinkets were delivered to the Bell house.

Charles was up to something else as he pursued Celine. Despite the age difference and several formidable rivals, he knew in his heart that this Connecticut girl was going to be his wife. And so he began the construction of a dream house, a honeymoon cottage.

Years earlier he'd gone out to Santa Barbara for a few days of ocean sport-fishing in the company of two business acquaintances. From their hired boat, Charles spotted a strategic prominence of land just south of the town. There was a Victorian home near the top of the property, but the rest of the surrounding acreage was undeveloped. The fishing guide said one family had owned the thirty-some acres for as long as he could remember. There was just a widow now, with a grown daughter living elsewhere. Thinking it a good investment opportunity, Charles had his attorney draft a letter to the widow asking if she might be interested in selling the place. After some negotiation, Charles purchased the house and 35 acres for 129 thousand dollars. He would build a sea-front hotel or perhaps a country club there, then turn the whole thing over for a handsome profit. He'd done the same thing before, with a lakeshore property near Chicago.

But then he met Celine, and it came to him: a more personally significant destiny for the Santa Barbara land. After knowing her for only a matter of weeks, he began planning a monumental residence. A mansion and gardens to outshine all others in the already estate-glutted community where it would rise. He interviewed the star architects of the day and selected one whose portfolio included Berkshire lodges and Manhattan banks.

As a model, he used an imposing seaside palace in Newport, Rhode Island; a house for which Celine had several times professed admiration. It was a solid and boxy edifice, with straight forward lines, a copper roof, and large windows facing the ocean. This template was refined, updated, and enlarged, resulting in plans for a two-story, ten bedroom, eleven bathroom, twenty-three thousand square foot manor house. There would be a swimming pool, tennis court, riding stables, three separate guest residences, servants' quarters and a Victorian greenhouse with a marble fountain. All this would be set amid acres of lawns, formal gardens, imported exotic trees, statuary, and meandering pathways leading to the estate's woodlands and ocean-side cliffs. Charles spent endless hours going over each detail and specification.

For the construction, he used his own chief engineer from the mining companies. The foundations and supporting structure would be of massive and perdurable design. Riveted steel I-beams were mounted on piers set fifty feet into bedrock. This was to be a house that would regard a major earthquake with mild amusement. An army of German carpenters and Italian stonemasons were imported to apply their skills.

The project bounded forward. Superb grey-flecked granite from Vermont was shipped in by rail: a dozen carloads. This was used to sheath the outer walls and build gutters for the driveways. Rare and special woods: Brazilian rosewood, African mahogany, Indian sandalwood, hickory from Virginia, clear Douglas fir from Washington, Sitka spruce from Alaska, aromatic cedar from Oregon, cypress from Louisiana, even teak from the rainforest of Borneo—all began arriving at the rail yard in Santa Barbara. Sculptors and finish carpenters were put to the task of carving elaborate fixtures, staircase railings and moldings. Intricate parquet flooring paved the hallways and large rooms. Not a door in the house was less than nine feet tall, every one of solid hardwood, carved and hand finished. All the hardware was custom-forged heavy bronze, made in Switzerland.

Outside, gardeners and laborers transformed the rough hillsides into an exotic paradise. Fully grown specimen trees were trucked in and carefully situated, forming miniature forests. Ponds were dug and stocked with Japanese carp, acres of sod were laid and rolled to perfection, rows of rosebushes and flower beds established, and vegetable and herb gardens were placed near the kitchen.

The garage was outfitted with a Packard limousine and a pastel yellow Duesenberg roadster with green leather seats.

Charles supervised this entire project from his offices in St. Louis. He conferred by telephone with the architect, and only once journeyed out to the coast during the construction. He had the buildings and grounds finished, the house furnished, and permanent staff in place, all inside of eleven months. This palace, his "honeymoon cottage", was fully completed two months before he even proposed to Celine Bell. The total cost approached ten million dollars, which in 1921 was a staggering fortune. But for Charles Stertevant it was justifiable. He was convinced that nothing less than the full realization of his vision was suitable for his beloved.

The architect asked Charles what name he would give to this magical place. Nothing jumped to mind—until just a few weeks before construction wrapped up. Charles was reading a magazine article about travel in Scotland. There was a picture of a romantic ancient castle, situated on the remote northern coast. It had withstood centuries of violent winter gales. Legend held that it was built by a feudal lord who won the love of a girl from a clan at war with his own. The castle was erected to protect his new bride from her own family. The place had an enchanting appellation: "Glenwhylden." Charles decided this was the perfect name for his own romantic castle-by-the-sea.

On the Fourth of July, 1921, he was a houseguest at the Bell estate in Old Lyme. The family had grown fond of him during his courtship with their daughter, and invited him to join their traditional festivities. It was a fun day, with the whole group going into the village to watch the parade, hear patriotic speeches and attend a Marine band concert in the park. Later that afternoon, Gerhardt Bell took Charles for a sail on his small sloop, "Caspian". While the two men were alone on the boat, Charles brought up an important and imminent decision.

As dusk fell, chairs were set up on the lawn near the beach in order to view the lavish fireworks display that was jointly sponsored each year by the most prominent beachfront landowners. Anchored a quarter mile offshore was a barge bearing the rocket mortars and the man who would set them off. Down at the public beach a short distance away, dozens of families from the village spread their blankets and settled back to watch the show.

The first rockets began to bolt skyward, and Charles asked Celine if she'd like to stroll down to the water's edge to get a better view. The ocean was calm as a lake, smooth water mirroring the spectacular pyrotechnics showering colors across the heavens. The couple found a seat on a driftwood log and gazed upward at the riotous hues for a few minutes. Then he dropped to one knee by her side.

"Celine, dear," he began slowly, "tonight I am compelled to ask your help in a matter of the greatest importance. I'm afraid this is something that just can't wait."

She drew a sharp breath and leaned toward him. "Charles, darling? What's wrong?"

"Celine, living the rest of my life without you by my side would be unbearable. So if you refuse to marry me, I'll destroy myself. Could you see your way clear to help me out of this mess?" With that, he placed a small box in her hands.

Those hands trembled a little, just as they had when she was clutching her handkerchief the first time they met. She opened the box, and in the flashing illumination of the fireworks saw an exquisite marquis diamond ring.

"Oh my heavens!" She fumbled to place it on her finger, finally succeeding. She grinned. "I'll do my best to assist you."

As the explosions overhead reached a crescendo, they kissed passionately, then succumbed to a terrible case of the giggles. Relieved and happy that the moment had passed and had turned out the way they both very much wanted, they walked back up the lawn to give the news to the rest of the family. Celine was surprised to see two magnums of champagne (having been hoarded in flagrant violation of Prohibition) already brought out in anticipation of the announcement. On board "Caspian" that afternoon, Charles had sought Gerhardt Bell's permission to ask for his daughter's hand in marriage. The father had let this news slip to the rest of the family during the fireworks display.

They were married on September 25, 1921, in a small Episcopal church near the Bell home. Despite the wealth in both families, the wedding was simple and small in scale. Celine wanted it that way, even though this had created battles with her mother as well as her future mother-in-law, both of whom had envisioned something much grander. But the bride prevailed. The chapel was decorated with gardenias and simple white ribbons.

On the other hand, the reception, held at the Bell estate, had been given over to the mothers to devise, and they had made up for their frustrations about the ceremony by laying it on thick at the party. Charles and his bride then set off for a two week stay at the Potter Hotel in Santa Barbara. Charles had successfully kept Glenwhylden completely secret. This had been a huge challenge, but he was determined that the surprise for Celine should be absolute.

They arrived in Santa Barbara, and checked into the hotel. The next day Charles suggested a morning of fishing. He hired a boat and guide, and directed that they be taken to a spot offshore from the prominent point of land just south of town. Once there, the anchor was dropped and hooks baited.

The boat swung around on the current, affording a spectacular dead-on view of the shining new Glenwhylden, haloed by the morning sun and grandly crowning the crest of the hill.

Charles did not have to wait long. Celine began to exclaim about the beauty of "that gorgeous house up there..." He cast his line into the water as his wife went on about how it reminded her of "that lovely old place in Newport, doesn't it, Charles darling?"

He allowed as how it did, and then agreeably wondered if they should someday have a little getaway cottage somewhere in Santa Barbara, it being such a lovely place and all. They remained at anchor in that spot for two hours, and were lucky with the fishing, hauling in a halibut and two sea bass between them. The entire time, Celine scarcely looked away from Glenwhylden. When she asked the guide about it, he professed ignorance, forewarned by Charles to keep his mouth shut.

That evening as they dressed for dinner, Charles announced that they had received an unexpected invitation from some local acquaintances he'd met on a previous visit. "They're charming people with a beautiful home," he said. "Would you like to stop by there, before dinner?"

"Why not?" she smiled, fixing her earring. "It sounds like fun."

He called down to the desk for their car, and off they went.

The darkening sky grew painted as their limousine pulled up to the bronze gates of Glenwhylden. An attendant waved them through and they drove ahead, the car tires humming pleasantly over the brick surface of the climbing driveway. They entered a circular motor-court and came to a stop at wide steps rising to the twelve-foot tall carved mahogany front door. A uniformed butler answered the knocker, and as they stepped into the front hall, Charles heard Celine gasp.

Hundreds of candles were alight and the grand hall was shimmering with their glow. The butler's heels clicked on the polished parquet floors as he led them to the immense main drawing room, with its lofty bank of windows facing the west lawn affording a magnificent view of the fading orange and purple sunset over the ocean. This room, too, was filled with glowing candles and fragrant flowers. They were seated on a couch facing the windows, and the butler turned to withdraw.

Celine leaned toward Charles and whispered, "Charles, isn't this the house we saw from the boat today? Isn't it? Why, this is the most lovely place I've ever..."

The butler interrupted her from the doorway.

"Allow me to be the first to welcome you home, Mr. and Mrs. Stertevant."

Celine turned. "Thank you," she said sweetly. She paused, watching him exit. Then, a look of puzzlement forming, she turned back to her husband, who now wore a maniacal grin. Suspicion growing, she eyed him, knowing his love of practical jokes. "Charles...what are you up to? Why did he just say 'Welcome *home*, Mr. and Mrs. Stertevant'?"

Charles could contain himself no longer. He leaped off the couch and strode to the bank of windows, chortling with satisfaction. With a sweep of his arm, he gestured at the sunset.

"Just look at that view, would you, Celine?" he bellowed as if addressing a large audience. "How about *that*? Is that something a person could get used to?" He was visibly wound up, dancing around, eyes like jumping beans.

Alarmed, she stood up to go over to him. "Charles, *please*..." she said in an urgent whisper, "you'll embarrass us in front of our hosts!" She shot a glance toward the door, fearful of seeing some dowdy couple standing there, witnessing Charles' inexplicable fit.

He took her hands. "My dear, I'd give you the moon, if only I could get it. Since I couldn't, I've had to settle for this place."

For a long moment she stared blankly, then a look of pure astonishment spread across her face. Her mouth opened and closed and silently opened again. Finally, she found her voice: "Charles, now—you mustn't...you can't be serious."

He began to waltz her around the room. "Ah, but I am, dear bride! This house is yours, all yours, my dear! I built it all just for you, just for you my darling Celine!"

The rest of the evening—the next few days for that matter—were delirium. She was overwhelmed. As far as Celine was concerned, Charles hadn't made a false move in his choices for the house. She loved every inch of it, every detail, and she made him repeat over and over the story of how he had done it all, the whole time managing to keep it a secret.

"And what if I'd refused your offer of marriage? Then what?"

"Then I'd have kept at it forever, my darling."

She wandered through each room, discovering all the little things, soaking it up. They took walks hand-in-hand through the gardens and woodlands, and some mornings they rose early to go down to the beach to dip in the ocean and watch the sunrise.

The beauty of Glenwhylden, its grandeur, and the magnitude of Charles' devotion to her in order to bring it into being—all stayed strongly in Celine's mind during the two weeks they spent there. That he would build such a palace before he had any real assurance that she would marry him was a true and tangible demonstration of his love. And in this perfect place, she was getting to know him better each day. There were facets to his character that were hidden during the formality of their courtship. Although he was conservative and restrained in most social or business situations, now he showed a more childlike and playful side. During their engagement, she worried that the span between their ages would result in problems communicating or sharing on the same level. During the honeymoon at Glenwhylden, it became clear that this would not be the case. He was becoming her best friend, and she found him approachable and understanding. He seemed genuinely receptive and interested. Spiritually, they had far more in common than she had ever hoped. And despite his reputation for inexperience—and much to her girlish delight—he was proving to be a passionate lover. She now began to be completely comfortable and settled with the idea that she would spend the rest of her life with Charles Stertevant, and they would raise a family together.

Charles golfed a bit, and told Celine of his desire to join a particular country club near the estate. Several of his local business contacts were members there, and they had invited him for a morning round. Celine wanted to do some shopping in town. So on the final morning of their stay in Santa Barbara, they decided to pursue these separate activities and then meet back at Glenwhylden for a late lunch.

As she stepped into the limousine at the front door, he leaned in and kissed her, joking, "Don't overdo it, dear. I've got this house to pay for, you know." The car pulled out of the motor-court, and she looked out the back window to see her smiling husband standing on the grand front steps waving at her. She started to wave back, but just then the car began its descent down the hill and she lost sight of him.

Charles took the Duesenberg over to the golf club, and spent an enjoyable morning on the links. His sponsors were companionable, and he was told to expect no trouble being accepted into membership. This particular morning his game had never been better, and there just seemed to be something about the course that suited him most agreeably. He felt on top of the world. He shared these thoughts with his friends: his joy in his young bride, the pleasure he was deriving from the new house, and his optimism for his businesses in the years to come. The day was spectacular, sunny, with just a little breeze out of the west. His drives were sailing long and straight, his approaching shots were landing right on target, his putts were true. For Charles Barton Stertevant, multimillionaire, newlywed, and lord of the finest manor in a town famous for its fine estates, life at this moment was indeed splendid.

In the dress department at Delmonts, Celine was perusing some of the fall offerings from Paris. She wanted several nice little somethings, with matching hats and shoes, to wear on the train back to St. Louis. Like her husband, she was feeling exceedingly fine. All the girls at the shop had clustered around to admire her engagement and wedding rings, and when she let it slip that she was attached to the new estate on the point, they had gone into orbit. They catered to her, bringing her this frock and that skirt, anxiously soliciting her opinion. She felt like she was a real princess, floating on a little cloud of her own, buoyed up by Charles' love. As the procession of garments passed before her, she scarcely paid attention, dreamily imagining the beautiful children she would have.

By now Charles was standing alongside the tee of the ninth hole, watching the other three men make their drives. He then teed up his own ball and surveyed the short, downhill par three. The green sat near the clubhouse in clear view of the terrace, which was now filling up with its coterie of members beginning the luncheon hour. His caddie recommended a number-two wood. Settling in his stance, he took a nice easy backswing and brought the club down through a perfect, natural arc. It connected with a satisfying whack, and the ball sailed up, out, and right toward the flagstick. Coming to ground on the edge of the green, it rolled purposefully across the manicured surface and plopped into the cup. A hole-in-one, his first ever.

The ninth was a spectator hole at this club; the tee, fairway and green could all be seen from the grill-room's terrace. Members dining alfresco gave much attention to the succession of shots being played out before them. At the moment of Charles' hole-in-one, there was a near full-house, and a loud cheer and applause erupted. Charles was so dumbfounded that he dropped his club. His companions began slapping him on the back, crowing. After handshakes all around, the group walked down the fairway and a joking suggestion was made that, in view of his current run of luck, Charles might do well to consider running for the club presidency during his first year of membership. The others chipped onto the green, then Charles stepped up to retrieve his trophy ball. He triumphantly thrust it over his head as the terrace once again broke into vigorous applause.

He turned to his group and grinned. "Well boys, that's it. I've got it all now!"

On the nearby tenth tee, stalwart club member Selmer "Mack" McArdle was preparing to tee off on the back nine. He was a large man, powerfully built, with a well-developed belly. This obstacle interfered with his follow-through. Annoyed by the nearby applause, he proceeded with his drive regardless, whereupon he launched off a mighty slice. His ball veered sharply toward the ninth green and impacted with devastating force on the left temple of Charles Barton Stertevant, still with golf ball held high.

As Dr. Dewayne Batchelder (who rushed down from the dining terrace) would later recount: "Charles Stertevant was dead before he even hit the ground."

Chapter 3

Roger hadn't forgotten about his letter to Celine Stertevant, but he'd just about abandoned hope of ever hearing anything back. It had been a long time—almost a month. He figured the mega-rich woman on the east coast had no time for some fringe-type in Santa Barbara with a hang-up about her house. What would you do, he asked himself. Would you reply to someone like that?

Anyway, it didn't matter. He was now planning to go over the wall instead of through the main gate. Maybe he'd even have to do it at night; that wasn't exactly what he wanted, but one way or another he was going to make good on his scheme to die at Glenwhylden. If he was going to shoot himself, he wanted to do it in a beautiful, majestic, exclusive place. It was a final choice no one was going to deny him.

After a long day at work, he wheeled up his driveway thinking about a six-pack of Coors in the refrigerator. He paused to empty the mailbox, and there it was: a cream-colored, fine stationery envelope. Adjusting his glasses, he read the Connecticut return address engraved on the back flap. With a shock, he realized who it was from. He decided to go inside, sit down with a beer, and ceremoniously open the letter.

July 10, 1989
Mr. Roger V. Caldwell
713 "B", Friar's Cross Road
Santa Barbara, California 93121

Dear Mr. Caldwell,

Thank you for writing to express your interest in Glenwhylden. I read your letter with engagement, and found your recollections and feelings about the property to be very touching. While we receive many inquiries about the estate each year, on advice of our attorneys we do not make the house available for visits or other uses.

Mr. Caldwell, you seem to have an unusual attraction for the house and you express yourself well. Would you like to have a chat sometime? Perhaps I could tell you some things about the house that you do not already know.

I have asked Phil Holmbard to contact you to see if we might arrange a visit, if convenient. Thank you again for your lovely letter.

Sincerely,
Mrs. C.B. Stertevant

Roger snorted, feeling sharp disappointment. It seemed she merely wished to talk on the phone with the nice young man. A courtesy, of sorts, to someone who had a personal interest in her property and had taken the time to write.

He tossed the letter aside and gazed out at the cool blue shimmer of the pool, inviting in the afternoon warmth. With a long pull on his bottle of beer, he decided a swim would be in order. He enjoyed the sensations of being underwater in the pristine environment of the pool, holding his breath and staying just under the surface, insulated from all outside distractions. Goggles allowed him to watch the blurred refracted sunlight traveling in soothing waves on the bottom. It was calming, his failing vision wasn't challenged to focus on any details. He slipped on his trunks, deposited the rest of the six-pack at the edge of the pool, then pushed off into the water.

Well, a conversation with the woman would be better than nothing, he reasoned. If he spoke with her maybe he could try turning on the charm, persuading her to let him see Glenwhylden after all. What did he have to lose? If it didn't work, back to "over the wall". One way or another, he was going to take action soon.

He floated face-down, arms and legs dangling, raising his head periodically to get a measured breath. This required almost no effort and induced a meditative state, soothing and contemplative. Once in awhile he'd swim over and swig from his beer.

Something struck him on the back and he splashed upright with a jerk. He could make out a long, slender pair of well-tanned legs at poolside.

"Roger! For God's sake, I thought you were drowned or something. What the hell are you doing, looking for something on the bottom of the pool?" It was his girlfriend, Gwynn Murck. She was got up in her typical outfit: shorts, designer tank-top, fluorescent white running shoes. She'd tossed a pebble to get his attention. He squinted up, shading his eyes.

"Hey, honey. No, I was just floatin'. You know, taking it easy." He had a basic policy of never trying to explain to her exactly what he was really doing, ever. Experience had proven this was best.

She looked exasperated. "Well, you're the only person I know who floats face-down."

He held apart upturned hands.

"You better get dressed," she scolded, pointing to her watch. "We're supposed to be over at Tommy and Susan's in half an hour, for the barbecue, remember?"

Gwynn was always unilaterally committing them. These events were usually with her friends, not his, but in general Roger tolerated them well enough. Interesting things sometimes happened, somebody making a scene or such, and this could be amusing.

He hauled himself out, flicking the water off his fingertips toward Gwynn. She squealed, dancing away.

Most of the time he felt grateful to have her. His friends told him he should be. She was beautiful, in the Southern California beach-girl tradition. Blonde, tall, tan, busty. Usually she was easy to get along with and made a better than average effort to keep things fun and light. But intellectually stimulating? No. Deeply intuitive? Come on.

"Susan's going to make her teriyaki swordfish, just like at the restaurant. They want us to stop and pick up one or two things on the way, okay Rog?"

"Yeah, sure." He was trying to shower quickly and get things on the road. "Let me guess, uh, must be two sixers of Bud light and a quart of Haagen-Dazs?"

Gwynn walked into the bathroom. "Roger, that's incredible! How'd you know that?"

"Coffee Chocolate Chip, right?"

She made a face at him as he reached for a towel. "No. Vanilla."

He looked at her knowingly. "Bullshit. Tommy hates vanilla."

She leaned against the basin counter, eyeing Roger's body appreciatively as he dried off. "OK, big man, if you're so smart and you know everything, tell me what I'm thinking right now."

He ran the towel briskly over his back, pretending to ignore her question. Looking in the mirror, he raised his eyebrows several times, studying the effect, then spun around, grabbed her and pushed her backwards into the bedroom. He muscled her down on the bed, climbed on top, and began growling and grunting into her ear. She shrieked, struggling madly under him.

"Roger! Cut it out, you're gonna mess me all up!"

He straightened, still straddling her. "That was what you were thinking."

"Was not," she lied, digging her nails into his thighs. "Now get off me, before my clothes get all wrinkled."

He sighed and rolled off. She ran to the bathroom mirror to check for any damage.

It was one of the things that bothered him most about Gwynn—her beauty was impressive, but so carefully cultivated as to be almost untouchable. Her overriding concern for always having a perfect appearance often put the brakes on spontaneous fun. She went to the nail bar once a week for a manicure and pedicure, and she had to get her hair just flawless or she couldn't leave the house, not even to go to the corner grocery. When they walked down the street together, there were stares. It was funny the way other women looked coldly at her. She was forever dieting and going to aerobics classes, maintaining the perfection. It showed—she was much like the models in the lingerie catalogs. Her favorite pages were clipped out and taped to her refrigerator door. She could cite the merits of each body part and why it was her goal to have her own conform to these ideals. She was glossy, polished, and animated, carefully in line with the commercial iconic images of femininity.

Fitting in was paramount to Gwynn. Gossip was the definition of conversation for her, but then, so it was for all of her girlfriends. Their boyfriends talked mostly of sports, so the whole arrangement worked out pretty well, with no one having to do much troublesome thinking. Like the popular beer commercial said: "Why ask why?"

Roger and Gwynne never argued much, it didn't seem worth the effort. And while their relationship presented a convincing face, it was in fact quite tenuous. Each had a non-expressed but well-defined agenda. These did not match. This division became far more defined when Roger found out he had Usher's Syndrome.

Now he had decided that his time was near. He'd made up his mind, he'd go on his own terms. But sharing this with Gwynn was out of the question. He knew she wouldn't understand. She'd try to "fix" things, interfere. Or worse, she'd panic and leave him. He didn't trust her to keep his secrets. She wasn't flagrantly indiscrete; she was just wide open with everyone in her life because she didn't have any reason not to be. Her parents were both alive and happily together; her older sister sold real estate in Visalia and raised two kids with her accountant husband.

Roger's mind had many dark corners where demons waited to pounce if he wasn't vigilant about compartmentalizing at all times. But Gwynn's life hadn't been complicated enough to create any of her own secrets. She'd never really known pain. Everything for her was simple, clear-cut, comfortable. Her mind resembled the "Gap" store at the mall: clean, well-lit, stylishly generic, always decorated with the latest cheery casual fashions. While her shallowness could be tiresome, right now she was at least a physical comfort. Roger didn't want to be alone in his final days. She was pretty much the last person left in his life, even if their relationship lacked all basic honesty. So he played her as an accessory, a temporary consolation—something nice to enjoy for this last little while. Even at her expense he felt he deserved this, seeing as so much else had been torn away from him.

Blissfully unaware, Gwynn viewed Roger as a good place in line, with potential. He was useful for the maintenance of her image. The relationship filled her essential needs; it was comfortable and secure. At least it would do until a really big fish came along or—also possible—Roger would become a fancy surgeon and start making a lot of money. Either scenario would be okay, because it really wasn't the who but the what that mattered; first reasonable man with the goods took the prize (which was how she regarded herself).

It was sad, really. Nothing was ever to come of it. But so many couples were that way. They were playing a game: winner take all. Each believed they held the wild card that would decisively change the picture, and they went along with the flow, waiting only for the moment when the card would be turned face up.

Roger was dressed and ready to go, jingling the car keys as Gwynn emerged with damage repaired and party visage installed. As they walked out, they passed the table where the letter from Celine Bell Stertevant lay, replaced in its envelope. Gwynn didn't notice it; her mind was on how she was going to look in a few minutes, roaring into the supermarket parking lot in Roger's hot little car. Maybe some of her friends would be around to see.

Roger squinted down through his glasses at the envelope for a moment, then leaned over and turned out the lamp.

The little envelope certainly didn't look like the wild card...but it was.

Chapter 4

Roger groaned as his wrench jerked sharply, snapping off the corroded nut he had been carefully trying to unthread from an old exhaust manifold.

"Damn it!" He tossed the wrench on the floor, grabbing a towel to wipe his perspiring face. It seemed that lately everyone and everything conspired to frustrate him. His mind had been churning all morning.

More than a week had passed since the letter from Mrs. Stertevant came, yet no one from her law firm had called. He wondered if he should just go ahead and call Phil Holmbard himself. It was almost noon. He usually checked his answering machine about this time, so he went over to the phone on the tool counter and dialed his own number. He listened as his greeting played, then entered his remote code. Three messages: Gwynn, wanting him to go shopping with her after work. Help her pick out new sheets for her apartment, oh god. Then his landlady asking if he might have seen her cat lately. And then, a raspy, bored-sounding voice came on the tape.

"Yes, Mr. Caldwell, this is Phillip Holmbard calling. You may recall I represent Mrs. Celine Stertevant. I'm presuming you received her letter; I have a copy of it here. She asked me to set up a meeting. Would you give me a call at your convenience? Phil Holmbard at Addison, Metz, and Diehl. 555-6712. Thanks."

Roger scribbled the number on a scrap of paper, then stuffed it in his shirt pocket. He hurried back to the mechanic's lockers and hung up his coveralls. After washing his hands and checking himself in the mirror, he paused at Franz's office, leaning in the doorway.

"Heading out for a bite, boss. Need anything?"

The shop owner was on the phone; he only glanced up over his reading glasses and waved. The walk to the corner deli took about three minutes, and every second Roger was aware of the note in his pocket. There was a courtyard behind the sandwich place, usually deserted, and a pay-phone with a bench beside it. That was exactly where he wanted to be.

The secretary put him right through.

"Oh yes, Mr. Caldwell, thanks for calling back," Holmbard said. "I...can you hang on just a second?" Roger heard the attorney place his hand over the mouthpiece. Someone else was in the office, and there were muffled bits: "...at the recorder's office by three. Got that? Thanks, hon. Yeah...heh, heh!" He came back on the line. "Sorry about that, let's see, where were we? Oh, yes. The thing is, Mrs. Stertevant would like very much to meet you. But, there are a few details we should go over together. Any chance you might have some time to come by my office?"

"Well, sure, no problem," Roger said, hiding his surprise. He tried to figure what was up. Was there some release to sign or something? Maybe she just wanted Holmbard to screen him for her—that was more likely.

"Good. Well—let's see here..."

Roger heard pages flipping.

"How's tomorrow afternoon, about one. Is that good for you?"

"Uh..." Roger paused, pretending to check his schedule. "Yeah, I can fit that in. One o'clock's fine. I think I've still got your address somewhere."

"34 West Mesa, Suite Four. Okay? I'll look forward to meeting you."

Roger hung up the phone, went around to the deli and got an avo-vegi sandwich on hearth bread, extra sprouts, a bag of soy bean chips, and a bottle of carrot juice. He couldn't remember the last time he'd had such a disgustingly healthy lunch.

The next day at noon, Roger stuck his head into Franz's office again. "Hey boss. I need a few hours this afternoon, for a personal deal. That okay?"

The older man smiled. "Of course, Roger. Take your time. Hope you have some fun for a change." He pointed his finger like a pistol.

Roger smiled, shaking his head amiably. He went home, took a shower, and changed into a suit and tie. With the top lowered, he leisurely cruised downtown, finding a parking spot close to Holmbard's firm. The elevator to the fourth floor opened into an elegant reception room. Paneled in dark wood, it had green leather chairs with high backs. A middle-aged woman, impeccably dressed, greeted him and asked if he'd care for a cup of coffee or tea while he waited briefly for Mr. Holmbard. She brought him his coffee in a fine little china cup with a saucer. Five minutes later a short, portly man in a dark suit came down the hallway. His red face contrasted with a thick tuft of white hair sticking up from the top of his head.

"Mr. Caldwell? How do you do sir, I'm Phil Holmbard."

He extended his hand. Roger rose to shake it and noticed that it was small, spongy, and a little damp.

"Sorry to keep you waiting. Please, come in." He led the way down the hall into a spacious office looking out over the red-tiled roof tops of the city. Large trophy animal heads festooned the walls. Roger glanced at photographs of manly sporting activities: Phil Holmbard holding a huge fish, Holmbard standing with a group of small naked black people with an unfamiliar-looking dead animal sprawled at their feet,

Holmbard again, in tennis clothes, with President Richard Nixon. As Roger dropped into a wingback chair the attorney went around behind his desk and sat down, palms smacking the desktop.

"Well sir! You wrote one heck of a good letter to Mrs. Stertevant." He cocked his head, a wry look on his chubby face.

Roger shifted in his chair and cleared his throat.

"Beg your pardon, sir?"

"Maybe I'm a little ahead of things here, uh, Roger. May I call you Roger?"

"Of course, sir."

"Oh, please don't call me sir. Phil's fine."

"Okay, Phil."

"Okay, Roger. *Well*. What I meant about the letter, it's just that, well, I've been representing Mrs. Stertevant's interests here for almost forty years and she gets lots of letters. Lots of people asking for things. But this is the first time anything like this has ever happened. Yes, sir. Most unusual. Know much about Mrs. Stertevant?"

"Actually, no sir—" Roger stopped himself. "I'm sorry, no, Phil, I really don't. I've just been interested in learning more about the house, for a long time. In fact, ever since I was a little kid growing up here."

Holmbard leaned back in his chair, which groaned under him. He clasped his hands over his stomach.

"Ah yes, the house. Very interesting story there, perhaps you'll be hearing more about that. Mrs. Stertevant's a remarkable woman, too. As I said, I've been her attorney here for almost forty years, and I've spoken on the phone with her numerous times, but I've never met her face to face. I can't say as I even know what she looks like. As a matter of fact, to my

35

knowledge, she hasn't ever been out here to see her house in the entire time I've been handling her affairs."

This confirmed what he'd heard for years, so Roger had to ask, "Why not?"

"That's not something I can tell you." He paused, then "I will share with you though, that I, *myself*, have never been inside the gates." He tossed this off wistfully.

Roger was astonished. "You're kidding."

"No, not kidding," Holmbard frowned. "She maintains a full staff over there...butler, maids, cook, gardeners. There's over a dozen people employed at the estate. None of 'em have ever met her, as far as I know. I *can* tell you that she's very interested to meet you, though." He picked up a yellow legal pad and scanned it for a moment, then looked back at the young man. "I've got a proposal here that I imagine you're going to find interesting. Mrs. Stertevant is quite elderly, you probably knew that much?" He raised his eyebrows, and Roger nodded.

"Right. Well, that being the case, she really doesn't care for traveling too much anymore. She lives out on the east coast. So, she's wondering if you'd be willing to fly out there for a few days, so she could meet you. Everything totally first class. She'd pick up all your expenses. Put you up in a nice hotel near her house. You'd have a driver to take you around. Would your schedule permit something like that?"

Roger was caught completely off guard. It was all starting to sound a little strange.

"Huh. Jeez. Really? I can...well, sure. I mean, my schedule's not a problem. But why does she want to go to all the trouble of flying me out there? Is there something going on that I don't know about?"

Phil Holmbard looked up at the ceiling for a moment, pursing his lips, then slowly leveled his gaze at Roger.

"Honestly, not that I know of. I spoke with her day before yesterday, and she just said that she'd like to visit with you. Told me to make the arrangements, if you'd agree. By the way, you wouldn't be traveling commercial. Not by a long shot. Mrs. Stertevant would send her own airplane out to get you. Airplane, hell—it's more like a small airliner. It's a Gulfstream jet with a full crew. I hear she doesn't use it much anymore. I've never been on it, but I understand it's quite luxurious." He squinted, pressing the tips of his fingers together. "I gotta say, Roger, I'm a little bit envious."

Now, this was too much. Roger laughed a little, shaking his head. He leaned forward and put his hands on the edge of the desk.

"Phil. Now let me get this straight. Mrs. Stertevant is going to send a private jet...all the way out here from the east coast...to pick me up...and take me there...and then bring me back here again?"

The lawyer nodded slowly. There was a long silence in the office.

"When?"

"Within reason, anytime soon. I'd do it soon, if I were in your position, Roger. I mean, God bless her, she's a woman in her late eighties." Holmbard raised his brows once more. Roger sank back into the big chair.

Now the attorney seemed irritated, as if dealing with a hunting partner who had the ultimate trophy in his sights but couldn't bring himself to pull the trigger. "Well. It's a lot to think about, isn't it? Want to take some time? You can call me when you decide." He glanced down at his watch, shuffling papers.

Roger straightened, remembering his purpose. "Actually, no, Phil. I don't need to think about it." He felt a flush of resolve. "You tell Mrs. Stertevant that I'll come anytime that's convenient for her. And please tell her that I'm honored."

Holmbard smirked. "Fine then. I'll get you the details as soon as I know. Can you find your way out?"

Just as Roger reached for the door handle Holmbard called after him. "Oh, just one more thing." He folded his arms across his chest. "Mrs. Stertevant is elderly, she has a lot of money and she's given a substantial amount to charities. But son, she's still sharp as a tack. I've never known anybody to put anything over on her." He tilted his head back, watching for Roger's response. "And of course, I'm looking out for her as well. Just so you know."

During the drive back to his house, Roger's mind buzzed. Just what was this all about? Why did he rate a personal audience with the mysterious Celine Stertevant when everyone else was denied...including her own lawyer? Yet, what was the worst that could happen? He'd get a nice ride in a fancy private jet; he'd never done that before. And a few days at a big mansion on the east coast. Kind of an unexpected bonus luxury vacation before the final act. And he'd have a real crack at convincing Mrs. Stertevant to let him see the estate, a tour with dignity. It was all good.

He took the beach road home, past Glenwhylden. Gardeners were out on the lower hillside, planting brilliant yellow and orange flowers. The color was spectacular, and Roger pulled over for a minute. He contemplated the whole thing before him. Here were these men, planting hundreds of lovely flowers, for a woman thousands of miles away who would likely never see them. What a waste it seemed. And beyond the trees there was a magnificent house, with a butler and maids and cooks, all with no one to wait on. The hubris of it all. Well, one thing seemed more clear than ever. Could there be a better place to die? It was as if it was all being done in preparation, just for him.

With a final look up at the gardeners, he shifted the Carrera into first gear and gave it the boot. The flat six screamed, redlining up through second and third. A moment later the mighty gates of Glenwhylden flew past on the right. He glanced down at the speedometer: a hundred and five in a thirty-five mile-per-hour zone. He pinned the accelerator, smoking the curve, blowing like a sidewinder missile past the startled other drivers.

Chapter 5

When Mack McArdle's golf ball struck Charles Stertevant on that bright September day in 1921, the event caused a plangent series of upheavals, extending deep into the business and social worlds Charles had so skillfully maneuvered during his relatively short life. His holdings and business dealings were complicated and far-flung; his circle of friends was wide.

Celine, of course, was devastated. She went through the process: the numbness, the support of family and friends, the gradual resumption of normal pursuits. To the growing dismay of her family, this did not include any effort to meet new men. Her mother gently encouraged her to find a new love, but Celine had no interest. She never discussed her exact reasons, but she had decided she would live the rest of her life alone, channeling her energies into pursuits other than matrimony and the raising of a family.

Although they had been married for only the briefest time, Charles had already redrawn his will, passing the bulk of his estate to Celine. There were a few charitable bequests and some cash and business properties conveyed to his parents, but these made only a superficial dent in the total fortune. At the age of 22, Celine Bell Stertevant inherited an estate estimated at 436 million dollars. This included cash, stocks, investment properties, various companies, sizeable tracts of undeveloped land in nine countries around the world, the house in Columbus (the one in St. Louis he had left to his family), and of course, the magnificent Glenwhylden estate in Santa Barbara.

Other young girls in this situation might have filled their days with leisure: shopping, opulent clubs, the social whirl. But Celine chose a higher path: the enrichment of the mind and spirit, the nourishment of the soul. She enrolled as a graduate student at Oxford. Two and a half years later, she received her doctorate in Eastern Religions. She traveled Europe and Asia. For about a half a year she lived at the ashram of a famous spiritual teacher in India, where she studied yoga and meditation. The intense experience with Charles followed by his sudden death made her ponder what it was all about. In her travels she sought, without much real success, to get answers.

Eventually she returned to her parents at Marsh Meadows house. They again urged her to remarry; there were lots of old beaus still interested. But that seemed the farthest thing from her mind. She gave her time at a children's hospital, was active in church fund-drives and fellowship gatherings, she volunteered at the zoological gardens. She also founded a monthly spiritual awareness study group which discussed books on religion and supernatural phenomena.

The Bell family continued to prosper. Guided by Charles Stertevant's former financial advisor, they anticipated the stock market crash of 1929. They divested themselves of stocks and moved into cash. The crash left them virtually unscathed, and they passed through the dark years of the Great Depression with no real change in lifestyle.

When war came in 1941, Celine worked with the USO in Hartford and New York, and volunteered for the American Red Cross. She donated blood and sat at the bedsides of convalescing G.I.'s, reading to them and giving comfort.

The Bells knew many families whose sons were at the front lines. More than a few were wounded or killed. Though the

Bells had no members directly involved in the war, other great losses came upon them at the end of 1945.

In late October Gerhardt took his sloop "Caspian" out for a final sail before the boat would be hauled out and placed in a shed for the winter. It was a yearly ritual, marking the passage of one season to another. On this overcast and blustery afternoon he'd been out alone for about three hours. Gusting winds made it cold and wet on the boat and Bell was straining hard to control the bucking craft. Tacking close-hauled, beating for the harbor, he stiffened in agony from an acute myocardial infarction. Just before dark, the drifting "Caspian" was spotted by fishermen on a trawler. Under the luffing sails Gerhardt Bell was slumped in the cockpit, the mainsheet and tiller still clutched tightly in his lifeless hands.

Celine's mother was never the same; she lost weight and strength quickly. December was bitterly cold and just before Christmas she developed pneumonia. She died alone in her bedroom early on the morning of the 23rd. The funeral was held in a snowstorm the day after Christmas, and Celine would remember that day as the darkest of her life.

Celine's sister Margrethe had been living in Florence, pursuing her passion for Renaissance art. When the war came she returned to Connecticut, intending to stay only for the duration. But after both parents died so suddenly, she reconsidered. The pain of that year had brought her and Celine closer, and she began to feel that she would no longer be happy so far from home.

The post-war years passed uneventfully, the two sisters living together. They each continued to pursue their own interests, their charity work and social engagements. They carried on the traditional seasonal rituals just as they had when their parents were living. Sometimes they traveled together.

Then in early 1969 Margrethe suffered a brain hemorrhage which left her almost completely incapacitated. She could no longer walk or speak, and required constant care. A full-time nurse came to live at Marsh Meadows. Margrethe hung on for a few more months, and then she, too, was gone.

Celine was now completely alone, empty. Her sister had been her best friend since their parents' deaths. They had shared everything and been of great comfort to each other.

A few friends tried to help, particularly one woman who'd been a member of Celine's spiritual awareness group since its beginning. Abigail Horvath was the most psychic of any of the members. She and Celine were the same age, they'd been at school together as teenagers. Now Abby provided her support after Margrethe's death. She called Celine or dropped by with something she'd baked; sometimes they'd go shopping. She had also recently suffered a loss: her husband, Ben. Happily married for forty-two years, their life together had been full and rewarding although they had no children.

In part because of their recent losses, as well as their advancing age and a shared sense of their own mortality, the two women often spoke of spiritual matters. As the bond of trust grew between them, Abby gradually revealed the true dimensions of her psychic abilities. With astonishing accuracy she could forecast the headlines in the newspapers a day or two in advance. Celine, rather than frightened or suspicious, was fascinated and envious. How did Abby acquire her visions?

"Just be open," Abby explained. "There's an inter-connectedness of things—living things and even events, in the present and the future. It can be vague, so drop your defenses. Be receptive to that connection. It's a whisper. That's how a psychic person sees what other people don't."

As the two friends entered their seventies, they developed a mutual desire to travel to places where advanced spiritual concepts were embraced: the homes of seers and great minds, whether in bustling cities or wilderness hideaways. Celine and Abby wanted to meet these people about whom they had heard so much and whose writings and teachings they had followed.

It was then that Celine decided to invest in a private aircraft, realizing that it would be helpful in maintaining a superior level of comfort and freedom as they visited these far-flung places and people. She purchased a brand new Grumman Gulfstream IV jet and had it fitted out with every comfort and convenience befitting a world-class home in the skies. She hired a full-time crew. And she had the big jet painted a glossy black, christening it "Arjuna", after the mythological hero of the Bhagavad-Gita.

Off they went, Celine and Abby, the peripatetic geriatric seekers of wisdom and truth. Jetting all over the planet: India, China, Peru, Australia, Greece, Egypt. It was a devout odyssey, and they were like children in a kind of cosmic amusement park. Arriving in such style and evincing genuine purpose, they were welcomed like royalty. They met many of the religious, spiritual, and philosophical heavy-hitters of the day. The Pope, the Dalai Lama, The Archbishop of Canterbury, Chief Rabbis, the Maharishi, mullahs, ayatollahs, shamans, witches, witch-doctors, high priests and psychics; all received and were charmed by the two spiritual ambassadors from Connecticut.

Conspicuous among the places they did not visit was Glenwhylden. Celine had tried a visit, just once. It was about a year after Charles' death. Her mother came along and they made the journey out by train, stopping off in St. Louis to visit Charles' parents. Celine hoped the trip would do her good—

maybe seeing Charles' parents and being back at Glenwhylden would help her feel close to Charles again. Perhaps she could find closure. But she only managed about three hours at the house, walking from room to room as she had during her honeymoon. It was too painful; she saw little things at every turn, and could not stop weeping. She simply had to leave, and they took the first train back East.

Over the following years, memories of Glenwhylden haunted Celine. It was a place in her mind, but of course, still a very real place as well, more magnificent with each passing season. She gave strict instructions that it should be maintained exactly as Charles had left it, no matter the expense. The estate was in constant readiness for her arrival at a moment's notice. She wanted to keep it prepared, just in case she should suddenly want to go there. It was an emblem: an enduring, highly personal monument to her late husband's great love, a love so suddenly lost. She truly meant to return; somehow it just never happened. And even as sixty years passed, she could not convince herself to sell it.

And so for decades, day in and day out, the tranquility within Glenwhylden's walls was perfect. The original staff Charles had hired stayed intact for a long time, only changing as someone would retire or pass away. As the nineteen sixties and seventies came, many of the staff began to be second generation. One man, Whitney Polk, the original chauffeur, was still on the job until his death in 1979. His son, Whitney Jr., became butler and head of the household staff. To a person, all of these workers were loyal to the absent Mrs. Stertevant and to Glenwhylden itself. Few had ever met her or even knew much about her, but it didn't matter. This was a magical place, in their care. From the beginning they'd been given a strict policy of not talking to outsiders about any of what went on there or what the place was like. This policy was religiously maintained; the staff was very well paid for their discretion and dedicated service.

On rare occasions Celine spoke with Abby about Glenwhylden. She described the house and gardens, the irreplaceable beauty and memories. The two women were close, sharing most everything, yet Glenwhylden was a delicate subject. Celine might begin talking about going back to see the place, but then tears would come.

"Honey," Abby finally said, "maybe it's better if you just never go back there."

Her investments were managed by lawyers and advisers, but Celine never allowed herself to be cut off from important financial decisions. Her father had taught her to keep a close eye on such matters. She read all the materials supplied to her, and she never signed any document before carefully studying it and asking questions. Once in awhile, however, something would slip past her notice.

It was an April afternoon in 1987. In the kitchen at Marsh Meadows house Celine and Abby were having tea, Celine opening the day's mail. There was an aerogramme envelope with a very foreign looking postmark and stamps; inside was a heartfelt letter.

Dr. Delia Larkin was a research zoologist, she wrote, working in the rainforests of Borneo and Sumatra. Her specialty was Orangutans, the rare and elusive red apes which exist nowhere else but in that obscure corner of the world. Larkin described the wonder and gentleness of these animals. She stated that they were highly intelligent, with remarkable learning abilities. So human-like were they, that for centuries the local Dayak tribespeople had referred to them as "Mawas", meaning "men of the forest". The lore held that Mawas could actually speak, they just chose not to because they feared they'd be made into servants. The letter extolled the glorious

46

and irreplaceable beauty of the Bornean and Sumatran rainforests, the natural environment of the Orangutans. She decried the accelerating old-growth teak and mahogany logging operations that were relentlessly invading and destroying the last remaining habitats of these reclusive creatures. The lumber crews were clear-cutting vast areas of pristine wilderness, leaving behind a useless and desolated wasteland where unprotected top soil was quickly eroded away by heavy rains. Creeks and rivers silted in with the runoff and logging debris, killing fish and aquatic plants. The logging at its current pace, Larkin claimed, would cause the virtual extinction of the wild Orangutans within a very few years, not to mention thousands of other species of animals and plants that relied on this same habitat for survival. Many apes were killed outright by loggers; infants had been captured to be sold on the black market as pets. A few animals had survived and ended up in a rescue station operated by Dr. Larkin.

Enclosed with the letter were photographs showing the rainforest in its natural state and others of areas laid waste by the logging. One photo depicted Dr. Larkin: a large, pleasant-faced woman in her late fifties, with curly black hair beginning to go gray. She sat on the front steps of a primitive building, and in her lap was one of the Orangutan babies that had been saved from starvation. A note on the back of the photo said the baby's mother had been killed by a logging crew when a huge teak tree had been brought crashing down. As there were sometimes upwards of twenty animals at the rescue station, money was invariably a problem. She and her associates also had to find other areas suitable for the displaced animals to be returned to the wild. This was causing them to go ever deeper into the wilderness in search of areas not currently being logged. And worse, the survival rate of these returned animals was very poor.

Then Dr. Larkin took Celine Stertevant to task. One of the biggest and most aggressive logging operations in her region was being pursued on vast tracts of privately held land—land owned by an American company called FiberMark. Dr. Larkin had asked colleagues back in Maryland to check out the ownership of this company. They reported that FiberMark was a closely held company, in which a seventy percent controlling interest was owned by just one person. That person was Celine Bell Stertevant.

The letter went further to declare that the monetary worth that could be extracted from logging the teak and mahogany trees was infinitesimal when compared to the scientific and spiritual value of the rainforest habitat of the Mawas.

"How can one person sitting back in Old Lyme, Connecticut," Dr. Larkin asked, "countenance the brutal and wanton destruction of the lives and habitats of these innocent and majestic animals, for no purpose other than to amass even more wealth, when that same person is already obscenely wealthy—possessed of far more money than could be spent in ten lifetimes? What's the point?"

Celine's hands began to shake as she read the angry words. The zoologist summed up: "I beg you, Mrs. Stertevant, as a woman, as a human, as a fellow inhabitant of this planet, to find satisfaction with the wealth you have already accumulated. Use your powers to cause the immediate discontinuation of the rape of these forests and the slaughter of these animals. I pray that you will read these words and look at these photographs, and then do the right thing. Please know that I am ready to aid this process at any lengths, and would greatly welcome a dialogue with you or your representatives anytime, anywhere. I thank you from the bottom of my heart. Sincerely, Elizabeth H. Larkin, Ph.D."

Celine was in tears when she finished reading.

"Dear, whatever is the matter?" Abby was looking at her with great concern. Celine shook her head, and wordlessly handed the letter and photos across the table to her friend. Abby read it, then expressed disbelief.

"Oh, surely she must be mistaken! This isn't true, is it Celine?"

Celine wiped the tears from her eyes. "I'm not sure, but I'm afraid it actually might be. I have seen the name of that company before, in some of my investment papers. I remember being told something about it. It was a land-holding firm of some kind, and the land was in several other countries. It dated from a long time ago, actually now that I think of it I do recall that. Charles had bought a percentage of the company, and back then it was called something else. But, Abby, I was never told anything about logging or Borneo or Orangutans or anything of the sort!" She paused and looked out the window, a distraught squint twisting her delicate features. "Oh, my God, Abby, I've got to find out about this right away." She struggled to her feet, pushing over the chair behind her. "If what this woman says is true, something must be done immediately!"

She got her investment adviser in New York on the line. She did indeed own seventy percent interest in FiberMark, a construction materials and textile firm based in Wichita, Kansas. The remaining thirty percent share was owned by the Markham family of Columbus, Ohio. The company had been co-founded in 1919 by Charles Stertevant and wholesale lumberman, Francis Markham, as a lumber supply business specializing in exotic hardwoods for fine furniture and interior finish applications. The adviser explained to Celine that the

49

information in question, about the company's activities in hardwoods logging, had in fact been presented to her in a meeting almost a decade ago, when the original company underwent a management change and a decision was made by the new management and their accountants to begin "utilizing some of the company's dormant assets in order to raise operating capital and increase shareholder's return on investments". Either she hadn't paid attention, or it hadn't registered on her at the time, but the "utilization of dormant assets" involved the cutting of timber reserves that had been purchased (for next to nothing) in Borneo back in 1920. It seemed that, for many years, the remoteness of the lands where the timber stood, as well as the ready availability of identical woods derived from more convenient source areas, made the extraction of the timber from the Borneo tracts economically unfeasible. However, over a long period of time, the demand for fine tropical hardwoods had continued to rise, while the supply of easily obtainable timber had steadily declined. Within the last ten years, the price of premium teak and mahogany logs had risen well into a range which now made cost-effective the investment in roads and equipment. The company was proceeding to profit from its long-held investment, and Celine was proudly reminded by her adviser that, to date, her accounts had benefitted to the tune of nearly three and a half million dollars from the Borneo timber operations currently underway. Noting her quivering voice and apparent agitation during their conversation, the adviser inquired if there was something wrong. Celine paused, gaining her composure, then steadily informed him that, yes, there was. She explained that she needed to think about things, asked him to send her a complete file of FiberMark's past and current activities immediately , and then said she would be back in touch very soon. She hung up, leaving the broker with an uneasy feeling.

As she put down the receiver, Celine was nauseated. She went over to a sofa and lay down, closing her eyes. Terrible images crossed her mind: stately, ancient trees toppling down, innocent creatures smashing into the ground, dying horrible deaths; deaths from which she was profiting. She began to feel truly dreadful, a combination of unbearable shame and guilt. She was a great, voracious, marauding, bloated old sow pig, she reproached herself. A pig that had already gobbled up everything in sight, and yet still snorted greedily about for any remaining morsels. Abby came over to hold her hand and try to comfort her, but it didn't help, not a bit.

This was a weight that Celine had never really felt before; the terrible mass of all that money—that "obscene wealth", as Dr. Larkin had referred to it. She'd always had the money; it was something that was taken for granted. It was as much an accepted part of her as her arms and legs. Where it came from, how it was generated was never a negative consideration. She thought she knew all about it and had a handle on it. Further, it had always been her view that the things her businesses did helped people; they were a means of getting things made, things that were useful, things that people needed in order to live comfortable lives. The businesses employed thousands of people and jobs were something people needed, certainly. She had always prided herself on using her power to help people and do good things in the world. She had always felt she was sharing. The money didn't just support her own luxuries, she had reasoned. No, just think of all the charities that had received millions of dollars from her, dollars that financed very worthy causes! The idea that one of her businesses could be doing grievous damage to something precious somewhere, that her pursuit of profit via her company's activities was destroying natural beauty, not to mention irreplaceable beings... well, that was just an idea that she had never had any inkling of. And now, here it was in front of her, in graphic detail. The letter and the photos, corroborated by the information from the investment counselor—it was undeniable.

Something had to be done. Celine sat up and started talking with Abby about what that should be. The logging must be stopped, they agreed, whatever the cost. That was first and foremost. Then, a program for helping Dr. Larkin accomplish her work should be undertaken. Money, people, materials— whatever was needed.

They wrote back to Dr. Larkin, explaining that it was Celine's intention to respond to her entreaties with no delays. Then a packet from the financial adviser was received, and it contained more horrors. There were plans to build even more roads in the very near future, expanding the logging. FiberMark controlled a gigantic area of forest, some five hundred ninety-seven square miles. To date, about fifty-five square miles had been fully "harvested". The government was cooperating with the deforestation process because it provided jobs for a largely unemployed rural population and resulted in land that was, however briefly, useful for farming or livestock grazing. FiberMark was engaged in a token reforestation and land-reclamation effort that appeared to be essentially ineffectual, designed to satisfy some regulatory technicalities.

The same day she received the information file on FiberMark, she called her attorneys and instructed them to structure an offer to the Markham heirs to buy out their share of the company. Above all else, she wanted action, not just the best deal. She wanted total control of that company and she wanted it now. When the lawyers attempted to find out what was causing this sudden interest in owning outright a company which she hadn't even mentioned in nearly a decade, they were curtly put about doing the requested work with no further explanation.

Soon a second letter arrived from Dr. Larkin. She expressed her amazement and relief that Mrs. Stertevant had chosen to respond as she had. She suggested that they speak by telephone as soon as possible, and gave a date and time when she would be at the nearest town where there was a phone. On the given day, she and Celine spoke for over an hour, with increasing mutual respect. Celine offered to fly Dr. Larkin to Connecticut right away to plan the preservation of the remaining areas of rainforest habitat. Who rather than she would know best what needed to be done? Celine also wished to introduce Dr. Larkin to some powerful friends who might help the cause.

Events went along pretty quickly after the telephone conversation. Dr. Larkin wanted to come to Connecticut, but suggested that Celine might visit Borneo first, to see for herself just exactly how things were.

Celine was then eighty-seven years old, and Abby eighty-six. The last time they had undertaken a real journey of this type they were a decade younger; yet this seemed to be an opportunity they could not pass up. So, after very little debate, orders were given that the jet be stocked and prepared for travel, and soon the two explorers were back at it, winging down to Malaysia. The visit was one of the most spectacular experiences in Celine's already remarkable life. The beauty of the rainforests; their spiritual, majestic peacefulness, the overwhelming profusion of life in its myriad forms, and the astonishing, almost otherworldly presence of the Orangutans. Never had either woman so strongly felt that they were in the presence of such sentience, represented by a "wild" animal. The place itself, and the "Mawas"; these brought a real epiphany for Celine and Abby. This was the direct connection they had missed in their other spiritual quests. Here was a primal contact with the higher powers. Abby pulled Celine aside and said "Any fool could see divinity in every corner of this place."

Dr. Larkin was an engaging host, and although the accommodations at the rescue station were, to say the least, somewhat less luxurious than what Celine and Abby were accustomed to, they were quite adequate. The travelers spent a moving and exciting week with the Orangs, and before departing they convinced Dr. Larkin that she should come up to the States as soon as possible. A lecture tour and other fund-raising and public awareness events must be staged. Her co-workers at the rescue station could manage without her for a couple of weeks. She had to agree; the benefits could be enormous. A date for her journey was set for a few weeks hence. On the scheduled day, Celine dispatched the jet down to Borneo to pick her up.

Celine and Abby had been making phone calls and doing as much advance work as possible. Thanks to their tireless efforts, Dr. Larkin's schedule would be full during her time away from the jungle. The hope was that the researcher's engagements and contacts would go far toward turning around what had become a terrible situation. And yet, it was still to grow worse.

Celine received an urgent phone call from her pilot, Chuck Bartholdy. He had arrived on schedule in Borneo to pick up Dr. Larkin and was met at the Sandakan airport by the foreman from the rescue station. Visibly distraught, he brought terrible news. On the previous day he and Dr. Larkin had traveled by jeep to Sandakan and checked into a hotel. At dinner, Dr. Larkin ordered curried chicken. Apparently she swallowed a bone, because she suddenly began to choke.

Several people tried the Heimlich maneuver. They pounded her on the back. Nothing worked. As everyone in the dining room watched in unbelieving horror, she turned blue and fell to the floor.

The foreman had tears in his eyes as he finished telling Bartholdy the story. "Sir, we are lost without her."

Chapter 6

"Use the pool whenever you want," Roger said, "but just make sure you've got your top on if you hear Mr. Tornquist coming down the tennis court path."

Gwynn was behind the wheel of her Honda, driving him to the airport.

"Got it. But it's okay not to wear my panties, right?"

"Oh, absolutely. It's not important if you're hanging reproductive organs out in front of my landlord. Just no boobs."

"Thanks, Rog. I'd never think of that on my own." She grinned. Using his pool while he was away would be fun, but she was deeply envious of what was happening to Roger. He told her he was flying to the east coast on a private jet, but fabricated the rest; a wealthy man in Connecticut collected old Porsches, Roger had worked on some of his cars, the guy wanted him to look over a rare car he might buy.

"But why is he flying you out there in his private jet?"

"The plane was gonna be out here anyway. It flew some big clients of his back out here from a weekend in New York or something, and it was just gonna go back empty so I'm hitching a ride."

Flying off on a private jet was something Gwynn would kill to do.

"If the plane's going to be empty except for you, why can't I just tag along? I don't weigh that much."

"Hah. No, see, it's not a loose kind of deal. It's a business trip, you know? It wouldn't be professional for me to ask if I could bring my girlfriend."

She wanted to sulk, but then reasoned that maybe she'd get to meet the guy who owned the jet. Maybe they'd make a connection. Someday he'd fly *her* somewhere. Maybe more. There was always that possibility, she thought. Things like that happened to girls like her.

"Here it is," he pointed to a parking spot by the Execu-Air hangars at the corner of the airport. As he opened the trunk for his suitcase, Gwynn walked to the end of a high barrier fence. Roger heard her gasp.

"Oh *my God.* Is that it?!"

He came and looked over her shoulder. The big jet with its cabin door open and stairs lowered screamed money: a sleek row of windows, the whole thing glossy black from nose to tail. The only markings were I.D. numbers on the tail and a demure inscription at the nose. In gold script, it said, "Arjuna". A catering van was alongside, and two men were loading boxes into the aircraft.

"Is that it, Roger?" Gwynn squeaked like she'd breathed helium. "That's the guy's name, right? Mr. Arjuna?"

"No, that's not his name. That's probably somebody else's airplane."

She scanned the area like a shopper at a sale. "Well, I sure don't see any other jets here. That's got to be it."

They walked to the office. A middle-aged man in a dark pilot's suit was leaning against the glass-topped counter, looking over a chart.

"Sir? I'm looking for a pilot who's supposed to be meeting me here?"

"You Roger Caldwell?" The pilot extended his hand. "I'm Chuck Bartholdy."

Roger introduced Gwynn and indicated that he had only the one bag.

"Well, you'll be glad to know we've got great flying weather all the way back. Nothing out there but blue skies from coast to coast. Pretty unusual." He looked out the window. "They're just about done loading lunch—you ready to hit it?"

Roger felt Gwynn's fingers digging into his back. "Sure am. Uh, could I ask you, if it's not too much trouble, would it be alright if Gwynn got to take a look inside the plane? She's never been in a private jet. I haven't either, but I guess I'll have time to see it while we're flying."

Bartholdy paused to look at Gwynn.

"As pretty as you are, Gwynn, I'd be happy to let you *fly* the plane back to Connecticut if you want to."

She giggled, and they all walked out to the big black Grumman Gulfstream. In the forward cabin there was a small galley against the bulkhead. An Asian man in a pristine starched white jacket was stocking the shelves and refrigerator. He turned and smiled, and Captain Bartholdy introduced him: Hwang-Shu, the cabin attendant. He bowed politely and stepped to one side so they could move into the main cabin. The seating area was simple, but very luxurious and comfortable; there were six high-backed swivel chairs and a small settee arranged about the cabin. These were all upholstered in a supple, light taupe leather. They proceeded on through the door at the amidships bulkhead and entered the bedroom. This cabin was roughly the same size as the forward seating area but altogether different in feeling. There were two single beds, one on either side, each covered with a colorful, tribal-looking spread. A little antique Persian runner lay on the floor between them. Mounted on either side of the after-bulkhead at the rear of the cabin were two gilt-framed oil paintings depicting characters from Hindu mythology. One was a warrior, standing with bow drawn-back, arrow aimed

58

skyward. The other portrayed an elephant god, holding several icons. To say that these paintings were exquisite would be a slight—they were magically attractive.

Gwynn studied them in amazement. "What are these? Like some kind of foreign cartoons?"

Chuck grinned. "Not exactly. The one on the left, that's Arjuna, the archer from the Bhagavad-Gita. That's an Indian fable about the great battles of life and spiritual evolution. He's the warrior this ship is named after. It's a really interesting story, you should read it sometime. And this guy over here, he's Ganesha, kind of a cross between an elephant and a man. He's one of the Hindu gods. There are quite a few temples in India dedicated to him."

Gwynn's nose was inches from the painting of Ganesha. It was something completely new to her. She turned to Bartholdy.

"Wow. I guess the guy who owns this plane must be kind of *spiritual* or something, right?"

Chuck knew the game. "I suppose you could say that. The owner is a person of many interests." He smiled in a neutral way. "So! That's the tour, folks." He looked at his watch. "We really should be getting underway." Roger shepherded Gwynn toward the door, his hands on her shoulders. She took a last dreamy survey of every detail. Roger went with her as far as the barrier fence, then gave her a big hug and kiss.

"I'm supposed to be back at around seven on Thursday evening, but I'll call you before to let you know. Okay?"

"Yeah, yeah, alright. I'll come pick you up, you lucky prick."

During the taxi out Roger was impressed by the hush inside the cabin—it seemed abnormally quiet. But then the jet accelerated on take-off with unaccustomed ferocity; he felt himself being pressed into the seat. His body tensed during the sharp, acrobatic climb after leaving the surface of the runway. It was quite different from commercial airliners. Hwang-Shu, sitting in the chair opposite him, must have noticed this because he leaned over and explained that Captain Bartholdy was an ex-Navy fighter pilot.

"He very smart man, very smart. Good pilot. I fly all over world with him, never worry one minute. Chuck no like waste time. He always go fast. Here, there, even in car he like go very fast. I trust him, he never have problem." He glanced out the window. "We level off in a few minutes. Now, Mistah Caldwell, what you have for drink befoah lunch? We got anything you want."

Roger asked for a ginger-ale and was sipping that a few minutes later when Chuck Bartholdy came ambling back into the passenger cabin. The copilot was at the controls and they would be attaining their cruising altitude of around thirty thousand feet shortly. Hwang-Shu looked at the pilot in a familiar way.

"Mistah Caldwell kind of nervous on take-off, Chuck. I explain him you one fine pilot, just a littah crazy is all."

Bartholdy frowned at the cabin attendant, then leaned over toward Roger, shaking his head sadly.

"Don't listen to this guy, Roger. My buddies pulled him out of a VC jungle prison and I think Charlie kept him up late a few too many nights. He doesn't have all his marbles." He held his index finger by his temple and made a circular motion.

Hwang-Shu shouldered in front of Bartholdy when he heard this. "Oh shuwah, he tahk! He the one in prison, not me! I get him out, no fool!" They both started laughing at this, their routine inside joke.

"Listen, Roger, what I really came back here to tell you is, Hwang-Shu makes a better Bloody-Mary than anybody else on the planet, and coming from me that's quite a recommendation. I've tried 'em just about everywhere. Now, I can't indulge while I'm flying, of course—we've got rules. But you've just got to try one of Hwang-Shu's Marys before lunch. It's a tradition on this plane."

Roger hesitated. "Well...I don't know. I wouldn't want to—you know, it's just a little early and all."

Chuck and Hwang-Shu looked at each other, mortified. Hwang-Shu consulted his watch in disbelief.

"Early?" Chuck spoke as if he were confronting someone who was tragically confused. "My God, man, it's nearly lunchtime. Don't worry, we'll take care of you." He motioned at the cabin attendant, who turned and set to at the galley. He returned a moment later with a small glass, beautifully topped with a celery stalk. Roger took a sip. Best damn Mary he'd ever tasted.

During the four hour flight to the east coast, Hwang-Shu was the perfect host. Lunch: salmon, asparagus, garlic potato timbales, aromatic salad, and a miraculous little chocolate soufflé with a warm chocolate cream bourbon sauce. Two wines. Although the meal came from the caterers in Santa Barbara, the presentation was the work of the cabin attendant, and he insured that everything was perfect. The weather was calm and clear as promised, and the flight was smooth and relaxing. When they were about an hour out of Old Lyme, Roger was invited to come forward to tour the flight deck, and Captain Bartholdy let him sit at the controls for a few minutes. It seemed like no time at all before they were descending for their landing at the small regional airport near Mrs. Stertevant's estate. The jet dropped rapidly, but this time Roger was prepared and the effect was exhilarating. The ground seemed to be rushing up to meet them, but just at the moment it seemed they would crash, Chuck pulled the nose up and touched down on the runway delicately. As they taxied over to a hangar, Roger saw a beautiful vintage Packard station-wagon driving out toward them. Bartholdy leaned out of the cockpit as Roger left the jet.

"Hope you enjoyed it, Roger. We'll be ready to take you home when you're done here. Look forward to seeing your girlfriend again. She *will* be picking you up, right?"

Roger grinned. "Oh, believe me. Thanks for everything, guys. See you soon." He shook hands and then turned to the driver who was waiting for him, a grey-haired man named Marcus. As they drove off the airfield, he spoke with a light British accent.

"I'll just take you over to the hotel to freshen up for a bit, if that's alright with you, sir. Mrs. Stertevant has asked me to tell you that dinner will be served at the house at seven twenty." He looked at his watch. "But they have cocktails first. It's quarter to five now—that gives you a little time to rest. I could be back to pick you up at about six forty five?"

"Sure, that's fine, Marcus, thank you." He looked around at the gleaming interior of the station-wagon. "This is an incredibly nice car. Super clean. Cars are my business, and I've never seen an old Packard wagon this nicely restored." He rubbed the dark green leather seat. "It's gorgeous."

"Oh, it's not restored, sir. It's entirely original. Mrs. Stertevant bought it new in 1940. It's just been maintained carefully, and it's not really used that much." He pointed at the odometer. "You see, sir? Only 7,830 miles on it. It used to go to the train station, now it goes to the airport once in awhile, that's about the sum of it." He chuckled softly. "I should know, I've been Mrs. Stertevant's driver since '46."

The hotel had all the requisite New England charm: antique Yankee furniture and understated floral wallpaper. It was a welcome change from the quasi-Spanish glitz of Santa Barbara.

At 6:40, dressed in his best dark suit and with stomach annoyingly full of butterflies, Roger walked out under the hotel's port-cochere, just in time to see Marcus turn in the drive. The distance to the Stertevant place was short, and they arrived just before seven.

Roger expected something like Glenwhylden, something grand and extravagant—but Marsh Meadows was far from that. The grounds were spacious and impeccably kept, yet there were no high walls or big gates, and the house, which was clearly visible from the road, was an average-sized shingle-sided two-story home with shutters. Climbing vines meandered up the corners. The impression was of sedateness, stability, reassuring permanence: good, old-fashioned American values. The Packard came to a stop alongside the front steps. Roger was surprised to see an elderly woman standing at the top, waiting for him.

"Ah, Mr. Caldwell!" She was beaming. "We're so glad you could come. I'm Celine Stertevant. I trust your journey was comfortable?"

"Oh, yes, it sure was, Mrs. Stertevant, it was fantastic." At the top step he shook her hand. "Thank you so much for inviting me."

Given her age, the woman's appearance was striking. Tall and slender, very erect posture, with crystal-white hair and nearly unlined skin. She had a broad smile and ethereally blue eyes—penetrating aqua-marine. She looked far younger than he had imagined. She energetically shook hands. It was almost suspicious, as if this was not the real Mrs. Stertevant. She could have been a younger woman whose hair had been bleached white to give the appearance of age. Phil Holmbard had alluded that Celine Stertevant was frail, geriatric. This woman seemed neither. She led him inside, continuing an amiable chatter as they moved into a sitting room. Another woman, grey-haired and older looking than Celine, was waiting for them. She rose a bit stiffly as Celine introduced her.

"Mr. Caldwell, may I present my dear friend, Abigail Horvath."

Mrs. Horvath was short and worn around the edges. But her gaze was also penetrating: sage and perceptive. Her voice was pure gravel.

"Well, Mr. Caldwell!" she rattled, "we've been so looking forward to meeting you. Please, won't you sit down? Did you have a good trip? May we offer you a drink? I'm just headed to the kitchen." She sounded as if she'd smoked a million cigarettes.

Roger lowered himself into a massive velvet sofa. "Sure, that'd be great. Whatever you're having."

"Right, then," said Celine. "That'll be three gin-tonics, extra ice and a twist, Abby." While saying this, but without breaking her stride, she turned her head away from Abby to coquettishly regard Roger. She kept her eyes on him while sweetly adding, "I would appreciate that very much, Ab."

Abby moved toward the far door, trailing sandy syllables. "Three GT's on the way. Be right back." She left the room slowly and closed the door, leaving a little hole in the fabric of the proceedings. Roger returned Celine's look, and after a few seconds of silence he felt compelled to resume the chit-chat. He drew a breath, but just as he began to speak, he was interrupted by the loud gonging of a grandfather clock behind the sofa. He dipped his head and turned to look at the formidable timepiece. Large gold hands stood at seven o'clock, straight up. He turned back to find Celine Stertevant's gaze still studiously fixed on him, her hand under her chin. She wore a curious expression, like a child who is puzzling over something. It seemed to take a long time for the clock to complete its noisy duty, but the gonging finally ceased.

"May I call you Roger?"

"Oh, sure, please do."

"Roger. I'm sorry if I'm staring, but you remind me a bit of someone I knew many years ago. Odd. At any rate, I'll bet you're a little curious about me, and why I've gone to all the trouble of bringing you here. Fair to say?"

Roger smiled. "Well, *yes*—Mrs. Stertevant. Fair to say."

"Thing is, I've got to admit, I'm not completely sure myself. You see, Abby," she nodded toward the door where the other woman had exited, "Abby has this way of knowing things about people and events; she can do things with her mind that are just amazing, Roger, really. Anyway, when your letter came, for some reason she got all excited. Now I thought that was a little queer, you see, because I've known her for the better part of seventy years..." she paused and raised her eyebrows for emphasis, "and, well, let's just say that she doesn't get excited about too many things. Maybe she's like that because she senses in advance when something is going to happen, and it's kind of hard to get too worked up when you already know the ending. Know what I mean?"

"I think so."

"So. Alright. Your letter comes, and she says to me, 'Celine, you've got to meet this man. He's so interested in your house out there in Santa Barbara, and he doesn't even know the *real* reason for that himself. He thinks he does but he doesn't.' That's what she said. And I said, 'Well Abby, there's lots of people who are interested in my house out there. We get letters all the time from people who want this or that, or want to sell it for me or some such thing.'" Her face clouded. "God, Roger, you just wouldn't believe all the stuff I

65

get from realtors. Some new kid on the block just got his license and thinks he's going to score the big prize right out from under the other guys. They send me *proposals*, that's what they call them." She sighed with irritation. "At any rate—Abby, whom I trust implicitly in these matters, told me, insisted, that I should meet you, because there is some reason or other—I mean beyond your expressed interest in Glenwhylden, some other way in which you are *fated* to the house." Her eyes narrowed. At that moment he felt she could see right through him, somehow knew exactly what he was up to.

"Uh, well—" he swallowed hard, "like I said in my letter, the place has always had a pull on me. Really, Mrs. Stertevant." He shook his head slowly. "And, this is all like a dream, sort of. Coming here on the jet and now sitting here with you talking about this. I wrote the letter because I'd been curious for so long. But I didn't have much hope that you'd ever write back, and definitely not...any of this."

The door swung open and Abby reentered with the three gin-and-tonics balanced on a small tray.

"Here we are!" she called out gaily as she hobbled across the room. Celine got up to help her.

"Abby, I thought you'd never get here." She reached out and gently took the tray. "Oh, Roger, I didn't mean I wasn't interested in our conversation. It's just that we look forward to the cocktail hour here, and it's best we get on with it." She lifted a glass from the tray and handed it to Roger, and did the same for Abby, who had settled back in her chair. Celine then offered a toast. "To our new friend, Roger."

Perhaps inspired by the first sip, Abby seemed to have an afterthought, whereupon she raised her glass again.

"And, to adventure!"

"Oh yes," Celine agreed, "to adventure." More clinking, more sipping.

"Ab, we were just discussing this whole business about Roger's connection, or whatever, to Glenwhylden, and how it happened that we had him come here to visit us. He was just telling me that he feels like he's in a dream."

Abby looked keenly at Roger. "Oh, truly? Hopefully not a nightmare, Roger?"

"Oh, no, of course not!" He squirmed, wondering if there really was some way they could know about his deception. "Just the opposite, actually. All this is so nice, the plane ride, the hotel, being here...I've never gotten to do this before. That kind of a dream, that's what I meant."

"Ah, yes." Abby smiled at Celine. "We've certainly had some adventures on that plane, haven't we, Celine? Yes, indeed." She took a hefty swig of her gin-and-tonic, finishing it. It had been in her hand less than two minutes. She brought the glass down, wistfully swirling the ice around.

Celine was nodding happily. "Roger, we've been all over the world on that plane, and met the most marvelous people. Did you see the little paintings in the sleeping compartment? Those were given to us by the former Majarana of Udaipur. They had been in his family for over a hundred years. I won't travel without them. They have powers, you know. They keep us safe on our journeys." Then suddenly her focus shifted. "Ab, did chef say dinner would be on time?"

"Yes, dear, I'm afraid so."

Celine looked at her watch. "Good heavens. We'd better hurry." She immediately bolted the rest of her drink. "Have another, Roger?"

He looked at his glass. Scarcely dented. "Uh, I think I'm fine, for now," he said, a little confused by their apparent urgency. Abby started to get up.

"No, no, Ab, don't you go. There's not time. I'll phone it." She picked up the handset on the table beside her. Someone answered momentarily, and in an excessively sweet voice she said "Auguste? Yes. I'm *so sorry* to bother you. Yes. Could you please ask Hwang-Shu to bring us two more gin-and-tonics? Oh, yes, in ten minutes, on the nose. I know. Thank you so much!" She put down the receiver, looking a little relieved.

Roger was struck by the obvious deference she had shown the person on the phone, and it must have registered on his face, because she immediately said "Auguste is a very good chef, Roger. He's an artist. They're most hard to come by, chefs like that, and many are quite temperamental, don't you know. He's from Switzerland, and, unfortunately, as a young man before he became a chef, he worked for the railroads. He is insufferable about time." She lowered her voice, as if afraid of being overheard out in the kitchen. "I'm not kidding. If we're not in that dining room, seated, in..." she looked at her watch, "nine minutes and fifteen seconds, he actually might start throwing things at us through the door."

Abby nodded gravely. "But, Celine, you've got to admit, the food's worth it."

"Yes, I suppose." She looked at her watch again, then crossly stared at the door at the end of the room. "Damn it! Where are those drinks?"

As if in answer to her question, the door whapped open, and quite at variance with Abby's previous entrance, Hwang-Shu came flying into the room with the tray held deftly aloft. He moved into position with the trained grace of an acrobat, deploying the cocktails on their napkins neatly in front of the two women. Without hesitation, they both began draining them in workmanlike fashion. Hwang-Shu stood with the tray at his side and looked at Roger.

"No mowah you, Rojuh?"

"No, thanks, Hwang-Shu. Really, I'm just fine. Thanks, anyway."

The little man shrugged his shoulders. Then he bent down towards Celine. "Eight minute, Missus Stuhtevant," he said softly.

"*Thank*-you, Hwang-Shu. We are quite aware." She motioned him off. "I'm sorry Roger, it's our little evening ritual. Two drinks before dinner, no matter what. We got started a little late, I suppose. But we'll have lots of time to talk about everything over dinner."

Right on time, they moved into the dining room and were seated at the long table. It was set formally, with perhaps a dozen pieces at each place. At the center was a bright spray of pink and yellow roses. Roger was startled to see a gnarled little man in a tuxedo sitting in the far corner of the room, holding a cello between his legs. He began to play as they were seated. Celine turned and smiled at him, and he nodded and smiled in return, continuing to play.

"That's Emil. We like to have a little music with our supper, Roger. You know, I believe that God wouldn't disagree with me if I said that food, wine, and music are the second Holy Trinity, don't you know?" She looked very relaxed now, and as the meal progressed, Roger began to feel ever more ensconced in a marvelous, therapeutic experience. He lowered his guard and had the two ladies roaring with laughter at his stories about the sports-car business and the people he dealt with. They had no shortage of amazing stories of their own. Different wines accompanied each course, and Roger saw labels he had only read about in food magazines. The bottles came and went, Celine and Abby seemingly possessed of a limitless capacity for consumption. He did his best to keep up, but by the time dessert arrived Roger was bombed.

After the dinner they moved onto the east veranda of the house, facing out on a sloping lawn which ran right down to the beach. There was the faint sound of gentle waves spending their motion on the sand. It was a beautiful, calm evening, with a glistening swath of moonlight striping the dark ocean. They settled into wicker chairs, and coffee and cognac, along with a formidable rosewood humidor, were produced. The two women made their cigar selection as Hwang-Shu held the opened box in front of them. No comment was made in connection with this; it seemed as normal as anything else one might expect of two distinguished senior citizens. Roger had smoked only two or three cigars in his life so he chose a small one. Hwang-Shu snipped the ends of each cigar, and then patiently went around with long wooden matches.

Finally the conversation turned to the subject of Glenwhylden—something which had been referred to only in passing during dinner.

"I appreciate the interest you take in the house, Roger," Celine said after a few thoughtful puffs. "It was built by my late husband, Charles, as a surprise honeymoon present for me." She paused again, this time longer. "Charles was a dear, dear, man, Roger. I've never met anyone like him since. He put so much into that house, so much of himself and so much of what he believed I would like. It was amazing, the first time I saw it. It truly was a...*reflection* of just how much he respected me, and how very well he understood me—because in every detail he had created beauty that agreed with my eye. That house made me certain that I had chosen the right man to marry. Understand, he was fourteen years my senior. And people—well, some of my college friends and such, actually— tried to tell me while he was courting me that he was a lecher, you know. He was just after me for my youth and beauty..." she laughed, "not that I was all that beautiful! But that's what

70

my girlfriends were saying. They told me that I wouldn't be happy with a man that much older." She raised her voice to a falsetto, mimicking their sisterly admonitions. "Oh, Celine, he'll have sophisticated friends and they'll make quick work of you. You'll feel like a fish out of water!"

"And, I must admit, I listened to that line a little bit. I can't say I didn't worry about that sort of thing." She raised the cigar and took a long draw, then launched three perfect, fat smoke-rings. "But—you know what happened? I got lucky. Charles was strong, Roger, truly strong. When I was being girlish or sulky or cross—and I was, you know, I was more than a little spoiled when he married me—he'd be most patient. He'd let me work through it, without rising to the bait. I learned a lot from him in the short time we were married, I learned a great deal." Now she spoke more softly. "And then, well...it was over so quickly. An *accident*. It happened on a golf course, of all places. And *during our honeymoon*." She shook her head and waited a bit before going on. "He was struck on the temple by another man's drive off the tee. The doctor told me later, if the ball had hit him just one inch one way or the other, then all that would have happened would be a big bump on the noggin and a whopper of a headache for a couple of days. Isn't that remarkable? Just one of those freak things." She took in a deep breath and let it out very slowly, as if to release the pain that telling the old story had caused her. "So, there I was, a very young woman, sitting in this huge, marvelous new house that my darling husband had only just made for me, only now I had no more husband. I simply couldn't continue living there. I tried to go back there—once—two years after the funeral. I took my mother. I couldn't bear it. The house *was* him. He was in every detail, and yet it didn't give me any solace, it just made me miss him more keenly. I think I was made all the more

71

upset by the fact that I'd not gotten pregnant before he was gone. I think if I'd had a child it might have been different. I was angry in those days. So very, very angry. I didn't talk of it or show it, outwardly, but I was. It felt so unfair. To be built up so high, and then just cut off, like that!" She snapped her fingers for emphasis. "So. That's why I haven't been back to Glenwhylden in all these years, Roger." She rolled her eyes and waved her cigar. "Heavens, not since 1921!"

The light was dim out on the veranda, just a couple of lanterns on the little tables around them, and in their mild, flickering softness she appeared remarkably young, even girlish. The yellow lantern glow made her white hair appear blond, and the blueness of her eyes seemed amplified.

"That's really something, isn't it Ab? I haven't seen Glenwhylden since 1921. It was a *new* house then." She said this as if recognizing the significance for the first time. Abby just grunted from within a cloud of smoke. Celine turned to face Roger.

"I know there are stories told in Santa Barbara about the house, and even about me. People think the house just sits there empty, unused, and that a few servants and gardeners are the only ones who ever get to be there. I know this...you see, there are garden clubs and the like—they send me letters through Phil Holmbard. They suggest it's my civic duty to let them use the grounds, have fund raisers there, or whatever else. They're good people, I don't blame them. I've donated money to some of those groups. A lot of money." She leaned toward Roger. "But, do you see why I don't let them go to the house? Can you understand that I've had a very real reason for not allowing other people to go there?"

Roger shifted in his chair, captivated by the story. "Hearing you tell it this way," he said thoughtfully, "I can see that you have."

"Yes. It is—well, certainly due in large part to my everlasting love for my dear Charles. I just can't stand to think of strangers walking through the paradise that he created for us. It's just too personal, even still, after all this time. I guess I want to keep it sacred. It's something I'm selfish about. I admit that it's *quite selfish*, but I've never changed my mind about it. Or maybe, I should say that, I haven't considered changing my mind...until now."

She sat up and looked over at the doorway to the living room. Hwang-Shu was standing there, at the ready. She motioned toward Roger's cigar, which had gone out. A match flared, and Roger resumed smoking. More cognac was distributed among the snifters. Celine waited for the servant to withdraw, then fixed Roger with a stern gaze.

"Now. Let's get to something you haven't bargained for. I will tell you, young man, that beyond the sacredness of my husband's memory, lately there's been another reason for privacy at Glenwhylden, and with no question it's a much better reason." She set the remainder of her cigar in a heavy crystal ashtray and clasped her hands under her chin. "Look. I'm not sure if you're just in the right place at the right time, or if you actually do have some spiritual purpose being here, but all that aside, after spending time with you I now feel I can trust you, Roger. To be honest, I need to trust someone like you. Because I need some serious help with a damned important situation. I'm going to reveal something else about Glenwhylden that almost nobody knows, so I must ask that you give me your solemn assurance that this will remain our secret. Even my attorney there doesn't know. A lot is riding on this. How about it?"

Roger felt the gravity of the forthcoming information. "I give you my word, Mrs. Stertevant."

Celine nodded. "Good. Well, contrary to all the stories, there aren't only servants at the house. No. There are actually others. Friends of mine, personal friends who are very dear to me. And they live there. Full time."

Well, this was news, true enough. But, nothing very big deal, as far as he could tell. So there were a few extra people living at Glenwhylden that nobody knew about. That was it? He kept silent, expecting more. But what she said next didn't exactly stand his hair on end.

"They're foreigners. Four men and three women. We met when I was traveling. They're in this country illegally, but they're all brilliant in their own right, and I feel strongly that they should stay here. I'd like them to have the same opportunities as anybody else."

Now he had the picture. She needs some local person to help these people get their papers and learn English and the whole bit. Huh. Why doesn't she just get Phil Holmbard to do it for her? That's what he's there for, after all.

"But you see," Celine seemed to search for her words, "they lived in very primitive conditions before they became my guests, and they're having a hard time adjusting. They have language issues and they need someone who can help them. You see? I mean, as they absorb the customs of our society."

He mentally patted himself on the back. Called that one. We're talking third-world people and they're in culture shock in America. Yep.

"Now, we believe," Celine looked at Abby, "that you might just be a very good person for a job like this, Roger. And, now wait, before you say anything, maybe you've never done anything even remotely like this, but I hope you won't react just right away. I brought you here so I could meet you and see what you're like. Once all the cards are on the table, then...you can decide. Okay?"

Roger didn't see how he could lose by playing along. He wanted to get inside Glenwhylden, and pretending interest in this job seemed to guarantee that. "Of course, Mrs. Stertevant. I'd like to hear all about it. I'd be very interested."

"Wonderful. Good, Roger. We'll talk more about it, then." She looked at her watch. "But now, it's getting a bit late, and I'm sure we're all tired—it's been a long day. Marcus will drive you back to the hotel, and then you could come back tomorrow for lunch and we can discuss all the details then. We like to have lunch at noon, so Marcus will come by for you at eleven forty-five."

They all walked out. Hwang-Shu was at the front door, and as it swung open the station wagon with Marcus at the wheel was waiting at the bottom of the stairs.

Roger turned to his hosts. "Well, this has been great. Thanks again, Mrs. Stertevant. I'll be ready tomorrow right on time."

"Sleep well, Roger."

Chapter 7

Roger grogged awake about ten the next morning (still on California time) suffering definite ill-effects from the previous night's drinking. Blearing at the sunlight hammering past the curtains, he momentarily recalled a dream he'd had during the night.

He was with a strange-looking old man, a wizened character with long, wild hair and a beard that grew out all around his face. He was explaining something in a solemn way, referring to a chart. It was dark blue, with white lines and dots, like a map of the nighttime sky. Roger could not remember the man's words—only that they had a powerful effect on him. He'd felt intensely sad; weeping, yet no tears would come, and no sounds either. As the little man talked, Roger had strained in profound distress, sobbing silently. That was all he could remember, and after considering it for a short while, he discarded thinking about it and got up. His head was throbbing. He showered and dressed, had coffee and an apple in the dining room, then went for a walk. He went down along the water's edge, and then on up through a quaint, older part of the village. Grateful for his sunglasses, he breathed deeply, trying to exorcise the poisonous residue in his system.

He arrived back at the hotel just in time to meet Marcus. Back to Marsh Meadows they went. This time it was Hwang-Shu who greeted him.

"Bell not necessary!" he grinned as he opened the door. "I see you come. Got good lunch ready today, Rojuh. You hungry man?"

"Well, I didn't exactly have breakfast, so I think I'll be interested. Where are the ladies?" Roger peered into the empty sitting room as he entered the hall.

"Ah! Everyone in sunroom, south side. Time for everyday phone calls."

Roger was led to a sunny, expansive screen-porch. Celine and Abby were propped up on chaises, the detritus of two or three newspapers strewn on the floor. The women were engaged in separate telephone conversations; Celine looked up and smiled, motioning Roger toward a chair. She cupped her hand over the mouthpiece of the receiver.

"Be right with you, Roger. Just finishing a little business." She resumed on the phone. "So...let's not waste a lot of time. Work out the details, John. I know the museum will love having the piece, and I'm sure lots of people will be very excited to come and see it. He has a price, I'm sure. If he knows it's me who's interested in it, he'll try to jack the number way up, so just act like you're buying it for yourself. Right. For your fireplace, good. I want to be fair, but not get robbed. So, I'm here if you need me. Thanks, darling." She hung up and smiled dreamily at Roger.

"I'm trying to get a wonderful little nautical painting for our museum here, and the dear man who owns it needs to sell—you know, a money thing." She sighed. "But... he's had it for many years, and I think he's quite attached to it. Damn. Got to be delicate." She glanced over at Abby, who was growling persuasively into her phone. "Abby knows the man's sister. Maybe we'll get in through that door."

Hwang-Shu returned and handed Celine a menu card. She read it intently. "Ooooh, *curried shrimp on Basmati rice* for lunch. I thought I was smelling curry. Do you like shrimp curry, Roger?"

He concealed his immediate reaction with a forced smile.

"I can't wait!" She flung the card over at Abby, who was just finishing up her conversation. She picked it up and grinned. No question, food was the big deal around Marsh Meadows.

"Now, Roger" Celine continued, "I should explain to you that at about this time every day we have a little lunch and take a conference call from our friends, the ones in California at my house. They're three hours behind us, so they're usually just having breakfast at the same time we're having lunch. It works out very well. Their English still needs a lot of work, but they love to talk. Some of them are quite opinionated, and very outspoken, so be forewarned."

At the mention of the word "outspoken" Abby snorted and folded her arms. "Outspoken? Hell, one of 'em plain old knows it all!"

"They're all very entertaining, Roger." Celine reached for a notepad that was laying on the table. "But at first it can be hard to understand what they're saying. Takes a little getting used to, that's all." She was jotting something down as she spoke, and presently she handed him the pad. There were seven names: Pongo, Artod, Trent, George, Emily, Betty, and Chloé. Roger squinted at the names, then looked back over at Celine.

"Don't all sound like foreigners, do they? Those aren't their real names. Or, I should say, those aren't their original names. When they got here they wanted to sound more American. They just went through the phone book one afternoon and came up with those..." she pointed at the list in Rogers hand. "They're like that, you know; very creative and spontaneous. It's one of the reasons they need someone to steady them. They need a rudder for their lives here."

The phone rang.

"Hello, Stertevant. Oh, good morning, Betty. Just talking about you. What, darling? Oh, yes, I know. Is it? Oh, well. It's that summer fog, you know. No. No. It's beautiful here, just lovely. Well now, listen, love, I've got a very big surprise for everyone today. Are you on the speaker? Well, put us on, will you? Is everyone there yet? Alright, go get them and I'll just hang on while you do." She grinned and covered the receiver. "Pongo and Artod are still out in the media room watching the end of "Good Morning America". They just love that girl that's on there...I think her name's Joan something?" She heard everyone coming on the line just then, and her face brightened even more.

"Oh, good morning, my darlings! Is everyone well today? Yes, we are. Yes! Yes, she's right here...now, wait just a second, because we're not on speaker yet. Just a moment."

She pushed a button and put down the receiver. Strange, strange, sounds now came out of the speaker. It sounded something like a chorus of small children, all talking at once through kazoos.

"Guhd murning, Ebby!"

Abby leaned toward the box and responded with her own squawking rasp. "Good morning! What are you having for breakfast, the usual?"

The kazoo chorus again. Roger thought he heard words like "grapefruit", "peaches", a very cautious and labored "cant-ell-ope". This subsided, then a slightly deeper voice piped up: "Wuffles!"

Abby burst out laughing. "Oh, it's waffles today, eh Pongo? What a treat!"

Celine took charge. "Listen, all. Today is a very important day. I have a wonderful surprise, so please pay close attention." She cleared her throat. "We've talked so often about finding someone—a special person, someone who could

79

come there to Glenwhylden and help everyone get to be better citizens. I know this is something you've all needed, and I haven't really done much about it, have I? I was quite concerned, to be honest, that I wouldn't be able to find the right person." She hesitated and looked directly at Roger. "But, now, it happens that a very fine young man from Santa Barbara wrote to me not long ago. He grew up there, and he has been interested in Glenwhylden since he was a little boy. Abby thought we should meet him, and so we asked him to come out here to Marsh Meadows for a visit. He was kind enough to accept, and he is...in fact he's sitting here with us right now."

There was complete silence on the other end of the line. Celine gave it a few moments, then offered a bit more information, to calm any fears of the stranger.

"I want you all to get to know him, as we've been doing here. Perhaps today you can all chat with him and get acquainted. His name is Roger Caldwell."

Still, a doubtful silence.

"Really, everyone, it's alright. Are you there, Pongo?"

Now the husky voice came over the speaker again. "Yus, Saylin. Ohkey. Uhhh...guuhd morneg Missar Cawdweo." He spoke slowly and uncertainly.

Roger leaned in close to the speakerphone and consciously tried to sound very gentle and non-threatening, like Mr. Rogers on Public Television. "Good morning, Pongo. Everyone, please call me Roger. Very pleased to meet you all."

The voices were exceptionally odd, textured and breathy. Roger pictured four foot tall tribespeople with painted faces and blowguns.

Once the ice was cracked a little bit, the guests began offering tentative fragments of polite chit-chat. Celine got them to reveal tidbits about their interests and concerns. Betty enthused about a pastry she'd baked using a recipe she found in Gourmet magazine. A raspberry layer cake. George was proud that a rosebush he'd planted was now blossoming.

Finally a cart laden with serving dishes was wheeled in. Celine raised her voice above the modest commotion.

"Give us just a moment, dears. They're bringing in lunch, and we're going to move over to the table."

Roger pulled out the chairs for the ladies, then seated himself. As they started on the watercress, apple, and walnut salad, Celine resumed with the conference call.

"Chloé, have you gotten those sweaters I sent you yet?"

The little voice wound up. "Ouh, yeass! I guht theym yastuhdeh effturnun, aynd dey arh sooo nize! Dey arh juhss wuht I wuhnted! Dankuo sooo mushz!"

"Szhee iss zo bootuhfoal, Ah thingk Ah'l maury hor!" It was Artod, making fun of Chloé and her sweaters. The others squealed and snorted.

The conversation meandered; for awhile Pongo and Roger discussed cars. Pongo wanted a ride in a really fast car. Roger promised that if they met someday, he'd make it happen.

Half an hour later Celine bade them all a good day, promising to call back with news about Roger's possible role in their new lives. Abby moved over to the chaise, lapsing quickly into the after-lunch nap.

"How about a little walk?" Celine said quietly. They went out the screen door and strolled across the lawn. "I think they all like you, Roger. I'm very glad for that. Our conversation was a good deal more lively today than it's been lately. I think your presence had something to do with it. Amazing, isn't it, how well informed they are? Keep in mind, they've only been here a short time."

"Their voices are so unusual. Are they small people? I get the impression that they're small people."

"Well, yes. They're somewhat short in stature. Their diet was poor, and they had it rough. They just need more practice with English. Their original language was absolutely *nothing* like English."

They entered a walled garden, with formal hedges, topiary trees, and a manicured lawn. She stopped and squared toward him.

"Roger, you're being so careful and polite, I get the feeling you're not telling us everything. The work with these people would take an open mind, a flexible imagination, a lot of patience. I need somebody I can count on. Are you that kind of person?"

He got a wave of discomfort. He didn't like having to lie to this nice old woman, it made him feel dirty, but it was the only way. He remembered his own grim reality. He had a purpose here, and it was getting inside the estate. He tried to give her what she wanted.

"Well, ma'am...I *think* I have an open mind. I'm usually okay with other people's ideas, as long as it seems like they have some kind of integrity. I've got my share of problems, same as anybody else, but I'm not an alcoholic or a drug addict or anything. I'm not a criminal. Of course I'd have to meet these people first."

Two peacocks paraded by. Celine watched their slow sashay, and said nothing more for a minute or so. She took hold of his elbow, and they turned onto a pathway that led down toward the beach.

"Alright then. Here's what I've decided. I'm going to allow you to visit Glenwhylden. I want you to meet the group there. I was thinking that a few days from now might be good." She looked out at the ocean. "And, also, I think it's time that I, finally...well, I should go back and see the place again myself. I need to do it, I should do it. It's been so long. Maybe all these years, possibly I've made more of it than was ever right or proper—keeping away, I mean." She nodded vigorously, putting the final seal on the decision. "We can wait to talk about the details of the work you might do—you know, hours, money, that sort of thing—until after you've had a chance to see things first-hand. I want you to be sure. I want them to meet you, too, so they can tell me if they want you to be their guy or not. It goes without saying, their opinion enters into it. Chemistry, don't you know. Sound fair?"

Roger smiled. Finally things seemed to being going right, even if it would all end with his suicide. His letter had been a gamble, scarcely expected to have this result, but here it was.

"It does, Mrs. Stertevant. Actually, I'll be very happy just to finally get to see Glenwhylden."

"Well, that much I can promise. We'll give you the tour. But Roger, I warn you. Things might not turn out the way you think they will."

He looked down. Oh yes they will, he thought.

Chapter 8

Earthquakes. In the overall scheme of things, in the life of the planet, no big deal, really. Just a mere shiver, a little localized shrug to deal with an uncomfortable build-up of opposing tectonic forces. A technical adjustment. Nothing more than a geological sneeze, as far as Nature is concerned. The stuff in the middle of the big ball is cooling down, progressively, and we all know what happens when things cool down—they shrink. So the more or less solid stuff on top, the stuff we all know as home, Terra Firma—it has to make allowances for that shrinking. A fold, a wrinkle here and there, a crease that wasn't there before. That's an earthquake. A perfunctory little event as far as the "big forces" are concerned.

Now, for us on the other hand, for the beings who walk on this earth and come from it and fall down to it when we stumble, for all of us a big earthquake is just about the biggest deal. A real occasion. Something to absolutely crap in the pants about. That stable stuff under our feet, that comforting blanket to cling to when the monstrously enormous vastness of the night sky presses down on us with all its impersonality and its repetitious, insistent posing of unanswerable questions—its chilling and bogglingly myriad swirls of prickly stars—the ground, that firm basis upon which we all live, begins to heave and pitch, and assumes the very qualities of a tossing, threatening, consuming ocean. That sort of event is paralyzingly disconcerting to us, and rightly so.

Then, there's yet another kind of earthquake, the kind where the ground doesn't actually move, but the people in the affected area would swear that it had.

The earthquake that occurred in Santa Barbara on the same day that Roger and Celine had their conversation in the gardens at Marsh Meadows House was of this last variety: extremely localized. The ground was perceived to move solely within the walled perimeter of the Glenwhylden estate. This event was experienced only by the staff and permanent residents of the estate. A massive plate (in the form of the full faith and expectation of the house-staff that Celine Stertevant would never again show up at Glenwhylden as long as she lived) abruptly being ground against another massive plate (a phone call, from Phil Holmbard to Whitney Polk, the butler and major domo at Glenwhylden) informing him that the house was to be immediately prepared for the arrival of Mrs. Stertevant and a small party on the following morning.

Holmbard and Polk were on a first name basis, as they had longstanding and frequent contact pertaining to the estate's maintenance. The two men had known each other in this association for nearly forty years, and they liked to needle each other over their mundane business. The lawyer's favorite joke involved placing a call to the butler—typically late at night, after a few highballs—claiming that Celine Stertevant was at the airport and would be arriving at the front gates within a matter of minutes. It was its quality of absurdity that always made this joke so satisfying. Over the years, the ploy would resurface periodically, always with some new twist: "Be forewarned," Holmbard once intoned to the butler, "I have it on good authority that Mrs. Stertevant is dressed as a beekeeper. Don't let on, no matter what, that you find this strange." Another time Polk picked up the receiver to hear the lawyer confiding earnestly that he had just discovered, to his absolute amazement, that Mrs. Stertevant had been at the estate all these years after all, masquerading as the pantry maid. "Now, Polk, you haven't been treating her abrasively, have you?" he demanded to know.

"You know, Phil, she calls me *directly*, I suppose it's only fair I should tell you," Polk lied expertly. "She's very unhappy with the way you're handling things. Oh yes, I'm serious, surely am. And she wants to know if I can give her the names of some better lawyers who aren't so damn lazy. Oops, sorry. Well, anyway, I'm just repeatin' what she said."

Given the lengthy tradition of this false-alarming poste and riposte, it is understandable that considerable effort, even histrionics, were necessary on the part of Phil Holmbard in order to convince Polk that this latest announcement was the real thing.

"No, really, Whitney! I mean it, goddamn it, *she's really fucking coming this time!*"

On the phone, Polk snickered. "Good one, Phil. Actually, I think this is the best one so far. You sound really fired up, man. Hey, well. I got stuff to do, so catch you later." He summarily hung up.

Holmbard scrambled into his ponderous Buick and roared over to Glenwhylden's front gates, punching the intercom button like it was a wasp that had gotten up his pants leg. Mystified by this behavior, Polk, contravening strict policy, buzzed him in and waited on the front steps for the car to enter the motor-court. It did a few moments later, going about sixty. As the lawyer rounded the last curve at the top, the Buick's white sidewalls squealed in protest, and he narrowly avoided running off into the azalea beds. Polk caught a glance of a crazed face as the massive sedan careened around the fountain. The car zoomed right toward the front steps, and for a terrifying moment, Polk thought it wasn't going to stop. But then Holmbard slammed on the brakes, and the car slid sideways over the cobblestones, coming to an undignified halt at the base of the steps. Holmbard propelled his substantial mass up the steps, two at a time. He was sweating like a plow-horse as he blew up to the butler, who now stood with his mouth open in amazement.

"Polk! You bastard! I'm not! Fucking kidding!" Holmbard wheezed heavily, the years of sedentary lifestyle in full evidence. He struggled to catch his breath, barking out short bursts. "She's coming! Here! Tomorrow! Get this fucker! Ready! Immediately!"

Polk backed up a step, staring through his owlish horn-rimmed spectacles at the streaming, reddened, inflating and deflating bag in the three piece suit.

"Damn, man. You're really serious? Come on, Phil, man, don't be shittin' me here. You're not shittin' me?"

This query further notched up Holmbard's agitation. He grabbed the impeccable lapels of the butlers' white service jacket, and hung on for a moment, catching his breath.

"I'm not *shitting you*, you moron. Listen to me. Celine Bell Stertevant, your boss, my boss, the person who owns all this, is coming here tomorrow for a visit. She's bringing some people. You've got 'till eleven o'clock tomorrow to get everything ready. Now get yourself in there, and get your staff off their asses and into gear, and get everything going, or else I will!" He started to push past the butler and reached for the massive bronze doorknob.

Polk was 6'4", 224 pounds, and ten years the lawyer's junior. He'd played some football in high school. He gently but firmly checked Holmbard's motion toward the door.

"Okay, okay, Phil," he soothed. "I believe you, man. Now, just calm down. You know I can't let you in there. I'm not even supposed to let you come up that driveway, you know that as well as I do. Calm down. Jesus, man, look at yourself. You want a cup of coffee or something?" He paused, absorbing the momentous news. "Holy shit, she's really coming?"

The lawyer nodded vigorously, his color beginning to normalize.

"Well, I'll be damned. Man. I never." The butler shook his head. "Then, yes, I got a lot to do. You just head on back out the gate, Phil. I'll take it from here. I promise you we'll be ready."

Holmbard's jowls drew taut in a beseeching look. "She's my bread and butter, Whitney. My biggest and best client, by far. You won't let me down, now, will you? Promise?"

Polk walked him down the steps, speaking in soothing tones. "Everything's gonna be perfect, Phil, I promise. Just go on back to the office and take care of your end. I'll have everything perfect here by eleven tomorrow. Slam dunk." He patted the attorney's sodden shoulders and opened the car door for him. Then, as the Buick muttered back down the drive, the butler turned and sprinted into the house.

Two miles away Gwynn Murck stood naked in Roger's bedroom, studying her image in the full length mirror. She'd been out by the pool most of the morning, perfecting the most impressive all-over tan in Santa Barbara. This "mirror time", her self-appreciation sessions, were immensely enjoyable to her, similar to what other people might feel when viewing a great painting or sculpture. Gwynn found scarce fault with her own body. She didn't like to admit it to herself, but she actually turned herself on. Sometimes she wished she could enter a man's body to see what it would be like to make love to herself. She liked Roger's bedroom mirror the most, because he was often there to witness her display. It was so satisfying, getting him all heated up, only to announce that she was late picking up her girlfriends to go shopping. "Take a cold shower, horn dog," she'd chirp, grabbing a towel and slamming the bathroom door.

Oh, she liked sex well enough. After all, it had an important purpose, didn't it? But she loved the concept far more. So much neater, cleaner. The way it happened in romance novels or in music-videos—tidy little three second bits. No icky mess.

She turned first one way, then another, allowing her long blonde hair to brush sensuously across her nipples. She admired the tasteful generosity of her breasts—levitated by countless dedicated hours on the pectoral cross machine at the gym—"not fake", she congratulated herself. Her nipples grew taut with the caresses of her hair. The phone rang. Shit. She eyed it balefully, reluctant to be distracted from her business. She waited for the answering machine to pick up. When she was alone at Roger's house sometimes she learned things about him that she might otherwise not have. It was fun, the illicit pleasure of hearing messages when the person on the line didn't know she was there, listening. But this time it was Roger himself calling. "Hey, babe. It's me. Gwynn...are you there? Pick up if you're there."

She reached over and grabbed the phone. "Hi, baby! I miss you!" She giggled expertly. "Are you coming home, Roger doll? I was just thinking about you." Her voice was practiced, ersatz elated.

"You were? So then, what're you up to there, exactly, Gwynn ? Let me guess, I'll bet you're on the bed with two or three...two or three..."

"Two or three what?"

"Magazines."

She fed him along, keeping it light. "Uh hmm, you're right about that two or three, Rogie, but they're not magazines! *Ooooh-wooooh!*"

He grimaced, yanking the phone from his ear, and felt a stab of nausea. It wasn't what Gwynn was saying, the fakery. Even the jarring squeal wasn't the problem. There was nothing strictly wrong with any of that. It was just...well, the whole exchange was a re-tread; she was making happy for him, doing *her job*. She was convinced this pleased him.

Experience in Montecito had taught her that most unattached wealthy men prefer their women spectacularly pretty and emotionally uncomplicated. Just look great and act like a kitten. Keep Daddy jolly. Don't get moody. So Gwynn had made herself into the kind of dream-girl most men fantasized about. But lately when Roger heard her pat little jive it made him feel dishonest and weak. He had to stifle an urge to blurt out something cutting and rude. And now, on this diverting journey, with his mind centered on weighty matters, the sound of Gwynn's voice on the phone fractured a mental screen of convenience he'd been maintaining. He had nothing in common with her. He had no respect for her, because although he was attracted to her sexually, there was nothing else about her that inspired him or commanded his attention. There it was. She looked great, she was good in bed, that was it. And if he wasn't so weak he wouldn't spend another five minutes with Gwynn Murck.

He'd run the scene many times in his mind, and the goodbye part always went smoothly. Strong and noble, a man of purpose, doing the right thing. It was the next sequence that gave him trouble. In that one, she hears him say "It's over", and instead of going to pieces, she's steel-plated. "You're a fool, Roger," she says. "If you don't want me, fine. I've got a waiting list as long as my arm. All winners, no problem." As she turns to walk out, his eyes travel down to her perfect little butt. A mocking little voice is saying "Stupid! Stooooopid!"

And he's the one who goes to pieces, realizing he's thrown away something irreplaceable.

He returned the phone to his ear. "I'll be home tomorrow, babe. I miss you, too. You're taking good care of my pad?"

"Well, it's a lot cleaner than it's been for a long time. I vacuumed under all the furniture yesterday. I don't think you've ever done that. So. Anyway, what have you been doing out there, partying all over the place without me? Did you guys find the right car or whatever it was?"

Roger paused, getting his story straight. "Uh, no. No, not exactly. They're gonna have to keep looking, I guess."

Gwynn pressed him. "No? Well, that's too bad, I guess. Aren't you having a good time anyway? You must be, I mean, what was that jet ride like? It must have been awesome! Are you staying in a nice place?"

"Oh yeah. Yeah, the jet was incredible. And this place where I'm staying is...really cute, you know. Real New England-y decor, comfy and cozy. I think you'd get off on the whole scene here, Gwynn. Lots of money, for sure. It's a pretty different vibe from Santa Barbara, though. I don't know, it just feels older or something. Just not as happening, but still really beautiful."

"That sounds great to me," she sighed. "I never get to go anywhere. Hey, when you get back, let's go up to the mountains, or something, you want to? I need a few days out of this berg, myself." She brightened. "I know! Let's go up to the wine country for a weekend, okay Rog? I saw an article about it in Bazaar and it had some pictures of this cool little hotel!"

"Yeah, sure. We'll talk about it when I get home, okay, Gwynn? I'm kinda tired right now. Listen, I'm gonna get a ride home from the airport tomorrow, so you won't have to come meet me. I'm not sure what time we're coming in, and they're gonna have cars there anyway. That way you won't have to get hung up. I'll just see you when I get back to the house, cool?"

"They? Who's they? I thought you were coming back on American, aren't you? Are some people coming back with you?"

Roger winced. "Well, *actually*, the way it worked out, these people needed to send the plane back out to the west coast anyway, so they're gonna stop off in Santa Barbara. I'm just gonna catch a ride again. It wasn't really planned, it just sorta turned out this way as of last night. So—I'll see you at the pad later tomorrow. Okay?"

Gwynn soured. "Oh great, I see. Jetting around without me some more, super. You're so lucky, you creep. I really need to get a life. Okay, I'll just wait here at home for you, prince." A sharp edge came into her voice. "Hey, you know, I'd like to *meet* these people, Roger. Why don't you *introduce* me? How do I know you're not just doing some rich babe who's flying you around as her personal plaything, huh?"

"Gwynn. Gwynn. Are you high? I've never heard you say anyth—these are *old* people for starters. And, listen, if the opportunity presents itself, of course I'll introduce you, okay? Don't get bummed because I'm having a little fun here, okay? Come on baby, it's not such a big deal."

Too late. She'd already decided a good sulk was in order, and she got it underway. "Roger, have a good time, don't worry about me, see you when you're available, okay? Ta."

Click.

Roger sank back on the bed, closing his eyes, affected by her pettiness. If he really loved her, he told himself, he'd have been able to naturally and playfully fix the tension. Maybe somehow he *wanted* her to get pissed off. The honest part of his being was pleased that she got huffy. He thought about calling her back. She probably wouldn't pick up the phone, he reasoned. Even if she did, then there would be more escalated shit-flinging. After another minute he sat up and looked hard at the phone, then shook his head. He went in and turned on the shower, shifting his mind to the evening ahead.

Chapter 9

The following day was rainy and foul, with the sharp wind bringing a soaking drizzle in off the ocean. At seven-thirty the small party of travelers assembled for an early breakfast, then were driven to the airport where the sleek black jet stood stocked and ready. Captain Bartholdy literally had the red carpet out for Celine and her guests, and it sogged underfoot as they dismounted from the cars and trudged the few feet to the gangway stairs. Bartholdy and the co-pilot stood in the chilly drizzle. Celine greeted them warmly, commenting that it had been quite awhile since they had journeyed together. The cabin of the jet was cozy and inviting, nicely warm. Before the ladies were seated, they went rear to see the magical little paintings, and they returned to the main cabin with wide smiles.

When the jet began to taxi out, the pace was noticeably slower than had been the case in Santa Barbara. Roger concluded that this must be due to Celine and Abby's presence on board. Sure enough, on take-off there was no acrobatic climb, just a smooth, steady ascent skyward, an almost immediate penetration of the low cloud deck, and finally a thrilling moment as they popped out of the grey overcast and into stippled sapphire, with sun-washed white cloud-tops carpeting the scene all the way to the horizon. Brilliant sunlight gorged the cabin. The windows, like multiple duplicate paintings at a modern art exhibition, displayed the fluorescent azure of a high altitude sky.

Celine and Abby smiled at each other and then at Roger as if they were angels escorting him on a celestial pilgrimage.

The plane banked gently and soon leveled off, racing west. Now the mood changed from subdued to festive. The day acquired a marvelous kind of energy. Spread out all around them was a most spectacular morning. Almost at once, the pleasure of consuming was begun, and along with delicious smells, little goodies began to issue from the galley. The flight back to Santa Barbara took a little over four hours, and as Roger had now come to expect, the time was filled with wonderful conversation and marvelous food.

As they neared the west coast, the ladies withdrew to the after-cabin for their midday naps, and Roger was left alone for awhile. He began to focus anxious thoughts on matters that had been put on hold during the getaway. Remembering his troubles keenly, the familiar curtain of depression began closing in once more. This trip had been a nice way for things to wind down. But soon, he thought, very soon it will all be over.

A short time later the hushed roar of the engines lowered and Roger felt the nose tilting a bit. They were descending over the inland desert. Hwang-Shu went aft.

"Missus Stuhtevunt! Missus Hohvath!" He addressed the closed door. "We land soon, you please come out for buckle down in seat?"

After a moment Celine came out, smoothing her hair. Abby followed, looking rested. Hwang-Shu helped them into their seats and then brought everyone glasses of iced mineral water. Celine turned to Roger and grinned.

"You know one of the main reasons I bought this airplane in the first place? I positively could not sleep sitting up in those airliner seats, not even in first class. Just couldn't ever get comfortable. There's nothing like having your own little bed to snooze in when you're flying somewhere. Some of the best naps I've ever had have been on this plane. I just love it.

I'm sorry we didn't have an extra bed to offer you." She reached over and patted his hand.

"Oh, no, no problem, Mrs. Stertevant. I really wasn't sleepy—actually, I was just using the time to...you know, think. Think about things."

Abby pointed her finger at Roger. "Young man, if you *weren't* doing some serious thinking right now, I wouldn't trust you a bit." Her jagged voice ground the words out like coarse pebbles. "This has all been a whirl so far, a lot of talk, hasn't it? You'll have your own business to catch up on when we get to Santa Barbara, I imagine."

Roger nodded.

"Well, we know, and we want you to take your time, don't we, Celine?"

"Yes, of course," Celine answered. Then, "Roger—do you have a girl?"

The question floated out innocently. He wondered why he hadn't been asked until now. Usually the first thing a sweet elderly woman will want to know about a young man is whether he has a girl.

He smiled and cocked his head, giving it a little bounce at the end like he was thinking of something dear and whimsical. "I most certainly do," he said. "I wouldn't trade her for the world." His own bullshit astonished him.

"Why, isn't that sweet! What's her name?" Abby leaned in, interested.

"Gwynn. Gwynn Murck."

Abby frowned and looked at Celine, then turned back to Roger.

"Gin Burp?"

Right, she hadn't heard him. The noise of the plane. He raised his voice politely.

"Uh, no, Gwynn Murck...*Murck*. Yes."

96

Abby opened her mouth and then sat back and repeated this news to Celine. "Gwynn Murck. She's named Gwynn."

Celine repeated dutifully: "Gwynn."

Why this little deaf act, Roger wondered, when the noise of the plane had been louder earlier in the trip and they'd had no difficulty hearing normal conversation then?

Celine continued. "Is she the girl of your dreams, Roger? I always like to hear stories about people finding their destiny."

Roger hedged. "She's...very nice."

The two women gave each other a significant look. Then Celine changed the subject. "Well, you need to have a little time to get things caught up, Roger. The day after tomorrow would be fine for you to come to Glenwhylden for your visit. We'll just get settled, and you can have some time to go back to work. Sound okay?"

"Yes, that would be fine. I do have a little list to cover, you're sure right there."

"Good. Alright then, it's settled. We'll drop you off at your place today, then you'll come see us on Saturday. By then I'm sure we'll have all the old cobwebs out of the place."

The plane now slowed noticeably and they could hear the landing gear being lowered. Roger looked down at the ocean, with dense fog banks spotting along the shoreline. Celine closed her eyes, having given some thought to this moment. She didn't want to catch a preview of Glenwhylden from the air. She wanted her first look in nearly seventy years to be from the perspective of the front gates, the way she remembered it.

A few minutes later the jet eased down on the runway. As they swung around to their final position on the apron, Roger could see a dark silver Lincoln town car parked on the tarmac. The driver stood beside it, his hat tucked under his arm. The man stepped up to the party as they came down the stairs. He bowed to Celine.

"It is my honor to welcome you back to Santa Barbara, Mrs. Stertevant. I am Whitney Polk, head of the household staff."

"Ah, Mr. Polk!" she exclaimed. "Of course. I remember your father. I'm so glad to finally meet you."

The servant seemed star struck. "Thank you, ma'am. Good to meet you as well."

Roger helped Hwang-Shu and Polk load the luggage into the trunk of the car. When they were ready to go, he went back over to the aircraft where Chuck Bartholdy was buttoning things up.

"Thanks, Chuck. I never had a better time."

Bartholdy shook his hand, frowning. "Roger, I've chosen to forgive you for not having your girlfriend here to pick you up. I think that was terribly cruel of you." He grinned. "Listen. Mrs. Stertevant seems to like you. She's been a great friend to a lot of people. You're lucky."

On the drive to Roger's place Abby kept exclaiming about the beauty of Santa Barbara.

"Yes, I'd forgotten a little," Celine said. "It's much bigger now, but still splendid."

At his driveway the ladies gazed at the main house across the lawn. "That's your place?"

Roger laughed, pointing at the little cottage to the right. "No, over there. I'm just a renter. But it suits me. I can't thank you enough for everything. It's been an experience I'll never forget."

"Oh, you haven't seen anything yet, Roger," said Celine. "Nine o'clock day after tomorrow, at Glenwhylden. We'll be expecting you, dear." As they drove off she waved from the car's window.

Roger went into the cottage and tossed his bag on the couch. Everything was spotless, uncharacteristically orderly. This was perfect evidence of Gwynn's compulsivity; she was unable to restrain herself from cleaning Roger's cottage in his absence even though she was mad as hell at him. He noticed a large note stuck to the refrigerator door. It was an unexpected apology; she wanted him to call as soon as he arrived. He crossed the room and dropped into the easy chair, picking up the phone. She wasn't in, so he confected a message for her answering machine, just saying he was back and couldn't wait to see her.

The swimming pool was shimmering in the early afternoon sun. Nobody around, warm and sunny. Looking good. He lost no time changing into his swim trunks, then grabbed a cold beer and a bag of potato chips. A few minutes later he was floating, face down as usual. He allowed the familiar peace to surround him. The bottom undulated with streams of light and warm sunshine pressed on his back. There was a sense of accomplishment; he would finally get to see the mysterious house and he'd have a fitting way to bring things to a close with dignity, under his own terms, in the most beautiful place he knew of.

Chapter 10

"It's the end of the world as we know it. It's the end of the world as we know it." The nasal lyrics bleated from the stereo in Roger's Porsche. He was flying along Sycamore Canyon Road on Saturday morning, top down, heading to his appointment with Celine Stertevant and his final fate at Glenwhylden. He had stayed up nearly all night getting things ready. There was a letter for Gwynn, and most of his possessions put in boxes for her to have, if she wanted. He'd even decided to leave her the Porsche, and signed the title over to her. After all, why not? It would make her beyond happy. And there was really no one else.

He remembered an old Indian saying: "It is a good day to die." And it was. A beautiful summer morning, the air warm and fragrant, just a few tendrils of fog at the beach. The pounding music coursed through him as he pushed the car hard into the curves, leaning to one side then the other, like a bobsled rider in a chute. He was hyper-aware of the hard lump in his trouser pocket, the .38 caliber snub-nosed revolver. There was only one cartridge in the cylinder, a copper-jacketed hollow-point. That would do the job without fail.

And then he was at the entrance to Glenwhylden. He adjusted his glasses as he sat briefly, looking up the driveway. Here it comes. In just a short time he would see all that this mysterious place had to hold; he would drink it all in with eyes and ears that mostly still worked, and then he would be dead. He struggled to slow his breathing. They say a condemned man notices everything around him in acute detail, hyper-aware in the last minutes of life. Roger now felt the same.

The gates were closed, as usual. Nothing looked any different from the way it always had. There was nothing to suggest that the mistress of this house had finally returned and was once again in residence after nearly seventy years absence. Leaving the engine running, he got out and went to the call box on its post. He pushed the button. No response. He politely waited thirty seconds or so, then pushed again. More waiting. Nothing. In an infernal impulse, he began to imagine himself the object of an elaborate joke.

Dreadful thoughts and notions began to muster in his mind, spiteful champions of the philosophy that the world and our life in it is forever and always a perpetual screw-job performed by a sarcastic Nature upon our gentlest and fondest hopes and dreams. The Supreme Being mordantly gives us tender hopes and high ideals, then guffaws uproariously behind our backs as we trustingly walk ahead with shining eyes and outstretched arms seeking the fulfillment of our aspirations, the cold wind ever more piercing as we advance, building to a roar and checking our progress, finally pushing us down for a face-full of dung, again and again, until finally we chance to look to one side and then the other, there to see all the other poor fools, hitherto unnoticed, camping out amidst the snow drifts, educated now, assessing their remaining penurious options—stymied, stalled, thwarted, curdling with rage and realization: the disenchanted, the defeated.

Fully two more minutes went by, but he continued to stand by the speaker box, staring at the grill and pressing the button, harder and more rapidly each time. Then finally, boiling with rage, he turned back to the car. He would park it, pocket the keys, scale the gates, walk up the hill, and finish his mission.

Two old ladies weren't going to keep him from his goal. Anybody else who got in his way, look out. Screw them. His hand shot out for the door handle of the idling Cabriolet, but just then he heard a scratchy noise, faint over the drone of the engine. He cocked his ear. There. There it was again, a screech like a parrot off in the back room of a pet shop. He reached in and switched off the ignition, looking back at the speaker box. It came once more, clearer without the motor noise.

"Whoever is there must speak his identification! Who is there, please?" A most distinctive voice, croaking and hissing amid the static. Abigail Horvath. Roger leapt to the box, leaning down to shout at the thing.

"Yes, yes Abby, it's me, ROGER!" he bellowed, as if the intercom was a stone-deaf relative. "ROGER CALDWELL. I'm here to visit."

The cube buzzed and crackled again now, an angry bee caught under waxed paper.

"Oh, Roger, *zzzzzggghhhhh*...hoping that was you! I, uhhh, hmmm. *mmmmmzzztch*...don't know a lot about how it wor...oh, dear. Yes, here it is, this button. This must be it. Come in. Is the gate opening?"

Just then the grand gates groaned, arcing slowly inward. Roger vaulted to the driver's seat, firing up the powerful engine. He slammed the shift into first, then squealed up the driveway. He was in.

At first the sports car climbed the hill athletically, jittering around on the bricks. Then he caught himself. Beauty and refinement were everywhere. Enjoy it, he thought. Slow down, let it bring you joy while you can still experience it.

There were boxwood hedges, palm trees, blossoms of myriad variety, and whimsical topiary scattered among the sections of lawn lining the drive. A dense shrub, trimmed to resemble a hand with the index finger extended, pointed the way up the driveway. He couldn't resist chuckling at the visual gag. He'd seen it often from afar; that hand was the last thing visible when looking up the driveway from outside the gates. Now as he drove past, it pointed to his fateful appointment. It seemed fitting.

He allowed the car to slow to a crawl. For the first time in months, a serene feeling came over him. Maybe it was the majesty of his surroundings or because this moment represented the realization of a lifelong dream, even if it was his last day on earth.

What would it be like to die? He'd fainted once, in grade school, when he had the flu. Just a fog closing in fast, then nothing. Would death be like that? He felt a stab of fear, but then resolve. No more bad could be done to him because now the sequence of events was under his control. Nothing could stop him.

The motor court at the top of the hill was almost exactly as he'd long imagined. In the center was an ornate fountain, around which the cobbled drive circled gracefully. It all focused on the main entry to the mansion. There were the solid, tastefully crafted stone stairs, imposing granite columns, and a towering mahogany door. Although he'd never been in this place before, he felt utterly at home. It was as if he had been far away, on sad and vexing errands, and now returned to find everything just as he'd left it. He parked, then walked up the steps, looking, trying to soak it all in. On the door a polished bronze knocker in the shape of a hammer and anvil awaited his hand. He lifted the hammer and let it fall. There was a resonating, deep-throated boom, like a huge kettle drum. It seemed to vibrate the entire house. Within a few seconds a tall elegant man in a butler's uniform opened the door and motioned him in. Roger recognized him as the man who'd picked them up at the airport. Once inside, Roger could see why the knocker had made that resonant sound. The spacious hall was all polished wood and stone, impressive as any old-fashioned government building. From high clerestory windows, dappled sunlight filtered down to the mirror-like floor.

"Good morning, Mr. Caldwell," said the butler. "If you'll follow me, sir, Mrs. Stertevant is expecting you."

He turned away, walking down the hall. Roger trailed, self-conscious of the squeaking his running shoes made on the polished floor. They came to a set of carved double doors and the butler opened one. An ethereal light issued out, like the light of the afterworld.

"I believe you'll find Mrs. Stertevant and Mrs. Horvath in here, sir."

Roger stepped through and gasped in pleasure. The heavy door closed behind him. He was in a broad hallway made of glass. The ceiling was domed, about twelve feet overhead, and fantastic tropical plants and vines curled and hung from many of the structural elements criss-crossing under the curved glass. Outside the glass walls, long reflecting pools with plants and colorful fish ran parallel to the corridor. Sunlight shimmered off the surface of the pools and bounced up into the hallway producing the most remarkable effect—it was like purgatory. The long hallway delivered into a Victorian-style conservatory, also made entirely of glass. This building expanded up and out to either side of the glass passageway. Roger walked down a short flight of steps and into the verdant, humid space. The profusion of shrubs, orchids, exotic trees, and flowering plants was boggling. Palms of multiple varieties, bromeliads, elephant ears, orchids, and ginger blossoms were everywhere. He looked up in amazement, toward the glass ceiling that was at least thirty feet up. A screeching tropical bird swooped by and vanished into the canopy of foliage that surged upward with rampant vigor. Electric blue sunlight filtered down in hazy shafts, playing along the tiled floor. It was a kind of stylized rainforest—a conceptualized version straight out of a Rousseau painting. The Garden of Eden. Close by, animated voices drew him through the jungle, and he eventually found Celine and Abby in a little alcove, examining a blooming plant. They were in white blouses and skirts, and Celine wore a white baseball cap and sunglasses. She looked up at the sound of Roger's footsteps.

"Oh, my dear young man!" she exclaimed, holding out her hand, "I'm so glad you've come. Awfully sorry about that business at the gate." She grinned at Abby. "We really don't quite have the hang of things around here yet. How are you, Roger?"

"Fine, Mrs. Stertevant. Hello, Mrs. Horvath. I can't believe this place!"

"Well, this is the conservatory, Roger. You know I had very different recollections of it from years ago. My memories were, well...it seemed almost empty then. And now it's positively a jungle! Some of the gardeners have been here for over fifty years. I must say, when I was in the car coming up the drive the day before yesterday, I thought for a moment I might be in the wrong place. Not really, of course, but it was all just so much more cultivated than I remembered. The gardeners have turned this into an absolute paradise. Abby thinks there are specimens here that don't exist in any other collection."

Abby pointed to a thorny, gnarled tree with spindly branches and outrageously bright purple-orange blossoms. "Now, that there, I haven't ever seen that even in a book." Her voice crackled with obvious delight. "We don't know whether these things were already here when Celine came a long time ago, or if they've been brought here since. The head gardener who started when the place was built passed away over twenty years ago, and he was quite secretive. His successor says he had never been told the names of some of these plants, or where they came from."

"And we're told some have medicinal properties," Celine added, lowering her voice. "In fact, there is a vine in here somewhere..." she squinted her eyes and searched, "which, if the leaves are boiled up into a tea, will supposedly rid a person of arthritis. What about that?" She folded her arms over her chest.

Roger stood smiling, shaking his head.

Celine continued, "Well. This is just the beginning, of course. I promised to give you the complete tour. It's going to take awhile. Shall we get going?" She patted his elbow and began leading him along. The three of them made their way back through the jungle, out the glass hallway and into the main foyer of the house.

The transition was remarkable again, from ethereal light and Eden-like greenery, to the formal, sober main foyer, smelling of mahogany and wood polish. From heaven back to earth. And each new turn in the massive house brought amazement to Roger: the fine large kitchen with its gleaming rows of copper pots, the dining room showcasing ocean views. There was a series of bedrooms, each charming and unique. Paintings and sculptures tastefully deployed everywhere, details of infinite taste and grace.

After an hour or so, he realized something. There had been no sign of the guests Celine had made so much of. In fact, she hadn't even mentioned them. He figured she'd get around to that part when she was ready. This was a huge place and there was no telling where she had them hidden.

They went outside and got into a golf-cart. With Celine behind the wheel, they proceeded through stunning gardens, alongside the marble rimmed swimming pool, and past several guest cottages tucked into wooded areas. Celine pointed out things as they went. None of it disappointed Roger. This was truly the place of his fantasies, even better. It was, as Celine had said, a paradise. His instincts had been right-on; if there was a better place to die, he couldn't imagine it. He kept getting the odd sense that he belonged here. At one point they paused and stepped out of the cart beside the cliff-top hedges. The soothing "shush-shush" of slow waves rolling onto the beach below lofted up to them. He looked down and felt a catch in his chest; in the distance he could see the exact place on the sand where he'd spent so many summer days with his mother and father. That was the place where he'd daydreamed, gazing up at the spot where he now stood. It was alright, he told himself. It was all going to be fine now. Soon the pain would be over and he'd be home to stay.

A few minutes later they were back in the central corridor of the main house.

"Now this might be my favorite room of all," Celine said happily. They entered a broad chamber with a coffered ceiling and fireplaces at each end. Fresh cut flowers were everywhere, complimenting the floral-motif overstuffed furniture. Tall windows fronted on rolling lawns, with the blue of the ocean's horizon describing a steady line to balance the room's other visual elements. Even though the couches and chairs were old-fashioned and stodgy, the overall effect was still cheerful: comfortable and soothing.

"The main drawing room," said Celine. "Right here is where Charles told me for the first time that this was my house. He was such a devil, that man. Loved practical jokes, the more elaborate the better."

There was a portrait above the mantle. Roger went closer and recognized the signature of the artist: John Singer Sargent. An attractive couple gazed out. The man had a self-assured expression, amused, almost wry. He was tall, stylish, with fine aquiline features. He wore his dark hair parted in the middle and tightly slicked back. His temples were dashingly grey. He stood behind the seated, younger blonde woman, his large hands resting gracefully on her bare shoulders. She sat on the edge of a chaise, attired in a light summer dress with narrow shoulder straps and a low cut neckline. Several strands of pearls encircled her slender neck. She was without a doubt the newly married Mrs. Celine Bell Stertevant, posing with her groom, Charles. Something about the image made Roger uneasy, but he couldn't quite put his finger on it. He looked more carefully at Charles Stertevant's face, and it came to him. Change the haircut and clothes, subtract a few years, and the man in the painting would be a dead ringer for himself. A wave of heat rose up his collar and he considered whether to comment on this. Abby decided for him.

"Celine," she began thoughtfully, "isn't it funny, but I just noticed this. Don't you think our friend Roger here bears more than a little resemblance to your late husband?"

Celine turned slowly and studied Roger's face for a second, then looked back up at the painting.

"Do you think so?" She cocked her head. "Charles was a very handsome man. Maybe the shape of the face—a bit." She gave Roger a benign smile. "Well. That's it, young man. Glenwhylden. You've seen almost all there is to see, Roger. Except for what's really the most important part. You've still got to meet our friends." She looked at her watch. "They should be waiting for us right now, just down the hall. Shall we?" With that she started toward the door.

Okay, he thought, jolted. This is it. Time's up, tour's done. No need to meet these other people, they'd only spoil the perfection of the day.

He had a plan at the ready. His blood pressure zoomed, but he managed to sound calm. "Would it be okay if I used the bathroom for a moment first?"

She turned back. "Why, certainly. Take your time. There's a powder room a few doors down on the left. Need me to show you?"

"No, no. I can find it. I'll just be a second."

Out in the hall he got his bearings. This was a big house, but not that big. He'd carefully remembered where the conservatory was so he could get back to it. He knew from the moment he saw the lavish indoor garden that it would be the place. End of this hall, turn right, then left through the big double doors. He strode urgently, not quite running, hoping that he wouldn't be stopped or diverted by a servant. Moments later he was passing through the glowing glass hallway and out into the fragrant, sheltering jungle. His hand went to his pocket, and there it was, nasty and cold, all business, the snub-nosed revolver. He drew it out and cocked the hammer, checking to see that the cartridge was in line with the barrel. There was no time to lose. An enormous tree spread its flowering branches right under the central dome. With his heart now racing, he knelt in the blossom-scented shade.

A wave of emotion engulfed him and tears rolled down his cheeks. He closed his eyes. "Mother...Dad?" he whispered in a little child's voice. "Can you hear me?" He could barely hold the pistol, his hands trembled so. "I'm frightened." He lodged the barrel just under his chin. Then he willed his finger to tighten on the trigger.

Chapter 11

"Roger? Roger?" A woman's voice came softly, from far away.

Was it his mother? There'd been no white light, his life hadn't flashed before his eyes. He could still feel his heart thrumming.

"Are you in here, Roger?"

Oh, no. No, it was not his mother. It was Celine Stertevant's voice, and she was in the conservatory, moving toward him. He'd waited a moment too long and she'd beat him to it. "Damn, damn, damn it to hell," he cursed silently. "Why can't things *just for once...*?"

"Roger?" She was nearby, still hidden by the plants, but getting closer.

In a flash he deliberated: Never mind her, go ahead, don't stop now, you might not have another chance.

But then, he couldn't. He just couldn't. After the shot she'd find him within seconds, she'd witness his body lying there twitching, head exploded, gore sprayed on the tree. It would be too much for her. It would be wrong, just terribly wrong. She might die herself, right there. No. He fumbled to uncock the pistol before shoving it back into his pocket. Then he wiped his face on his sleeve, struggling for composure.

"Uh, yes...yes Mrs. Stertevant." His voice was a hoarse croak. "I'm in the...I'm over here."

She came around the tree just as he was stumbling to his feet.

"What happened? Did you get lost?"

"Oh…I, uh—no, no. I just, uh…well, it's so nice in here. I wanted to see it one more time."

"Well, are you alright? You don't look so well. Right after you left the room, Abby got most alarmed. She said I should come get you in the conservatory immediately."

"She did?"

"Yes. Is anything the matter, my boy?"

He forced a smile. "Oh." He shook his head with exaggeration. "No, of course not. I'm sorry. Here, see, I didn't get much sleep last night…I was so excited about coming here. You know. That's…I shouldn't have wandered off. Just wanted to get some air, before meeting the people. But I'm fine now."

She studied him a moment longer. "Well, perhaps we should wait to meet the guests. Would you feel more comfortable—"

"No, Mrs. Stertevant, really. Let's go right now." He was already seeing a "Plan B". Just play along a few more minutes, that's all. Then he'd have another go. "Everything's great," he said, steadying. "I'm ready."

"Well. If you're sure."

They walked back out. In the echoing main hall, Celine began speaking in a grave voice.

"Roger, I must ask you right now to give me your solemn promise that no matter what happens next, whether you end up working for me or not, when you leave here you will not breathe a word about this. You will not cause anyone else to know. I'm trusting you. Do you promise me this, on your honor?"

Roger reflected on what would be the absolute integrity of his word.

"I promise you, Mrs. Stertevant. On my honor, no one will hear about what I see here. It won't go out of the gates."

She nodded sharply and extended her hand to him, sealing their pact. They arrived before a door they hadn't entered during the tour. From behind it came the sounds of commotion, laughter and music. Seeping out was the tang of cigarette smoke and liquor.

Great, Roger thought. A party. Just what I'm in the mood for.

Celine hovered a moment, her hand resting on the knob.

"I hope you're ready for this." She swung the door inward and they moved into a cavernous, smoky, darkened chamber, with flickering blue light bouncing off the walls.

It took a moment for Roger's failing eyes to adjust to the darkness and register what was in the room. The bluish light came from a huge wall of television screens. These all displayed different programs: game shows, soap operas, CNN. A few screens seemed to be computer monitors displaying lists or charts. Inexplicably, each screen had its own individual audio turned up, so that fifteen or twenty different programs competed with each other in a kind of gang-channel-surfing cacophony. This accounted for the chaotic party noises Roger had heard. Spread in front of the screens was a group of recliner chairs. In silhouette, squatty figures hunkered, chatting to each other and occasionally pointing up. A lazy cloud of cigarette smoke hung over the grouping. As he observed a finger jabbing up at a leering image of Bugs Bunny, it struck Roger that the arm the finger was attached to was absurdly long. So was the finger, for that matter. Celine grabbed Roger's elbow and whispered to him.

"This is the media room. They spend a lot of time in here." Then, turning toward the video wall and fairly shouting to be heard over the din, she announced their presence. "Hello, everyone! Our visitor is here!"

Within a scant moment, all activity at the far end of the room ceased. Someone's finger must have touched a remote button, because all the screens went silent. Back-lit by the flickering monitors, large hairy heads leaned out from behind the high backs of the chairs, craning around to get a look at the new arrivals. Roger shielded his eyes from the video screens, still not able to make out their faces. No one uttered a word. The only sound was the quiet squeaking of the leather chairs as the occupants shifted around. Celine led the way, and as they neared the recliners, she paused and snapped on a lamp.

Roger could now clearly see the faces peering at him and he felt the filaments on the back of his neck lift up.

The occupants of the recliners were all large, red-haired apes. He blinked, looking hard at them. He had seen such creatures at the zoo and in books, but it took him a few seconds to remember what they were called. Orangutans. Right. But unlike zoo animals, these apes were all clothed, in a mish-mash of outfits. One wore a long dress and a sweater. A couple of them held cigarettes. Celine took up a position beside the largest one and affectionately patted his shoulder. Then she did a fine imitation of June Cleaver trying to jump-start a birthday party with a bunch of neighborhood kids.

"Everyone, I'd like you to meet our *new friend*. This is Mr. Roger Caldwell." Like a game show model, she looped her upturned palm toward Roger. He was frozen. This was crazy, what did she expect him to do? He stared at the apes and they stared back. For the second time in this day, it seared across his mind that he was the object of some kind of elaborate joke. He was being played. Maybe all this was being video-taped. Cameras. Where, concealed in the darkened recesses of the room? Zoom lenses scrutinizing his comically confused expression? He scanned around, peering into the corners. Still no one moved.

But then at Celine's murmured invitation and gesture, the largest ape rose heavily from his chair and advanced toward Roger, who instinctively took a step backward. Clad in a black satin warm-up suit, the animal was massive, perhaps five feet tall and easily weighing more than three hundred pounds. His face was as wide as the moon, with great, dark half-discs of flesh on either side of his closely set black eyes. He lifted his chin and extended his hand slowly; Roger hesitated before taking it. When he did, he felt the huge, roughened fingers gently encircle his entire hand and wrist. While holding on, the ape did not immediately shake Roger's hand but looked over at Celine, as if for guidance.

"It's all right, Pongo. He's all right."

To Roger's unbelieving astonishment, the creature turned back to him, still holding his hand, and uttered a breathy, slow greeting.

"I'm plizzed to mit yew, Rujehr. Mar nam izz Pongo." His mouth had moved strangely, awkwardly, but he had unmistakably spoken. *Spoken.*

Roger could only gape. The ape shook his hand a few pumps, then released it and shuffled back a few paces, looking down at his feet. He seemed embarrassed that the young man had not said anything in response to his clumsy introduction. Now each of the others stood and approached. The one in the dress and sweater lumbered forward. Smaller than the big male, she swayed from side to side on bowed legs. She stopped about three feet away and bridged the gap with a long arm, placing the knuckles of her other hand against the floor. She took Roger's now slightly trembling hand very gently. Her skin felt cool and dry and her wild little upturned face seemed sweet and polite in the soft glow of the table lamp beside them.

"Hallo, seer. Vaway nize tuh mit yewuh. Ah emm Ameelee Fahruhstol." Her voice was high pitched. Roger recognized it from the speakerphone call at Marsh Meadows. And she smiled, pulling her enormous lips apart and bobbing her head. She was obviously older than the others, with a little gray hair around the sides of her face.

Dislocated from reality, Roger swallowed hard and attempted to find his own voice. "Huh...hello. How are you?" he said, in little more than a wheeze.

There were five others. Another female, very young, wearing sweatpants and a Jane Fonda Workout sweatshirt. Her name was "Klo-wee Poh." Two more males, "Ahrtahd Mohahjee" and "Trayuhnt Aluhnuhdayuhl" introduced themselves. One wore blue sweatpants and a white Cleveland Indians t-shirt, the other was done up in a silk paisley smoking jacket with a polka-dotted dickey. That one seemed surer of his speech, speaking more rapidly and clearly than the others. Then there was a smaller male who visibly made a great effort to hold himself as erect as possible as he shook Roger's hand. He spoke his name shyly: "Joworsh Veelowfruhnko." He was wearing khaki work pants and shirt. "Iyah ayam dee garuhdenuhr."

"George is interested in gardening," Celine explained. "He does very fine work." The red ape nodded gravely.

The last was a little female in a full-length Hawaiian Mumu. She took Roger's hand between both of her own. "Hairlo, Wuhjuh. Arhm Behddi Roodeen. Gledd tu miet yur. Ar hohp yur weel veesiht wiz uhz menni tahms." She looked down shyly, giggling with a wuffing noise.

Roger kept looking at each of them: no wires, no phony looking fur or skin. They were breathing. What in God's name was going on?

"Well. Thank you very much everyone," Celine then said. "I'm very proud of you. We'll have lunch in about an hour, but now Roger and I have some things to discuss. Okay? See you soon." She beamed at all the apes, then turned to leave. Roger felt like he was walking on jello, his mouth dry as sand. One of the apes restored the sound to the screens and the blare again filled the room.

When the door had closed behind them, Celine turned to Roger.

"You okay? Want some water, or something stronger?"

Roger just shook his head. If this was a hoax, it was flawlessly done. "I, uh. I don't get it. Was that real?"

"Oh, yes, absolutely. And that's why you're here." She paused, assaying his expression. "Look, you need some explaining. Anyone would. So, I've got that all arranged. Come on, let's head up to the library."

She took off at a fast clip. Interesting things passed by on each side but Roger didn't notice, his mind was racing so. His thoughts were now a confused jumble, his fatal plan derailed. He was aware again of the potent lump of the revolver in his pocket, thumping his leg as they walked. But how the hell could he go through with his original plan now? If he shot himself at Glenwhylden, it would certainly bring the police inside the gates. Before, when he didn't understand what was really happening here, that hadn't mattered. It had even been sort of a plus. His death would be noticed, even covered in the newspaper, because of the prominent place where it had occurred. But he had given his word, hadn't he? "Not cause anyone to know." And beyond that, what about these creatures, these apes that could talk. What if it *was* real?

Up a wide polished mahogany staircase, down another long hall, then into a formal library. Waiting in a wing-backed chair was the tall butler who'd met Roger at the front door.

Chapter 12

"Roger, I don't believe you've been formally introduced to our head of household staff," Celine said. "This is Mr. Whitney Polk, Jr."

Polk rose and shook hands while Celine poured a little whiskey from a decanter and handed the glass to Roger. He looked at it uncertainly.

"Whether you want it or not, just in case. I sure needed a bracer when I finally met them. Have a seat."

He sunk onto a couch, then bolted the entire contents of the glass in his hand. Celine suppressed a smile and poured him another shot.

"Okay, take a deep breath. Look, what you just saw down there is entirely real. Not some kind of fakery. I swear to God. Those are all real Orangutans, born in the wild, and now they can all speak and think, just like us, and believe me, that's just the tip of the iceberg. If you still doubt it, we're going to have lunch with them in a wide-open dining room with plenty of daylight and you can fully convince yourself then. Alright?"

"Yes, ma'am," he croaked.

"Are you alright? Do you need a minute?"

"No, ma'am. I'm okay."

She sat down opposite him. "Very well then. So, how did they get this way? Well, it all began two years ago because I failed to pay attention in a meeting. Seems one of my many businesses was involved in a logging operation on an island called Borneo. One of the most beautiful places on earth. Well. This company of which I was a principal shareholder owned large tracts of virgin teak and mahogany timber. The trees were undisturbed for years and years because they were very remote. The value of the wood didn't make it worth going in there and taking it out. But over time, exotic wood got scarcer and the prices went up. Changed the whole picture. So the managers in my company started bulldozing roads and going into these rainforests. They claim they told me but I sure don't remember. And they were cutting down thousands of these magnificent old trees. Bad enough, but that also caused the deaths of, I don't know, could be millions of animals. And maybe I would never have realized this if I hadn't gotten a letter from a wonderful scientist who was trying to stop the logging and protect the animals. She wrote me, I finally understood the situation, and I immediately bought out the other partners and closed down the whole operation. Done, stopped. But then, as I was right in the middle of trying to help this dear woman get the logging stopped elsewhere and help these animals survive, she died. Hell of a thing. Choked on a chicken bone. After all that time in the jungle. Can you believe that? She'd been running a shelter for some of the displaced animals from the logging areas, mostly Orangutans. And I had met these animals and just fallen in love with them. Also I felt responsible that they were in this predicament to begin with. Then I get a phone call from the head assistant there at the rescue station. He says he and the others are shutting it down. I offered him a lot of money to keep things going, but he refused. I found out later that there were threats against the shelter because when I folded my logging company it put people out of work. There was a lot of resentment about that. So. It was a rock and a hard place, don't you see? Truthfully, though, I was never uncertain for even a moment that I was doing the right thing."

She sighed. "Okay. Now I had a real problem, because right at that time there were these seven Orangutans living at the station. They weren't ready to be put back into the wild; they had health problems and other issues. But the shelter was closing. I couldn't stop that. All I could figure to do right away was to send my plane down there to collect those animals and bring them to Glenwhylden. I did it on impulse, but I thought that, well, at least they'd be safe here. There would be plenty of people to take care of them. The climate here was warm, not too far different from where they'd been. That was my reasoning. So, that's what I did. I sneaked them up here on my jet. Yes, it was illegal but I did it. Here at Glenwhylden one of our big greenhouses was converted into a habitat for them. I got a very nice local veterinarian to care for their health and not tell anyone. He's done a fine job. His little granddaughter started coming along with him and she kept the secret as well. As a matter of fact, she still comes to visit them often. She's really just about their only outside friend, other than her grandfather. Anyway, Roger, I know this is getting to be quite a tale, but we haven't even gotten to the good part yet. How did they get the ability to talk? Well, Mr. Polk here witnessed the whole thing. Whitney?"

"Yes, ma'am." He turned to Roger. "Well, I'll just tell you sir, that I don't sleep real well. I'm up at all hours. Sometimes, I step out on the back lower terrace, there—" he gestured in the direction of the rear of the house, "and look at the ocean. Now, this one particular night, I guess this was about a year and a half ago, I was out there about three and it was fixin' to storm. Lot of wind and the moon just about to go under the clouds. A whole bunch of lightning going off. So, I'm watching this, then I see this real strange thing. These four black dots, like balls, up in the sky in a formation, you could say. At first I thought I was seeing things. But I blink real hard and rub my eyes and they're still there. These dots in formation, flying *super fast* along this storm cloud. Just darting, back and forth. They'd stop on a dime, then shoot off a whole other direction, almost faster than you could follow 'em with your eyes. No airplane could fly like that. No, sir. They came *real* close, and didn't make any noise at all. I ain't never seen that before. So I believe these was *some of them UFO things*." He was getting excited with his story, moving onto the edge of his chair.

"Now, sir, I got a real good look. No mistake. And I'm about to go get a camera because nobody gonna believe me without a picture. But right then, these things got hit, KAPOW!" He slammed his fist into his other hand. "A shot of lightning just *zapped* 'em. Then they start to wobble and lose formation. And I think "They're coming down."

The butler took a handkerchief from his pocket and drew it across his brow and lips. Eyes widened, his voice now lowered to a near whisper.

"*And they were coming right at the house.* I just froze. I'm dead, for sure. Well sir, they miss the house and shoot behind the trees over the rise and boom, crash. Looked like a flash-bulb going off." He placed his finger-tips tightly together, then burst them open wide. "And then a big stripe of green light shot off up into the sky. Now I'm just shaking, seeing this, but then I realize, *man!* The monkey-house is over there! I got to go check on them. I get a flashlight and I'm running in the rain, thinking oh my God, what has happened? I come up over the rise and there's this...well, *green fog* lying in that hollow. The monkey-house is in the middle of it. And sir, it's *glowing* there. I ain't never seen *that* before either."

He paused for a moment and sighed, fanning himself.

"Well, now, I didn't know if that stuff was poison. Could'a been. But I went on down there, scared for the critters. But up close, my throat burned and I got all faint. So I think again, poison. I backed-off right quick. Funny, this whole time the wind was blowing, plenty strong, but this mist was staying put right there, just laying all around the monkey-house. I looked with the flashlight, but I couldn't find any parts of them things that crashed. Not a scrap. I thought, Polk, okay now, go get some help. I start back up the hill and when I got up a ways, I turn around and now that stuff is all gone. One-hundred percent. My back hadn't been turned more than thirty seconds. So I run to the monkey-house, and outside everything looks normal. I don't smell nothing or feel faint, so I go in and turn on the light. Then, man, my heart just sank like a rock. All the critters, they're all laying out around in there, and it looked like they've all been sick to their stomachs. Bad. I couldn't see for sure if they were breathing—but it didn't look like it. I thought, they're dead, poisoned, and you best be getting the hell outta here too, and maybe it's already too late. So I took off and ran up to the servant's house and got Ron."

Celine broke in, "Ronald Okizuta. He's the head gardener."

Polk barely broke his stride. "Yes ma'am. I got Ron up outta bed, and we go back down there into the monkey-house. Ron goes over to one of the animals and took hold of its wrist to feel for a pulse. Yes, but barely there. He say "Polk, what happened?", and I tell him, and he's just looking back at me and at all those animals lying there. He didn't say nothing when I finished, nothing at all. He checked another one of the critters and says go call the vet right away. So I get to the phone and get the vet down here. He stayed until morning, working on the animals. He said he couldn't exactly tell what's wrong, says maybe they've been poisoned somehow. He said they're all close to dead. Man, I'm just all shook up now. And worse, all the staff that knows about this, now they think maybe *I done something* to the critters. Ron had told them my story, see. And they're sure I'm cracking up, or on drugs, or some such. But, man, I love them little dudes, I'd never have done anything, ever, to hurt them. And, God as my witness, that story I just told you is true, every word." He held his hand up, testifying. "Well now, 'course they didn't die, and after about three days they start to come around. All of a sudden like, they're all better. Better than ever. And they start right in to doing things they never did before. Like letting themselves out of their cages whenever they felt like it. No matter how good we'd fix them latches, they'd just show up after awhile, walking around on the lawn. A few days later, they took a newspaper out of the gardeners cart and they're all in the monkey-house down there, sitting around looking at it real close-like. Like they're trying to figure out what's written there, or something. One of 'em sneaked up to the barn the next night and made off with a radio out of the gardener's office. They plugged it into the socket down there at the monkey-house and the next morning, you know, when the man came to feed 'em? They's all gathered around there, listening to the news. Plain as day, that's what they're doing. Like to stand the hair up on the back of your neck, to see that stuff."

He took a long pause, looking down at the floor, shifting his feet a little. When he resumed, he placed all the gravity he could muster in his voice.

"And then, long about two months after that thing crashed—they start in to *talking*." He nodded emphatically. "Man, we just ran for cover then. It was that one, Trent, he was the first one that actually said something, that we know of. Ron was in there giving them their food, and Trent walks up to him and he says, "Thanks for the grub." Just like that. "Thanks for the grub." Ron says when he heard that, he liked to about have a heart attack. And he tells it that Trent, after he done said it, acted all proud in front the other ones, like he'd been practicing or some such. And the other ones, after he done it, Ron says they're all snickering, sort of. Well sir, after that, it got on to bigger every day. Pretty soon they're *all* talking. You walk down there at night and listen outside the door, and they're all in there with a little TV on, the one Ron gave them, and they're all practicing their speech on each other. Not so good at first, but doing it. Just like that. One thing led to another, and pretty soon we've got no choice but to treat 'em just like they're people. We had to let 'em come on up and start living in the house! We can't just leave 'em down there in that monkey-barn, now that they're talking to us—lord! We told Mrs. Stertevant about all this, and of course at first, she couldn't believe it none. But the vet, Doc Lewis? He called her and told her yes, it's true, then he puts Trent on the phone and they talk awhile. That was it. Yes, sir. Now they're all just like family. And we love 'em all."

With that, Polk seemed to have spent the last of the agitated energy he'd displayed during the relating of his tale. He fell silent and looked at Celine.

She praised him with a broad smile. "Thank you Polk, you told that very well. I think Mr. Caldwell has a much better understanding now. So. I'd like to discuss a few things with him and I know you'll want to go see about lunch. We'll be down in a few minutes. Would you please tell the others?"

When he'd gone, she went to the window, drawing open the brocade curtains. Brilliant midday sunlight flooded in, making the colors of burnished wood and leather jump to life. She turned back, sizing up the young man's expression.

"Okay Roger. You're in the club now, whether you wanted to be or not. Still think it's some kind of trick?"

He hesitated. "I think I saw a UFO myself once, when I was camping in the mountains. It kind of acted like the ones he described. But then, maybe it was something our own government was doing. You can't rule that out, can you?"

"No, I sure can't. But that's not the point. All I know is *what they did*. One more time. It's not fake, I swear." Now she sat beside him. "Look, we can discuss this a lot more, but let me ask you a question first. Do you like your job, working with the cars? Is it what you want to do for the rest of your life?"

"For the rest of my life?" Roger stood up and paced, jamming his hands down into his pockets, once again fingering the revolver. For the first time in months, that phrase sounded different. "That's kind of a tough question at the moment."

"Okay. Let me tell you my issues here." She leaned forward. "I'm eighty-nine years old. I've had a wonderful life. Dear me, I've been *beyond* blessed. If you took all the bad things that ever happened to me, the good would far outweigh them. And everybody has to get old and die. I'm not afraid of that. No. But this situation here, with these Orangutans, this is a monumentally significant thing. Maybe nothing like this has ever happened before on earth. It has implications that, well, just beggar the imagination. You haven't really had time for it all to sink in, you probably feel like you've been on a carnival-ride. But when it does sink in, and you get the whole idea of where this all could lead, my boy, you're going to need more than just a drink. To be honest, I feel better already, just having somebody else in on it. But I've got a huge responsibility here, see? I think that God or the Power of the Universe placed these creatures here in my care for a reason. I've got to do the right thing by these remarkable beings, and by the rest of the world as well. I don't think that's an exaggeration. Just imagine what could happen—put your mind on it for a second—if this ever became public knowledge.

What would most of the dingbats out there—the people who scarf pizza and swill generic beer and rent action-adventure videos every night—what would they do if they got it positively confirmed that there really are extraterrestrial beings coming here, to this planet? For real, not just in some piece of Hollywood hokum. Think maybe they'd go off the deep end? You better believe it. So, I've thought about it plenty, and this whole business has to remain an absolute secret. It must, Roger, because these creatures, they're so wonderfully sensitive. You've got to understand this." She leaned in, eyes burning. "The *last* thing I'd want to do is get the scientists in on it. I know exactly what would happen. Those Orangs would get taken away, poked at, and prodded. They'd be tested and experimented on for the rest of their lives. They'd be turned into media freaks, that's what. Every one of them would end up as completely miserable wretches. And I won't allow that to happen!" Her hand slammed down on the arm of the couch. "God knows, they've had enough trouble in their lives even before all this crash stuff. So make no mistake, Roger, they've got me here to protect them, me and my money, one hundred percent. As long as I'm around, they're going to be protected and taken care of. That's for certain. Now. That brings us to the real problem. As I said, I am eighty-nine. I'm still very healthy, and I get around well for a woman my age, but things can happen very suddenly when you're pushing ninety. Statistically, it stands to reason that I might not have a whole lot more time to be here. You break a hip, you get pneumonia, you have a stroke—my sister had a stroke. One minute she was there, practicing her cello, and the next, on the floor, drooling. She didn't go right away, but she never spoke another word. Never got out of her bed. I'm not even sure she knew who I was after it happened, and we'd been close as could be for over seventy years." Her eyes watered a little, and she looked past Roger, focusing on the trees outside.

He waited for her to go on. She raised her hand to her face and stroked her cheek with the backs of her knuckles a few times.

"So you see, I need someone younger to take this responsibility with me. I need someone to take over. Someone who's capable of understanding the full dimensions of what's required here. I've realized this just about as long as I've known about the situation. But unlike almost everything else that's ever happened to me, I was having a hard time figuring out what to do. I admit it. I was caught in my own little cage, wanting to come here and get started with this, but then I hadn't been here for so long and I was frightened, really. That's probably hard to fathom, isn't it? I have it on good authority that I'm hosting a bunch of talking Orangutans at my estate and yet I don't come immediately to see for myself. Well, I was just delaying, really. I meant to come, and I was getting up the nerve to do it. It would have happened soon. But I knew *something else* had to happen, *someone else* needed to emerge. Because we're not talking about a mere job, it's a whole life that would be needed. This isn't nine-to-five. Abby and I sitting having tea, talking about this very thing, neither of us having any really good ideas. I mean, what would you do? Put an ad in the classifieds? 'Wanted: visionary individual, full-time, to supervise the development of seven possibly extra-terrestrial-mutated Orangutans.' Of course not. How do you find the right person, how do you decide who to trust? We were thinking of the household staff here for awhile. But no one was right. We were stumped." She turned to face him. "And then...your letter came. When I read it I sat up in my chair. I showed it to Abby. Right off she said 'Celine, this is our person. He's the one we need. Let's get him out here to meet us.' That's how it happened, Roger, just that way. That's why you're here. And I think you must realize by now that you have the opportunity to do something extraordinary, historic. I wish I were younger, even just ten years, because if I was, I'd do this job myself. We wouldn't be having this conversation. But I don't have the energy for this now. I don't want to start something I can't finish. These creatures have minds like insatiable sponges. They have a capacity for absorbing information that seems without limit. Did you see, they've got *twenty-five* televisions going all at the same time! They keep asking me if they can get more. They keep the sound turned up on all of them. And you know what? They can keep track of what's happening on all of them, simultaneously! They want to learn about everything. And they want to go out and *do everything*. Obviously, we can't let them do that—like I explained. But, if it's handled properly, there are many things they can do, and I don't want to keep them prisoners here." At this, she smiled. "We can arrange things, somehow. You see, they're brilliant, and very innocent, and they need a personal guide, a kind of all-encompassing concierge for their new lives." She halted, looking for his reaction.

"I don't know," he slowly shook his head. "What if I screw it up somehow? I mean...wow, my head's spinning. Listen, I'm not all that great. I've got problems. I mean serious problems. I haven't been completely honest with you. In fact, to tell you the truth, I actually came here today to..." He stopped short.

"To what?" she almost seemed to know. "What? To get your head totally messed with?" She surprised him by bursting out laughing. "Everybody's got problems, Roger." Pushing up, she walked over and flung the door open, turning back toward her confused guest.

"Ahhhh. Know what I think, young man? Let's give it time. We're both about half-crazed from hunger. I'm being a very poor hostess. Let's go join the others. You can get to know them better. They're *very* entertaining. They'll make you laugh. We need to relax for awhile, okay? We'll have plenty of time to talk more later." He rose and followed her out into the hall. A slight draft was moving up the staircase as they descended, carrying enticing aromas from the kitchen.

Chapter 13

Orangutans, as they exist in the remote lowland swamps and rainforests of Borneo and Sumatra, are known to be mostly solitary creatures. Small family groups have been documented, but these are the exceptions. Lone males, feeding and traveling among the tree-tops, will routinely not see others of their kind for weeks or even months. Unlike most of the other Simians, they are sparingly vocal and do not display nervous, jerky movements. Orangutans are normally non-aggressive and non-confrontational, mostly dealing with conflicts among themselves by avoidance, not violence. Because of their secretive lifestyle, the red apes have been difficult for researchers to locate and follow in the wild. In the public mind, they are known for their comical, dead-pan facial expression. Maybe for this reason they are perceived to be thoughtful, even contemplative. In fact, recent research has found them to be the most intelligent, curious and ingenious of all the apes. Their learning abilities most resemble those of humans. In the wild they use various tools, such as employing a leaf for a napkin, or constructing a leak-proof cover of branches for their beds. In captivity, their skill at manipulating mechanical objects is legendary.

Orangutans mate only once a year. They will skip a year if the conditions are not right. Impregnated females gestate for a period of approximately 270 days, virtually the same as humans. They give birth to a single offspring, which the mother carries and nurtures through the periods of childhood and adolescence. Young animals reach a state of sexual maturity at around age eight.

"Mawas" (or "Men of the Forest") have near mythical status among the local humans. In the lore of these people, the Mawas are revered for their solitary ways and their awesome physical strength. In the wild, man is the only formidable enemy of Orangutans.

Roger learned all these facts from Celine. They had long discussions about the crash of whatever it was and how that might have led to the apes' phenomenal development. Roger was fascinated and transformed. On that first eventful day, he rushed home to his cottage and unpacked his belongings. He tore up the note to Gwynn, and the pistol went back into the sock drawer. The unfolding events at Glenwhylden had made him decide to wait—at least for a little while.

He was invited back to the estate three more times in the following days and spent more time with the Orangs.

The largest male, Pongo Pygmaeus, was the only one to choose a name that was not human. "Pongo Pygmaeus" is the Latin name for the species Orangutan. He settled on this as his name after he was shown a chapter on Orangutans in an illustrated zoology book. Pongo was the most physically imposing of the animals. His age was estimated to be around 23 years. Like nearly all of the other animals, he had been injured when he was taken into captivity—his shoulder was separated when the giant teak tree he had climbed was felled by loggers. He had fought hard against the capture nets and been clubbed into unconsciousness. He was taken to Dr. Larkin's rescue station right away, however, because a high-ranking member of the National Forest Resources Ministry happened to be there inspecting a timber stand at the time. Pongo was released into the wild very soon after his recovery from his injuries. It was thought that the release was successful, but within a few months he had apparently wandered down from the remote release area back into the logging tract. This time he was not significantly injured but was netted and subdued and again taken to the Larkin station. He had been there for only two days when Dr. Larkin died.

After the crash incident at Glenwhylden, Pongo had been the most severely affected. He was ill longer than the others and lost more weight. Of all the animals, he was the one the vet was most concerned might die because he was still in his coma when all the others were coming out of theirs. He did recover, of course, regaining consciousness about two days later than the rest of the group. He was moody, and often went off to far corners of the estate to be alone. He read books, like all the others, but his real fascination was with machinery, especially fast cars. He adored riding on the gardener's electric cart. They had to take the key out of the cart if they left it somewhere because twice Pongo had tried to drive it off by himself. The first time the cart ended up hanging on the edge of a reflecting pool. In the second incident, it careened down a steep hill and overturned at the bottom. Pongo got a sprained wrist and Celine severely scolded him during the next morning's conference call. He religiously kept up with all the car magazines, never failed to watch "Motor Week" on Public Television when it came on each Saturday.

"Emily Forrestal" was about 26 years old, the oldest and most respected female. She was very sweet and kind to everyone around the house, always taking an active role in caring for any member of the household staff who might be down with the flu or some such thing. She loved all music, but classical music in particular. In comparatively little time she'd built up formidable knowledge of the genre and could discourse as a scholar. Celine encouraged her and had given permission to use her credit cards to phone-order CD's from catalogues. Eventually, Emily had written to the local paper, describing herself as a disfigured shut-in with an avid and extensive interest in classical recordings, and actually managed to convince the editor, entirely through correspondence, to give her a monthly column in which she reviewed new classical recordings. This feature became quite popular, and Emily was soon receiving dozens of complimentary CD's each month directly from the manufacturers, in addition to many letters from her avid readers. She often received invitations to concerts and recitals and was sorely pained at turning these down.

Emily's daughter, "Chloé Poe" was around nine years of age. She had been an infant when a logging crew destroyed the section of forest where she and her mother were living. They were both captured with nets and held in a crude wooden cage at the logging camp for three weeks. Salvation arrived in the form of Dr. Elizabeth Larkin when they had been nearly starved to death. She rescued them and took them to the conservation shelter where they were nursed back to health. Both mother and daughter bonded with Dr. Larkin and were resisting being returned to the wild at the time of the scientist's death. After her transformation at Glenwhylden, Chloé acquired a love of all things pertaining to youth culture: MTV, any kind of new young fad or fashion, especially whichever slang words happened to be in vogue. She was always pumping the veterinarian's granddaughter, Kerri Lewis, for details about what the girls at school were wearing and which bands they thought were cool. She was also forever asking about boys and what it felt like to fall in love.

The second youngest of the males, Artod Mohadjhi, also had a close relationship with the Lewis girl. He was approximately nineteen, slender and soulful. His facial disks were developing, but not to any great size, so his look was still a bit on the juvenile side. He loved to read poetry, and had begun to produce some very fine works of his own. Artod had an affinity for American literature. He was never so happy as when reading a section of a book that he found to be fabulous, then later relating insights he had gleaned.

"Trent Alanadale", a year younger than Artod, was a wannabe jet-setting society-boy trapped in an Orangutan's body. Unlike most of the others, his entry into captivity was not characterized by violence or trauma—quite the contrary. He strolled into the rescue station one day and calmly joined the resident animals during feeding time. He refused to leave, and was fed and allowed to remain. One of the workers taught him to shake hands and bow and after that, he was forever going around introducing himself to everyone, over and over. He was short and stocky and had become fond of the gourmet food and fine wines at Glenwhylden. He wore a smoking jacket around the house, like his favorite TV character, Thurston Howell III, from "Gilligan's Island". For some reason, his speech had progressed faster than the others and during the earliest periods of their development he often did the talking for the rest. Celine called him "The Ambassador".

Food, in fact, was of overarching interest to every one of the Orangs. For twenty-one year old "Betty Rudeen", the art of cooking reached near-religious significance. She always wanted to be in the kitchen, learning how it all worked. She subscribed to all the food magazines: Gourmet, Food and Wine, Bon Appétit and others arrived at the Glenwhylden mailbox each month. Betty would sequester herself, memorizing every page, and then head to the kitchen for a go at preparing whichever dishes had sparked her imagination. The staff had set up a corner work area for her, complete with all the implements she needed to turn out ever-changing culinary masterpieces. If Betty needed some unusual or exotic ingredient, all she had to do was inform Mr. Polk. She soon eclipsed the accomplishments of the house chef. She could sew, arrange flowers, loved housework, and was developing a finely honed telephone manner. In short, she'd make someone a great little wife. This was something she repeated to anyone who would listen. When Roger first met Betty, he noticed the long scar running down the back of her scalp, crossing her neck and zigzagging to a halt on her left shoulder. Celine later told him the story behind it. The massive scar was the telling remnant of perhaps the most horrific of any of the seven apes' experiences with the logging crews.

On a pouring monsoon afternoon, Betty had been flushed out of a tree when it was felled and managed to reach the ground relatively unscathed. She made a desperate dash for another stand of trees, some hundred yards distant. But as she raced across a clear-cut area, a pack of four large dogs owned by the logging crew ran her down and attacked her. Outnumbered and cut off from any escape into the branches, she turned and fought bravely. For nearly a minute, she managed to stand them off, although she was being badly mauled. One of the loggers saw the fight, and ran over with a long machete. He waded into the fray and took a powerful vicious swipe at the hapless Orangutan. The razor sharp blade struck Betty's thick skull, glancing off then slicing down her neck and into her shoulder. She was knocked unconscious by the force of the blow. For some inexplicable reason, the logger did not allow his dogs to devour her on the spot. Perhaps he intended to portion the meat out later, one can only guess at his reasoning. At any rate, taking her for dead, he called off his animals and dragged the Orang over to a truck, tossing her in the cargo bed. At this point, she was bleeding profusely and only minimally breathing. Another half hour would have seen her doom.

Dr. Larkin (once again) had learned that, as a matter of course, any time there was active logging in her area, a sympathetic native observer should be discreetly stationed nearby in order to watch the proceedings. Fortunately for Betty, such was the case on this rainy afternoon, and a message regarding the events was immediately relayed to the rescue station via two-way radio. The doctor and several male staff members raced to the scene, where a confrontation ensued. Elizabeth Larkin was accustomed to such reactions from the loggers; they regarded her as an unrelenting nuisance, standing between them and the unfettered pursuit of remorseless money. After examining the body and ascertaining that there was still a flicker of life present, she wisely avoided informing the crew of this since they had already lied to her and maintained that a saw killed the animal during the process of felling a tree. She demanded that the crew surrender the body of the 'dead' Orang for research purposes and loudly insisted that any other course would be strictly against the law, with a report to be made to the district authorities immediately. The crewmember who had possession of the animal resisted, and the argument rapidly escalated to a screaming match, halting all work. They were near coming to blows when the crew chief happened to pull up in his truck. He saw people screaming and gesticulating, but much worse than that, he saw an entire crew not working. He interceded, ordering them to "give the lady the damn dead monkey," or words to that effect.

Betty was rushed to the station where she barely clung to life for more than a week. But sutures, antibiotics, pain-relieving drugs and constant loving attention pulled her through. Dr. Larkin spent many long hours just holding Betty, cradling her bandaged body and talking to her encouragingly. Subsequent to her recovery and in spite of this harrowing experience, Betty grew to love being around people very much. At Glenwhylden, she was among the most shy of all the animals, but arguably the sweetest and most approachable. She was resolutely loved and fussed over by virtually everyone on the staff.

And then there was "George Villafranco", about twenty. Amazing, quiet, astonishing, gentle little George. He lived in his mind like a remote hideaway, occasionally venturing out to give color and form to his evolved concepts. He was a skilled gardener and spent days on end working with plants in the conservatory. At the beginning, he just tagged along with the gardeners on the estate, watching them go about their work of trimming, mowing, fertilizing, and potting. He learned to help them, and quickly caught on about the right ways to nurture plants.

A pivotal event happened one day when he observed one of the gardeners grafting a branch onto a fruit tree. He was shown how to do rudimental grafting, and after that, he just went ballistic all on his own. He began to select different plants and trees to work with, mysteriously creating entirely new varieties with remarkable properties. Some would produce brilliant flowers never seen before by the resident gardeners. He took fruit trees and combined them with melon-vines and somehow got the cross-breed to work. The resulting fruits were occasionally more than curiosities; some were quite delicious (his pear/watermelon was divine). He concocted his own mixtures of fertilizer, with stupefying results. In the controlled atmosphere of the greenhouse, he created a new strain of corn that boggled the rest of the gardening staff. On thick stalks that were only three feet high at maturity, the individual ears weighed up to two pounds, with a length of one and a half feet or more. The bright yellow kernels were near marble-sized. Not only was the new variety tremendously productive, it also had a very sweet flavor. Later George topped himself, creating a variation of popping corn.

The popped kernels had the circumference of a golf ball. When the other gardeners tried to get him to demonstrate how he was doing these things, George would hug himself and look down at his turned-in feet.

"Oh, Iuh don't know," he'd mumble. "Can't ruhmember."

In addition to communing with plants, George utilized—and thoroughly understood—computers. George displayed a high degree of interest anytime something about computers appeared on television. Excited, he'd rise from his chair to move closer to the screen as though he feared he would miss something. Each of the group began to ask Celine for the things that they found interesting. The thing that George wanted without any doubt was a laptop computer. He carried it around, sitting out in the greenhouse or under a tree on the lawn overlooking the ocean, just staring into the screen and filling up disk after disk with data. It was as if he instinctively understood the explosive potential these machines held for the future of creating and shaping higher knowledge. George was besotted with information. Of all the group, he was the most intelligent, the most astonishing, and the most opaquely secretive. Even as he was with the others, participating in their activities, his thoughts often appeared to have him elsewhere.

Celine and Abby regaled Roger with story after story about the track of the Orang's unfolding personalities. Their minds were insatiable, capable of stupendous daily absorption of knowledge. They seemed to require far less sleep since the transformation. Before, they would spend from eight to ten hours sleeping each night, with a one hour nap after lunch. After the crash, their total daily sleep hours dropped to around four or five, with no loss of energy or vitality. Quite the opposite.

For decades Glenwhylden had been a quiet refuge, a tranquil place suspended in time. With the coming of the change in the apes, the daily pace sped up abruptly. They were so inquisitive, so excited to learn about everything, anything. At first, this had been cute. The staff functioned much as before, with the Orangs just tagging along and observing. But soon the Orangs' hyper-curiosity was overtaxing the ability of the staff to accommodate them. They begged to be taken out, to be allowed to see and feel what they knew was out there, waiting for them. Celine grew worried that they would soon take matters into their own hands and just go over the wall. The result would be disaster; another reason why a full-time "minder" was now a necessity.

On his fifth visit to Glenwhylden, Roger once again was taken into the little upstairs library. Celine laid out for him exactly what she expected. If he accepted the challenge, he would be the person most responsible for the welfare and development of the Orangutans. He would be with them a great deal, far more than just forty hours a week. He was to be their absolute best friend and guide. This wasn't to be so much a job as a lifestyle, she emphasized. There were no rules she could provide him with, no predictions for what kind of course the next months and years might follow. It was anybody's guess just how far these apes might evolve. So far the change had been meteoric, with no slow-down in sight. Could he cope with all this? Had he had time to weigh all these factors?

She crossed her arms and stared at him. "And you know I haven't said anything about the money yet, have I? So. This is serious business here. I'm asking you to make a long-term commitment and I'm expecting you to change your whole life. I need you to move here to Glenwhylden and spend most of your time here. If you take this job, you won't really be able to live like you have been. Maybe you won't even be able to live any kind of normal life, so to speak. I think you should be paid an amount commensurate with those requirements. To start, a million dollars a year enough?"

Roger's jaw dropped. They shook hands on it.

Three days later Celine and Abby returned to Marsh Meadows. Celine missed the weather on the east coast and wanted to check on her charity projects and business matters. She missed all the things in her old family home—she felt she belonged there. She'd made peace with Glenwhylden and no longer felt sad or unhappy thinking about it. Now that the Orangs were there and Roger was in place to care for them, she knew the big house would be full of life, the way it should be.

And so Roger Victor Caldwell, aged twenty four, erstwhile Porsche mechanic and once-suicidal Usher's Syndrome sufferer, improbably came into a new job, and at least for the moment, a new life. He would now carry on with living in the mansion where he'd planned to die because at the last possible moment a miracle had happened. A necessity for his damaged life was created, and though he had been planning something else entirely, he now saw little choice but to respond to it. It wasn't the money, really. He had no one to spend it on or leave it to. Something else was telling him to stick around. And as for his ebbing sight and hearing—well, he had at least a little time left, didn't he?

Chapter 14

Pongo held the hose with care, playing the stream of water over the hood and fenders of Roger's Porsche. It was just the two of them, washing the car out by the garages. Pongo fixated on the little coupe from the first moment he saw it. He pestered Roger to take him for a ride, if only just to the bottom of the driveway. Just anywhere at all. Roger kept putting him off. Finally, he gave in and took him for a sedate spin down the road to the greenhouses, then looped back along behind the tennis courts.

"Gowuh fastare, gowuh fastare!" Pongo begged, his eyes on fire. But there wasn't enough road. They didn't even clear second.

On this clear September morning Pongo sprayed the last of the soap suds off, then they went to work with the chamois. When the car was dry, Roger demonstrated how to apply and polish the wax. They were chatting amiably as the job progressed.

"It'z jess so enterustink tuh me how boofully thizz musheens auhr put tugevver, Rujuh. Awhl dese pahrts, dey ahwl havta wuhrk jes riyuht an not brayek. Iss so wunnerfull that pipple cud thingk thisz up and mayke it sow fayust and stihl bee so boofuhl. Ah gehssz yew no jess bout evrthung arbowt theese musheens, downt yew?" Pongo's huge face was animated when he talked about machines. He rubbed the wax carefully in small circles, just the way he'd been shown.

Roger worked on his own patch of the hood and grinned over at his friend. "I know a lot compared to most people. But it's my job. I've been working on these things for a long time.

What you said about all the parts—man, you're absolutely right. There's thousands of parts in this thing and they work very well." Roger paused and shook his head slightly. "Look, I'm sorry I can't take you for a fast ride, Pongo. I think it's just too risky."

Pongo stopped what he was doing. He came around the front of the car clutching his wax rag and stared intently at his new friend. "Now lissen tur me fur a secuhn will yuhr, Rujah? Ah thing ther's a way thuht yeyw can shohw me whud iss lakh tuh gowah relly fayst. We got sum mayusks thet we hayad fuhr a Hellowin partiy lest yeahar an' thers thisz wuhn thad luhks jes lahk uh lidduh owld mayuhn. It fidts me perfeck. Ah cuhd puht id owuhn an ride wis yew. Ah rilly, rilly wuhnts dis. Izs funnay how yew brut thiz up becauwsz Ah wuz gunnah ayusk yew eenyway." He was swaying back and forth, wound up in the selling of his scheme.

Roger leaned on the car and studied Pongo for a moment. In the short time he had known him he had become familiar with the ape's amazingly well-developed dry humor.

"A mask? A Halloween mask? Come on, Pong, you gotta be kidding." Roger snickered at the thought of a Halloween mask pulled over Pongo's huge head. "Right, I'm gonna drive around with you sitting in the passenger seat wearing some kind of Halloween mask. You'd look like a movie monster."

Pongo threw his rag down and hopped a little. "Oh, oh yehuh? Dat isz rawung, Rujah! Yew jesz wait riyuht heyar. Ah'm gunnah goa an geyut thayut mayask an puht ohn sum cloz Ah haz, an yull see, yull see how id cud bee okayie!"

He turned and hustled into the kitchen. He was serious. He was going to go get himself into some kind of disguise. Pongo wanted speed so much it was driving him nuts. "I shouldn't make fun of him just because he wants to go fast," Roger thought. "It's a serious thing to him and in a lot of ways he's just like me." Maybe it could happen, somehow. They could go late at night, into the countryside. In the dark there would be little chance of anyone seeing them.

Roger had moved on to the rear fender when he heard the kitchen door slam, then the sound of shuffling. He turned around, and despite his very best efforts, fell to the driveway laughing. Pongo was advancing earnestly, in a ludicrous get-up. He had on an ill-fitting old brown suit with a stretch sports-shirt underneath. A latex mask, the face of an ancient man, was stretched down over his outsized head. He looked like fat, balloon-headed Methuselah. Pongo walked over to where Roger was lying on the driveway and spoke up indignantly.

"Yew duhnt nowuh howh mush Ah hayut beyeeng stugh heyuhr an nod beyeeng abule to gowh anuhwhuhr, Rujuuh! Thiyes diskice miyut nuht beh purfac bud itd wull wuhrk! Ah jesh rully wowuhnt tuh gowah for uh dryuhv wid yew. Pleehz? Ah promishiz tuh bee verah kwite an guhd. Pleehz, Rujuh."

Roger looked up and could see Pongo's intense little eyes peering out from the holes in Methuselah's face. He stifled another fit of laughter and sat up, remembering what he had been thinking a few moments before. If they were careful it would be okay. It was worth taking the risk, considering how happy it would make him.

"God, Pong. That's the funniest thing I've seen in years. Okay, man, if it means this much to you, I suppose I'll have to take you out for a spin, but I'm not so sure you shouldn't just go regular, instead of wearing that outfit. I'll have an accident if I look at you and start laughing again."

Pongo pulled the mask off and beamed. "Thadas greyut! Thehnk yew so muszh, Rujuh! Weyan kann wee gowuh? Riyut nowuh?"

Roger stood up, wiping his eyes. He was just beginning to say that they might go for a ride that evening when he heard someone else burst out laughing behind him.

He spun around and saw a lanky figure only a few feet away. At first he thought it was a young man, then realized otherwise. Somehow he had not heard the tomboyish girl approaching. She was giggling with one hand over her mouth, pointing at Pongo. When the ape looked up and saw her, he exclaimed with affection.

"Kaeree! Yew uhr bayack! Wee uhll misszed yew so mushz!" He dropped the mask and lumbered over to her, grabbing her vigorously for a huge hug. Roger stood where he was, waiting to be introduced. The girl held Pongo, then pushed him back a little and started teasing him.

"What a set of threads! What's the story, huh?"

Ah, yes, the veterinarian's granddaughter, thought Roger. She chucked Pongo under the chin, then turned toward Roger.

"Hey there." She had a disconcertingly deep and breathy voice for such a young girl. Pongo silently stood by and looked at Roger, uncertain about how to handle this new situation.

"You must be Kerri. I've heard a lot about you. I'm Roger Caldwell." He extended his hand. The girl's crushing grip was rough as any carpenter's.

"Well thanks, I hope. Been hearing about you, too. I guess you met my grandfather yesterday." She looked over his shoulder at the Porsche. "Nice car. Yours?"

"Yeah."

"Wow. That's hot. Maybe I can get a ride sometime." There was just a touch of provocation in her tone. "Well, hey, congratulations on your new job here. These guys have been needing somebody like you for a long time. You're just about the luckiest guy on the planet." She playfully pushed Pongo, then smiled at Roger.

She was striking, but in a primitive way. Her eyes were the pale green of a cougar, turned up at the corners, set under thick dark brows nearly joined together. The look of a predator. She had a wide mouth with full lips which, when drawn apart in her wary smile, revealed wolfish white teeth with a gap in the middle. Her short-chopped chestnut hair was dappled with blonde, left to bunch itself in careless spikes. And she was tall—almost six feet, with a noticeably developed musculature. Big shoulders for a girl, boy-hips, and ram-rod-straight posture. She was wearing a plaid flannel shirt and a shredded pair of cut-off jeans. As she stood holding Pongo's hand, Roger couldn't help noticing her powerful legs, with scraped knees and scars. Runner's legs, he thought, or even bodybuilder's. Lean, corded thighs and unshaven bulging calves. She was shoeless (that's why he didn't hear her walk up) and her ankles were encircled with leather thongs strung with little trinkets: seashells and beads. She fixed him with an unsettling gaze.

"So. What do you think of all this?" She raised an eyebrow. "Interesting?"

He gave out a high-pitched laugh. "Oh, it's *definitely* interesting. No question. You, uh...you've been coming here for a while, haven't you?"

"Yep. Since I was sixteen. These guys are my best buds." She and Pongo were swinging their hands now. "How's everybody else doin'?" she asked the ape. "They all in the TV room?"

Pongo nodded and tugged her toward the house. "Lesz gowah inn dere an suhpriyes dem, Kaeree! Dey weel bee so happiye to szee yew. Come owuhn, Rujah, gowah wid us." He led off excitedly in the direction of the kitchen door with Kerri still happily holding his hand.

In the kitchen they found Betty and Emily chattering away, a lively string quartet issuing from a CD player. Betty was peeking into one of the ovens. Judging from the aroma, she was making chocolate cake or brownies, or maybe fudge. Emily was on a stool smoking a cigarette and drinking a cup of coffee.

"Hey, girlfriends!" Kerri bellowed from the door. Both apes whooped and came running to hug the tall girl.

"Kayree, yewh luug szo guhd, hunny! Did yewh and yor grehnspa haff a guhwd tahm up in thuuh mowuhntuns?" Betty wiped her hands on her apron, looking for all the world like a normal little mother busying away in the kitchen.

"Oh, Grandpa and I had a great time in the Sierra. We hiked way up to this secret spot he used to go to when he was a boy and you know what? He said it was exactly the same as he remembered it. It didn't seem like anyone had ever even been there. There's this awesome little lake. The water was sooo cold, but I went swimming anyway. And then, there's this stream with a waterfall not too far up from where we camped, you know, and we got some good fishing in. It was perfect. I'm glad to be back though—I really missed all you guys."

Emily got back up on her stool and wriggled around, swaying a little to the music. She winked at Kerri. "Weyehll Kayree, iss been puhrtyh interuhstin heyehr. Yew problee huhrd, Sayleen kaym tuh vihsiyt uhsz. Shee isz jus thuh mose wunnerfuhl ladiy in thuh hohwl wurl! An nowuh, weeyuh goht Ruhjare tew tayke cayer uff ahwl uff usz. Iss uh lot bedduhr. Weeyur gohnnuh hafv uh loht mowehr fun nouh!" Emily put her big hand up to her lips and blew a big kiss over at Roger. He blew one back.

"Yep, so I hear." Kerri looked appraisingly at Roger again. He was struck by the directness of her gaze. Most girls her age are uncertain of themselves, but she seemed cocksure, downright powerful beyond her years.

Cacophony floated with clouds of cigarette smoke in the media room. The other Orangs were lounging in their recliners, jabbering about programs on the screens. When they saw Kerri it was a repeat of the scene in the kitchen, all of them jumping up to hug her, excited and happy to see their friend. Trent quickly returned to his chair to resume watching a re-run of Gilligan's Island. All of the others clustered around Kerri to hear about her camping trip. Roger sat down beside Trent, but from across the room he was unable to take his eyes off Kerri. She was the most riveting person he'd met in recent memory. Trent noticed him staring.

"Kerri's quite a girl, isn't she Roger?" he commented softly. It was amazing how advanced his speech and vocabulary had become. Talking was his thing and he'd worked very hard on it. He'd progressed rapidly, even just within the past few weeks.

"Yeah. I guess you've all known her and her grandfather for a long time."

Trent nodded, then tapped Roger's forearm. "She can kick your ass, too, my friend."

Roger looked at him blankly.

"What did you say?"

Trent snorted. "You heard right. I said she can kick your ass. That girl is one of the strongest humans around, and a real mean fighter. Since she was a little kid she's been coming here with her grandfather, and she's always wanted to be as strong as us. Way before everything got different—I mean, before all these changes happened to us—I remember wrestling with her, and she'd always get mad when I could pin her so easily. But she'd never give up, so I'd just pin her down, over and over again. It made her really angry. So she does things to get tougher. She wants to be just like us."

"She does? Wow. Well, she sure looks strong."

146

Kerri was up on the coffee table, re-enacting the capture of a rainbow trout for her giggling audience. Artod was playing the fish, flopping around the floor.

"She works out in the gym that Celine put in for us here, just about every day. You know that weight bar thing, what do you call that thing? A press, or something?"

"Bench-press?"

"Right. Bench-press. She can lift two-hundred pounds on that thing, eight times."

Roger frowned. "No. I can't even bench press two-hundred pounds eight times, and I'm no wimp. No way."

"I've seen her do it, Roger. I told you, she can kick your ass. And she climbs up a rope we hung from a branch on a great big tree down the hill. I mean, we can climb it real easy, it's nothing for any of us, but I never thought any of you humans could do it. It goes way up there, and she can do it with just her hands, all the way to the top. She does a lot of other stuff, too, like swimming in the ocean. She swims way out there all by herself, even when it's cold and rainy. She never wears those black suit things like the surfing men we can see through the telescope. And she runs over here after she gets out of school. Polk says that's two miles away. When he's out in the car he sees her on the side of the road, running on rocks and broken glass and stuff, with no shoes, to make herself tougher and to get used to pain. She always says no if he offers her a ride. And she does those sit-up things, you know. Five hundred of those things a day."

Roger shook his head, not sure what to think. Trent stirred his vodka and orange juice with his finger.

"I heard her grandfather telling Polk that he's worried about her cause she's angry so much. She's been getting into trouble at her school a lot, I guess. For not dressing right and for fighting. She doesn't have any friends. All the girls and even most of the boys are afraid of her. They call her "Scary Kerri". A few weeks ago, some boy at the school was teasing her like that, calling her that name. He pushed her, I guess, and she punched him back. He was a big strong boy, a football player. Dr. Lewis told Polk the boy was trying as hard as he could to beat her up, but Kerri kicked him in the face and knocked him out. She knows how to do all that jumping, kicking stuff like in the fighting movies on TV. I've seen her practicing. She kicks this big heavy bag that's hung up down at the barn and she punches it with her fists too. It makes a loud noise. They had to take the boy to the hospital because she kept on kicking his head after he fell down. She hurt him real bad and he didn't wake up for awhile, I guess. They were afraid he wasn't going to wake up at all. The police came and then the school said she couldn't come back there for two weeks, and that's why Dr. Lewis took her up to the mountains to go fishing. That's why. I think he wanted to talk to her about what happened. He's all the family she has, except for us. Polk says her father left her mother before Kerri was born and her mother ran off with some other man when Kerri was two. Then the mother was in prison after that and somehow she got killed there. We all really like Kerri very much, Roger. Of course, *we* can still kick *her* ass, so we all get along, no problem."

Trent bared all his teeth and got up from his chair. "I need some more ice."

Roger went over to collect Pongo. The ape was telling Kerri that soon—perhaps tonight—he would actually be leaving the estate, for a ride in Roger's Porsche. A fast ride. This had been promised to him. They both looked up at Roger.

"So," Kerri said, "breakin' Pongo out, huh Roger? That should be fun."

"Well, he wants to go pretty bad. I'll take him up the Gibraltar Pass. There's nobody up there at night. And let's not forget, he'll be wearing his perfect disguise, too. Nobody would ever suspect."

"You know something, Roger, how about lettin' me come too? You don't mind, do you Pongo?" She looked at the ape for support.

"Okeh wiss me."

"Well, there's not much room in the back seat. There's not even really a back seat, just some fold-down benches. You're pretty tall. I don't know how comfortable you'd be."

"Oh, I don't think I'll have a problem. I'm *very* flexible." She smiled wickedly. "What's the matter, afraid we're gonna roll you and steal your car?"

Okay, he thought. She's gonna test me for awhile. That's how she does things. No problem. She wants to go for a ride, I'll take her for a ride, no big deal.

He was careful not to let his expression change.

"Hey, no problem then. As long as it's okay with Pongo." He casually let his eyes wander over her shoulder, feigning distraction.

"Cool!" Her smile was sunny. "When do we go?"

"Well—after dinner at least. The pass road'll be deserted by then. Okay?" He looked back to Pongo. "If we're gonna take that drive, we better go finish waxing, right?"

"Owah yeshz, Ah uhlmowst furgowt!" The two of them repaired to the driveway and resumed working. After they had the car looking perfect, they spent the rest of the afternoon watching the television wall with the others. Roger usually couldn't do this for long. It gave him a headache, the onslaught of light and noise. To someone accustomed to watching just one program at a time, it was too chaotic and annoying. Kerri was apparently used to it because she was sprawled out on the carpet contentedly gazing up at the jumble of programs.

The media room had originally been a billiard room. This was, of course, before the Orangs had developed their insatiable interest in television. The old billiard table was still there, but it now occupied a spot close to a wall. No one used it. A high bank of cathedral-peaked windows were kept fully obscured with heavy dark draperies. This allowed the Orangs to concentrate on the televisions, undistracted by the time of day or even the weather outside.

Recently George had confided to Roger how remarkable it seemed, that creatures once so in tune with the natural rhythms of the days and the weather were now so disinterested in it all. They all had clear recollections of their lives in the rainforest, long before events brought them to Glenwhylden. The contrast was acute; where before they'd been unprotected and absolutely responsible for their own welfare, now they were in the lap of luxury, amid totally controlled circumstances. Now, everything was provided for them. And although the rainforest is a place where in fact a lot happens, to the Orangs all these things were routine. True curiosity was blunted. When you woke in the morning, it wasn't as if you were going to learn a lot that day. You couldn't choose to go where new things could happen to you. No, you just went about your business, foraging and eating, doing your best to stay calm and avoid significant trouble. Once in awhile, according to the established and ordered natural agenda of things, you got the urge to mate. Even that didn't associate with any great pleasure, completely unlike everything they were now learning about the sexual exigencies of humans. For Orangutans in the tropical rainforest, life had been a certain way for hundreds of thousands of years. But within the last hundred years, man and his machines had progressively encroached on their pristine world, and more change had come in that brief time than in all the previous millennia.

George watched television with the others, and like each of them, he had his favorite programs. However, two of the screens were reserved for the display of his computer. While everyone sat watching and discussing, George had a keyboard on his lap, entering notes as the viewing went on. Roger soon realized that George was doing formal research, without ever having been trained. He was assimilating and recording important information. Sometimes it was easy to understand: paragraphs expressing opinions about some behavior, or questions about customs or slang he didn't comprehend. Other entries were mysterious, long sequences of numbers. George was racing to understand everything about his new world. One night Roger watched an old Cary Grant movie on one of the screens. During a commercial break, his eyes wandered over to George's computer screen.

Two sentences were written there:

"Evolution is the cause of revolution, not its symptom."

And, "Revolution is the cause of evolution, not its symptom."

George was hunched down in his chair, fixating on the words, oblivious to everything around him. He gave the impression of a machine which had become locked due to some malfunction in its logic circuit. Roger kept glancing over during the next ten minutes and George remained motionless, contemplating the two opposing concepts. Only after nearly half an hour did he reach a point of resolve, clearing one sentence from the screen. Roger read the remaining one: "Revolution is the cause of evolution, not its symptom."

George hadn't looked at anyone else nor discussed his dilemma. He'd simply reasoned it through, finding his own solution.

Dinner was the usual romp, with everyone talking pretty much at once. All of the Orangs in the group, save Chloé, had ceased to be vegetarians, although they rarely ate any meat more potent than chicken. Chloé's adherence to the meatless diet probably had more to do with what she was seeing on MTV more than any health considerations. All the others loved king-crab legs and these were on the menu tonight. They liked twisting the shells to crack them open, extracting the sweet meat, then dipping it in melted butter. It was ideal finger food, and they dove in with alacrity. There were heaps of fresh steamed vegetables, as well as very textural salads. Large bowls of whole fruit were never ignored by anyone. Roger enjoyed eating with them; the conversation was always fascinating. It also gave them a chance to work on their speech skills. At least one dish at each meal would have been contributed by Betty. Lately, this had been dessert—she was on a pastry kick. This particular evening she had outdone herself with a lemon-kiwi meringue pie with lime sauce. Exquisite. Following the example set by Celine and Abby, there was always a generous supply of wine with dinner and post-prandial comforts included cognac or port and of course, Cuban cigars.

All during the evening Roger tried to avoid resting his eyes too often on Kerri, who was seated across and down from him. He had failed. She caught him looking quite a few times because apparently she had more than a little curiosity about him as well. They exchanged only minimal conversation with each other directly but the eye contact was profuse.

It was late, almost ten, when Roger, Pongo and Kerri finally walked out of the service door and got into the Porsche.

It was a warm evening and absolutely clear, one of those Santa Barbara nights when the stars seem amplified and rippling. True to her word, Kerri folded her long legs into the tight space behind the front seats with no problem. She turned sideways and braced her feet against the leather panel under the side rear window. Roger helped Pongo fasten his seat belt, then fired up the engine and dramatically began the descent down the twisting driveway, heading for the front gate and the outside world.

"Ahw haff beyehn heyuhr foruh yeerzs, anh Ah haff nayvehr beyehn outsahd uff thuh gayets!" Pongo squeaked with delight.

"Well, you're going out in style tonight." As he braked at the bottom of the hill to wait for the gates to open, Roger glanced in his rearview mirror. All he could see were Kerri's eyes, glowing out from the darkness of the backseat. The hairs on the back of his neck lifted.

The ponderous swing of the gates completed, Roger stuffed the accelerator and they were off, hustling vigorously up Shoreline Boulevard, then turning abruptly onto a darkened short cut—a twisting coastal-canyon lane that would deliver them to the base of the Gibraltar Pass road. As they halted at the stop sign where they would turn right to start up the mountain, Roger paused to check on Pongo. He and Kerri had both been silent for the five minutes or so that they had been clipping along the backstreets of Montecito. Roger wanted to make sure Pongo was actually having the good time he had anticipated, not getting carsick or frightened.

"You doing okay? Having fun?" Roger looked over at the ape hunkering in the passenger seat, then reached over to make sure the seat belt and shoulder harness were properly fastened.

Pongo seemed calm, almost serene. "Thiyes isz wuhnderfuhll, jesz wuhnderfuhll," he murmured, turning his head a little toward Roger. He had his enormous hands folded neatly in his lap.

"Kerri? Ready?"

He felt unexpected fingers ruffling his hair.

"I thought you'd never ask." The voice was a sultry growl and it came from lips so close to his ear he felt warm breath.

A shiver shot down Roger's spine and crash landed right between his legs. Trying to ignore it, he opened his CD box, pulling out Z.Z. Top's "Afterburner". Perfect for lawless driving.

He punched the play button, simultaneously stomping the accelerator pedal to the floorboard. The initial stretch of Gibraltar was relatively straight and flat and within the first eight seconds they were at the top of third gear and making better than ninety miles per hour. Z.Z. roared from the three-hundred watt dual-amplifier stereo, shaking the seats beneath them. "You're just a dawg, a dirty dawwwwg!" Roger knew this deserted road intimately, it was his unofficial test track and it was standard for him to spike a hundred forty-five miles per hour before reaching the first serious hairpin turn, less than a third of a mile from the stop sign where they had started. There was a specific way to accomplish this. At the top wrap out of second gear, he shifted to third and briefly thumbed the nitrous oxide injector switch on the stick shift, feeding a burst of super combustible vapor into the screaming power plant. This was like kicking the car in the ass with a giant boot. Sixteen inch Pirellis on the rear wheels spun loose for a split second, even though the car was already clocking better than ninety. Then the sticky rubber caught again, and in the next head-snapping instant, they blew through third and into fourth, the speedometer needle jumping up like a pin to a magnet. At 145 mph, they rocketed toward the treacherous, banking hairpin curve. Roger was on a preset program now, concentrating fully on what he was doing. The car projected at the sharp curve with the all the purpose of a laser-guided missile. Closer, closer, too close. It now seemed all but obvious that they would never be able to slow down quickly enough to negotiate the sharp turn out in front of them. Faintly, a prolonged and unearthly scream wavered from the back seat, just barely audible above the howling engine, squealing tires, and pounding rock-and-roll. The adrenalin floodgates were wide open and a smell of terror mixed with giddy ecstasy and burning nitrous filled the car's cramped cabin. When they were less than fifty feet from legitimate disaster, Roger abandoned the accelerator and stood on the brakes with practiced force. Oversized pads seized all four perforated discs, chattering from the computerized pulses of the ABS system. At the same time, he double-clutched and downshifted to third, allowing the engine's torque to further retard their forward motion. The little roadster initiated a controlled drift into and across the turn at around seventy-five mph. Wide tires left a dark calling card on the pavement, documenting their course through the bend. A yellow sign flickered as the halogen beams swept it: "Sharp Curve, 25 mph". With perfect timing, near the middle of the slide, Roger released the brakes and popped the throttle again, torqueing the rear of the car into line with the front, immediately goosing the speed back up above 100. Somehow, the turn was now behind them and they had ghosted through it without ever falling below seventy miles per hour. It had taken less than two seconds to pass a significant hairpin turn that a normal motorist would need to spend ten seconds or more negotiating safely. Out of the curve, the acceleration resumed. Razor sharp guitar riffs slashed menacingly across the top of an obscene pile-driver of drums and bass. "Git that dawwg offa my lawn!" The road straightened, climbing steeply, but the grade was no match for the customized Teutonic fire-dragon which slobbered and gorged under the Porsche's engine cowling. With all the modifications and refinements, Roger had succeeded in raising the engine's total horsepower to near four hundred fifty, up from the stock figure of two hundred eighty nine. This degree of power was mounted in a little go-kart frame that weighed less than twenty-two hundred pounds. Even heading uphill and carrying the passengers, the car's thrust was stupefying. It didn't accelerate so much as attempt to take flight. The stretch of road comprising the climb covered one half mile to the next serious curve, skirting a cliff with more than two hundred feet of vertical drop to a boulder field below. Two more spurts of nitrous near the top of second and squarely in the power band of third and they were right back into the heady realm above one hundred thirty miles per hour. The blue-white sear of the car's illegally powerful driving beams shocked the dry tufts of grass blurring past on the sides of the narrow road. Objects in the field of vision became softened and fuzzy, first leaning anxiously toward the glare of the approaching rocket, then instantaneously recoiling as the shock wave ripped past. Each successive curve fell behind much as the first, amid impossible geometry and noise and vibration. The serpentine road climbed and flattened, dove and swooped, split giant boulders and glanced off sheer pitches. Roger was giving his passengers the full treatment, going all the way to the top of the mountain. When they were near halfway up, Roger noticed out of the corner of his eye that Pongo had begun to hold his hand rigidly outstretched, pointing the direction of the vehicle's probable trajectory as each new twist in the road arrived. He held the hand flattened and turned on its edge, chopping down as if it were the blade of a sword. He seemed to be imagining that he was setting, by force of will, the certainty of the car's passage through each undulation of the road surface.

Along the entire route, they encountered no other traffic. This was an unusual luxury; it permitted the spell of speed and danger to remain unbroken until they crested the final rise, then slowed and pulled off onto the shoulder. A majestic carpeting of city lights spread below. Roger rolled down the volume knob on the CD, allowing the resonant idle of the engine to be heard. They sat there for a few moments with no comment from anyone. Then he shut off the engine and stereo. The sounds of night breezes and crickets in the tall grass were all around, in marked contrast to the mechanical chaos of the previous few minutes.

"You guys like that?" Roger asked. He heard shifting in the back seat.

"Oh my God." Kerri sounded like she'd just had an orgasm. "That was so awesome. This car is unreal. Dude, you're an incredibly good driver." She started laughing, the adrenaline rush wearing off. "That was the most fun I've ever had. Let's do it again right now!"

Pongo turned toward Roger. "Kann we geht ouyut heer anh look dowuhn?"

Kerri answered for him. "Of course, Pongo. We can get out for a few minutes, right Roger?"

The road was visible for the better part of a mile below and if any other cars were coming, Roger knew he'd be able to see them a long way off. "Sure, stretch our legs for a minute. No problem." He swung out of the car and went around to open Pongo's door for him. Kerri wriggled out of the back seat from the driver's side and then strolled across to the edge of the overlook to gaze out.

"Wow. I've lived here all my life and I don't think I've ever been up here to see this view at night. It's so cool. I think I can probably see my house from here."

Pongo moaned a little bit, seemingly overwhelmed by the experience he'd just had, and by the beauty of the glowing city. He pointed down, long finger tracing the snaking line of car lights on the freeway, incandescent cells pulsing along a dark artery.

"Sohwuh menny masheens down theyuhr" he murmured. "Masheens yew peyuple thowuht uhf, ayand yew peyuple kuntrohuhl. Isz veryuh mizzteriuhz, veryuh wuhnderfuhl."
They stood for a few more minutes, enjoying the warm breezes that wafted up the slope.

Finally, Roger glanced at his watch. "I don't want to get the others worried. How about we head back down, okay? We won't go so fast this time."

They protested, wanting another wild ride, but Roger knew it was far more dangerous to go fast on a down slope than on a climb. The evening had been a lot of fun so far, and he didn't want to spoil things by having a mishap. On the descent, he held the speed to a sedate eighty miles per hour.

It was nearly eleven when they reached the gates of Glenwhylden. Roger let Pongo push the button on the remote control and the big gates responded. They climbed up the hill and parked behind the kitchen. Pongo ran inside, eager to tell the others about his adventure.

"Guess I'll head home," said Roger to Kerri, as the girl slowly extricated her long limbs from the back seat. "Been a long day."

She stood beside the open passenger door. "Hey, would you mind giving me a ride to my house? I live pretty close, but it's kind of late and I don't like to freak out my grandpa on school nights. I'm supposed to be home by eleven."

"Oh, no problem. You should have told me, I would have gotten you back sooner."

"No way. I wouldn't have missed that ride for anything." She smiled that threatening smile again. They drove out of the estate and she directed him along the mile or so route to her house, which turned out to be not so very far from Roger's cottage.

Before she got out of the car, Kerri paused a moment, still looking forward, then said, "Hey Roger. I'm really glad you're the guy Mrs. Stertevant got to take care of the Orangs. They all really like you and...I like you too." Then, before he could reply to this, she leaned over kissed him on his neck. Sort of a kiss. But it was more like a bite. Roger felt the pinch of sharp teeth. It all happened within the space of a second, and it was something for which he was unprepared, to say the least. "Hey!" He spun toward her but she bolted out and sprinted up the walkway, vanishing through the door.

He drove on slowly to his cottage in a thoughtful mood. His fingers kept going up to his neck, exploring the double-crescent welt where the young girl's teeth had marked him. He couldn't believe it—she had definitely bit him. Why? Why would she do that? How strange, he kept thinking. What an odd girl, so totally unlike any other he had ever met. She had such an aggressive, in-your-face kind of vibe about her, but yet was so kind and gentle with the Orangs. A couple more things: she way too young for him and she really wasn't his type at all. Yet there was no denying that he found her unusually attractive. He was mulling all this over as he coasted into the driveway at his cottage. The Porsche's headlights flicked up to the carport and he felt his stomach tighten. He had company. Gwynn's red Honda Prelude was parked there and a light was on in the cottage.

Chapter 15

In Gwynn's mind it was a simple deal. She had all the right stuff to serve some rich guy as a very presentable trophy wife. No, she wasn't intellectual, but for the role she desired, not a bad thing. Smart usually meant contentious and contentious wasn't cute. She was very beautiful, with conformations acknowledged by popular culture. She'd prepared for years, reading the fashion magazines and paperback guides to being a "total woman". She and her girlfriends mercilessly evaluated each other. Gwynn was supreme among them. She worked hard perfecting her image, with regular work-outs and tanning. She was brightly cheerful, always skirting portent or dissidence in conversation. She kept it light. Her topics befitted her purpose: shopping, other women's clothes and bodies, leisure activities, men as a generalized concept. Beyond that, no true opinions. Being opinionated was not a quality well-liked by the type of man she saw herself marrying. Opinionated was like contentious: not cute. She'd done her best to become great in bed. Her personal hygiene was exemplary and her vocal expression of an orgasm—at just the right moment—was top notch. She understood that a great blow job could confer a kind of power that "good girls" could not even begin to fathom. All along she'd paid attention where it mattered, learned her lessons well. And now, she felt it was time. Time for the payoff.

She should be in the right place at the right time to meet a single man of substantial wealth who would identify her assets. He would be attentive and generous and she'd reward him in the manner he found most desirable. Within a reasonable period of time—months, not years—he'd propose. The ring would be impressive. She would accept, breathlessly. The wedding would be a victory roll where she'd relish turning from the altar to see the drooling, jealous faces of her girlfriends. Thus would begin her life of leisure and style, no longer concerned with money, content to busy herself with decorating the life and house of her new husband. If he *insisted*, a child or two would be a sacrifice she would endure. Icky, but okay. That's what nannies were for.

What could be simpler? She saw other women doing this very thing every day. They were everywhere in Montecito, there was no issue to contend. They had a certain identifiable look, a patterned deportment. Goddamn it, *they looked happy*. They figured it out, they played the game well, and now they had it good. This was how it worked, everybody knew that. Gwynn wanted nothing more or less than what these other women had. She deserved it.

Her current problem, as she saw it, was with Roger. Specifically, his failure to give her faith that he would soon convert into the financial specimen for which she could accept no substitute. He was just a mechanic, not a doctor, and even if he eventually became one it would be years from now. As if all that wasn't enough, recently he hadn't demonstrated proper appreciation for her great value. He wasn't calling her often enough, not returning her calls as religiously as he used to, not making enough dates, behaving remotely on the ones he did make—and, more important than any of that—he was disappearing for whole afternoons and evenings at a time with no valid explanation for where he had been. He'd been acting just downright mysterious, ever since he came back from that trip to the east coast on the private jet. She didn't know if he was seeing another woman, or what. What she did know was that he wasn't living up to his end of the bargain and she had carried him long enough. There should now be a good accounting, an apology, and correction of the errant behavior. If not, it was over. After all, he had been given his chance. If he couldn't provide her the life she deserved, then she should move on, no looking back. There were other qualified men out there and she should grab one before someone else did. Available, rich single men were in short supply, and you had to be dedicated to land one. Yes, sir. Oh, she still thought Roger was attractive, that much was fine, but this was business, damn it, and serious business at that. Emotions should be kept the hell out of it, until that big diamond ring was on her finger and the sprawling house, club memberships, and forest-green Jaguar were firmly in place. Her next birthday would be her twenty-third, she reminded herself. Youth was a powerful and irreplaceable playing card. She was well along in the game. Time was of the essence.

When Roger came through the door, this was the potent body of logic awaiting him: seated on the couch, attired in a silver and blue warm-up suit, cradling a vodka and cranberry juice in her hand.

"Hey, Gwynn. This is a nice surprise." He smiled, sensing something ominous. He walked over and kissed her lightly. She looked up, studying his face, then patted the cushion beside her.

"Roger, we need to have a little talk. How about sitting down here with me?" She raised her glass and took a hefty pull on the contents, the ice cubes tinkling sadly in the hushed atmosphere of the dim room.

He sat down resignedly. He knew his behavior of late was bound to bring this moment. He hadn't been upfront with Gwynn about what was happening, any of it, and he felt guilty. But how could he? Trouble was, he hadn't been able to figure out how to keep both her and his new job. Gwynn wasn't the kind of girl who would just accept a story that he was busy with clients. She knew him too well for that, knew his patterns and the way he did things. She was used to being right there for every part of his life, and the way he'd acted lately was not cool at all. It wasn't fair for him to treat her the way he had—he kept promising himself that he'd resolve the situation, but he had procrastinated past the point of no return.

Although he felt like a real shit, a part of him seemed to be relieved that this was finally happening. He hadn't been able to fully explain this to himself. As he had reasoned so many times before, he liked Gwynn, but there was just some key element missing: that noble, heroic bond that a man feels for a woman who truly inspires him. He wondered if this element actually existed for any man in real life. Perhaps what he had with Gwynn was as good as it got for anyone, ever, and he was just a prime fool to allow it to go by the wayside. He hated being wishy-washy, it wasn't like him, but he didn't seem able to be otherwise in the context of this situation. He felt confused. Maybe events were now causing something to take place that he just hadn't had the resolve to bring about on his own.

Gwynn's face was tired in the weak light from the end-table lamp. Had she been crying? She reached over and squeezed Roger's hand when he sat down, and this act of tenderness heightened his already guilty feelings.

"Honey," she began in a soft voice, "something's really wrong. You aren't acting normal, you're not treating me the way you ought to. And I'm... I, it's making me really unhappy. Roger, we've been together for two years, and if something's going on that I need to know about, then I want you to tell me about it, right now. So. What's with you lately? Did you meet somebody else?"

Roger sighed. "No, no. Well, not exactly. I mean...no, I didn't meet *somebody*, that's not it. Before I...look, let me tell you, I feel like a total jerk right now, Gwynn. You're right, I haven't been acting the way I should toward you. I've been trying to figure out how to handle what's happening to me. And it's not you, really, you're any man's dream, you know that. The deal is, well, I've just had some things happen lately, kind of odd things, just by chance more than anything else. And...before I knew it, I got all wrapped up in these things, and I haven't been able to sort out how I can make everything fit into my life. The whole thing, you included. I guess I always just assumed that I was a lot more together than this, and right now I'm feeling pretty humble, especially about you. See, I really want to apologize to you about—"

She interrupted. "Wait a second Roger. If I'm every man's dream, then why aren't I *your* dream? I'd just like you to be honest and tell me. How is it that work and me can't both fit into your life? What you're saying doesn't make sense to me. Don't apologize to me, just tell me what's going on, okay babe?"

Roger looked down at his hands, clenching and unclenching in his lap. He moved over and sat on the coffee table opposite her.

"I don't know if I can do things like before. There's a time thing here, everything's changing so fast. Things have been happening, just really crazy stuff. I'm in a situation now where I need to be more independent because I have things to do that are important. I'm at a point where I have to make changes, because the things...I don't have any choice. Don't get me wrong, I'm not saying things have been bad with you, they haven't."

Gwynn had been listening intently. She sat with her arms crossed, rocking back and forth, her features hardening. Her eyes had never left his face, and now they were black as marbles.

"Well, Roger, are you going to tell me what these...*things* are?" She tilted her head in sarcasm, lifting her eyebrows, and her voice was clouded and shaky. "I mean, if it's going to change our scene so much, or maybe even break us up, don't you think I've at least got the right to hear what's doing all this?" Now she took the tone of a parent speaking to a foolish child. "I'd really like to hear it from you, Roger. Come on. It has something to do with the people who own the jet, right?" Her eyes trailed down to his neck, where they remained fixed for a few seconds, a look of astonishment stealing onto her hardened features. "Or maybe I should say, it has something to do with the *person* who owns the jet. What the hell is that on your neck?" She thrust an accusing finger toward the teeth marks. "Is that a hickey?"

His hand came up to cover the marks, just as he felt a wave of crimson spreading over his face.

"No, of course it's... it's not a hickey, Gwynn. Jesus. I was, I just accidentally leaned against part of a, uh, hot engine at work, is all. It's just a little burn."

"You're a fucking liar." The words boiled out and she pulled her mouth into a sneer of anger. "I want to know about the whole thing, Roger. I want you to tell me, right now, or we're done. Done, do you hear me? You're obviously trying to cover something up and I'm not going to put up with any more of this bullshit. *Are you seeing someone* ?" She glared, an ultimatum.

But Celine's admonition of absolute secrecy hung over Roger like a sword. "Uhm...well, indirectly, I suppose. I'm not seeing *anyone*. That's not important. I just need some time to—"

"Not important?" Gwynn's voice rose. "*Not important?* The hell it's not important!" She reached for her cocktail, sloshing a bit on the floor. She gulped a furious swig, then slammed the glass down again. "Let me tell you something. You know Roger, I've never seen you acting so chicken-shit ever before. Why are you being so goddamn secretive? What's the big deal? Are you such a total coward that you can't just be honest about it?"

The situation was going exactly as he hoped it wouldn't, with Gwynn growing enraged. Venting was all that could happen now and he had to endure it, because he couldn't for the life of him think of anything else to say that would actually soothe her. He tried to focus on her caustic expression and the way her glossy red nails picked at the sofa upholstery, in the hope that he wouldn't find anything attractive remaining. That would make it easier when she struck him and then stomped out the door, two actions which he knew from experience were likely to occur.

"Sweetheart, I...look, probably you won't be satisfied by this, but the fact is, I just can't be any more specific about what I'm—about what's involved. There's a very good reason, really, but I just can't talk anymore about it. I'd like to, but I'm not allowed to." He faked a smile. "You understand?"

At that her face went completely slack and she sat stock-still for about ten seconds. Her gaze appeared to float, transfixed on a spot in the air, just above his head. For a fleeting moment, he thought she'd gotten control of herself or just become resigned about the whole thing.

But, no.

"ASSHOLE!" Lightning fast, she launched the contents of the cocktail glass. Roger clenched his eyes just as ice cubes and freezing cold liquid slammed into his face.

Fleeting images jumped into his mind, like the desperate calculations of a small animal cornered by a predator. He knew full well that she was prone to getting even. His car was out in the driveway, beside hers, and although it was not blocking the Honda, it certainly would present a strategic target as she was departing in a highly irresponsible state of mind. This galvanized him in a way that even the iced cranberry-juice-and-vodka facial had not. He resorted to something unusual. Dripping pink goo, he moved over beside her and tried to hug her. Mistake. He never got close, but rather found himself sprawling back over the coffee table, propelled by the business end of one of her Reebok Super-Aerobic Pros. From his supine position he saw her rise to make what he presumed would be her dramatic exit. Instead, she strode over to the phone on the kitchen counter and fished a scrap of paper out of her purse. Wrenching the receiver off its cradle she forcefully punched in a number and then drummed her painted nails on the counter-top, waiting for an answer.

Roger was astonished by what he heard next. The change in her voice was stunning. She bubbled into the phone, sounding the very model of relaxed coquettish charm.

"Hi, Jeff ! Me! Yes, it is, you big stud. What are you doing? Did I wake you up? Oooh, good, so you're already in bed then. Well...I'm bored. Nothing. Just watching TV, thinking about you. Tee-hee. You are, huh? Well, I was thinking I might come by, what do you think? You would? Well, whatever dream you were having, you're just about to have a much better one. Uh-huh. Oh, you'll see." The voice was Marilyn Monroe, breathless and contrived. "I'll be there in a few minutes, so get ready, hunky muffin. Oh, I will. Okay. See you in a few!" She hung up the phone, still wearing her stage smile, then abruptly turned toward Roger. Her features instantly resumed a stony scowl. Pulling out her key ring, she peeled off his key, hurling it at him.

"I've got a handsome, successful doctor who's been chasing me for months. I've been fending him off, can you believe that? I can't imagine what I've been thinking. You're an idiot, Roger. Too bad. Look, I've got a few things in your closet and bathroom, so I'll call you when I've got time to come get them. In the meantime don't call me or come by my place for any reason. We're done. I don't want to talk about this anymore and I don't want to see you at all, understand?"

Roger was standing by the couch, wiping himself off with his shirt. While she was on the phone he decided that restraint was the only appropriate response for all this. He wasn't without emotion about what she was saying to "hunky muffin". The prospect that she was about to go sleep with another man—he was actually feeling a desperately sad kind of nausea. But he also realized he couldn't blame her all that much. It was his own fault it had come to this. What's more, witnessing her performance, it was clear that things would never have worked out anyway. Her shallowness and dishonesty were breathtaking.

He answered in a calm, steady voice. "Whatever you want, Gwynn. I won't stand in your way. I'm sorry. I know it's my fault. I don't blame you for being angry. I honestly hope things go well for you. And...I'll miss you. Good luck."

For the first time, he saw her face quiver a little, and tears came to her eyes, but then she hardened again and shoved the door open. Roger followed at a discreet distance, fearing for his car. In the doorway he stood ready, but she went right to her Honda, backed out, and screeched off down the street.

He lingered for a long time, looking out at the ivy curling over a stone wall across the way. Moonlight danced on the shiny leaves and the wall became a phosphorescent caterpillar.

The last wisps of the exhaust from Gwynn's car drifted by. Roger didn't move from his spot at the door, not wanting to analyze what had just happened. He didn't want to go back inside and see the empty room. He didn't want to clean up the pink juice on the floor or look at the empty glass with her lipstick. He didn't want to consider how he might feel in five minutes or five hours or five days. He didn't want to think about whether he had been right or wrong. Dim light from the room washed around and past him, and his shadow stretched away, a distorted void in the yellow area. His eyes wandered around its outlines.

Finally, shirtless and damp, he noticed the cold. The late-evening air seemed to be seeping into his bones. He turned to go back inside, slowly closing the door.

Chapter 16

It was now a glorious mid-October of 1989 in Santa Barbara. Roger was borne along on a tide of change. As with Gwynn, most of his friends had vanished from his life, or more accurately, he had vanished from theirs. He no longer had the time to spend with them or do the things that they had done before. Once in awhile one of his cronies would see him at the drugstore or the gas station and ask where he'd been keeping himself, what he'd been up to. "Oh, around, you know," he'd answer vaguely. "Doing some independent jobs." And that was true; while he'd left fulltime employment at Eichthaller's, he was still cordial with Franz, and he did some bid-out work in the garage at Glenwhylden, more as a hobby than anything else.

He'd moved to the estate by now, settling into the thatched-roof English cottage in the redwood forest beyond the formal gardens. It was cozy and secluded, with a tree-framed view of the ocean. Kerri began coming to visit him there. They talked about the Orangs, of course, always.

"I guess I have a lot in common with them," she confided. "They're oddballs, outsiders. So am I. But they're survivors, too. In lots of ways I look up to them. The shit hit the fan for them more than once, but they all made it through bad times."

As her trust in Roger grew, she opened up more about the troubles she faced in her own life. Almost from the beginning she had never fit in. It was hard for her to make friends at school; she was marked as strange. Everything normal had been ripped away from her. Nothing could be counted on. No father, no mother. She had to be ready to fight at any moment, she was convinced. She had to rely on herself. Her only solace was her grandfather, but he was old and her terror was that the morning was coming when she would walk into his bedroom and find him dead.

Roger never gave her advice, never tried to tell her what she should do. They were each facing their own problems. He didn't let her know about his illness. She liked black coffee, strong as paint remover. While she stretched out in the window seat, Roger would make her a cup, then take a chair and just listen. She fidgeted as she spoke, like she couldn't ever get comfortable. Her eyes darted to the window, keeping a lookout. The muscles in her scarred legs knotted, and her hands with their calloused knuckles often clenched into angry fists.

Sometimes on her way out the door she hugged him, but he strived to keep things from going any farther. He was drawn to her, the way you can be drawn to a beautiful and dangerous animal. But his concern wasn't for himself. For one thing, she was young, just going on eighteen. But more importantly, why start something he couldn't finish? Kerri might be tough in many ways, but she was also emotionally vulnerable, he could see that. She had been hurt over and over again. It would be selfish and plain wrong to hand this tormented girl one more hard knock by getting involved, then leaving her abandoned as he shrank into a shell of sensory oblivion.

His vision and hearing kept ebbing. It was a slow process, but relentless. He took medication and some days he could convince himself that he had gotten better, but it was wishful thinking. The disease was evaporating the incredible new world he'd stumbled onto. It was dissolving, day by day. It was torture, but he'd decided to wait as long as he could before doing what he'd originally planned. He hadn't shared any of this with Mrs. Stertevant either. He wasn't in denial; he reproached himself almost daily. But he wanted to keep it all going as long as he could. He'd know when it became untenable.

The assumption that the Orangs would continue changing rapidly had also held true. They had all made great progress with their speech. Still a bit husky and squeaky, but they were no longer difficult to understand. It had been thought impossible for apes to master speech, but such was their intellectual superiority and adaptability, they had evolved ways to use their vocal chords and shape words remarkably well.

Other characteristics emerged. Personalities amplified and some behaviors weren't so charming anymore. Trent was often cranky, he'd snapped at Roger a few times. Chloé had sullen days, as did Pongo, and Roger sometimes found himself wishing that he did not have to spend the entire day with them when one or two were acting out. The cause of their disgruntlement was simple: mounting frustration. The apes were now emotionally and intellectually far more like humans than Orangutans. They knew so much about the world outside the walls of the estate—it was drilled into their highly curious minds every day through television. Their isolation thwarted any opportunity to experience directly the wonderful things they were seeing on the screens in the media room. They wanted to get out there and be a part of it all, and the more Roger explained the obstacles to this, the more frustrated they became.

So far, the only one to have ever been outside the walls was Pongo, on the night he went for the ride in Roger's Porsche. He had regaled the others with this story many times, and they all then clamored for their own outside adventures. Your first few weeks on a new job—you're just going to make mistakes, because you don't know any better—and Roger had come to realize that taking Pongo out that night was a mistake. He couldn't just take all the others out as well; it was simply too risky, there was too much at stake. So. He had to keep making explanations, all the while trying to figure out just how much longer he could hold back the tide. He feared they might take matters into their own hands and just go over the wall someday when he wasn't around to stop them.

To keep it interesting, he planned special events for the apes. Little parties and such, things they could prepare for and participate in. It gave them an outlet for their considerable creativity. They loved theme parties, especially with costumes. Of course, they adored Halloween. By coincidence (or perhaps not) Halloween also happened to be Kerri's 18th birthday. Roger asked the Orangs about what kind of party they wanted to have, and it was Emily's idea that they should combine their Halloween celebration with a birthday bash for Kerri.

Everyone was excited, devising their costumes. Betty and Emily worked with the kitchen staff to bring off a wonderful, whimsical Halloween dinner, complete with a special cake for Kerri. They did up the main dining room with jack-o-lanterns, ghosts, witches, and goblins. Roger settled on Zorro as his guise. Pongo wanted to be Captain Hook, Artod would dress as an astronaut, and Betty would be Medusa, with a crown of snakes. She was trying to get Kerri to help her figure out a way to use live serpents. George—true to his heart—would be in a white lab coat and fright wig: The Mad Scientist. Chloé had decided to be Persephone, Goddess of Spring. Trent, of course, would attend as Thurston Howell III, and Emily couldn't wait to become Mother Goose, complete with bonnet and shepherd's crook. The birthday girl didn't have to think twice about her outfit. She would be Sheena, Queen of the Jungle.

The big day arrived. Toward late afternoon a storm was blowing in off the leaden, white-capped ocean. An east wind rose steadily, making a dull roar in the cypress trees around the house. Most of the staff had been given the evening off, so the big house was deserted and gloomy as dusk closed in.

The mood was different in the main parlor. Logs crackled cheerfully in the fireplace and jack-o-lanterns glimmered on the mantle. Pre-dinner cocktails were being served, with Pongo tending bar, yar-harring with a Captain Hook eye patch lashed to his huge face. Roger sat on a couch chatting with Emily. She was a ludicrous sight, sweet old ape mug smiling beneath a frothy bonnet streaming with ribbons, and this atop billows of voile and lace skirts. The others were slowly filtering in, and as each came through the door, there were hoots and howls for the new arrivals' costume. Betty's green make-up and writhing headdress of sinuous rubber snakes (real ones had been impossible to achieve without cruelty) had everybody doubled over.

Then, just as Emily was telling Roger about the effects of classical music on brain wave patterns, the parlor door swept open. Enter Sheena. Kerri stopped the show cold, striding right to the center of the room and planting herself, surveying the domain.

Under his Zorro mask Roger's jaw dropped. Kerri was all but naked—just a few strategic scraps of ragged leather covering her vital areas. She looked about ten feet tall. Her hair was spiked into a wild crown, a thorny aura framing a face painted dark with lines and patterns, like a tribal mask. Green eyes glowed like back-lit emeralds. She was darkly tanned and her muscles seemed carved of marble. With everyone staring she flexed her biceps and gave a ululating jungle call that rang off the rafters. The Orangs blasted off, hooting and jumping around in their former feral personas.

Almost unnoticed, Dr. Lewis came through the door behind his granddaughter and now stood by the bar observing with amusement. After Pongo poured him a Manhattan, the vet sidled over to Roger.

"Pretty nice bash, Roger," he said, raising his voice to be heard over the din. Kerri had switched the music to pile-driving punk. Dr. Lewis was concerned about the Orangs' worsening habits of drinking, smoking and eating rich foods. They were also not getting enough exercise, he declared. "Why not make a couple days of the week exercise days, Roger? Tell 'em no television on those days and give 'em a good exercise program to get into." He pointed over at Trent, whose gut was protruding visibly over the waistline of his velvet lounge pants. "See that, Roger? That boy's gonna have problems if he keeps gaining weight like that. They used to have a real healthy diet in the wild, you know. Mostly fruit and leaves. And they had to travel a lot, you understand? Swingin' through the trees to get to where the food was. Now, they've got everything handed to 'em on a silver platter and they don't really have to move a muscle. Plus, the stuff they're eating is darned different from what they used to get in the forest. All this stuff—" he gestured over at the hors d'ouevres table, mounded with caviar, sliced meats, and deviled eggs, "ain't exactly good for 'em. They need to eat better and get some exercise. And, man, they gotta quit this smokin' crap. That's crazy, I keep tellin' 'em that. You gotta make 'em toe the line, Roger, that's kinda your job description, ain't it? Can you make a go at that?" He looked over the tops of his glasses at El Zorro, who was himself just then scarfing down one of the deviled eggs, by now a little self-consciously.

Roger nodded, swallowing. "You're absolutely right, Mark. I actually do talk to them about this, you know. Tell you the truth, I can barely stand being around all this damn smoke all the time myself." He picked up a cashew, then accurately lobbed it across the room at Trent, who was regaling Chloé while puffing grandly on a Kool filter king. The nut bounced off the ape's head and he pivoted to determine the source of the missile. Roger pointed at the cigarette, miming that he should put it out. Trent stared blankly back for a moment, then calmly raised his hand and shot the finger. He turned back and resumed his conversation with Chloé.

Roger chortled. "See what I mean, Doc? They aren't easy to push around, and to tell you the truth, it gets harder every day. Maybe I need to get a book about it or something."

Dr. Lewis shook his head. "There ain't no book, Roger." He downed the last of his drink, then set his glass on the bar. "Gotta run. Got a date, if you can believe that. Nice gal from the bank, been droppin' hints for awhile now. Listen, I'm sure Kerri's probably gonna sneak a drink or two after I leave. No big deal. Just don't let her walk home, will you? Maybe she could stay with you guys tonight, that way I won't worry."

"No problem. I'm sure her room's available for her, as usual. Got a hot date, huh?"

"Oh, yeah. Yeah. Nice widow. She's a teller. We're goin' to that new restaurant over on the water, should be fun. I don't get out much, you know. Man of my age." He winked at Roger, then slapped him on the back as he walked away.

Dinner was announced a short time later, and everyone repaired to the formal dining room. The vaulted room was lavishly decked out with haystacks, jack-o-lanterns, false cobwebs, and yards of orange and black crepe paper. The diners entered the room with oohs and aahs, and Betty and Chloé were given a short ovation for their wonderful decorations. Immediately after everyone was seated at the big, candlelit table, George stood up and rapped on his water glass, uncharacteristically taking center stage. He spoke in a quiet voice, keeping his eyes on the table in front of him.

"I want everyone to enjoy Halloween, uh...I mean, this is a great party so far. And, Happy Birthday, Kerri." He looked over at Kerri, smiling shyly. She beamed. "I'd, uhm, just like to share some of my homemade special stuff with everyone, you know—before we eat dinner. Just a little treat, sort of." He reached under his chair, bringing out a wooden box. Some of the apes giggled, apparently already clued-in to whatever this was about. Opening the lid, George walked around to each diner, proffering some of the contents. First Pongo, then Chloé, then Emily each dipped their fingers into the box and extracted a wad of material that, from where Roger was sitting, appeared to be whitish twigs. They popped the substance into their mouths. George had moved on to Artod when Roger, squinting to get a better look, realized just exactly what it was they were eating. It was familiar, he'd seen it before. Dried psilocybin mushrooms. He shot to his feet, holding up his hand like a panicky traffic cop at a busy intersection.

"Hold it, guys! Wait a second now, what's going on? What are we doing here? George?"

George paid no heed, continuing his rounds like a priest administering the sacrament. Pongo spoke up.

"No big deal, Roger. We've done it before, don't worry. Just a little giggly buzz, that's all. You've got to have a bit yourself, you know. It's everyone together."

The others all broke into uproarious laughter at this. Roger tried to figure out what to say, wishing he hadn't already had three glasses of champagne.

"Look, guys—" he looked around the table, trying to seem the voice of reason. "I don't know if this is a good idea. I mean, I'm...I have to be responsible for what goes on around here."

Kerri was seated beside him and she pulled him back down into his chair.

"Roger," she husked with a huge smile, "I'm the birthday girl, and I give you permission to think it's all right."

The others applauded. The Queen had spoken, and that was that. At that point Roger elected to just go with the flow. He raised his glass in a resigned toast, and when the box came around to him, he took a pinch and ate it. It tasted terrible. Kerri took a generous plug and swallowed it, then grabbed a little more and tried to push it between Roger's lips. He jerked his head back, resisting.

"Come on, Roger," she chided. "Don't be a wimp. It's not any good if you don't eat enough. Just loosen up and let's party, okay?" She tried again to feed him, and this time he allowed her to succeed.

Within forty-five minutes all rules, elements of normalcy, and predictability of behaviors ceased to apply. Dinner was served and eaten, sort of, but there was just so much hysterical laughter, jumping up and running around, and bizarre utterances that the meal had ceased to hold much interest.

Meanwhile, the storm outside had built to an intense level. Large tree branches were falling, torrents of rain sheeted sideways with the battering wind, and lightning forks were snapping down to rake the ocean and pop at the coastline. Near-constant thunder rocked through the walls of the big house, rattling the window panes.

No matter. Everyone in the dining room was rushing hard from the mushrooms which, as Roger had feared, had turned out to be quite potent. Hardly just the "giggly little buzz" Pongo had claimed. In addition to hallucinations and a distinctive "body-high", the overriding effect seemed to be uncontrollable laughter, and nearly any little thing that was said or done by anyone convulsed everyone else. Most of the dishes were cleared from the table and more champagne appeared. Roger had resigned himself to it all. He was having a damn good time. The absolute bizarreness of the scene all around him—a bunch of Orangutans dressed up in costumes, partying with abandon and conversing in human speech—was frying his synapses. Add to that, Kerri had been periodically rubbing her bare foot up and down his leg and grabbing his thigh under the table. It was all he could do to resist doing anything in return, especially when at one point she turned and smiled luxuriously, flashing gleaming white teeth, then ran her tongue in a slow circular motion over her full lips. She looked positively luscious. The mushroom-champagne combo had diminished his self control and he was now sailing into uncharted waters.

Eventually, "Happy Birthday" was sung for Kerri and a chocolate-raspberry layer cake—her favorite—was brought out, eighteen candles glimmering on top. The girl was laughing so hard she barely managed to blow them out. Gifts were produced, all of them carefully wrapped and decorated. Each, when opened, struck everyone as progressively more idiotic than the previous one. Under normal circumstances, these things—books, a little video game, a sweatshirt, a seashell necklace, would have seemed sweet and thoughtful gifts to give a young girl on the occasion of her eighteenth birthday. But under the influence of the mushrooms and the champagne, they were so foreign and comical and useless that they caused fits of laughter. All the smokers were now puffing away and the room mushed into a haze.

Waving his hands in the air, Artod called across the table to Kerri.

"Oh, Queen! Queen, do your dance for us! Please dance, Queen of All Beasts!" He pointed his nine-inch index finger at Roger. "I'm sure Roger would *love* to see your dance."

Kerri stood up and bowed deeply to Artod, while all the others began to applaud, chanting "Ker-ri, Ker-ri, Ker-ri." In one smooth motion, she bounded up onto the table, kicking aside the last few remaining dishes, one of which skittered over into Trent's lap. He howled, picking the food off his trousers and flicking it around at some of his dining companions. The tall candelabras were quickly pulled out of harm's way and someone raised the volume on the stereo. The after-dinner show was on.

Kerri went into a trance, eyes heavy-lidded, sensuous; she traced her fingertips over herself, moving in rhythm to the driving music. Artod (doubtless her accomplice because he took action at the appropriate time) pushed a large ashtray heaped with crumpled paper out onto the table, then struck a match to it. Kerri danced with the fire, prancing in and out of the flames. Then came an astonishing display of contortion. Springing up, she landed in a split, then lay forward, her legs swung behind her. Bending her torso, she threw her head back and touched her heels to her nose. Next an elbow stand, arching her back to the extreme, with her feet somehow dropping past her face: a human circle. In this position she glanced at Roger, making sure he was catching it all. The apes went bananas, jumping up on their chairs and hooting.

The near-naked young beauty dancing on the table along with the warp of the mushrooms, pounding music, and catcalls of wild animals, seared a voodoo-strength sexual arousal into Roger. He was possessed. Grateful for the draping tablecloth over his lap, he squirmed in his Zorro tights. Kerri slithered around like a snake, writhing and baring her fangs. Then the finale. Striding to one end of the twenty-foot table, she pirouetted and launched herself in a full lay-out flip, landing square on both feet at the other end of the table. She thrust her arms toward the ceiling. Standing ovation. Roger attempted to rise with the others, but due to factors beyond his control, he was forced to maintain a crouch. Pongo and Trent pulled Kerri up on their shoulders and paraded her around the room.

And then the music stopped short, strangled. Wall sconces flickered and expired. The storm had now reached the public-utilities-damage stage, taking out the electricity to the estate, probably the whole neighborhood. Since candles burned all around the room, the party wasn't plunged into darkness, just momentary silence. The boys lowered the Queen to the ground, and right away, Trent started in persuading everyone that it was a perfect time for a game of "fugitive search." This was the Orang's version of hide-and-seek, in which the fugitive, chosen by lots, gets five minutes to abscond somewhere within the main house and then the rest go hunting. The first one to find the fugitive gets to set the punishment for the criminal: some degrading act that must be performed in front of the others. This might involve the perversion of food, usually in a state of complete undress. So paper straws were torn from a newspaper and held by Emily. Being the matriarch, she was never the criminal. Poor Chloé got the short one, so off she went, trotting up the hall into the darkened vastness of the huge house. The others consulted the clock in the hall, just to be fair, and then decided that the immediate consumption of another bottle of champagne would be necessary to fortify the search party for its task.

"I'm spinning already." Roger announced. "I'll be in the upstairs library with some coffee if anybody needs me."

Kerri put her arm through his. "That sounds good to me, too. Maybe we can build a fire in that little fireplace up there?"

Grabbing a candle to light their way, Zorro and Sheena took off, with Zorro trying not to feel too apprehensive about leaving the others to wander the house inventing such activities as their drug-addled brains might devise.

There comes a point in the mushroom experience, roughly about three quarters of the way through, when the giddy, rushing high begins to roll off, replaced with a more quiet, contemplative mood. The laughing and vivid hallucinations ease, and body awareness becomes heightened. A tranquility seeps in; things of a tactile nature grow more attractive.

Roger and Kerri arrived at the upstairs study. He opened the door and placed the candle on the desk. But just as he turned to the fireplace, Kerri pulled him back through the doorway.

"Hey," she said, pointing down the shadowy hall. "Know what's down there?"

Roger paused. "Sure. The master bedroom. But nobody can go in there. It's always locked. Mrs. Stertevant wants it that way."

"Oh yeah? Well, how about if we just cruise down there and see if we can look through the keyhole or something? I'm just curious."

"If you want to. But I doubt you're gonna see anything." He laughed a little. "It's pretty dark, wouldn't you say?"

"I can see fine. I'm part cat." Tall windows interrupted the gloom, with random flarings of electric blue lightning. The wind was screaming, clawing at the panes. Kerri padded along, prancing and pulling on his hand. She was up to something, but in his altered state it pleased him not to put any effort into figuring out exactly what. Then they were standing before carved double doors. He tried the latch. Locked, of course.

"See? The only person who ever gets in there is the maid, and that's only once a month or so."

"I know the story. Sad, isn't it?" She reached out to the door, stroking the wood as if to comfort the pain that Celine had felt at her husband's death.

But then she turned, grabbed Roger's neck, and kissed him with immense passion. Now he couldn't resist. After a moment, she leaned back a little and sighed.

Roger caught himself. "Listen Kerri, I shouldn't—"

"Hush," she interrupted, clamping a rough hand over his mouth.

Her voice became breathier than ever. "I'm eighteen tonight. And everybody gave me lots of nice things. But the only present I really want doesn't come in a box. What I want is in that room."

Roger looked hard, trying to make out her features in the darkness. "In there? What is it?"

"How about if I show you?" She fumbled with her leather top and leaned close to the door, feeling with her fingers. Roger heard a metallic noise, then a decisive clank. Kerri swung one of the heavy doors inward.

Roger whistled. "You got a key. But, hey, Kerri, really—I don't know how you got that, but we can't go in there. We just can't. I don't want to do anything against Mrs. Stertevant's wishes." A sweet smell came wafting out through the opened door, powerfully floral.

Her lips pressed to his ear. "Celine *gave* me the key. She said there'd be a time when I'd have a use for it."

Her warm breath went right into the pleasure center of his brain. With no further protest, he allowed himself to be led by the hand once more, and they entered the dimness of a large room with a high ceiling. He heard the door being closed and latched, then her hand was in his again. He wondered if she truly was part cat, since she apparently *could* see in the dark. There were large window seats at the eastern end, that much he could see. Gardenias were scattered all around. At a broad chair in front of one of the windows, she gently pushed him down and then slipped sideways onto his lap.

She whispered again. "Have you figured it out yet? What it is in this room that I want?"

"Well, I can't really see anything else. So it's me, I hope."

"You're so smart."

The chair was plush and comfortable and the tall girl on his lap was determined. As they began kissing, there was the sense that Kerri hadn't done much of this before. After a few minutes she took her arms from around him and wriggled a few times. Roger's appreciative hands could feel that she had rid herself of the little scraps of leather. He slid his fingers along her iron-like thighs. Her stomach was a washboard of muscle and above that, the angle of her ribcage expanded to meet her broad shoulders. Had he not known better, Roger could easily have believed there was a young man on his lap.

She stood up abruptly. "Shuck that outfit before I tear it off with my teeth," she commanded while thrusting a small foil packet into his hand.

The room felt chilly as soon as he was naked, but Kerri's warm body again pressed into his. Roger lifted her, depositing her on the satiny deep cushions of the window seat. Then he was on top of her.

Maybe it was the mushrooms, or his partner, or a combination of the two, but his stamina was the best he could ever remember. He felt like he was thirteen years old and the damn thing just wouldn't ever go down.

Roger had been accustomed to Gwynn's cultivated smoothness. She was firm but softly manicured from head to toe; lotioned, perfumed, and powdered. She also knew all the tricks and performed them well. Kerri, on the other hand, knew no tricks whatsoever and was more than a little rough:

hooking her thumbs into his mouth, gripping his face as she bit his neck. There wasn't a smooth part on her entire body. Her technique was borderline assaulting; at times it seemed more like a fight than making love. But fighting was what Kerri knew best. She wrapped her legs around the small of his back, violently clenching. As the lightning flashed, he caught glimpses of her face, savage in the covering of tribal paint. Roger would never have foreseen himself being with this type of girl, yet he wasn't put off in the least. Quite the opposite. When it was finally over, they panted, listening to the storm's muffled fury.

Then stilled, they began to feel the cold. Kerri nestled closer. "Let's go get in the bed."

"The bed?" Roger felt a twinge of guilt. "Do you think we should? I mean, Mrs. Stertevant's honeymoon bed and all. I don't know".

She laughed softly. "You still don't get it, do you? Celine wanted this to happen. She wants us to use the bed."

Across the room, a gargantuan vessel reared up like a ghost-freighter in a fog bank. It was a four-poster, with a soaring canopy at least ten feet high. Kerri tugged at the covers and they wrestled playfully under the goose down comforter. The sheets had a unique slickness. Wow, Roger thought. Silk.

Kerri sighed. "Well, that was a lot better than I expected."

He gave out a bark. "Gosh, thanks! I'm so glad I didn't disappoint you."

"Oh, not you, Roger! You were great. I just meant this was my first time."

"What?!"

"You were my first, Roger."

He sat up to face her. "Are you serious? Why in the hell didn't you tell me that before?"

"Because then you wouldn't have done it. I knew that. This was something I wanted to do for my birthday. And I got what I wanted," she laughed wickedly.

"You sure did. You caught me off-guard when you brought your own protection."

She laughed again. "A girl's gotta be prepared."

He shook his head, incredulous. A psychedelic mushroom costume party with talking Orangutans, then wild sex with a virginal girl. What would be next in this place?

Down in the kitchen Betty, Emily, and Chloé were all clustered within the circled sanctity of about two dozen flickering candles. Earlier they bailed from "fugitive search" (Chloé hadn't been too inventive; she hid in the front hall coat closet. She was found in ten minutes. She was made to toss a deviled egg in the air and catch it in her mouth. Success on the first try.) The boys had gone to play cards and smoke cigars. Now the girls were drinking Kahlua-and-coffees, smoking Bel-Air filters, and scarfing a batch of outrageous caramel-macadamia-popcorn they had concocted. As a team, they were attempting to get through the latest Cosmo "Love and Sex Test". Like a bunch of adolescents, they were having a riot with the officious tone of the questions. Betty held up the magazine and squinted at it, trying to divine the next question in the puny light of the candles. She cleared her throat.

"Okay, here you go. Number twenty-seven. 'Can your man's orgasms be improved by...mmphhhffftt!'" She stopped in mid-sentence and sprayed a thimblefull of coffee out her nose, seized with laughter at the question. The others, likewise plotzed, doubled over along with her. She waved her hand for order, regaining her composure, then wiped her dripping chin with the back of her sleeve and resumed. "Can your man's orgasms be improved by stimulation of the...*rectum*?" She wore the "dumb-cheerleader-slumber-party" look, one corner of her mouth quivering.

Chloé placed her finger to her temple while exhaling a thoughtful cloud of smoke and grappled with the question. She furrowed her brow. "You mean, can you get him to boil faster if you stick your finger up his ass?"

Emily and Betty wailed, dropping their popcorn and teetering off their chairs. Emily lay prone on the floor, sobbing and slapping the tiles. They were not going to get much farther, it was clear. Betty stood up, wiping her eyes, and then heaved the magazine in the direction of the waste bin.

"Oh god. That was too funny, you little moron. What a load of shit that is. You guys want to go watch TV or something?"

Emily began dutifully picking up the scattered bits of popcorn. "Power's still off, honey."

They were silent for a moment, resignedly coming to the conclusion that bed was the only good option left to them. Suddenly, Betty thought of something.

"Hey. You realize who disappeared completely, hours ago?" She raised her eyebrows. "The birthday girl. And Roger. Wonder what happened to them—suppose *they* went to bed?"

They all looked at each other but nobody said anything.

In the parlor, a marathon gin-rummy game had fizzled to an end. Pongo leaned against the mantelpiece, patiently sucking on a Montecristo Number Two as he poked at the dying embers in the hearth. Artod, Trent and George had drawn up chairs around the fireplace, presenting their outsized palms, gathering the warmth of the glowing coals.

"Well. I know one thing," Trent intoned. "You're all a bunch of goddamned cheaters, that's what."

Artod regarded him dolefully for a moment. "And you're not."

Trent nodded gravely. "Right."

Silence then prevailed for a few minutes. They were all tuckered out, coming down off the mushrooms and champagne. Their costumes, so meticulous during dinner, were now missing pieces here and there. And there was a feeling they were all thinking alike.

"You know, we've got to talk to Roger," Pongo finally said. "Parties are fine, but we need to get out of this place, folks." He let that sink in. "You guys agree, don't you?"

They nodded in alliance. They had reached a critical mass of sorts. All of the Orangutans were intellectually and emotionally outgrowing the physical and psychic limitations of the estate and boredom was beginning to tell on their morale. This evening's festivities had provided a measure of much-needed relief but had also served to whet their appetites for still more stimulation: new experiences, new sensations. They liked feeling good and they wanted to feel good some more. It had been discussed before. Yes, there were problems that would be encountered beyond the protection of the walls, but somehow, they had to get out. It had to happen, the sooner the better. It was a great big world out there and they were not going to allow themselves to be secreted away for very much longer. It would drive them crazy if they did.

Pongo stared into the failing glow of the hearth, then took a potent last toke on the big cigar and launched it into the coals. He dipped his head decisively.

"Alright. We'll press our case with him tomorrow, okay?" He scanned around the assembled group, drawing support from the solemn faces. "I think it's become obvious to everybody. It's time."

Chapter 17

The previous night's storm had blown in a whole new set of ground rules. Conditions had changed, and the atmosphere in the loggia during the late breakfast the next morning was heavy with impending transposition.

The detritus of the party had been efficiently cleared already; the maids had returned to work that morning at seven. Roger was feeling very irresponsible and vulnerable, and that put him in an edgy mood which he was working to contain. He silently reproached himself, evaluating the possible fallout of the previous evening's grand indiscretions. What if Celine were to hear about all this? Even if she didn't, there would still have to be damage control, that much was certain. But, first things first, and all the reconciliations and accountings would be much easier if not undertaken on an empty stomach.

There hung in the air that vague pall of guilt commonly observed in the breakfast rooms of cruise-ships and other holiday venues, when the same guests who were all gaily misbehaving with reckless abandon during the booze-soaked party the night before, now meekly sit and sip their orange juice, stealing glances at each other, cold sober and hung-over, all-too-painfully repossessed of their inhibitions, piecemeal recalling with horror little snatches of their swashbuckling exploits of a half-dozen hours before, now mercilessly exposed in the bright daylight.

Kerri was unusually quiet. Unlike some of the others at the table, she was looking fresh as a daisy. All the tribal paint had been scrubbed off and her hair was still damp from the shower. She had a pleased little smile curling the corners of her mouth.

They had not stayed the whole night in the honeymoon suite. Roger awakened with a jolt at around four a.m. He roused Kerri, whispering that it might be prudent for each of them to decamp to their separate quarters before morning. She protested sleepily, but he insisted, so they got up and hunted for the odd scattered bits of their clothing, then crept downstairs, leaving the suite re-locked behind them. Roger escorted her to her guest room and kissed her softly before she closed the door.

She whispered, "Don't think you're gonna get off with just this one time, Roger. We're gonna be seeing a lot more of each other from now on."

At the breakfast table, the boys were reviewing the previous evening's mushroom high and fugitive hunt. Roger listened with a bland smile, but inwardly he was feeling distress at his lack of control over what had happened. It seemed strange to him, as he recalled the details of just exactly how it came to take place. Kerri had looked into his eyes and he had simply surrendered control. It was like hypnotism.

Trent laid down a half-finished melon crescent and lifted his chin toward Roger, baring his teeth amiably. "Wow. Those are some nasty marks." He pointed at Roger's neck. "How'd you get all bit up like that?"

Roger grimaced. "Oh, just...never you mind, Trent."

The Orang chortled. "Well, anyway big guy, what's on your program today? Anything pressing?" He was artificially upbeat, like the emcee at a Lion's club luncheon. Roger knew right away, something was up.

"Actually, now that you mention it, I do have a little errand to attend to." He glanced at his watch. "I have to run up to a house on East Valley Road and pick up a car from a client of mine, Fred Tasselmere. He wants me to tweak a few things for him." He paused here, looking in Pongo's direction. The big male was staring absently out the bank of windows, absorbed in the activities of the gardeners, who were clearing the lawn of the night's debris. "It's a car I'm sure you'll be interested in, Pong. It's probably the fastest street-legal Porsche Carrera in the country. The owner's a nut for speed. It's a brand new '90 C-2, custom three-point-eight liter engine, sequential turbo-chargers, chopped body, highly modified block, amped suspension, nitrous, the whole box. It'll kick my car's ass."

Pongo's head had swiveled at the start of Roger's description and he was now paying close attention. "Really? And you say you're bringing it here?"

"Yep. Gonna have it here for a few days. Putting in a new set of brake line seals. No big deal really. The Concourse in wine country is coming up two weeks from now. Fred's taking it up there. You can help me work on it if you want to. Sound good?"

"Sure it does. I'd like to do that with you." Pongo seemed genuinely brightened by this prospect. Roger turned toward Kerri.

"You want to ride up there with me and follow me back down here in my car, after we pick up Fred's car?"

She stared at him. "You mean it? You're going to let me drive your Porsche?"

"Hey, I said follow, *follow*...got that? We're going slow, back roads all the way. You do drive a stick shift?"

She whooped. "Damn right I do! Grandpa's truck's a five-speed. Alright!" She pushed her chair back and sprang up, shadow boxing. "Ready to go, big guy? I'm all set when you are!"

He wondered just how crazy he was, but, what the hell, it was insured, and there wouldn't be any traffic on the back road. He had a feeling Kerri wouldn't let him down. After all, he did need somebody to follow him back down and he couldn't get just anybody, could he? He'd already asked Polk, but the butler was too busy to go until that afternoon. Roger wanted to get started on the brake job earlier than that.

"Okay, okay, let me finish my coffee here." He pulled on Kerri's shirt tail. "Calm down, you're making me nervous."

Trent reasserted himself, not to be forestalled in his mission. "So, Roger, you're going to be around later on? Sure would appreciate it if you could give us a few minutes, okay? We need to ask you about something."

Roger caught the significance in this. He looked around at the other faces, trying to get a clue. Poker mugs, every one.

"Something you want to talk about? Sure, that's what I'm here for. Anything, uh...anything I should prepare for?"

Trent kept up the Lion's Club patter. "Heh heh. No, just the usual. One of our ideas. It'll keep 'till you guys get back."

Roger shrugged, inwardly dreading whatever it could be. "Good enough. I'll come find you guys in about an hour, cool?"

All the males nodded in unison. Trent gave a thumbs up.

On the way to Fred Tasselmere's house, Roger and Kerri stopped at an upscale neighborhood grocery for chocolate bars. For some reason they both had been craving this all morning. They found what they were looking for: Cloud-Nine dark chocolate bars loaded with roasted espresso beans. They were waiting in line at the check-out, when the front door swung open. Roger's gaze had been wandering absently along a low rack of exotic potato chips by the door. Now a very familiar pair of legs crossed through his field of vision. Gwynn Murck and a short male friend made their entrance, both of them in tennis wear. There was no avoiding a direct meeting. It would have been simpler to get past a bull in a loading chute.

Roger felt a physical sense of discomfort as he resignedly waited, trying to present an unaffected expression for the few seconds which would elapse before he would be seen and then have to engage in some kind of exchange. One second, two seconds, ten. The stylish couple were tantalizingly distracted—as if this scene had been scripted to build the suspense—by a display of Chilean mangos. They paused, her pointing at the fruit and him commenting inaudibly in the busy hum of the Saturday morning bagels-and-coffee crowd. After what seemed like a full minute, they turned to enter the main part of the store. Bammo. Gwynn's eyes came up and made Roger. Her features, only a moment before looking fairly relaxed and even peaceful, instantly clouded and cracked, like a ball of hot wax dropped into ice water. She visibly stiffened and changed her step in midstride, in the manner of someone who has just spotted a snake on the path. She couldn't escape either, not now, so there was nothing for it but to come forward, quickly fumbling to place her hand on her as-yet unaware companion's narrow shoulder. She fixed Roger with an artificially pleasant look. Kerri, standing directly behind Roger and happily humming, chose this precise moment to engage in her very first public display of affection. She slipped her arms around his waist and rose on tiptoe, putting her chin on his shoulder and looking at the line of people in front of them. Gwynn and whoever-he-was moved within range and she fired the first shot.

"Well hello there, stranger. How you doin' Roger?"

"Hey, Gwynn. How are you?" Okay, he thought. Maybe that'll be all of it. That'll do.

Nope. She stopped, apparently having some gain to make here.

"Roger, I want you to meet my fiancé, Doctor Jeff Riesmiller. Jeff, this is Roger Caldwell and..." she looked at Kerri expectantly, raising her brows as if meeting a very young child. She looked back at Roger, requiring an introduction. This sudden juxtaposition of startling news (she had unmistakably said "fiancé") and haughty condescension toward Kerri gave Roger a sharp sense of contempt for this woman with whom he had recently thought himself so close. He swung his arm around and brought Kerri forward, a tacit declaration of allegiance.

"Kerri. Kerri Lewis. Gwynn Murck, Jeff Riesmailer."

"Hi," Kerri nodded, amiable.

The short blonde man extended his hand, very genuinely polite. Apparently he didn't yet have the script.

"It's Riesmiller, nice to meet you both." His voice was high, thin. His hand was as soft as a silk handkerchief, with a wispy grip to match.

"Oh, sorry. Riesmiller." A stumble. "Well..." The action in the store seemed to ratchet into slow motion all around them, there was a deadly pause, with Gwynn openly making a withering head-to-toe appraisal of Kerri. Her eyes lingered smugly on the girl's scarred legs, dirty bare feet, frayed clothing, and whimsical body ornaments. What is more coldly intimidating than that certain look women give each other in these situations? Kerri was unfazed. She was used to such disapproval from other women. Roger tried to revive the conversation.

"So. Engaged, huh, Gwynn? Jeff? Congratulations to both of you. Sure you must be very happy."

Gwynn leered with smarmy self-satisfaction. "Thank you, Roger," she warbled. "Yes, we've been engaged for, what, two weeks now?" She extended her left hand with its prominently beringed finger. "So, is this your new lady?" She turned a faked homecoming queen happy-face toward Kerri.

Roger felt his lip curl slightly. What the hell. "Yeah." Just as he said this, he felt Kerri's hand gently running up his spine.

"Oh, really?" Gwynn exclaimed. A flash of shock clouded her face, but this was quickly replaced by a mask of smug contempt. "Well. Nice to finally meet you, Kerri. Roger's a great guy, but I'm sure you know that."

Now Kerri's voice came out husky, even threatening.

"Yep. I know." She stared through Gwynn. This was a look she might give someone she was about to knock out. Knowing his ex-girlfriend quite well, Roger saw she was more than a little unglued by the power in Kerri's voice. He glanced to his right, saw that the line had moved, and realized that within a few more seconds the business of cashier and money and "bag-for-your-purchase-sir?" was going to save them all from anymore of this. He bridged the gap by changing the subject.

"Uh, aren't you a dentist, Jeff?"

The short man smiled broadly. "You bet. How'd you know that?"

"Oh, I think I must have seen your ad in the, uh, Yellow Pages? I remembered the name." This was a lie. Roger recalled that last night with Gwynn, and her taunting bit of business about the "gorgeous doctor." He later heard from a friend that the "doctor" was in fact a D.D.S. He had been laboring with an erroneous picture of the man in his mind, to say the least.

"Well, that's great, Roger. Glad to know my advertising's working." He grinned again, flashing miniature teeth like bleached baby corn.

Now Roger picked up that he was truly just a nice, decent guy. He began to feel sorry for him.

"Yep. I always say, teeth are my thing!" Jeff had this personal motto right at the ready.

Roger couldn't think of anything else to add so he repeated after the genial dentist. "Teeth are your thing."

Taking no meaning, Jeff gleamed with enthusiasm.

The check-out line moved again, and now they were up. Roger gratefully smiled at the cashier, taking the chocolate bar out of Kerri's hand and laying it on the counter with his own. He brought out his wallet, and as he handed the money to the girl and then waited for his change, he could feel Gwynn's eyes boring into his back. He wondered which of them would have the most disturbed thoughts after this. The cashier dropped the chocolate into a glossy bag. Roger turned back to the tennis couple.

"Well. Sure nice seeing you guys. Nice meeting you, Jeff. Hope you have a good game or whatever. And, uh, hey...congratulations again. Bye-bye."

Jeff continued to smile, unfazed, but Gwynn's expression had soured further. Her eyes had gone to Roger's marked-up neck, then back to Kerri. She said nothing as they turned and walked away.

Back in the car the air of tension vanished. Kerri unwrapped her chocolate and began to bring the bar up to her mouth, then suddenly, theatrically, sat up straight and hyper-animated her features.

"TEETH are my THING!" She laughed derisively. "Okay, Roger. Let me guess here. She has to be your ex, right? Has to be."

He smiled over at her, impressed with her grasp. "Well, actually, yeah. I'm a little embarrassed to admit that...but, yeah." He paused, starting the car and backing out of the parking spot. "Strange, isn't it?"

Kerri shrugged. "Hey, listen. Dude, she's very pretty. She looks like the girls in my school who get all the guys. I mean, she's...older, of course." She took a thoughtful nibble on the chocolate. "So. I'm your new lady, am I?"

Roger winced, turning out into the street and accelerating. "Okay, sorry. That wasn't cool. I just needed an ally right then. I was kind of caught off-guard."

"Oh, you were, were you?" Kerri was enjoying her position on top of the moment. "Well, since you said it first, I'm going to be holding you to it." She turned in her seat and leaned over to him, kissing his ear sensuously.

A few minutes later they were standing with Fred Tasselmere, looking at the glowering mechanical apparition hunkering in his garage. The coupe looked formidable, even menacing, just parked there. It was matte black, with all blacked-out trim, like some kind of military stealth aircraft. It was lower and wider than the stock machine. Outsized fat tires were mounted on plain-looking wheels. The front air dam sported two enormous intake ports, protected by black wire mesh, and around the back, twin exhausts protruded, approximating the diameter of coffee cans. There were no license plates, just a small document taped to the inside of the windshield. The windows all around were almost opaquely tinted. The thing looked ready to suck up the road and blow it out its ass.

Fred was explaining to Roger about a few other things he wanted checked: a little rattle in the steering column, a slight pull to the left at 110 mph in third gear. Kerri looked through the opened door into the cockpit. It was almost completely stripped. A fighter-aircraft seat with a four-point harness. There was no other seating in the car. The dash had been removed and replaced with a drilled, blacked-out titanium board. Only essential instruments were mounted in a small cluster, right beside the steering wheel. The floor boards were bare aluminum, spray painted matte black. The only refinements were a cellular phone mounted on the floor and a stereo unit with large speakers bolted in the rear.

After a few more minutes of discussion, Roger sealed the door and fired the thing up. It cranked briefly, then caught. The ensuing roar conveyed the certainty that unholy hell resided in the engine compartment. Roger gave a thumbs up, like a pilot about to be launched from the deck of a carrier, and Kerri skipped over and jumped behind the wheel of his car. As they headed down Sheffield road she performed flawlessly, never missing a shift, as far as he could detect from his constant monitoring of the rear-view mirror. He even had the confidence to give her a mild thrill, momentarily elevating their speed along the straight stretch between the golf-course fairways to near sixty. He could see her back there, grinning and bobbing. They arrived at the gates without incident and proceeded to the garage. Roger had set up a fairly complete shop there, where he worked on his own car as well as the occasional customer's machine. After parking the race car he climbed out, exclaiming to Kerri as she walked up.

"Man, that thing is dangerous. Ridiculously overpowered. No telling what would happen if you really popped it open on a curve. It's way too light for the power."

"Well, good. More the better, right? I had a good time with your car, too. Can I keep these?" She dangled his keys.

He smiled, taking them from her smoothly.

She leaned against Fred's Porsche.

"You know something, Roger, I was thinking when I was following you. I've seen lots of flashy fast cars. I mean, this is Montecito, after all. Ferraris are a dime a dozen around here. But this thing..."she pointed at the black beast, "this is the first car I've ever seen that actually looks psychotic."

He nodded respectfully, running his hand along the matte finished fender.

"I know. It's bad, huh?"

"Oh my GOD!" It was Pongo. Hearing them drive in, he had run up to the garage from the house. He approached the blacked-out Porsche like it was some kind of altar, stopping a few feet short of it to stare, awestruck.

"I've never seen anything like this, even in the magazines. How fast is it?"

"Not sure. I don't think the owner's even had it to top speed. But, well, definitely over two hundred. I thought it could make about six hundred horsepower, but Fred told me this morning it's actually closer to seven hundred with the nitrous. It's a death trap though, Pong. It's way too light for that much juice. The engine's all drilled out, it's a like a bomb just waiting to blow. It felt pretty skittery, even just going sixty coming down here. It runs like shit at low speeds. I had to keep the throttle up a bit at the stop-signs to keep it from just taking a dump."

Pongo was mesmerized. He circled the machine, looking at every detail. Roger turned to Kerri.

"I guess I better go find Trent, he wanted to talk to me about something. What are you up to?"

"Well. It's a really nice day." She smiled invitingly. "Sunny, nice breeze. Want to take the boat out for a little cruise?"

He warmed to this. "You know, that's a good call. Yeah, we'll go for a sail. Let me see what's up with the guys, then I'll come find you." He looked over at Pongo. "Are you in on this Trent thing? I'm going in to find him. You coming?" Pongo stepped back from the car reluctantly. "Don't worry," Roger reassured him, "we'll work on it later."

"Oh, yes, yes. Please, could we do that?" His eyes were as bright as shiny black marbles.

They all headed into the house. Kerri went to bag a few sandwiches and some sodas, then strolled down to the boathouse. Inside was a sweet little thirty foot mahogany plank-on-frame masterpiece, made in Sweden in 1920. The yawl was named "Logos" after the Greek word for reason, the controlling principle of the universe. Charles Stertevant had sent it out from New York, via flatbed rail car, around the time the construction was wrapping up. Like everything else, it had been maintained to perfection and never used. With Celine's permission, Roger had taken it out twice since he had been at Glenwhylden. New Dacron sails had to be fitted, since the original ones were made of Egyptian cotton; now too weakened by age to hold the wind.

The boathouse sat on high concrete pilings at the bottom of the cliffs, accessed by steep stairs. Over the years, winter storms had come and gone, but like the rest of the estate, the boathouse had been built to withstand the test of the elements. Safely ensconced, "Logos" still looked brand-new. Kerri lowered the boat from its hoist and jumped aboard, getting the craft ready for what she was certain would be a blissful afternoon.

Chapter 18

Roger and Pongo found Trent and all of the others in the media room—where else? They gathered on the couch and chairs over by the billiard table. Trent opened with an air of moment and dignity.

"Roger, we all had such a great time at the party last night. Yes, indeed. But what I really want to tell you right now, though, is that all of us are feeling kind of unhappy lately. In general. We don't want to sound ungrateful, really. We're not spoiled. It's not the food or the things we get to do here or...and, well, it certainly isn't about you, that's not it at all. Gosh. Listen, Roger, we all sure like you. We're glad you came to be with us." The others shifted and mumbled their agreement. "The real problem is, we're anxious to get out of the estate at least once in awhile, you know? Pongo got to do it, and now the rest of us want to as well."

Artod held out his hands. "That's right, Roger. It's only fair, and it's just that, well, we've all been here for a long time—and there's just so much more out there for us to see and do."

"We keep learning more, every day," added Chloé. "I'm young, and I feel like the world is passing me by. I don't want to let it go by. We think about it and talk about it all the time. I'd give *anything* to go to a rock concert." She sighed deeply.

Now Emily spoke up. "There's something else, dear. We seem to be changing every day, in our bodies. We aren't clear about what it is that's happening to us anymore than you, or Celine, or Dr. Lewis, or anybody. We just know it's happening. We can feel it. Maybe we're having some kind of delayed physical reaction to what happened to us. It's a little scary."

"Maybe, just like we're advancing mentally, it could be we're advancing physically, as well," Artod added, sitting on the edge of the couch. "Maybe we might all get sick or even die soon. Who knows? Can you tell us? Nobody can, Roger."

Pongo had been nodding soberly at all this. "Roger, all we wanted to say here was, thinking about all that, we've just gotten to feel closed-in lately. Like we're prisoners, sort of. It's really frustrating."

Trent smiled, trying to keep it pleasant. "Of course, we know we're not prisoners, you're only thinking of our safety. But still...we want to see some of the world for ourselves. Not just on television. Understand?"

Roger leaned forward, resting his elbows on his knees.

"Oh yeah, Trent. As a matter of fact I do, real well." He looked around at the others. "I don't blame you, any of you. It's perfectly natural to feel like that." He clapped his hands together. "So. Here's what's up. I'm going to immediately start working on some ways to make it happen for you guys. I don't know how we'll do it but we'll do it. I'll have to talk to Celine. I, uh...well, I don't know if you have specific things in mind. If you do, tell me and I'll see what can be done."

"Disneyland!" Betty chirped. The others laughed, relieving some of the tension.

Roger grinned too. "Well, let me work on it, Betty. Hell, you never know what's possible. There are lots of talking animals there, maybe we'll slip you in." He leaned back in his chair and his tone grew serious. "Look, I probably don't need to go over all this, but since we're more or less on the subject, and you mentioned safety, Trent. You all do realize, don't you, the possible—no. The *inevitable* consequences if someone, the wrong person—say, a reporter or a government official—

were to find out about you guys? About how you got to be the way you are now? It would be completely berserk. Your lives wouldn't be worth living anymore. They'd take you all off somewhere and study you like some kind of science experiments. If you think your freedom is restricted now, just imagine what it might be like to be locked in a cell in a government laboratory, undergoing tests and stuff like that, probably for the rest of your lives. Maybe they'd separate you. I'm not trying to scare you, I just want to make sure you understand why Celine has gone to such lengths to protect you here. She knows how things work in the real world, and she doesn't want anything bad to happen. She loves you, and she's only trying to keep you safe. You all know that, right?"

Everyone nodded in unison.

"So—all that means is that we're gonna have to come up with things for you guys to do, and situations where they can be done, that are safe. We have to be reasonable about what we want to do, so that no one gets hurt, or worse. Everybody see how that is?"

More nodding.

"Okay. Just give me a little time, I'll ask Celine, then we'll all talk some more about it."

The meeting broke up with everyone feeling hopeful. Roger poked around the house looking for Kerri, and out in the kitchen Polk gave him the message that she was already down at the boathouse, waiting for him. He dashed to his cottage, changed into shorts and deck shoes, grabbed his cell phone and loped off across the lawn, heading for the cliff stairs.

Kerri had the ketch all rigged. She was sitting on the bow with her legs dangling, riding the gentle rocking motion of the boat as the swell moved under the dock. She had even remembered to open the barn doors at the gable peak of the building's roof, to allow the masts to pass through. Roger whistled as he came into the boathouse.

"Pretty as a picture!"

She looked up and smiled, the last traces of a far-away look lingering on her face. "Let's go, sailor boy."

Roger jumped on board and started up the inboard auxiliary. It sputtered to life, spewing a fat cloud of diesel smoke from the exhaust port. Kerri cast off the lines, and the little ketch slid smoothly out of the shade of the boathouse and into the brilliant autumnal blue. The seas were glassy smooth, a remnant of the storm rain runoff. A ruffle of breeze traded whispers with the ocean's surface. They cleared Glenwhylden's short rock jetty, then rounded up into the wind and hoisted the new main and genoa. Bearing off, "Logos" took the mild power of the wind on her rig, gracefully heeling to leeward. Roger sheeted the sails in a bit more, then put the prop in neutral and cut the motor. Heaven. "'Logos'" narrow hull slipped along effortlessly. Kerri finished stowing the halyard tails on the cabin top, then came aft and nestled under Roger's arm. Far offshore, Santa Cruz Island rose from the low mists with purple and golden majesty, beckoning them out into the calm channel.

Back at the house, Pongo selected an ice-cream sandwich from the boxes in the walk-in freezer. He was feeling optimistic; it seemed the talk with Roger had gone in the apes' favor. He ambled out the back of the kitchen, munching pleasantly, letting the screen door slam behind him.

Wandering toward the garage, he hoped to have a closer inspection of the street racer sulking in the far bay. The garage doors were closed and nobody was around, so he went through the side door and snapped on the lights. Yep. There it was. He could swear he heard it breathing right then and there. He walked over carefully, as if it might suddenly rear up and snap at him. But then, as he got alongside it, he began to feel it was calling to him, drawing him in. He reached out and tried the door handle. Roger certainly would have locked it.

No. The door popped open, allowing the spoor of hydraulic fluid and Teutonic machinery to waft out. Beguiling. He stuffed the last morsel of the ice cream sandwich into his mouth and then carefully wiped his fingers on the front of his bib overalls. He touched the black leather of the driver's seat exploringly. Nice. There were some papers, Roger's work invoices, laying on the seat. Pongo held back a moment before placing those down on the floor beside the seat. Then slowly, so as not to make any wrong moves, he slid in behind the wheel. Oh, oh, oh. So comfortable—it felt like a big hand was gripping his bottom, holding him perfectly in place—safe, come whatever surprises the road might bring.

He removed his baseball cap, closed his eyes, and permitted his long fingers to encircle the fat little wheel. He imagined being out on the road, shooting up the grades and sliding around hairpin turns. No worries. Speed, baby, speed. No problems. Always in control, amazing, amazing. He saw himself accelerating, blasting through one-thirty, then thrusting the gearbox into fourth and flicking the nitrous, his head slamming back as the coupe rocketed up through two-hundred on a straight stretch. His left hand involuntarily fell off the wheel to seek the nitrous button, and as it did it struck something, causing a little metallic jingle.

He opened his eyes in terror, fearful that his big clumsy hands might have broken off a part. Then he saw what had made the sound. It was the medallion on a regulation Porsche factory keychain, dangling from the *ignition key*.

The key, the ticket, the passport, the power. There it was, right there. In the ignition. No shit.

He couldn't believe it. He fixated on it for a minute, fondling the medallion between his fingertips. A curious burning sensation ran up and down the back of his body, from his neck to his ankles. The keychain and medallion sparkled, flashing with promise.

In the kitchen, Polk was rubbing paste polish on a Queen Anne tea service that was on today's rotation of silver polishing. There was so much silver at the house that a schedule was required. Once every three months, on a cycle, every piece in the inventory came due. No sooner had the list been completed than it was time to start at the beginning once more. Nearly all the domestic staff put in time with the polish rags a few hours every week. Polk hummed. He actually didn't mind polishing; he had managed to convince himself that it was meditative. His attention was distracted by a low, throaty rumble down on the driveway by the north side kitchen windows. He leaned over and looked out, just catching a glimpse between the trees of a low, black sports car moving (a bit uncertainly?) down the drive, heading for the motor court. That's funny, he thought. Didn't Roger say he was going sailing with Kerri awhile ago? Well, they must have changed their plans. He went back to polishing.

A moment later, a small red light on the security panel over the butler's pantry door winked on, indicating that the main gate was being opened. Okay, Roger must be taking that car out for a test drive or something. He finished buffing off the last bit of paste on the tea pot, then went out into the dining room to return the piece to the second shelf of the Chippendale highboy.

He positioned it carefully, then stepped back a bit to admire his handiwork.

He was about to leave the room when an obscure element of the view from the tall southern windows caught his eye. It was something far out on the sparkling ocean. He squinted, trying to make it out. Odd. He could swear it was the varnished hull and brand-new sails of Mr. Stertevant's little ketch "Logos" skipping along smartly in the afternoon breeze.

Chapter 19

Pongo's heart was racing and his mind was a battleground of opposing persuasions.

"Go back now. Just turn around and go back. You're already in trouble, but if you go back now it won't get any worse than it is now. Go back! This is crazy!"

Then, from the other side: "NO! Keep going. This may be your only real chance ever to do something like this. You could die tomorrow. If you're lucky, no one will find out. You'll take a spin and have the car back in the garage before anyone knows what happened. Anyway, no matter what, it'll be worth it!"

He tried to concentrate on just driving, doing his very best to remember the turns that Roger had taken to get them up to Gibraltar road the last time he had been out of the estate. So far it was going okay. The other cars on Shoreline whizzed by menacingly, but no one seemed to really notice him. True, he was a little shaky on his shifting, but he had spent long hours sitting in the parked gardener's truck on many late nights, just practicing the moves and running the pictures in his mind.

Right now, he was very nervous. His legs were trembling and he was breathing hard. The car felt like a surpassingly fine and magical steed underneath his body. The suspension was stiff and muscular and the accelerator pedal was tender—frighteningly responsive. The least little bit too much pressure caused the car to leap forward violently. It was somewhat hot in the cockpit because he was keeping the heavily tinted windows rolled all the way up, so as not to be seen. He had pulled his cap low over his eyes and tried to hunker down as much as possible.

He got off the main road coming up from the beach, working on his shifting technique, and made his way into the quieter neighborhoods skirting the foothills. He was able to relax a little then, because all the streets were sleepily deserted, and as he came up to a corner with a large oak tree and a bus bench he was delighted to recognize the surroundings. This was definitely the correct place to turn right, he remembered clearly now, and then the next street up would be the mountain pass road. He stopped and carefully looked both ways for oncoming traffic. Nothing.

He let out the clutch with the shift lever in first gear and turned, easing along the street, up-shifting conservatively, feeling better all the time. Momentary tension seized him as a figure appeared suddenly on his right. It was a man mowing his lawn, and he was wearing sunglasses and a walkman. He didn't even look up as the black sports car moved by. Hi, neighbor. Then, at the end of the block, the street sign he had been looking for: Gibraltar Road. He sighed. Great, now just a right turn and then I'll be out in the country. Home free. No more intersections. Maybe get to see a little bit of what this baby can do. Yep. Give her the boot and fly. He began to accelerate, tentatively at first, then, as his confidence built, more aggressively. The lower sections of the road were flatter and had fewer curves than the higher elevations. Pongo fed more and more fuel to the engine, realizing that the true personality of the machine wasn't even beginning to emerge at these lower speeds. He ran up a small incline and found himself at the start of the long, straight stretch that Roger had zoomed down that night, right before they dramatically hit that first climbing hairpin turn.

He saw no other cars ahead, so he stuffed the accelerator. It was mind-numbing. The coupe bounded forward, leaving a cloud of rubber smoke in its wake. The sky—so compellingly blue—the greenery flashing by on either side of the road, the rocks, the lines on the road: to Pongo at that particular moment, everything was nothing less than perfect. He loved the sensation of the machine vibrating under his feet, the vistas of deserted highway, the promise of limitless possibilities. He was free. This was surely the very best moment of his life. But it got better.

As the speedometer jumped through 100 mph, something unexpected happened. As if a switch had been thrown, Pongo began receiving new sources of sensory input, like a "heads-up display" coming on inside his brain. He was able to "feel" the car and its interaction with the road, as if all were enmeshed parts of the same organism. Electrical pulses shot from his fingers into the steering wheel, and return pulses echoed back. In fact he felt full of electricity. Where was it coming from? Temperatures, stress-load factors and mechanical limits of the car; how performance changed with acceleration, braking, or steering: it all flowed to him. He looked at his own arms and hands with wonder. Blood circulation patterns and muscle efficiencies were somehow visible. This had never happened before. George had told him how he could "see" plants growing. Maybe this was the same thing.

It was another notch in the pervasive changes, but a big one. For Pongo it felt natural and easy, like slipping on a familiar old jacket. The tension drained out of his body. Pumping the accelerator and brakes, he marveled as the displays variated. From here on, it was just like painting by numbers.

He began to drive in a manner that would seem to be sheer insanity. He hurled the car into steep curves with lunatic ferocity, but never spun out. He braked to the absolute limits of the equipment—not one iota beyond—but never skidded. He ran the engine up to its peak output in each gear, finding ultimate performance with no real effort or risk since he was operating from an unimpeachable chart.

He recognized a series of switchbacks—he was nearing the top. He told himself he'd stop up there and look at the view, just as they had done the last time.

Then, just as he screamed down the final straightaway on the ridge bordered by scrub-oaks, a glint passed through his peripheral vision. He lifted his foot off the accelerator, feeling a telepathic prick of nausea. Checking the rearview mirror he saw a black and white vehicle with a bright red light attached to the door scramble from concealment and accelerate, fishtailing, out onto the road. It was coming after him. It was coming after him, going very fast. Headlights flashing alternately, side to side. In a near-suicidal instant, Pongo realized that this was a police car. The police. He was being pulled over by the police. The police, the POLICE! Oh, god. God. He slowed down a little more, trying like crazy to think. Rear view again. POLICE car, closing up on him very, very quickly. Lights flashing, siren wailing.

Now the overlay of information, still in his vision, seemed a damnable distraction. It would not go away. Pongo had seen "True Adventures of the Highway Patrol" on television about a hundred times. He knew what would happen here if he tried to outrun the police car. He might be able to get a little distance ahead, because there was no way in hell the police car had anything like the power or suspension of the highly specialized Porsche. But this was the middle of nowhere—probably there was nowhere to run to. Also, the road ahead was an unknown to him, it might even dead end right over the top of the hill. He just didn't know.

All of that didn't really matter anyway, because he knew for sure that if he didn't pull over immediately, the police officer behind him would make a radio call, and right away there would be many more police cars converging on their location. Maybe there would even be a helicopter overhead. That's what they usually did in a pursuit, and that's what this would become in about twenty seconds if he didn't stop: a pursuit. No. No, he had to stop, and then figure out some way to deal with the situation after that. Okay. He braked and pulled to the side of the road.

Suddenly, the bright day seemed like a pitch-black nightmare. With his eyes now glued to the rearview mirror he saw the cruiser skidding in behind him, then a large uniformed officer jumping out and trotting up toward the Porsche. His right hand was ominously poised atop his holstered handgun. He approached along the passenger side of the car, crouching, trying to see into the heavily tinted windows. Pongo's visual overlay showed the man's elevated blood pressure and thrumming heart rate. He was clearly in a state of excitement. Peering in the passenger window, the cop rapped the glass, shouting to shut off the engine and roll down the window. Pongo killed the ignition, looking at the cop's terrifying face. He then leaned over and turned the window crank.

Sergeant Butch Turnbull, aged fifty-two, California Highway Patrol, had been lying in wait between the scrawny windblown oaks which Pongo had hurtled past at a radar-indicated 155 miles per hour. Turnbull had been in that spot specifically because there had been complaints from trailer and camper owners driving back to town over the pass. Young punks in hot cars were driving far in excess of the speed limit up there, endangering the law abiding folk. People had been run off the road. Pongo was the latest punk to snare himself in Sergeant Turnbull's net.

As the blacked-out glass descended, Turnbull's expression did not perceptibly change. Pongo said nothing. He reasoned that he should not use up the element of surprise before the most opportune moment. The sergeant also remained silent for a long moment, sizing up the bizarre thing sitting behind the wheel. Then he backed up a half step and barked out a command.

"Driver. Get out of the car and put your hands on the roof. Do it now."

Terribly frightened and filled with dread, Pongo did as he was directed, unlatching the door and hoisting his rotund frame out of the narrow seat. He drew himself up to his full height and placed his huge hands on the low roof of the coupe. The late afternoon wind was gusting hard up along this section of the pass and Pongo could feel its force buffeting the little car. Nearby trees and grass were jumping like crazy. The cop came around the front, one hand still on his gun butt, the other reaching around behind his back, presumably for his handcuffs. He took up a position behind Pongo.

"That some kind of monkey suit? Halloween was last night."

"It is not a monkey suit, sir. I am not a monkey. I am an Orangutan."

Only the roar of the wind came from behind him for a moment.

Then, "Yeah, right. Put your right hand on top of your head."

Pongo pivoted his head but didn't move his hands. He realized he must do something decisive within the next few seconds, or this situation would go from being very bad to being absolutely tragic.

"Please, sir. I *am* an Orangutan. An ape. I am the result of scientific experiments. I have used this car to escape from my captors." He began to turn slowly. He was now thinking with remarkable clarity. Two things must not be allowed to happen. The patrolman must not use his radios, either the one on his belt or the one in the car, and he must not be allowed to draw his handgun.

"Don't turn around, shithead. Stand still."

Over the wind's clamor, Pongo could hear spiking tension in the man's voice. He turned around anyway, and the officer, who had been just about to grab the ape's wrists and place handcuffs on them, shuttled backward and shot his hand down for his gun. However, Pongo saw the officer's nervous system cueing this event and he moved near simultaneously. The ape's reflexes and muscle coordination were vastly superior, so he got there first and ripped the pistol from the officer's still contracting grip.

"God damn! Drop it boy!" Deprived of his firearm and facing a bizarre huge ape-apparition dressed in Farmer John overalls, he began to panic. He tried to back away but Pongo's other hand wrapped around the officer's bicep, pulling him off balance. Yanked up, he landed on the ground more or less face down.

Now Sergeant Turnbull began to struggle and howl with the violence and desperation befitting a man convinced that he is engaged in a contest for his life. Pongo sat astride him, using his weight and strength to pin the patrolman. He threw the gun into the wind-raked bushes, getting it out of play. Although one arm was caught under his body, the officer used his free hand and pulled his nightstick, twisting around enough to use it. This time he got lucky and Pongo didn't quite cut him off in time. The stick glanced off the side of the ape's face. It stung like hell, and Pongo was briefly more pissed-off than scared. He wrenched the stick from the man's fingers and thumped him hard, once, on the back of his head, before lobbing the stick away.

"Listen, sir! Calm down. Do you hear me? PLEASE CALM DOWN!" He yelled into the patrolman's ear. "I don't want to hurt you. Just be still a moment and we'll talk, okay?"

But Turnbull now struggled even harder. Pongo read his synapses firing, like fireworks. The ape reached for the man's neck, trying to stop his wriggling, but the outcome was unintentional. On contact with the officer's perspiring neck, there was a blue spark from Pongo's fingers, like static electricity, but far bigger. "Pzzaapppp!" Shrieking, the officer stiffened, then trembled violently. His bellows were reduced to gurglings. Pongo himself began to panic now, seeing that the man's nervous system was being short-circuited. Fearful of what he'd done, he struggled to sound calm.

"Are you okay, sir? Sir? I'm sorry, that was an accident. I didn't mean it. *Please* listen to me. Stop fighting, I won't hurt you. I really am an Orangutan. I can talk because of a scientific fluke. I am at least ten times stronger than you."

The patrolman still seemed paralyzed, jerking spasmodically.

Pongo pleaded with him. "Your gun and stick are gone. So here's what. Listen to me, sir, please. I am going to take off your belt and throw it away. I only want you to let me go and not tell anyone about this. Do you understand? It would be very bad, for a lot of people, if anyone found out about me. Okay?"

The man gurgled less urgently. He seemed to be coming back to normal now. Pongo rolled him onto his side, still keeping him pinned. As he fumbled at the belt buckle, the radio crackled in its holster, a woman's dispassionate voice reciting a series of numbers. Pongo worked the fastener open, then stripped the belt off the officer. He flung it down the hill as far as he could.

"Okay. Now I'm going to get up. Please be calm, won't you?"

"Unnhhh!"

Pongo took his weight off him, keeping a firm hold on his arm. Sergeant Turnbull looked up, his eyes the very picture of terror. A thick cord of drool trailed from the corner of his mouth.

"What...are you?"

Pongo got up and pulled the man to his feet, vigilant for any sign in his nervous system of a renewed attack.

"I told you. I am an Orangutan, an ape. I've been the victim of scientific experiments. Here, let's go over to your car, okay sir?" He pulled the still trembling but now cooperative officer over to the open door of his cruiser, keeping tight hold. Leaning inside, Pongo pulled the keys out of the ignition. He threw those as far as he could, another direction from the belt. Tearing the microphone out of the radio, he hurled that as well. Next, he ripped the shotgun from its locked mounts, launching it. He then faced the man. Turnbull's chest was heaving and he was streaming with sweat. Mud smudged his face and covered the front of his uniform. Pongo eased him against the side of the car, holding both of his arms.

"I apologize most sincerely sir, for messing you up like that. I hope I didn't hurt you, I certainly didn't wish to. Now, sir, all I ask is that you sit in your car here for awhile, maybe half an hour, and let me get away from here. I really don't think anyone is going to believe you if you say you stopped a talking ape in a Porsche and he took your gun and your radio. Do you? Excuse me if I'm wrong about this, sir, but you would appear to be of senior status for a man in your profession. You would be eligible for retirement soon, yes?"

Turnbull nodded dimly, in complete bewilderment. His breathing grew more labored.

"I thought so. Well, I don't think you'd want any crazy story like this to appear on your record. No one would believe it. So. Can I count on your help? Will you wait quietly here for a few minutes while I drive away? Could you forget about all this and not tell anyone? I'd be most grateful for that." Pongo looked at the man steadily for another few seconds, making sure that he was not going to come at him again. Glassy-eyed, the officer nodded. Pongo let him sit in the driver's seat.

"Alright, good. You're going to be fine now, sir. In awhile you can get out and go look for your gun and your keys. And please, sir, don't talk about this. Really. I need your help very much." Then Pongo leaned in the door and kissed the astonished highway patrolman on his forehead. "Have a nice afternoon, sir."

With that, he closed the patrol car door and ran like hell for the Porsche. The driver's side was still open, and as he jumped in something swirled past him, a piece of paper. Too preoccupied to notice, he slammed the door, fired the engine, and spun the car around to face down the mountain. Shaking like a leaf, he drove steadily, not too fast, anxiously checking the rearview mirror often to see if anyone was behind him. Amazed, he reached the bottom of the road with no problems.

As he retreated from his encounter with the patrolman, the visual overlay gradually diminished, and now it had disappeared. He tried to find his way back through the neighborhood, but he was all rattled and became confused. He was lost. He pulled into a shady spot to think, and sat with the engine running, feeling terrified. For all he knew, there might have been an extra radio somewhere in the cop's car. He realized all the things that might happen now, especially if he didn't get the Porsche back to Glenwhylden right away. His eyes travelled over the interior of the car. Could there be a street map somewhere? There wasn't. There wasn't even a glove compartment.

Then he saw the cellular phone bolted to the floor. He picked it up and examined it. He had never used one before. He began pushing the buttons experimentally. Ah, yes, the numbers stayed on the display screen. He looked at the other buttons. "Clear". Numbers removed. Logical. It suddenly came to him. He remembered quite well the number for Roger's cellular phone. All the Orangs had been required to memorize it, just in case of emergency. He entered the numbers carefully, then waited for the phone to ring. No ring. He pressed 'Clear' and tried entering the numbers again. Nothing. He studied the key pad again—perhaps he was missing something. Aha..."Send". Worth a try. He pushed that button. Yes. Now it was ringing. One ring, two, then three. He began to feel panicky—maybe Roger didn't have the phone with him. A fourth ring. Then, an answer. It was Roger.

Chapter 20

The afternoon of sailing had been wonderfully relaxing. Roger and Kerri tacked up the coast, looking at the beautiful beaches and the chic homes lining the waterfront. They shared things with each other...talking about their lives. They ate their sandwiches, drank ginger ales, laughed, and kissed a lot. Roger forgot his troubles for awhile.

They were heading in, only about a half mile off the Glenwhylden boathouse, when the phone rang. Kerri's sharp ears picked out the electronic chirping coming from Roger's tote-bag. She reached in and fished it out.

"Your phone, sir," she said with a giggle.

"Hello...oh hi, Pong. Well, we're still out on the boat, just off the house actually. We'll be back in about fifteen minutes. What's up, everything okay?"

He then listened without speaking for at least thirty seconds. Kerri glanced at him, then stared as the blood drained out of his face. He began to shake his head slowly, over and over. He absently took off his sunglasses and dropped them on the cockpit deck.

"What is it?" she whispered. He waved her away.

Finally he rasped, "Oh, Pongo, damn it to hell, shit!" He stood up abruptly, staring toward the beach, steadying himself with one hand on the boom. "Okay, I see. Yes, I understand that, Pongo. Are you okay? Is the car okay? Oh, thank God. Man, I can't even believe this." His voice dropped. "Yeah. Okay, tell me the street name. Can you see a sign? Okay. Is there a big blue house over to the left? Good. Go straight for two blocks, then turn right on Sycamore, then come all the way back down to Shoreline. Turn right, then you'll come to the estate on the left. Can you remember that?" There was another long pause. "Oh, for sure, Pongo. I'll definitely meet you at the garage. You should be home in five minutes. And *don't* speed. Right." He clicked off the phone and sat back down, ashen. "Pongo stole Fred's Porsche and took it up Gibraltar Road."

Kerri's eyes widened. "No he didn't!"

"Yes. He said he was having some kind of psychic experience, driving the car. Then he got pulled over by the police and got into a fight with the cop who stopped him."

She clasped her hands over her scalp, like a helmet. "Oh my God. No. Where is he? What happened to the cop?"

Roger shook his head again. "I don't know. He says he got away somehow. Says he shot energy from his finger into the guy. He's in Montecito, driving home right now. He got lost, that's why he called me. He needed directions." He looked off across the water, at the big mansion on the hilltop. "We gotta get back right away. Let's start the kicker and get in."

They powered in as fast as the little engine could push them. At the boathouse Roger jumped onto the dock and took off running up the stairs. Bursting into the garage a few minutes later, he was thoroughly out of breath. To his great relief, the black Porsche was parked in its stall, apparently undamaged. Pongo sat on the ground, his head cradled in his hands.

"Pongo!"

The ape looked up, mournful and dazed. "I did very bad things, Roger."

Pongo was shaking violently. Seeing this Roger didn't have the heart to yell at him. He sat down beside him and put his arm around his shoulders.

"Yeah, it sounds that way. But listen now, Pongo. I've gotta hear exactly what happened so I can figure out what we need to do. That's the most important thing right now. So calm down and tell me everything, right from the start."

With his voice breaking, the ape gave a detailed account. How he had handled the confrontation with the policeman, what each of them said, and so forth. He explained about the visual overlays and the spark from his fingertips. He asserted that, as far as he knew, he hadn't been followed or identified in any way. Roger questioned him about other witnesses; had there been any other cars going by while all this went on? Pongo was certain there had not been. It was just him and the cop up there, the whole thing had taken only two or three minutes. He described the patrol car and uniform. Definitely California Highway Patrol.

"And he never used his radio. I never saw him use it."

"Well, that's probably wrong, Pongo" Roger said sharply. "They always call in a stop in progress, before they even get out of the car. So, the dispatcher knew the guy was pulling somebody over and there was a description of the car given as well. That's the way they do it, I know. You sure you weren't followed?"

Pongo nodded. "I didn't see any other police cars the whole rest of the time I was driving back down here, honest. Nobody was behind me at all, I was looking the whole time."

Right then Kerri ran in and rushed to Pongo. He jumped up to hug her, starting to shake all over again.

"Oh Kerri, I'm so sorry. I've messed everything all up. I'm very, very bad" he blubbered.

She patted his back, comforting him. "Pongo, you big ninny. Why did you do that?"

"I...I just couldn't help myself, you guys. I'm so sorry. I know it was so wrong, but, well, the keys were in the car, and

I just found myself starting it and driving out the gates. It was like being in a dream or something, really it was." He turned away and beat his hands on the top of his head. "Oh, I have the most awful headache right now. It's killing me." He began rubbing his temples with his fingers. "But what was so weird is, like I was telling Roger, while I was driving really fast these...displays, sort of, kept coming into my vision. It was like I was, I had become one of George's computers, only I was a computer with feet and hands, and I was just made for driving a car. I was able to do things. Impossible stuff. Electricity was flowing through me. It was amazing. Roger, I was making some of those twenty mile per hour turns at eighty and ninety, and I wasn't even out of control at all, not at all! In fact this car and I were like a single machine."

At this Roger turned white and began to look the car over very closely, checking for damage. He dropped onto the floor and peered under the chassis, then ran his hands around behind the wheels and under the rear bumper. He got in and started the engine, revving it and listening closely. He popped the hood open and leaned down, poking through the hoses and wires. After a few more minutes of examining the entire machine, he killed the ignition. He turned back to the others, a blank look on his face.

"Pongo," he said gravely, "are you really telling us the truth about all this? Are you sure it really happened?"

Pongo stared at him, halting the kneading of his temples. "What? Am I...yes, of course I'm certain!" He squinted. "What, do you think I made all this up? Why would I do that?"

"Hang on, I didn't say that. But, maybe you dreamed it or something. Is that possible? Because I can't find anything really wrong with the car. There'd be wear lines on the tire sidewalls and brake dust in the wheel wells, that sort of thing.

I'm a mechanic, I know. You drive a car that hard, there are signs. But it's just a little dusty, that's all. The engine's hot, but I don't see how you could have been going as fast as you say you were. You know? Maybe you just got in it, and started it up, and then just sat here in the garage having some kind of hallucination."

Pongo shook his head slowly, looking at the car, then back at Roger. He weaved on his feet, trying to comprehend. Then he looked down at his hands.

"No! It's not possible. Look at my hands, see the mud on my knuckles? I got that when I was wrestling with the policeman. There was a puddle by the side of the road, from the rain last night, and we fell into it when we were wrestling. He got mud all over the front of his shirt, I remember, because afterward I told him I was sorry it had happened. And I got mud on my pants, too, see?"

Roger looked at the mud stains and heaved a long, long sigh. "Okay then, listen. For the time being, we're just going to assume that it all happened, and we'll also assume that what you said was true, about not being followed. If the cops have anything, it'll have to relate to the car, because that's really all they can go on. They can't trace a talking Orangutan. I think you said the right things to him, Pongo. It's true, nobody would believe him. Maybe, if he's smart, he sat there and decided that it would be for the best if he just found his stuff and went on about his business as if nothing had happened. Who knows. One thing I do know is that cops hate getting beat out of their authority. So. We'll just wait and see. But I guess I'll have to call Celine—won't that be fun." He squared toward Pongo. "And now, let me tell you something, mister. I'm pissed off as hell at you. I don't care what your reasons were for doing this or what you felt like. There were no good reasons, there was no excuse, it was just totally, totally stupid.

You just put everybody at risk, and I mean big-time. Aside from that, which is the most important part, you also risked losing or damaging a very valuable machine that I'm responsible for. I'd be the one who'd have to pay if it got lost or damaged. That makes me think that you don't care about other peoples' concerns, Pongo. I'm very disappointed. I'm going to have to re-evaluate the way we do things around here because of this. Am I going to have to watch all of you, every minute, like babies or something?" Roger was venting now, pacing up and down. He shot his finger out at the ape. "Another thing. I don't want you to say one word about this to the others. Not a word. It'll just get them all fired up, and we're a long way from knowing just how bad this might become. You got me?"

Pongo hung his head through all this. He nodded weakly.

"Alright. Let's all go up to the house and keep a lid on this. I just hope this is the end of it. I sure as hell do."

Chapter 21

C.H.P. Sergeant Turnbull did not "just forget" about the incident on Gibraltar Road. Further, he ignored Pongo's advice to "not tell anyone about it."

Moments after the black coupe fled the scene, Turnbull jumped out of his car and began a frantic search for his firearms, belt, keys and portable radio. Cursing and thrashing through the bushes, he hunted up all the items within about twenty minutes. Using his belt radio he called in to report his fight with "a man in a monkey suit". No license plate, but he gave a good description of the unusual sports car. Dispatchers then broadcast a bulletin for all other units to be on the lookout for the suspect vehicle with the driver wearing a full-body disguise. Turnbull advised "consider armed and dangerous".

As he was about to leave, Turnbull spotted a piece of paper snagged on a low tree branch. Grabbing it, he saw it was an invoice with the Porsche's description, along with a local phone number and post office box address. There was also the car owner's name and a description of the work to be done: "Reseal brake lines. Prep for show." Bingo.

Turnbull gunned his cruiser down the mountain, siren blaring. He was hoping that by some miracle he might catch up to the suspect's car. If he was so lucky he wouldn't waste the opportunity; he told himself he'd shoot first and figure out who was in the monkey suit afterward. Beyond reckless driving, the suspect had committed first-degree assault on a peace officer, destruction of public property, resisting arrest, and flight to avoid prosecution. Other police units were now circulating the area as well. But there was no sign of the car or the man in the monkey suit. They had simply disappeared.

Back at headquarters Turnbull's detailed account of the incident to his Lieutenant sparked an immediate investigation.

"That fucker had to be some kind of Judo expert, L.T." Turnbull exclaimed. "He pinned me and zapped my neck with a Taser. Couldn't move. I think he had it concealed in his glove or something. Son of a bitch."

Turnbull was mad at himself, humiliated. Never before had a detained suspect gotten away from him. In almost twenty-five years of service as a highway patrolman, he'd never lost a hand-to-hand fight. Having his gun taken away was particularly painful. The sergeant was a big man, an instructor in self-defense. Nobody pushed him around. His pride was hurt, and he was embarrassed. The "King Kong Incident" (as some of his fellow officers were now calling it) was already being mocked around the station. Worse, the asshole in the monkey suit had been right, he *was* near retirement. He didn't need a thing like this dogging him on the way out. The monkey suit guy was going down if it was the last thing Turnbull did.

He rubbed his face, then scowled at his C.O. "Another thing. The guy was on PCP or something. Maybe tweaking. He must have been, to be that strong. Insane. Hell, you should go out in the shop and see where he ripped the shotgun out of my unit. He did it with one hand. It was *locked in the security mount.* He had a hold of my arm with one hand and he just reached in there with the other one and tore the gun mount out like it was made of cardboard."

The lieutenant paused from taking notes and looked up at Turnbull. "He did that with just one hand?"

"Yep."

"Damn."

They were in a glassed-in office. Glancing around to see if anyone was watching, Turnbull leaned across the desk. "The guy kept telling me he was part of some science experiment. He was using the car to escape. He said stuff like 'just let me go.' But I'll tell you this, L.T. That was the best damn monkey suit I've ever seen. It really had me going when he rolled down the window. Even when we were fighting, it looked totally real. It didn't feel like rubber. And it didn't slow him down one bit, either."

Two detectives were already at work tracing the car owner's name and physical address: Tasselmere, Frederick. 6204 Chula Prieto Drive, Montecito, CA. The registration brought up a "VIN" number that matched the car's description: black 1990 Porsche Turbo Carrera, specially modified in Germany.

Later that evening Fred Tasselmere's wife answered her doorbell and was surprised to find two C.H.P. officers standing on her porch. She invited them in and answered their questions. Her husband was out of town, in San Francisco on business. He'd been gone for two days, flying commercial, not driving. She believed his black sports car was at the mechanic's shop. She wasn't sure where that was, exactly. No, she had not heard anything about the car being stolen.

"Is Mr. Tasselmere a large, strong man?"

"Fred? Goodness, no! Fred's sixty nine years old. He has rheumatoid arthritis." She showed them a picture of her white-haired husband.

"Does he own a monkey suit that you know of?"

Mrs. Tasselmere stared back in confusion. "Do you mean a tuxedo?"

The officers gave her their cards and left, now confident the car's owner wasn't the suspect. They began to focus on the mechanic or someone else at a repair shop that might have had access to the car.

A call to the mechanic's number wasn't picked up and there was no answering machine. But another cross-check of records revealed a link between the mechanic's phone number on the invoice and a certain very high-profile luxury mansion. The phone company confirmed that the line with that number was located inside the garage at the exclusive "Glenwhylden" estate.

Chapter 22

"Well. That's really great. When did this happen, you said yesterday afternoon?"

"That's right, Mrs. Stertevant. About four o'clock or so." Roger had just finished relating to Celine the news about Pongo's misadventure. It was early Sunday morning at Glenwhylden and Roger was still in his cottage. He hadn't been able to sleep much.

"I guess by the time he got back here and we got all the details out of him, I figured I'd just wait and call you this morning. I wanted to be sure that I had all the facts, as best I could get them. I'd just like to say how very sorry I am, Mrs. Stertevant. I feel responsible in more ways than one. I left the keys in the car for one thing. And then, of course, I was out sailing. I'm just sick about it, really. I just never dreamed anything like this would happen. I was totally caught off guard."

Celine's voice was matter-of-fact on the other end of the line.

"Roger. C'mon, listen, that's bull. There was no way anyone could see this coming. It's like I said, they're going to be doing things from out of left field and you've just got to be ready to react. But, listen, do you think he actually got away clean, without the car being identified? You said it has no license plates, right?"

"No plates. But whether he got away clean, I'm not sure. Who knows if everything he told us was true or not. But there is one thing. There aren't that many cars like that anywhere. They're extremely rare. So that narrows it way down right off the bat. Then of course, the other thing is, would the cop risk reporting the incident, officially, when it just sounds so outlandish? If I were in the guy's place, I might be inclined to just let it go, like a bad dream or something. If he found his gun and his belt and his keys, he might have just covered the whole thing up. You know?"

"Shouldn't bet on that." There was a long silence. "But I guess we hold the fort and see if anything happens," she finally went on. "Just in case, I'm going to have Chuck bring the plane out there today, to have it on standby. If you had to get them out of there for some reason, I want it ready. Don't leave the estate at all for the next few days, okay? If something were to happen I want you there to deal with it."

"Oh, yes. Absolutely. I'll be right here."

"Good. Now, I'll have Chuck call you when he gets in. Probably be fairly late this afternoon. And, Roger? He doesn't know anything about the changes the group have gone through. Did you realize that?"

"I didn't know if he did or not."

"Well, he doesn't. Like I've told you, I'm keeping the circle as small as possible. He'll remember flying them up there from Borneo. But, of course, there was nothing abnormal about them back then. They were in animal shipping crates. So if something were to happen and they had to be flown out as they are now, we'd have to figure out how to deal with that aspect of it. I suppose, as long as none of them talks or does anything too human-like, there wouldn't be all that much to it. Okay, so you just sit tight, my boy."

Roger went up to the main house. Polk and one of the cooks were in the loggia setting the table for breakfast, as usual. Roger sat down and knitted his fingers anxiously.

"Nothing new?" Polk asked. Roger had told him the tale the previous evening.

"No. Mrs. Stertevant wants us to just sit tight."

Polk shook his head. "No way that's gonna be the end of it. No, sir."

As Roger perused the paper and sipped his orange juice, some of the group began to wander in. Betty and Emily came first, wearing new silk kimonos that Celine had just sent them. They looked very colorful and Roger complimented them on their style. Some of the others began to arrive—no Pongo yet—and Roger decided to pick up the phone and check his voicemail for messages. These had lately dropped to near zero, owing to his absence from his old social circles, but every once in awhile there was a little something from a friend and he had resolved not to lose all touch with everyone. His mailbox picked up and played his droning greeting. He entered his code. One message.

"Roger? Fred Tasselmere. I'm calling from out of town, but my wife told me that two Highway Patrol officers just came to the house about the Porsche. Asked if it was stolen. Is everything alright? She told them it was in the shop. Would you call me right away? I'd like to know what the hell's going on." He left a number at the end of the message. The voicemail was time-stamped at 9:55 PM.

Roger hung up and sat there biting his lip for a minute. Okay. This was very bad. It meant something was happening; the incident was being investigated. Major bad news. He was probably going to have to answer questions from the Highway Patrol. Who should he call first? Fred? Celine? Jesus, how the hell had they found out so fast whose car it was? The amiable chatter of the others having their breakfast sounded echoing and far away.

Roger rose, walked into the small formal card room down the hall and closed the door. He sat down beside the phone and pulled it into his lap, continuing to think. Celine first, right.

She'd want to know what's happening. Hwang-Shu answered, and moments later he heard Celine's voice.

"Hello again, Roger. What's happened, something wrong?"

"I'm afraid so. I just checked my messages and there was one from the man who owns the car. Called me late last night. He's still out of town, I guess, but his wife told him the Highway Patrol came to his house about his car, the Porsche. They asked where it was yesterday or if it had been stolen. The wife told them the car was in the shop. I haven't called Fred back yet. I wanted to tell you first."

Celine's voice remained deliberate. "Alright." She paused for a few seconds, coughing softly. "Call the man, the car's owner, and tell him there's been some mistake. Tell him the car's fine, it hasn't gone anywhere or been stolen. If all they've got is a stolen car inquiry, and the owner says it wasn't stolen, maybe it'll go away."

"Yes, ma'am."

"Good. Just do that for now. Chuck should have the plane in the air within the next hour. That would put them on the ground out there by about one or two o'clock your time. He'll give you a call when he's there. I told him to have the plane fully serviced and provisioned, ready to leave on a moment's notice."

"I sure hope that won't be necessary."

"I do too, but it's better to be ready. There are government-types involved now."

"I'll call the owner right away."

"Okay. Do the others know anything about this?"

"Only Polk. And Kerri, of course. I thought it would be better to keep it quiet."

"Right." Her voice lowered. "Keep your cool, you hear me?"

He hung up. He didn't feel cool at all. He called the number Fred Tasselmere had left, reaching a hotel in San Francisco. The desk connected him. Tasselmere sounded irritated.

"Is my car okay, Roger?"

"Hi, Fred. Got your message. Yeah, it's fine. I don't know what the deal is. It's out in the garage with the wheels off. Hasn't been anywhere since I picked it up yesterday."

"Boy, that's a load off my mind," Tasselmere sighed. "I guess there must have been a foul-up somewhere. Maybe it's another car that looks like mine. That really had me going. You know better than anybody, Roger, that car's my baby. I'll call the detective guy back and tell him it must be somebody else's car. So, how's it going, will you have it finished this afternoon? I'll be back in town around eight."

"Yeah, it'll be done way before then. No problem. I'll drop it by your house in a couple of hours."

Roger hung up, hurried through breakfast, then went out to the garage and finished the work on Fred's car. When he was done he vacuumed the interior and his attention fell on the cellular phone. Then he realized: Pongo had called him from the cell phone yesterday. That call would appear on Fred's bill at the end of the month. Of course the billing wouldn't show where the call was placed from, exactly, but it would reflect that a call was made on Saturday afternoon, at a time when Roger had claimed the car was sitting in the garage. Well. Maybe he'd overlook it, it would only be one short local call. He started looking for the work invoice, so he could complete it. But it wasn't where he thought he'd left it, nowhere in the car. Probably around here somewhere, he thought, but I don't have the time. He quickly filled out a new one and got the car ready to drive back up to Fred's house. Taking it back out on the road worried him. What if the same cop who stopped Pongo should just happen to be cruising down Sheffield at exactly the right time? It would be better to wait until dark, but he couldn't; Fred would be back before then and he wanted to see his car. Resigned, Roger found Polk and asked for a ride back down from Montecito after he dropped off the car.

The delivery went off without incident. No one was home; he left the car in Tasselmere's garage, tucking the keys above the visor like usual. He began to relax a little. The black Porsche was back at its rightful home, the authorities had been informed by Fred that his car had not been stolen. Perhaps now that would be the last of it.

Nearing suppertime the big house was quiet. Roger peeked into the media room. Almost everyone was there, watching the usual mélange of programs. But not George—the computer screens were idle.

"He's out in the conservatory," said Chloé. "He said to tell you to come find him. That's where he'd be."

Funny, Roger thought. Wonder what he wants. He cruised down the hallways and opened the door to the glass passageway. He hadn't been out in the conservatory for quite some time, and as the earthy smells of lush foliage and super-oxygenated, humidified air greeted his nostrils, he instantly felt more peaceful. Evening light cast deep shadows. There was the faint sound of water from a hose.

"George? George, you there?" He stopped, waiting for a reply. The watering sound ceased.

"Roger? I'm over here."

He found the ape squatting, with a hose and a few mixing bottles by his side, ministering to a remarkable fern. It was oversized, hallucinatory green, with the tips of the broad leaves shading into purple, then bright red. George looked up mildly.

"Hi there, Roger. How you doing?"

"Okay, George. Wow, strange plant. What do you call that?"

"I'm not sure what it's called. I just like the way it looks, don't you?"

"Yeah. It's pretty cool." He squatted alongside George. "Chloé said you wanted to talk with me?"

"Yes. I had a vision about something. I want to ask you about it." George leaned back and produced a bag of Oreo cookies from his smock pocket, offering it. "No? Okay. Well. Do you know where we're all going tonight, Roger?"

Roger stared. "Where we're going?"

George nodded slowly, munching cookies.

"We're not going anywhere, George. As far as I know."

"Yeah. Well, it seems like a place that's really far from here. It's different, too. There are big mountains, it's really cold, and there's snow on the ground. But first we have to go through a dark cave, then we're getting into a big airplane."

Roger laughed. "Oh, I think you're imagining things, George."

"It's because of what Pongo did yesterday."

"Oh?" Roger darkened. "Did Pongo tell you what happened yesterday?"

"No. But I know about it."

"Really. How, George?"

"It just comes to me. He took your man's car out of the garage and got into a fight with a policeman. The policeman got a piece of paper with your name on it." He dug into the bag, extracted the last Oreo, then plugged it into his mouth.

Son of a bitch. The invoice from the car. That's why he couldn't find it. Somehow the officer had gotten it, it had fallen out of the car. Of course, it had his name, all his business information on it, as well as Fred's name and address. The make and model of the car. There was also the telephone number for the separate line at the estate's garage. Everything. Roger felt his guts begin squirming madly.

George sounded just as sure as if he was reading the newspaper. "And Roger, other men are coming here tonight. They're wearing black clothes. They have guns, and they'll all be right in here where we are now."

"George. George. Hang on. One more time. How do you know that—all of that? I need you to tell me, it's important."

George nodded, finishing his last mouthful while meticulously collapsing and folding the empty bag. He shrugged his narrow shoulders.

"I can't fully explain. I don't know how it happens myself. It's not all that different from watching TV, really. Except the reception might be bad. It's not exact. You see things, maybe just bits. Abby told me the same thing has been happening to her for a long time, and she doesn't know how it works, either."

"But you're sure? You're sure about the men-with-guns part of all that?"

George closed his eyes for a moment. "Yes, later. It's dark outside. Chloé's crying. She's scared."

"Well, George, that's very interesting. I hope you're wrong about all this."

"Yeah. We'll be leaving in a big hurry."

Roger stiff-legged out of the conservatory, feeling dizzy. He headed for the kitchen, realizing he'd skipped lunch. Polk handed him two messages. One was from Chuck Bartholdy. He and his co-pilot were now at the Biltmore hotel and the plane was at the Execu-Air hangar, all set to roll. It was stocked with food and other provisions, enough to service a fairly lengthy flight. The other message was from Celine: "Urgent, please call at once."

The card room, again. He snatched up the phone, punching in the number for Marsh Meadows. It rang only once, and Celine herself picked up the receiver.

"Roger. I think we're going to move on this one. Abby says she has a very bad feeling."

"Well, George just predicted there would be men with guns coming here to the estate. I think one of my invoices fell out of the car while Pongo was pulled over. It had all my information on it. The phone number at the garage here, too. Anyway, George had some vision or something, that men in black clothes will be here and also that we're leaving to go somewhere in the mountains. Something about a cave, too."

Celine gasped. "He said all that? Well, he's got one thing on target. The best place to go will be my mountain lodge outside Sils Maria, Switzerland. It's very private, very remote. There's an airfield in Samedan, just down the mountain from St. Moritz, and the Customs people there know me and my airplane. There won't be any problem getting the group into the country and then up to the house. Hang on, Roger."

She covered the phone and Roger heard a muffled urgent conversation. It began to sink in. She was going to move the whole lot of them to Switzerland, of all places. Seven tropical rainforest apes, dropped into winter in the high Alps. Of course, he thought. She has a lodge in the Alps. What else?

"Okay, Roger, sorry about that. I can't listen to two people at once. Here's the deal. You're definitely going now. It's decided, get on it right away. Abby is calling Chuck and he'll be at the airport within a half an hour waiting for you. Try to get airborne before midnight. Got it?"

Roger was shaking his head, which by now was beginning to throb. He tried to sound unfazed.

"Uh, you mean, we'd all just get on the jet? And, fly straight out of here and put down in Switzerland? Could that work? I mean, it's winter there, Mrs. Stertevant. Wouldn't the Orangs be a bit out of their element?"

"Roger, the house is heated, so I'm not concerned about the weather. And we'll buy them all parkas or something. I don't see this as being for a very extended period of time. What I'm most concerned to do right now is to get them as far away as possible from any kind of police who might suddenly show up. Switzerland is a great place to hide things. Just pack a few essentials, Roger, there's not much time. Abby and George are seeing the same scenario. I don't know about George, he's kind of new to this sort of thing, but Abby has a hell of a track record. So get busy, Polk can help you. Like I said, Chuck will be ready to go as soon as you get there."

Roger tried one last time to put the brakes on things.

"Mrs. Stertevant, I understand what you're saying, and of course I'm here to do whatever you feel is best, but just for the sake of argument, is it possible we might be leaping ahead here? George's vision aside, even if the police were to find out that I had possession of the car at the time of the incident, and even if they were to question me, they'd still have no probable cause to do anything else. Right now, all they've got is the story the officer told them, and maybe a piece of paper with my name on it. That's hardly reason to issue a search warrant and come in here looking around. Do you think we should be taking the animals to Switzerland before they even contact me?"

Celine turned sharp. "Stop arguing. Bad things are about to happen. Believe it. The time to act is now, while there's still a little time. For years people have wanted to get inside Glenwhylden and see what's there, and that includes police people. Don't put it past them. If they can link you to that incident, and then place you or the car at Glenwhylden, there could be a search warrant, bingo, just like that. They've got probable cause. A highway patrolman was beaten and a suspect escaped. That invoice is all they need. They've already gotten as far as knowing who the car belongs to and who had it the day of the incident. So just do what I'm telling you. Pack up the Orangs now and get them aboard the jet."

Roger gave up. "Of course, Mrs. Stertevant. Right away."

"And, listen. No one else is to go, just you and the Orangs, understand? Don't tell the staff where you're going. Not even Polk. That way, if he's asked, he won't have to lie."

He got off the phone and grabbed a sheet of paper, jotting a list of everything he'd need to do in the next few hours. Sprinting to his cottage, he pocketed his passport and stuffed a few other things into a duffel.

Then he went looking, and found everyone except George in the media room.

"Stay put, okay?' he announced after the blaring TVs were turned down. "I'll be right back. I've got big news for you all." He went off to George's room. The ape was sitting on the floor, absorbed in a cache of books and papers.

"Well, George, congratulations. I don't know how, but you got at least part of it dead right. We're taking a trip on an airplane."

George was placid. "Yes. It seemed clear."

Roger could only sigh. "And the others? Do they know about this?"

"I don't think so, Roger." George fingered his tee shirt. "What about warm clothes? We don't have any."

"We'll take care of that. Let's go tell everyone else right now. But listen, don't talk about the men in black clothes, okay? I don't want to scare everyone."

George nodded.

Roger wanted them to believe, at least for now, that this was the magical mystery tour they'd asked for, rather than a flight to avoid danger.

The news that they would leave tonight for a faraway place caused much excitement. Everyone loved the idea of being in the snow. Roger explained about the cold, and how important it would be to have the right clothes. For now, they should bring whatever they had (there were sweaters and light jackets). More appropriate clothing would be arranged once they arrived.

Trent was beaming, convinced this journey was the direct result of his skillful lobbying.

"Can't you tell us where we're going, big guy?" he asked. "Why all the mystery?"

"Celine just wants it this way. She thinks it'll be more fun for you guys if it's a surprise. It'll be an adventure, okay? But we have to hurry. Now, if you'll all go to your rooms and start—"

"Roooogerrrrr!" It was Polk, hollering out in the corridor. Then he was at the door, motioning furiously. He grabbed Roger's arm and pulled him down the hall to the butler's pantry. "They're here," he hissed. "Lots of them."

"What? Who's here?"

"The cops, man! Deputies! Calling from the gate box." His finger jabbed up at a monitor showing the grainy black-and-white view from the gate security camera. Roger's heart almost stopped. Lights were flashing, and men in helmets with machine guns were clustered there. A SWAT team.

"They say they got a search warrant and we got to open up! What we gonna do?" His voice cracked with panic.

It was all going to fall apart, Roger flashed. Everything. He should have goddamned shot himself while he had the chance.

Now the buzzer sounded again on the intercom, and an angry voice followed. "Sheriff's officers! Search warrant. Open this gate right now or we'll bust it down!"

Roger fought for self-control. "Oh shit!" he exclaimed to the butler. "Stall them if you can. I'll get the apes and we'll run for the trees. We can probably get across the lawn and over the far wall before they're up the driveway."

Then they heard a thunderous clatter raining down outside the windows. A helicopter. There was a helicopter circling low over the house.

The two men locked eyes. Polk's normally peaceful features were twisted in fright, under a sheen of sweat. In desperation the butler remembered something. "All of you get down to the basement. Over by the boiler, there's a big flood drain. Shaft goes all the way out to the beach. There's a ladder, I been down there once, a long time ago."

Roger's chest was heaving. No time for questions. He sprinted back to the media room. "Everybody get up and come with me!" he barked at the startled animals. They all froze. "NOW!" Roger bellowed. With that he scooped up Chloé and started running. His hoarse scream and blanched face must have convinced the rest of them this wasn't a game or a joke. Chloé weighed over seventy pounds, and he'd snatched her like a ragdoll. The rest bolted up and followed.

"Roger, what's the matter?" Chloé cried, clinging to his neck as they all tumbled down two flights of the rear service stairwell.

"We're in big trouble, honey. But don't you worry, I've got you."

Moments later they were in the dimly-lit basement, trotting toward the hulking shape of what Roger hoped was the boiler. And there it was, no more than two-and-a-half feet square. A heavy cast-iron grate on the floor. Roger set Chloé down and began furiously tugging it upward. It wouldn't budge. The others gathered around.

"Okay Roger, tell us, what's going on?" demanded Pongo.

Roger spun on him. "The cops, that's what, goddamn it!" he snapped. "A SWAT team, and they're here at Glenwhylden, looking for you, probably about to come through the front door right now. So we've all got to get the hell out of here. We have to get to the airport somehow. Okay? That's what's going on!"

The ape stared back for a split second, then moved Roger aside and grasped the plate. With a rusty grinding it came jumping up out of its frame. They all peered down into pitch darkness, seeing only iron handholds spaced on the shaft, receding from sight within a few feet. A damp fetid odor rose from the hole.

Betty's shaky little voice broke the silence. "Oh my God," she whimpered, "we're all running for our lives again."

Roger reached to her in a vain try to bring calm. "Listen, Betty, sweetheart. They won't find us. Polk says this shaft is a way to get to the beach. We're cut off up above, so we're all going to climb down this thing, together. We've got no other choice." He hadn't even thought about a flashlight. Too bad. "I'll go first. Pongo, you're the strongest. You go last and pull the cover plate back on when you're inside."

At that same moment a beacon-pulsing swarm of black-and-white vehicles, led by an armored car with a turret, exploded into the motor court. Officers in battle gear jumped out and ran in all directions. Polk was standing at the open door, trying to show that no resistance would be given. The gesture was ignored. The front hall was instantly aboil with helmeted cops.

"Sheriff's Department search warrant!" they yelled. "Show us your hands!" Guns were pointed everywhere, and Polk was roughly pushed to the floor. He was handcuffed, then placed on a chair under the watch of a deputy. Other officers were spreading out, calling "search warrant" up and down the halls and staircases. Polk could hear stomping and assorted crashes. Five other staff members were rounded up and brought to the front hall to wait with Polk. They were all beyond rattled; two of the maids wept in fear.

The helmeted officer standing over them was a rookie with a smooth face and tiny, close-set eyes. His finger was poised on the trigger guard of a submachine gun. "Any of you know about a black Porsche kept here? Seen it? Anybody got a monkey suit?"

Polk hesitated and finally looked up. "Sir, we don't know anything about why you're here. Are we under arrest? May I please be allowed to call the estate's attorney?"

The deputy snorted. "You're not under arrest at this point, just lawfully detained. Why do you need a lawyer if you don't know anything?"

One of the senior officers conducting the search knew quite well what he was looking for. In addition to having conducted the traffic stop of Pongo, CHP Sergeant Butch Turnbull just happened to be a seven year veteran of the county multi-agency SWAT team. Serving this search warrant was his call-out. His heart skipped a beat when he spotted a Polaroid snapshot stuck on a mirror in a downstairs bedroom. It showed a small red ape wearing a "Romeo Void" sweatshirt. The ape didn't look like the same one that attacked him, but it confirmed there was actually something to all this. They were barking up the right tree. Studying the photo Turnbull noted that this looked like the real thing: an ape wearing human clothing, not a person in a monkey suit. He called for the evidence team to collect and document the picture.

Roger knew he was claustrophobic, but like most who have the condition, he'd always avoided situations that could trigger it. Now climbing down the dark narrow drain-shaft brought sheer panic up in his throat, and he sucked in the foul air, fighting not to become ill. He concentrated on feeling his way, feet and hands one after another on the ladder. Within moments there was no light, period. Cold as a tomb. Shortly, echoing from above, he heard the grating clang back in place, along with the rustlings of the others climbing down after him. They were all in. The rungs were damp and slimy, and after fifty or sixty had come and gone, his grip started waning. How much deeper did this thing go? Maybe the Orangs could climb indefinitely, but not him. The fear of falling weakened him further, and a tremor set in. Down, down, down. He could hear Chloé crying now, and he called up to the others. "Everybody okay? We should be almost there." But he didn't know that, of course. And they weren't. Perhaps fifty more rungs, and now he was barely clinging on. His fingers defied him...going rubbery and numb.

Finally he halted, legs quaking violently. He didn't know which Orang was directly above him, but he touched a hairy leg and said, "Listen, I'm...I'm not so sure I can hang on."

A powerful hand came down, taking firm hold of his forearm. Emily's calm voice said "I won't let you fall, honey. Keep going."

So they went on. But suddenly he swayed, feeling only vacant space where the next rung should be. With his arm still firmly gripped by Emily, his feet kicked into emptiness, and the narrow shaft seemed to widen.

"Hold on everybody," he warned. "Stop. There's no more ladder down here."

Along with his own hammering heart, he heard murmuring and labored breathing above him in the shaft. Roger furiously tried to think. Right. Probably the ceiling of a horizontal storm sewer tunnel. Likely. But in utter darkness, how could he know? And how far to the bottom? Maybe the shaft just got larger and went down further with no rungs. Then he remembered. Coins in his pocket. He fumbled for one, and dropped it. There was a moment of silence, then a splash. It sounded farther down than he'd like. For a split second he thought about telling the others to go back up. But there was a limit. That was over a hundred feet and they were all exhausted. They were much closer to the bottom than the top.

"Okay, Emily," he finally gasped. "Let me go."

"Let go? Are you sure?"

"Yeah. There's...there's water down there. I don't think it's too far."

The strong hand hesitated, then did as he asked. He lowered himself and dangled a terrifying moment from the last rung, then surrendered his grip.

The next instant was a hundred years. Eyes squeezed shut, he felt the accelerating rush of air around him. His shoes hit hard, splashing into water, but then striking concrete and mud perhaps two feet under the surface. Bumping his head on the bottom he saw stars and got a mouthful of liquid beyond foul. He pushed himself to his knees and vomited heavily.

"Roger?" came the alarmed call from overhead. "Roger, are you okay?"

Soaked in sewage, he was gagging, his ankles and wrists ached, but he seemed otherwise uninjured. He guessed the fall was a dozen feet or so.

"I'm okay...it's okay," he stammered. "It's, uh, about twelve feet down. Wait just a second." He stood up and waded in the odorous stagnant water, kicking away clumps of debris.

His instructions to the others reverberated in the flooded tunnel. "Okay, listen. One at a time, come down to the last rung. Hang off as low as you can, then drop. You'll hit water about two feet deep. Try not to land flat."

He stood back a bit. Presently there was a mighty splash and he heard Emily mourn, "My new pink dress." Then she called to the rest: "No big thing. It's like jumping from a tree into swamp water."

When they'd all safely made the drop, Roger felt for the walls. Curving, and about ten feet apart. But which way to go? They paused, listening. There was a slight movement of air, and from the same direction, a faint rhythmic whispering.

"The beach is that way," he guessed aloud.

They waded blindly along toward the growing sound, tripping over debris. To Roger's enormous relief, the faint outline of an opening appeared. But his momentary optimism turned sour. An opening, with closely-spaced heavy metal bars blocking it.

Chapter 23

So near, yet so far. In the starlit darkness, there was the sand, right outside the tunnel opening. Gently breaking waves were a few yards beyond. Cursing madly, Roger felt around the bottom and sides of the thick bars for a release or a hinge. If there was one, he couldn't find it. Polk had said nothing of this. Maybe he'd forgotten, or the bars were something new. Roger started searching in the muck for a piece of wood, anything to use as a prying tool. But it seemed hopeless, the bars were far from flimsy. Pongo stopped him.

"I got us into this. Maybe I can help get us out," he said gently. Reaching up, his huge hands encircled one bar about halfway from the top. Then he swung his body sideways and braced his feet against the adjoining one. For a couple of seconds the three-hundred-pound Orangutan hung like a bat on a window screen, grunting. Then there was the faint sound of rending metal. And then the louder snapping of welds, and the wild clanging of the two bars ripping out of place.

They all spilled out onto the sand, freed from the nightmarish drain shaft. But now what? They still had to get to the airport, a dozen miles away, and not be seen by anyone. Roger's mind raced. The boathouse was close by. Maybe they could all fit into the sailboat and motor up the coast. No. Too risky. And maybe the police were searching the boathouse, who knew? The main house had to be swarming with them by now. Then there was the circling helicopter. From the beach they could periodically hear the staccato pop-pop-popping of its blades. Then he remembered: there was a small beach park a quarter-mile away. It wasn't popular, the bottom was too rocky for swimming. And it closed at sunset so it was likely deserted by now. There was a pay-phone there. Kerri and her grandfather had gone to Bakersfield for a horse show, so he couldn't call them. But there was another person he was thinking of, the one person who would be duty-bound to come get them all and secretly take them to the airport. Roger had that person's unlisted home number memorized.

It took another half-hour of clambering over slippery rocks and wading through shallow surf to get to the park. At one point the police helicopter made a wide swing out to rake the cliffs with its intense spotlight. Roger saw it coming and shouted for them all to duck behind a boulder. The searing beam swept by, jittering, but after one pass the helicopter returned to its vigil directly over the estate. Pressing on, they finally could see the beach park's solitary street light and empty parking lot.

"Wait here," Roger whispered in the shadows. "Stay together. And keep quiet, we don't know who's around. I'm going over there to make a call."

After a few rings a heavy voice answered, a little slurred, like there'd been a cocktail or two involved.

"Who did you say this is again?"

"It's Roger, Phil. Roger. From the estate?"

Phil Holmbard had been advised of Roger's position at Glenwhylden when he started the job. He was there to accomplish unspecified projects for Mrs. Stertevant. They'd shared a few brief phone conversations, during which the attorney seemed openly distrustful of the young man's sudden insider status.

"Oh. Oh, *Roger*. Caldwell, yes. Of course. Well...how are you, son?"

"To be honest, I've got a little problem right now, Phil."

The lawyer snorted. "In jail, are you?"

"No, no. Listen. I need a ride to the airport. Right now."

There was a pause, with the sounds of a televised football game in the background. "This a joke?"

"No, Phil. I'm totally serious. I need you to come get me, right now. I'm at the Arroyo Leon Beach Park, and I have to get to the airport immediately. Could you come at once?"

Now there was a tone of irritation. "Ah, listen Roger, what the—why don't you just get Polk or somebody else from the staff to take you? I'm in my slippers here, I'm watching the Cowboys game. This is most unusual, what's this all about?"

Roger knew just what to say. "Phil, listen. I'm acting on Mrs. Stertevant's direct orders. She wants you to do this, it's urgent. If I have to, I'll call her back right now and you two can take it up directly."

That worked. "No, no. Okay." Heavy sigh. "Damn it. Alright, I'm coming. Where did you say you were?"

"Arroyo Leon Park. At the pay phone. And Phil, bring some towels, would you?"

"Towels? What the hell for?"

"I don't have time to explain. Please just do it, okay?"

"This better all be for a really good reason, son."

"Oh, you won't be disappointed, Phil, believe me." He hung up and retreated to wait with the others.

Fifteen minutes later the hidden group watched as the yellowed headlights of Holmbard's '75 Buick Le Sabre swung into the dim parking lot. The car lumbered toward the pay phone, and Roger waited a moment, trying to make sure who it was. Then he caught a glimpse of the driver's tuft of white hair.

"Here's our ride," he announced softly. "Remember, absolutely, positively no talking. No human behavior. You're just regular Orangutans. And keep low in the car. Cover yourselves. We're in enough trouble already."

He trotted out, waving his hands and whistling. The Buick halted beside him.

"Jesus, you're a mess," Phil frowned as the passenger door opened.

"Yeah, sorry. Thanks for coming. Got the towels?"

Holmbard jerked his thumb at the back seat.

Roger grabbed one, wiping at his face. "Gotta get to the airport."

"Well? I'm here, aren't I son? How come you're hanging around this dark parking lot? Get in. You'd better tell me what the hell's going on."

"Just a second. A few others are coming with us." Roger turned to signal, and Phil Holmbard gaped as seven red apes attired in badly soiled human clothing loped out of the shadows. Roger threw towels around them, hustling them into the sedan.

The lawyer freaked. "Oh now, goddamn it, what the HELL?" he bellowed at Roger. "Monkeys? A bunch of fucking monkeys?" He turned to peer into the crowded back seat. "You can't be serious! They smell like turds. This is ridiculous, get them out of my car! I won't have it. Out, do you hear me? I don't know what you're trying to pull here, boy, but I—"

Roger leaned in and grabbed Holmbard's shirt, yanking the startled man halfway across the seat. "Don't screw with me, Phil," he snarled. "It's been a bad day. We're going to the airport, one way or another. You drive, I drive, we leave you here, I don't care. These are Mrs. Stertevant's personal pets, she wants you to do this, and if you like your job, then shut up and do it." Letting go of Holmbard, Roger then pushed the last ape, Trent, into the front seat and jumped in beside him. He slammed the door. "Get going."

And they thought climbing down the drain shaft had been tense. Behind the wheel Holmbard was silently furious, screeching the car around corners, stomping the accelerator, honking his horn, driving way too fast. He had to slam on the brakes to avoid broad-siding another car at the turn for the freeway on-ramp. The apes in back hunkered down, cowering under their towels.

"Back off a little, Phil," Roger admonished. "I don't want us to get pulled over."

That was all the lawyer needed to start another tirade.

"Why no, I'll just bet you don't, boy. No, sir. Because you're up to something no good, aren't you? I didn't like you the first time I laid eyes on you, son, and now that you've got Mrs. Stertevant buffaloed into giving you a whole lot of money for who knows what, I can see my instincts were right. Oh yes, I see your paychecks. I don't know how you did it, but I'll find out and then your con-game will be up. You're a shifty little prick and this whole deal right here tonight proves it. What are you doing anyway? Smuggling stolen circus animals?" He shot a look at Roger, slitting his eyes. "In fact, I've got half a mind to just drive you and all these stinking monkeys to the police station right now. Get to the bottom of this. The chief's a personal friend of mind, you know that?"

Roger sat and took it, biting his tongue. He worked to regain his composure. But he heard Trent indignantly clearing his throat, and he grabbed the ape's thigh, squeezing hard.

"Phil," Roger lowered his voice, "I'm sorry about this. I apologize for yelling at you back there, okay? I'm just doing exactly what Mrs. Stertevant wants. These are her pets, her airplane is waiting for us, and we're going someplace where they can get medical treatment. It has to be secret. You're her attorney. She said we could count on you."

Holmbard's head and jowls weren't so much shaking as vibrating. "Oh, you bet she can count on me, alright. Thirty nine years, son, I've been taking care of her affairs. There's never been anything even remotely like this happen. She's a sharp woman, but she's getting old and maybe a young sweet-talker like you finally took her in. I'll drive you and these shit-plastered animals to the airport for now, but I'm going to check you out thoroughly after this. Not that I haven't already. Car mechanic, right? You've covered your trail pretty well, but I'm not done. You don't fool me. I don't trust you as far as I can throw your candy-ass." He glanced back at the apes with a sneer. "Perfect company for a grease-monkey like you, Caldwell. Stinking monkeys. You're in your element."

A few minutes later they were at the gate outside the Execu-Air private hangars. Chuck Bartholdy was standing there, ready to let them in. He leaned down when he saw Roger in the front seat.

"First hangar on the right," he pointed. "It's secured. Drive on inside."

The Buick eased into a vast space that was unreally bright, blazing orange from sodium vapor lights. A few other planes hunkered in the corners, but the main attraction was the glittering black Grumman Gulfstream IV, "Arjuna". It was poised in the middle of the hangar, regal and ready to fire. The gangway was deployed. Roger quickly got out and started helping the apes, shepherding them up the stairs to the cabin.

Bartholdy trotted in. "Sheesh, Roger. You been mud-wrestling?" He watched the succession of grubby apes climbing the stairs. "Man, they must be a handful, huh? You sure you got this under control? My orders are to get wheels up the second you're all aboard. We gotta hurry, the fog's coming in."

"Don't worry, Chuck," Roger sighed. "They'll be cool."

Most were already inside, a few more still mounting the gangway. There was just one ape left in the car. Roger leaned back in to grab Trent, taking hold of his sleeve. But, too late.

The ape and a scowling Holmbard were staring each other full in the face. "You *pompous* motherfucker," Trent enunciated calmly.

The lawyer's eyes popped, his lips forming a perfect pucker of outrage. Roger grimaced and snatched Trent, resisting the urge to smack him.

Holmbard vaulted from the car and charged around to the other side as Roger was pushing the Orangutan up the gangway.

"Oh, I see!" he was yowling. "Ventriloquism! More of your stupid circus fakery, Caldwell. Think you can insult me and get away with it, do you?" He seized Roger's collar with both hands, and Roger involuntarily drew back his fist. Chuck Bartholdy separated them.

Quivering with rage, Phil turned on him. "You work for Celine Stertevant? What do you know about all this?"

The tall, ex-Navy fighter pilot looked down calmly. "And you would be?"

"I am her attorney, sir, that's who. And I *demand* an explanation."

Chuck's lip curled. "Well, I just do what the boss tells me. And she didn't tell me to talk with you." He jerked his head at the Buick. "Now you better move your car or I'm going to run it over with a forty-six thousand pound aircraft."

Most of the apes' faces were pressed to the windows, and they could see Holmbard shaking a chubby fist and shouting up at Roger in the hatchway. "You'll get the bill for cleaning my seats!" He stormed back to his car, and the clumsy land-yacht spun around to fishtail out of the hangar, trailing blue tire smoke.

Bartholdy witnessed this, then sprinted up the ladder, retracting it and latching the door. "Wound a little tight, isn't he?" He surveyed the cabin, seats filled with apes. "Well, this is something. You'll have to buckle them in. Sure they'll behave? I mean, they were in cages when I flew them up here before." He pointed at the huge form of Pongo seated at the rear. "That big boy there could be a real problem if he gets antsy at 30,000 feet over the Atlantic."

Exhaling, Roger leaned back against the bulkhead. "No Chuck, he'll be alright. They all will, I've spent a lot of time with them. Anyway, they're tired, they'll probably sleep."

"Okay, if you say so." He hesitated. "But what about their, you know, bathroom needs? It's going to be a very long flight."

Roger smiled. "Believe it or not, they know how to use the facilities. They're housebroken. A little messy once in awhile, but not bad. No problem. But would you mind buzzing me if you're gonna come aft? They'll stay calmer if they don't get surprised."

The pilot took one more look around, assaying the animal's mood. They were placid.

He turned back to Roger. "Okay, sport. You're in charge. There's lots of food and drinks in the galley. The bar's stocked too. You look like a drink might be good for you. Here we go. Bring me some coffee around three o'clock, if you're awake."

It was hushed now as they felt the jolt of a tractor pulling them out onto the flight line. The engines started, whining, building to a muffled roar. The lights in the cabin dimmed, and minutes later they were airborne, skirting over the enveloping curtain of fog pushing in from the ocean. The apes were all looking down, but there was nothing to see. For awhile they conversed in whispers, hearing the story of Pongo's transgression, the reason for the police raid. Roger reassured them. They'd fled with none of their extra clothing or other possessions, but they'd be fine once they got to Celine's house in Switzerland. Everything would be taken care of, they'd be safe. This trip wasn't so mysterious after all, but maybe it could still be magical. At least it would be a real change of scenery. Everyone was worn out, the adrenaline of the past few hours wearing off. The plane banked inland, gaining altitude into the night, heading eastward.

Chapter 24

Returning from the airport with the stench of sewer-soaked apes still lingering in his dignified old car, Phil Holmbard simmered with rage toward Roger Caldwell.

"Punk bastard," he muttered. "Telling *me* what to do, like he's the boss. Grabbing my shirt, ordering me around. Dickhead. And where'd he get all those monkeys? Celine Stertevant's pets, my ass. I've never seen one thing about monkeys being at the estate. Not one invoice, nothing. Bullshit lies, that's what. I should've called his bluff." Then another thought made him pound the top of the steering wheel. "Damn. I bet he's trying to cut me out of the picture!" He screeched into a self-service carwash so he could vacuum out the interior.

When he finally got home an urgent message on his answering machine added to his distress. "Phil, this is Whitney Polk. Call me as soon as you get this. It's an emergency."

The main number at Glenwhylden rang just twice before Polk answered.

"Whitney? It's Phil. I just got in. What's the matter?"

"Well, the police were here awhile ago, Phil. They served a search warrant and went through the house. I thought you should know."

"Hold on, hold on. Are you serious? The police just searched the house? Searched Glenwhylden?"

"That's what I said. Actually, it was city and county SWAT."

"SWAT? Jesus! Well...why?" Holmbard's hands began to tremor as he switched the receiver to his other ear and searched for a pen. "Did they say what they were looking for?"

"Looking for some black car is all I got. Something to do with an assault on an officer yesterday."

"An assault? What the hell? And a car there at the estate was involved? Well, did they find it?"

"Nope. No car like that here. But they took some other stuff, I think. A few papers from my office...and a couple of pictures."

"Pictures? Of what?"

"I don't know, exactly." Polk sighed. "That's why I'm calling you, man. Look, Phil, I'm pretty ticked-off, okay? They were a little rough with us and put us in cuffs. They pointed guns at us. They asked us some questions but we didn't talk. So, all I know is, you're our lawyer, the house just got searched, and you probably need to get involved here."

"Of course, of course. Just help me out a little here, Whitney, I need to ask a few more things before I start calling people. I'll get to the bottom of it, don't worry. So, you say nobody was arrested or anything like that?"

"No. They just detained us while they searched. That's what they called it. Lawfully detained. They released us when they were done."

Holmbard's mind raced. "Was Caldwell there while all this was going on?"

There was a pause. "No. No, he's been out somewhere all evening. Haven't seen him."

"I see. Okay." Holmbard shielded his eyes from the glare of the table lamp, trying to think beyond the ligatures of a now skull-pounding headache. This had been the evening from Hell. First the crazy drive to the airport: Caldwell being an ass, and all those reeking monkeys in his car. Then the ugly face-off in the hangar. And now this. Glenwhylden estate, his responsibility, *his turf* had been searched by the police. Violated. The first time outsiders had ever been inside, and it was cops with a search warrant. Beyond that, the first he hears of it is from the butler. For crap's sake, *he himself* hadn't ever been allowed in that house even after decades of representing the owner's affairs! The lawyer felt control of his domain slipping away from him. Roger Caldwell was behind all of this, he was sure of it.

"Polk, level with me. Do you know anything about Caldwell having a pack of pet monkeys? Maybe there at the estate? Have you seen anything like that?"

After a moment of silence, Polk responded "Say *what*, Phil?"

Now Holmbard realized he might have slipped up. If those animals really were Mrs. Stertevant's pets, and she meant to keep them a secret, then his question to Polk might have violated attorney-client privilege. He abruptly ended the Q&A.

"It's nothing, Whitney. Forget I asked. I'll call the D.A. right now and find out what's going on. I'll handle this and get back to you in a little while."

Chapter 25

Bright morning sunshine flooding the cabin awakened Roger, and he quickly sat up and surveyed the others. They were awake as well, glued to their windows. The jet was circling a deep green valley, passing the tops of jagged peaks crowding in on all sides. A topaz-blue lake shimmered in the light. It looked like a lost kingdom, impossibly beautiful and majestic. Roger spotted the field below, a simple asphalt airstrip. It seemed alarmingly short. Bartholdy ran "Arjuna" up to the end of the valley at slowing speed, lowering the flaps and landing gear. He positioned the jet with precision, then plummeted suddenly toward the valley floor. It was a thrilling approach, the ground rushing up with menace. When they were low enough to see the laundry flapping on the lines behind tidy homes, the jet stood on its ear, banking sharply. Roger felt his stomach fall and there were squeals of fright from some of the Oranges, but then, just as suddenly, they leveled off and the wheels kissed the runway. Brakes and counterthrust brought them to a noisy halt near the end of the strip. They taxied to a hangar where a Mercedes limousine and driver waited.

Instructions probably weren't necessary but Roger cautioned the apes again anyway.

"Remember, no talking at all until we're up at the house and by ourselves." He pointed at Trent. "You got that, yacky-doodle?"

The gangway was lowered and Roger descended, feeling invigorated by the cool, clean mountain air. There was a welcoming trace of wood smoke and after the long flight, the airfield seemed extraordinarily silent. A dapper, middle-aged man with a pencil moustache introduced himself.

"You are Mr. Caldwell? Ah, very please to meet you, sir. I welcome you in Switzerland. I am a Scartaino Scarpita. I will assist you with the arrangements here in Sils Maria." His English had a central-casting Italian accent. He was dressed formally, in a somber black wool suit, fluorescent white shirt and dark red tie.

Roger extended his hand. "Mr. Scarpita? Thank you, very glad to make your acquaintance, sir." Roger was bleary but he did his best to be formal and proper. He'd heard that counted for a lot in this country. "Are you with Customs here, Mr. Scarpita?"

"No, sir, the Zoll, the Customs, will be here in only a few more minutes. I am work for Mrs. Stertevant to care for her property here. We have not seen her for several years, but I a understand that she is well, yes?"

"Yes, sir, she is quite well." He gestured at the plane. "As you may know, sir, I have seven Orangutans on board. They've been cooped up in there for a long time. What will the Customs procedure involve?"

Scarpita waved dismissively. "Only is a formality, Mr. Caldwell. The Zoll, in a few minutes they are here, look over the plane and the animals, give us a papers, no problems." He scissored his downturned hands. "Already everything is done." He looked to the open door of the jet. "You like to have them come down?"

Roger scanned the airfield, wary of anyone watching.

"That okay? I'll bring them out to walk around right here until the Customs men come. They won't be upset if the animals aren't in cages or boxes, will they?"

Scarpita smiled benignly. "Oh, no sir. No sir. All arrangement made. They are already told what to expect. Mrs. Stertevant is well known here. No problems."

Coming down the steps in the sun, the mud-spattered apes were a real sight. Minutes later a Customs officer buzzed up in a Fiat. He was young, maybe twenty-five or six. He was remarkably calm in the presence of seven large apes grouped just inside the hangar of the community airstrip. The uniformed man conversed with Scarpita in Romansch, a dialect of the area. Glancing at the animals, he smirked only a little. Then he addressed Roger in English.

"Good day, sir. Welcome to Switzerland. Passport, please?"

Roger froze. Passport. Thank god he'd shoved it into his pocket before they fled, but with the climb and the fall and all that wading, was it still there? He felt for it. Yes. A little spongy, but in one piece. The officer gave it little more than a cursory glance, then returned it. He went up the stairway of the jet and stopped at the door, looking inside for a moment, then came back down. He looked at the animals one more time, counting them. Opening a binder he wrote on some forms, then tore out a copy and gave it to Scarpita. They shook hands and he drove off sedately. Customs, over and done.

"He is good man, these fellow." Scarpita enthused. "His father my friend. Everything in order, animals have six weeks permit to stay here. This can be extend with permission. If a you move them, you must a tell the authorities. You say me, I take care this, okay?" He smiled broadly, and for the first time Roger noticed his very fine gold tooth. "Now. You like go to the house, no? You are all tired, like to rest?" He motioned toward the waiting car. Roger looked over at the group. They huddled by the jet's stairs, hair matted, clothing smeared.

"Yes, sir. To the house, please. Is it far?"

"Pshhh. No! Just a fifteen minute is all. Very lovely drive, I a show you some nice sights.

"Roger, I called ahead for a room at Badrutt's in St. Moritz," Chuck interjected. "I'll tend to a few things with the plane here, then the hotel will send out a car. Call me if you need me." He slapped Roger on the back softly.

Roger orchestrated the passenger load-up. The route was spectacular, with mown meadows, postcard vistas, and Heidi-houses everywhere. Scarpita kept up a commentary on the various points of interest. Presently they turned in at a rustic gate, two granite boulders, and a barrier of sun-darkened timbers. High across the top there was a mammoth log, ancient letters carved into its surface. Scarpita read the inscription for Roger: "Blauhimmelheim": Blue Heaven House. Scarpita jumped out to open the gate, nothing automated here. Then they were motoring through a druidic, old-growth conifer forest. Sunlight shafted in patches through the towering trees, piercing the gloom along the mossy forest floor. After crossing a timber bridge over a rushing creek, they finally emerged into a rolling meadow. Rising beyond was a steep mountain, with patchwork slopes of forest and rock. And at its base was the house.

The house did its own talking. Straight out of a fairy-tale book. Two stories, all rough-hewn timbers and ginger-bread. Mullioned windows with planter-boxes spilling red geraniums. Shutters bright with old Engadiner patterns. There were river-rock chimneys and weathered porches and steeply pitched roofs covered with moss. Cows lounged around the emerald pastures in perfect deployment. Roger was astonished at Celine's reach, once again. He could only shake his head. They proceeded slowly up the circling gravel drive, lined now on both sides with split-rail fences. As they stopped in front of the house its full effect registered. The view from the veranda was a jaw-dropper: rolling meadows falling away to towering conifers, and beyond that, an array of jutting snow-capped peaks. No other houses, roads or power lines within view in any direction. The sound of softly clanking cow bells floated through the sparkling air. There was an overpowering sense of peacefulness, security, order, and majesty. Roger leaned on the hood of the car and just gaped. Scarpita had shared this moment with other visitors. He kept silent, knowing talk would only dilute the moment. Blauhimmelheim was, in much the same respect as Glenwhylden, a monumentally inspiring place, with a spirit all its own.

They were led up broad granite steps and through the cathedral arched front door. Inside, more magic. Santa Claus could live here, Roger thought. The house was a double for the North Pole workshop. Deer antler chandeliers on gnarled chains hung from rough-hewn beams. The floors were wide oaken planks, pitted and scored from over a century of use. Coarse and rugged hand-loomed rugs were scattered about. The furnishings were alpine, utilitarian, sturdy. Nothing fancy and nothing an afterthought. Everywhere the eye settled there was wholesome, solid comfort; perfect for a little mud on the boots or some good honest dirt on the seat of the pants.

Scarpita was talking again now, asking to show Roger the living quarters, the fully stocked kitchen, the bathrooms. On the second floor there were nine bedrooms, each with its own bath. Some were modest, one was quite grand.

"Anything more you require, Mr. Caldwell?" he finally asked.

"No, sir. I think we'll be just fine here. Thanks for all your help."

Turning to leave, the caretaker handed him a card. "Is my phone. I am just down the road," he said. "Anything, anything at all. No one will disturb you." As his car crunched away down the gravel drive, Roger sank wearily into a chair and closed his eyes.

"Jeeesus!" Trent howled as Scarpita's car disappeared. "I had no idea how hard it would be to shut up for so long!" He came away from the window, grandly gesturing at the interior of the house. "Good show, Roger. Truly grand. This place is great! Boy it's cold in here. How about some drinks? Who's for a cocktail? Where's the bar? I'll mix." He dodged off, seeking the liquor cabinet.

"Roger, this is wonderful, really." Betty came over and rubbed his shoulders. "I'm sorry I was so frightened last night. It all brought back bad memories."

He gave her a squeeze. "Betty, honey, if anybody had a right to freak it was you. And don't worry, nobody's going to chase us out of here. We're safe."

The first thing was to get cleaned up. They'd been living with a coating of sewer slime for a full day now. After their baths, the Orangs began a further exploration of the house, digging odd bits of warm clothing out of closets and chests. Roger found a telephone in the study and placed a call to Marsh Meadows house.

"Oh, Roger, thank heavens. I was about to call there to see if you'd arrived. Is everyone alright?"

"Yes, I think so. It was pretty hairy, though. Have you talked with Polk?"

"I have and I got the whole story. Wow, I didn't expect all of that. I guess it just shows you. But you all did splendidly. I'm quite impressed with how you handled it. Let's not get into the details here but I think it's all going to work out okay. I have my New York attorneys on it, they flew out there immediately. Oh, by the way, my Santa Barbara lawyer called this morning. He was a bit rattled by you and your friends. I hear you can throw your voice."

Roger smiled. "Oh, that? Yes, I learned it at the circus."

"I guess you're a dangerous type as well. Not at all what we thought. So I'm warned."

"Yes, ma'am. Got the wool pulled all the way down over your eyes."

They laughed, a welcome bit of comic relief.

"Well, anyway, the lawyers tell me nothing conclusive so far from the, uh—shall we say 'official tour' of the estate. My team says they're putting everything to rest. They say there wasn't any real evidence they could use. So we can at least hope that's about the last of it. I'm just glad no one was hurt and you made it out. My goodness. We'll talk more about it all later. Is the house there okay? I know you'll need some things. We're working on that as well."

Roger chuckled. "Mrs. Stertevant, the house is more than okay. It's incredible. We'll be fine. So you're saying we can relax a bit?"

"My word on it. Just lay low, don't make any calls if you can help it. I'm going to have a secure line set up for us within a day or so. My man there will handle your other immediate needs."

"Yes, he's great. Really nice, really helpful. We'll just hang out then. I guess I'll be hearing from you again soon."

"In a day or two. Get some rest and take care of my darlings."

After he hung up, Roger examined the gaping fireplace in the living room and saw that it was already laid with logs and kindling. He decided to set a match to it since the afternoon was closing in. A hearty blaze was soon crackling, and Emily flitted about, lighting a few candles and setting the big, informal dining table in the living room with some colorful plates she'd found in a cupboard. Ancient phonograph records were discovered on a bookcase shelf and they provided a scratchy background ambiance. Everyone was tired and jet-lagged but they pitched in and put together a nice, simple meal: some pasta, vegetables, garlic bread, sausages, and hearty Italian wine. Then came dishes of vanilla ice-cream, rich as sin.

During dinner, Artod raised a critical issue. "Roger, we've looked everywhere and there's only *one* television in the whole house. It's over there in the kitchen. It's pretty small. I had it on for awhile and it only gets *three* channels. Another thing: the programs are all in French and German. None of them are in English. I've checked, personally." He was knitting his fingers anxiously, looking and sounding like a heroin addict facing cold-turkey deprivation.

"Oh, really? Only three channels?" Roger hadn't even thought about this yet. But television was a huge part of the apes' lives and a great babysitter as well. "Okay, well, first thing tomorrow, I'll see what we can do. But, hey," he brightened, "maybe this is a good time to stop watching so much TV." He pointed at the bookcases. "Lots to read here."

Dead silence around the table. Finally, Artod responded "That's not funny."

The jet lag finally won out after dinner, and all the Orangs went off to bed. The house settled into peacefulness. Slipping on an old leather barn coat that he found on a hook by the door, Roger stepped out on the front veranda to take a bit of pristine alpine air before retiring. No stars overhead. Scattered snowflakes drifted down, illuminated by candlelight from the windows. His breath created great clouds—it had grown markedly colder. Without a TV forecast he could only guess, but with the temperature change and flakes already falling, by morning their surroundings would likely be a great deal whiter than when they arrived.

He went back in, and the worn staircase creaked agreeably as he climbed to the second floor. Undressing in his snug room, he slipped under a fluffy down comforter. The threat they had fled was, at least for now, far away.

Chapter 26

When Pongo got in that Porsche and drove out of the gates of Glenwhylden, he wasn't merely acting out an adolescent fantasy. It wasn't just the thrill of speed, or his love of machinery, or even the danger that compelled him to steal the car and go joyriding. Something more important, irresistible, and significant made him do it. He was being beckoned by a monumentally powerful force.

All of the Orangs were heading somewhere. They were transforming. Daily, their awareness increased of the workings of things in the world and of their own developing minds. How did all this happen?

"Revolution is the cause of evolution, not its symptom."

It is a fact that for many centuries, even millennia, beings from other parts of this universe have been visiting this planet. It's no big secret, and it's no big deal, either, at least not to thoughtful people. It's how things are. If you need any verification, just go outside on a clear, moonless night in a place free from human lights, and gaze upward. Look at the Milky Way. That vast smear, trillions of spots of light, isn't just individual stars; many points are entire galaxies, with billions of stars and planets *within them*. Now really, seriously, looking at that, doing the math, can you really tell yourself that *we are alone* amid all that? We're *the only ones*? No. And while we're not exactly the village idiots, we're definitely not the most advanced of all beings either. We can hold our heads up; technologically, we've made some good progress. But compared to the real aces out there, well, we've still got *a lot to learn.*

Okay, so. Other beings come here—primarily for scientific reasons, it is to be imagined—but doubtless there is probably a percentage of the traffic that could be classified as recreational. We're a nice-looking destination. All that blue water, those white clouds. Pretty appealing if your home planet is an incinerator with a poison-gas atmosphere. And there is no shortage of places like that. A lot of them got that way after their occupants did sufficient damage so that the whole ecosystem got out of whack and just keeled over, leaving the technologically advanced residents to live in a shit-heap of their own making. A lot of people believe that is precisely what we ourselves are doing here at this very time. That might well be, but the fact is that we have not yet fully accomplished it. So at least for now, we still have a damn gorgeous piece of real-estate. An inviting place to visit.

Some will ask, "Well, if they're so superior, why don't they just attack us and take us over? Maybe eat us or something? Like in the movies?" Okay, let's clear that up. Once you've developed the ability to travel across vast space, and you've conquered much of the physics of the universe and you have a scientific culture on that level, pretty much the *last thing on your mind would be* "Great, now let's get out there and destroy the lives of lesser sentient beings and rip up their planets and crash their whole worlds!" See, that's the reasoning of a lower-developed (stupid) consciousness. Highly evolved beings are way past such foolishness; that's something you do when you're infantile—sort of like bashing another kid's head during a dispute for possession of a plastic bucket in the sand-box. Once you've got a Ph.D. you're just not there anymore. It works for movies, but in the real universe—no. The reality is, the higher the development of consciousness, the more love becomes the controlling element in the scheme of behavior.

So, beings who have the means to get here from far away simply aren't going to zap us with their death rays.

Most people would be shocked to learn just exactly how many beings are out there who *have* those means. During various segments of our history these "aliens" have had either fairly direct contact with us, or else they've seen problems with that and deemed it necessary to give us the silent treatment. We are presently in just such a time of sequestration. They're not talking to us right now.

Why is our government so damned secretive about this whole business? You'd best believe they know all about this; *they know all about it.* They've got files and documentation that fills warehouses. So, why not tell? Because they believe that to do so would scare the crap out of Joe and Mary Sixpack. As long as it's confined to science-fiction movies and books, no problem. But you start in with the authorities giving it all color and form and, boy howdy, you're going to see some real foaming at the mouth and tearing of the hair. It doesn't dovetail terribly well with some of the popular dogma, either. Therefore, no one with credibility from either side of the ionosphere is owning up. That's it.

So what happened at Glenwhylden in 1988? Nothing more than a weather-related aircraft accident, but wrapped around a classic bad-luck-good-luck, good-luck-bad-luck situation.

Seven Orangutans from the remote jungles of Borneo initially had the bad luck to be displaced from their ancestral habitats. They then had the good luck to be rescued and removed to a beautiful, safe place where they were living quite comfortably. And then there were some unidentified visitor-types who had the good luck to encounter severe Earth weather conditions they were interested in observing using their drone-craft. They then had the bad luck of having their probe get nailed by lightning, whereupon it crashed and disintegrated right smack on top of the place where the previously unlucky and now lucky (?) Orangutans were domiciled.

What wasn't clear at all was how the material from the downed drone—the plasma or vapor or whatever it was—took its effect on the Orangutans. What physical processes facilitated their remarkable new abilities? When they arrived in Switzerland the answers to these questions weren't known, even to George. But soon, these and other even more intriguing questions came to be resolved in stunning fashion.

On the first morning, Roger opened his eyes and dreamily gazed up at the timbered ceiling in his bedroom. The air against his face was sharply cold, so different from the balmy climate of Santa Barbara. The house was quiet. He turned over and looked out the window. Incredible: judging from what was mounded on the window-sill, perhaps two feet of snow had fallen overnight. The pastoral scene surrounding the house was transformed into a glorious winter wonderland. Nothing was stirring out in the whiteness. He swung his legs out of bed and pulled on his freezing clothes. Celine said the house was heated, but with the fireplaces blazing he had neglected to think about turning on the system the previous evening. Better find the thermostat and get the place warmed up before the Orangs awakened.

Heading downstairs he soon found it—a modern thermostat on the living room wall. He dialed it up and heard creaking and groaning noises. Baseboard radiators were protesting as they came to life. He went over to the fireplace and stuffed new paper, kindling and split logs in on top of the previous evening's embers. In no time the fire was popping joyfully. Now for something to warm the stomach. Out in the kitchen he got a kettle on and rummaged through the pantry. It was stuffed, though all the boxes and cans wore labels in

German or French. He managed to find coffee, tea, cereal and jam, then went over to the big refrigerator to pursue butter, eggs, cheese, fruit, milk, and juice. It was all there, in great variety. Clearly Scarpita had been to the market and it seemed that he'd thought of everything. There was delectable looking ham and bacon, and the bread box held six or seven different fresh loaves. This was shaping up to be a stellar day. Roger was in the process of setting the big rough-planked kitchen table, when Emily came in, shivering. She had a blanket pulled over her head and wore a huge grin.

"It's all white outside! That really is snow out there, isn't it Roger?" She stage whispered, as if the sound of her voice might cause the pristine snowfall to vanish like a delicate dream. "I've been looking out at it for quite awhile—I can't believe how beautiful it is! I didn't want to get up and wake the others...but I thought I heard somebody down here."

"Yep, that's really snow," Roger grinned back. "Did you sleep well? You look very cold. I just got the heat on a few minutes ago and a fire's going in the main room. Why don't you go in there and sit by it? You can warm up while I get breakfast ready."

She looked over all the ingredients Roger had brought out onto the table.

"Oh, no, honey. I could never let you do all this by yourself. Don't be silly. I'll be fine once I move around a little. Let me help you with all that."

The house was soon comfortably warm and the others straggled down. They had on most of the clothing they had found, just layered one thing on top of another. They chattered away about the snow, the mountains, the house, their rooms.

The phone rang around eight-thirty: Scartaino Scarpita. Everything okay? He would be on the property later in the morning with workmen to clear the roads and take care of the cows.

A string of cold, bright sunny days ensued. Boxes filled with the best snow-gear soon arrived. Although the stuff didn't fit the Orangs exactly, it was quite adequate to allow them to go on walks with Roger, tramping through the woods behind the house, and to sit out on the back terrace, protected from the wind, and bask in the sun. After some measurements were taken, custom clothing was ordered from a shop in Zurich. With amusement, Roger imagined the likely puzzlement there about the odd dimensions.

The television issue had been taken up with Scartaino Scarpita. He explained that they could get a large satellite dish installed, but these weren't very popular in the valley. The looming mountains limited the range of satellites the dish could pick up to the east and west. So a dish never did get installed. The apes still watched some television—they got a few more sets but spent far less time glued to the screens than they had in Glenwhylden's media room. The language problem was easily solved: within weeks they all learned to understand German and French, just by watching the programs. They all became fluent and even spoke the languages with skill. Roger was confounded as they talked between themselves in French while enthusing about food. In German they abused and cursed each other.

A few weeks passed and the winter days grew shorter. Absent all that television exposure they began to get more involved in reading. The library at the house was large, but they also asked for books to be sent over from America. Favorites were passed around; Emerson was a hot item (they loved his essay on self-reliance) as were Proust, James Thurber, F. Scott Fitzgerald, Descartes, T.S. Eliot, and Einstein. They plowed through thick volumes on religion and philosophy, reading the Bible, the Torah, the Bhaghavad Gita, the Upanishads, the Koran, and the Book of Mormon, as well as tracts on Buddhism and Native American religious practices that Celine and Abby had collected along their travels. In addition to all that, they had newspapers delivered daily, in three languages, and they read them all. At any given time Orangutans were curled up in wing-back chairs by the fireplace, in window-seats, or retreated into far corners, deeply absorbed in some book or paper.

It was a sea change, all this, and their whole manner began to shift. The atmosphere was like a university faculty library. Contrast that with Glenwhylden's media room where the apes seemed casual about absorbing knowledge. That wasn't a probing, scholarly kind of interest in the subject matter, it was more a relentless vacuuming of anything and everything.

Once at Blauhimmelheim, the switch to books as a primary knowledge source created a different way of relating to the information. It was measured, more spiritual, scientific. What they were learning from books was arguably of greater consequence than what could be gleaned from television. Although they hadn't completely ignored the "good" programs in the media room back at Glenwhylden—after all, they had over twenty screens going at once—there was still bigger interest in the mindless sitcoms and action-adventure crap. Switzerland brought peaceful evenings around the fireplace, the setting for lively discussions of things that had been read during the day.

Roger began to find himself in over his head, not familiar enough with the subject matter to offer any significant contribution. Sometimes he saw them all sitting in a group, earnestly talking and showing each other notes. In scarcely a month the apes had developed a new level of intellect vastly superior even to what they had formerly possessed at Glenwhylden.

Switzerland had drawn them all much closer and the old frustrated tensions had vanished. They were now a lively family. In fact, there was only one real problem lately: headaches. All of the apes were getting them on a near daily basis, and Roger kept doling out the Tylenol. On the phone, Mark Lewis offered that it was probably the altitude. Blauhimmelheim sat at 8,400 feet, and the Orangs had spent their lives near sea-level. "The headaches will probably clear up, Roger," he said. "I wouldn't worry too much. Just get 'em to exercise, their bodies will adjust."

So a good walk everyday became another new fixture of life in the mountains. Roger usually had three or four companions for the daily tramp through the woods. They went, no matter the weather. If it was blowing hard and snowing, they bundled up and shortened the route, but never canceled. Some days the hike would take them to an overlook above the house. There was an ancient warming hut there, and the hiking party would sit on the porch, eating chocolate and talking.

One morning it was Roger and George, just the two of them. The day was overcast and sullen, with snow imminent. During the hike up George was quiet, but once they reached the porch and sat down he turned to Roger with a sense of purpose.

"Roger, I'm glad we're alone. I need to talk with you about important things. Have you talked to Kerri lately?"

"Well, actually, I have, George. Let's see, I called her a few nights ago. She's doing well, just about to get out of school for Christmas. She misses you guys."

"Yes. Well, I'm glad you're keeping in touch with her."

"You are?" Roger smiled, pleased. "Mind if I ask why?"

"It's because of something that I've been learning about lately." He looked away and scanned the valley below, stretching out his fingers, tracing the wispy fog-banks that braced against the shins of the mountain slopes. "The ways people, and just about all other things, really, are connected. You and Kerri, you and Celine, Abby, me, the others. All of us. There's a lot going back and forth that I didn't really have much awareness of until just lately."

"What's going back and forth?"

"It's...matter, actually. But really fine—very small *things*." He slowly looked over at Roger. "You and Kerri have material in your bodies that is identical, because it came from the same place a long, long time ago. It's a little hard to describe. Let's just say that you and Kerri are made from the same stuff, at least in part. That's one of the reasons why you like her so much, and why she likes you. It's powerful when two beings with a lot of the same stuff in them come together and focus on doing things. Accomplishing things. Like Celine and Abby, or you and Kerri. The connections have a random element to them, but then there are also bigger, cyclical forces." George waited, concerned he wasn't getting his message across. "Roger, do you know anything about turbulence?"

"Turbulence? You mean like the weather?"

George shifted on the bench, holding his boots out and tapping them together, watching snow clumps fall off. "Yes, the weather. But any kind of turbulence. See, if you made a slow-motion film of the snow falling off my boots here, you'd be able to see the way the particles fell—very random. I could tap the boots a million times, and the pattern would be different a million times. Turbulence causes the randomness, in effect. But, now, what I've learned lately, is that there are patterns of repetition in everything. Even randomness isn't really random, if you look at it on a large enough scale.

Everything eventually repeats. If you go far enough, you will come back to where you started. Everything is a cycle. Little ones inside of bigger ones, on up. But along the way, there can be diversions, like eddies in a current. That's turbulence. And what may look like chaos in the short term is actually organization on the finest level. See?"

Roger struggled to understand, at least a little. Maybe he'd experienced this as he floated face-down in the Tornquist's swimming pool. He'd felt peaceful and orderly, surveying the bottom of the pool, soothingly crossed and re-crossed by the refracted light lines resulting from the surface ripples. Turbulence. Patterns. Random, and yet somehow organized. But he still didn't quite get where the Orang was going with this.

He looked into George's round face, the eyes black and hypnotically full of moment. At that moment he and the little red ape were in a bubble, high in the Swiss Alps, with all the time in the world. Nothing else mattered, and all he wanted to do was hear what George would say next.

"Roger, there are problems. Our own kind of turbulence, I suppose. It's time you should know."

He stood up and shuffled, leaving wing-like patterns in the fine dusting of snowflakes that had drifted onto the porch.

"The beings or entities involved in the crash of that spacecraft are beginning to contact us. We've spoken about it among ourselves and we all seem to be having similar experiences. It doesn't involve words. The closest I could come to describing it would be the way you can download information from one computer to another. It's not sequential. I think it's actually instantaneous, it doesn't take any time. At first it happened at night, in our sleep. But early this morning, when I was just lying in bed, I might have been awake, I had a short bit of contact with these kindred beings."

Roger was astonished. "Contact...with kindred beings?" He squinted. "Are you sure? Maybe it's just dreaming."

George pulled at the parka he was wearing, adjusting it on his shoulders, cinching the hood tighter around his moon-face.

"No. I thought that too, at first. That's logical. But the messages are identical between all of us. And they happen at the same time. We didn't get around to comparing notes right away. I didn't want to start in on it until I had a better idea of whether it was real or not. I just had my suspicions. Then Pongo read an article about astronauts, how in the future there would be a helmet where you just think commands for the machine and it would do that thing. Something just clicked from that, and he told me about his experience with this information coming to him. He said he had felt like a machine responding to someone else, or to the mind of something else—that sort of thing. He described the feeling he'd gotten from the message, and it was exactly the same as what I'd gotten. It happened on the same night. We asked the others and Emily said she had it, and it was the same thing, exactly. The others, also."

"Everyone?"

"Yes."

The day was not getting any lighter—the clouds were thickening and a breeze began to stir in the tops of the snow-covered pines around them. George exhaled a cloud and leaned forward, resting his gloved knuckles on the floorboards of the porch. This primitive pose was something the apes rarely did anymore. His mild voice darkened.

"Now, Roger, they are warning us of a danger. It's the headaches and our brains. Our brains are growing, you see, because of how fast we can absorb information. It's something that came from these other beings, from that thing that crashed over us. It got into us, became part of us. It's like a new operating system for a computer, but this is a new way of functioning for our brains. A new way of uploading and interpreting things. That's why we're kindred with them now." Then George pivoted toward Roger and tapped his own head with his finger. "But because our skulls are hard bone, they can't expand for the new cells. We weren't designed for this. So if it keeps going this way it will kill us."

This was like a punch to the gut. "Oh, George," Roger said urgently, "please don't say that. That might not be true at all. Mark thinks you guys are just having altitude sickness."

"Mark is a good doctor. I think he saved our lives after the incident. But he's wrong this time."

Roger chewed like he'd tasted something bitter. "What should we do then? There must be some way to deal with it."

"I'm not sure there is."

"There has to be. If it's true, we'll figure something out, George. I promise you." Roger heard a note of desperation in his voice even as he made the assertion.

"I hope so, Roger. But it makes you think, doesn't it? Why did it happen *to us*? Orangutans. Not to humans; not to René Descartes, or Leonardo DaVinci, or Albert Einstein. Why?" He paused, scanning the distance.

As Roger floundered for a response to this, George, just like he had the time he'd resolved the opposing statements on the computer screen in the media room, came up with his own answer. "Well, there it is. Turbulence. Randomness. An accident, but not really."

He lowered himself back onto the bench. "You know what I said about accomplishing things, Roger? Since this has come up, it's made us all focus. And we've decided, as a group, that if our time is limited, we want to do something important while we're able. We want to use what time we've been given."

"Really? What would you like to do?"

"We're working on an idea, a plan for a real accomplishment. I think we'll have it figured out in a few more days. We'll tell you then." George folded his arms, finished.

Roger fell silent, too, trying to wrap his head around all he had just heard. They sat awhile, watching the weather change. The cold began to seep through their clothes. When Roger could feel his feet and hands getting numb, he stood up and stamped around.

"Well, George. No point in us both freezing to death up here. How about we go back to the house and get warm?"

They crunched down the trail, with the wind rising around them, knocking cascades of powder, randomly, from the branches of the trees.

Chapter 27

Butch Turnbull leveled a blank stare at the rows of garish cereal boxes in the Santa Barbara Wal-Mart Superstore. Normally he would have just grabbed the old favorite, "Wheat Chex", but his shopping experience, like the rest of his life, had changed. Now he had more time to decide what he might buy. He told himself he should relax, try different things, break with tradition. Live a little. Maybe get that new stuff he saw advertised on TV all the time, "Blueberry Crunch Clusters". Supposed to be good for your heart. Turnbull pulled the box down from the shelf and perused the label with all its new-age decorations. He snorted, tossing the box into his cart.

Six weeks earlier he had retired with honors from the California Highway Patrol. Now, for the first time in twenty-nine years, he no longer had to roll out of the sack at five a.m., hurriedly pull on his uniform, grab his gun and badge, and hustle down to headquarters to begin his shift. He had always told himself, on those seemingly endless afternoons sitting along some baking-hot stretch of deserted road waiting for a speeder or an expired registration to pass by, that when he retired he'd live the good life. Go fishing, finally hunt elk in Colorado, maybe even get an R.V. for a tour around the American West. Turnbull had been married once when he was much younger, and the brief bad experience had kept him solo ever since. No kids, thankfully. He figured his job would make having another wife a little tough anyway; that's how it was for most of the other officers he worked with. Long hours, unpredictable schedules. Lots of stories about disharmony, lots of divorces like his. He didn't need that bullshit; he could date a little and get his rocks off once in a while without having to buy the whole package. It worked for him. Turnbull always figured the right lady would turn up once he was retired. After all, he was only fifty three—still young and in damn good shape. The pieces would fall into place.

Yet now that he was actually off the job for good, he was having a little trouble adjusting. For one thing, there wasn't any action as a retired CHP officer. At least when he had been on the job, there was the occasional high-speed chase, or a fight with a drunk, or something to get his adrenaline flowing. He had served for years on City-County SWAT: some of those call-outs had ended in gunfire. Turnbull had two fatal "O.I.S's" (officer-involved-shootings) on his record. That was all behind him now. The days of retirement had already become boring and predictable and he had to battle the frequent urge to phone his old colleagues and ask how things were going at the station.

But beyond the humdrum there was something else bugging him, and it wouldn't go away. It was the face of that huge "ape" thing, if that's what it really was. That enormous face, that unbelievable strength, the *talking*, good god. The way it bested him with ease, then kissed him goodbye before fleeing the scene of that bizarre traffic stop high up on Sheffield Road. In fact, *that* might have been the most troublesome impression of all: that the thing, in the midst of subduing him, still seemed *to love him in some way*. It was being kind, despite the confrontational circumstances. He could not reconcile this with anything he'd ever experienced before. The whole tableau was seared into his mind. Turnbull had nightmares about it, waking up in a sweat, wrestling with the sheets. Sometimes he'd see a black Porsche in traffic and it all came raging back: the utterly transformative four minutes of that encounter.

The investigation following the raid on the big house hadn't given him any great satisfaction. Beyond a few pictures of apes (like the one he spotted on the dresser mirror), nothing much else could be found to prove that the house or anyone in it had any real connection with the humiliating fight he'd been in. Maybe some guy had used the garage to work on cars, but again, no physical evidence of the specific Porsche used in the crime. And the old woman on the east coast who owned the house...well, she possessed more wealth than many small countries. She wielded immense power; her lawyers had mounted a strenuous defense, effectively stopping any further investigation of the incident dead in its tracks. Turnbull's ears reddened with anger when his commander called him in for one of his last meetings before he retired.

"Sarge, we're dropping the assault thing with the uh, you know, the ape, or whatever. It's not panning out." The lieutenant looked out through his office window, clearly wanting to get this over with. It had been a bit of an embarrassment and one reporter had already been sniffing around. Not good. "So, chalk it up, Butch. The D.A. says we've got other cases to work and this thing goes in the files."

"Are you saying you don't believe me, L.T.?"

The commander's face darkened. "I didn't say that, Turnbull. And it doesn't matter anyway. I said we're ending the investigation. Understand?"

It wouldn't have been so bad, but Turnbull had a few enemies around headquarters, and there had been some merciless ribbing after he insisted that his account of the fight with the ape had been accurate, talking and all. Shit, he knew what he'd seen and heard, damn it. He hadn't hallucinated. Still, he was left to retire with a feeling that after all the small victories of his career he'd lost the really important contest at the end. It was shaming.

He hung out at the gym and the driving range, went to the movies, puttered in the yard and garage. One day he dropped into Jake's Bar and Grill for lunch. The place was a favorite watering hole for aging attorneys and the old-school Santa Barbara law enforcement crowd. Dark walls covered with pictures of retired judges, ex-police chiefs, that sort of thing. The simple food was great and the bartender didn't scrimp on the pour. Nobody cared if you had a smoke.

It was coming on Christmas; there were a few cheesy decorations and scattered strings of colored lights festooning the bar. Looking around the dim room, Turnbull spotted a long-time acquaintance sitting alone at a corner table, enjoying the prime rib, reading a paper. He walked over.

"How you doing, counselor? Keeping yourself busy?"

The older man looked up, startled. "Well, hey Butch! This is a nice surprise. I was wondering about you. Heard you hung it up." Phillip Holmbard extended his hand as he wiped meat juice from his chin with a napkin.

"Yep. Got my time in. Guess I'll be in here a little more often now."

"Well, yeah, why not? You worked hard." Holmbard motioned at an empty chair. "By yourself? Why don't you join me?"

The attorney had already downed two martinis, the empties sitting by his elbow. But now he called for another one. Turnbull ordered a Miller High Life and a ham sandwich.

"Martinis for lunch. Boy, you lawyers sure have the life."

Holmbard grimaced. "I know. Listen, I usually don't. You know me. But it's a been a little tough lately."

"Yeah? How so?"

"Oh," Holmbard waved his hand dismissively, "I can't say exactly. Just work, that's all. Things have been sort of crazy."

Now Turnbull remembered: Holmbard was one of the attorneys working for the rich old woman who owned the estate that he and the SWAT team had raided nearly two months earlier. In fact it was well known that managing the estate was the lawyer's only substantial gig. He bit his lip, suddenly wanting to ask a few things from an old friend. But he also knew quite well, there was a limit. Client privilege and all. He'd have to be careful.

"Really? Sorry to hear that, Phil." He paused for effect, then "Ohhhh, I think I get it. You mean all that stuff that happened with the house and all." For a moment he halted as the waiter came to set another martini and a tissue-wrapped bottle of beer on the table. Then he resumed with an ingratiating leer. "Well, now, Phil, we both know *a little something extra* about *that business*, don't we?"

Holmbard managed a sloppy smile himself. "Yes, Butch, we do. We sure as hell do."

After that ugly ride to the airport and the embarrassing search of *his* estate the same night, Holmbard had been put to work on little details of the clean-up. Mostly he was elbowed aside by Celene Stertevant's crack team of New York attorneys. They'd flown into Santa Barbara within a day and were quickly in charge of the whole affair, knocking down any further attempts by authorities to re-enter Glenwhylden. Holmbard felt like a lackey, sent to file a few motions at the behest of the big boys. They treated him with faintly concealed contempt; it was clear he was nothing but a glorified janitor: the local yokel. It rankled him mightily. But beyond that, Holmbard was convinced that Roger Caldwell was out to get him fired. He had finagled "face time". The old lady had fallen for the gigolo; he was getting paid ten times more than Holmbard and now he was moving in for the kill. As far as the attorney knew, Roger was currently off traveling on Mrs.

Stertevant's jet, but he'd certainly be back. The young man was clever and scheming, it was clear, and he aimed to get rid of anybody who might stand in his way. Holmbard was losing sleep, consumed with paranoia and hatred for his rival. If he wanted to survive, he had to find a way to stop him.

"Of course, I'm retired now, Phil," Turnbull continued deliberately, keeping a steady gaze on his old pal. "Got nobody to really talk with these days, you know how lonely it can be for us old cops. So stop me if I'm out of line here, but I guess I can ask you if you at least saw the original incident report?" He glanced around casually, making sure no one was within easy earshot.

Holmbard hesitated, knocking back half the martini. He knew his job, he knew where the line was, but right then he dearly needed a friend. He'd been keeping it all inside. "Yes, Butch, as a matter of fact, I certainly did." He lowered his voice. "And I guess we need to get it understood, all we talked about here today was golf. Am I right?"

Turnbull nodded, hand around his beer.

"Okay then. The way I got it, seems you had some kind of a road-side dust-up involving the driver of a sports car," Holmbard muttered, raising his eyebrows. "And let's just say the driver you tried to arrest for speeding was a little bit...unusual. You could say, he...was *something very unusual*."

"Uh-huh. Right. You could sure say that."

Bleary-eyed, Holmbard leaned over closer. "Well. Suppose I told you something *similar* happened to me?"

Turnbull's butt cheeks tightened, raising him a full half inch in his chair. "Is that so?"

"Yep. That *is* so. And you know, Butch old buddy, I probably should just shut the fuck up right now. But I happen to know you're not happy about the way things turned out, and the fact is, neither am I."

"Think you'd be right about that, too."

Each man had skin in this game. Both of them had worked long, professional careers and both had recently been made to feel deeply humiliated. Both were older single men with no families and very little to look forward to. They understood each other.

For a long moment Phil Holmbard stared at his dining companion and Turnbull could see the wheels turning. He took a big gulp of his beer, hoping it would encourage Phil to drain the rest of that third martini. It worked.

Poking at the now-cold remnants of beef and horseradish sauce on his plate, Holmbard lowered his head and hunched his shoulders with resolve. "Butch. I happened to, uh, end up at the airport...on the night the house got searched," he growled. "Was at a private hangar. Just so happens." He was barely audible above the background noise of the lunch crowd. "Got a surprise call to give some folks a ride. And well, I think I might have seen *that same driver*. He, uh...*said* some things to me too. Called me a 'pompous motherfucker'. Not the kind of thing you'd forget. Close as I am to you right now. At first I thought it was a trick, who wouldn't? You follow me? Then later I saw your report." Holmbard's eyes narrowed. "Well, now, that got me to thinking, that's for damn sure. I was actually hoping I'd run into you. In fact, I was maybe gonna call you. So I don't know. But something really strange is going on, Butch. I don't think there's any doubt. That's what I've been thinking since then."

Turnbull exhaled, beyond overjoyed it had been so easy. "That makes two of us. Well, I'll be. And...it was the *same driver*, you think?"

"Well, look at at what happened to you and me both. I'd bet on it."

Holmbard pulled himself back before he went too much further, but he still let it slip that the "driver" and some "other critters like him" had gotten onto a big private jet that night. A black jet. And yes, there was a connection to the estate. "So maybe if you do some checking on your own, Butch," he concluded, "you might just find out some things that you and I have both been wondering about. I'd kind of like to hear about it if you do. In fact, I'd really like to hear about it. Could mean a lot to me. And, hell, I can't stop you from having yourself a little fun, can I? Now that you're retired and all?"

Chapter 28

Four days until Christmas. Especially since his parents died, Roger had dreaded this time of year. It wasn't the holiday itself, or the idea of giving gifts. And he didn't begrudge the rest of the world the fact that he was alone at a time when families were together. He didn't dislike the traditional holiday meal of turkey and trimmings, the champagne, the eggnog, all that. The decorations? Within reason, not unpleasant. No, what truly spoiled it for him and made him wish he could just skip it entirely, was all the unholy hype that was crammed down the collective throat, starting even before Halloween. All the merchants, desperate to wring the absolute maximum of those all-important Christmas dollars out of the beleaguered shoppers, launching non-stop barrages, salvos one atop the other, festering all over the airwaves and engorging the billboards, newspapers and magazines: buy, Buy, BUY, BUY FASTER, DAMN IT! People on the streets wear a crazed look as the deadline approaches. Yes, it was the advertising, and the hardly-if-at-all veiled implication that if you didn't buy something for each and every deserving individual in your sphere then you are a stingy bastard, a regular tightfisted Scrooge of the most determinate rank.

And then, the most annoying element in the whole mélange, central to all the hype, the core structure upon which all the other frippery gets hung: the Christmas music. Synthesized, sampled, cutesified, twisted, molded, pumped-up and pressure-injected into everything, everywhere. Relentlessly repeated: commercials, social gatherings, office co-workers whistling, little electronic-chip-loaded pop-up cards, small children with their mothers in the supermarket check-out line lamely re-running only the first bar of one of the anthems, over and over and over. You could not get away from it. Someone once said that there are only eight Christmas songs. A sarcastic observation, yet not far off the mark. As far as Roger was concerned, this onslaught, building to a screaming fury on the Christmas-day television and radio programs essentially ruined the holiday for him. Maybe he was a scrooge...it didn't seem to bother any of his friends. Gwynn reveled in it, worshiping the decked-out department stores, ogling the bangle-trash like a three-year-old supplicant. But for Roger it was painful, it was harassing, it put him in a funk.

He awoke this day in his snug bed by the dormer window of the cozy bedroom in Blauhimmelheim and realized this could be the best Christmas in years, perhaps in his entire life. There had been no commercialism to endure, no guilt-inducing advertising, no force-fed music. Oh, the house was decorated with fragrant pine boughs. There were candles and candy. Cookies were being baked. There was hot apple-jack and there was a tree, embellished with popcorn chains and little home-made figurines that the Orangs had fashioned out of aluminum foil. No sequentially twinkling electric lights. He was assured by Celine that there would be carols sung around the old piano. And there would be gifts, of course, because the Orangs looked forward to them with the conviction of children. But there was no hype. This was more like it, this was Christmas. Hallelujah.

But beyond that, there was something else most delicious for Roger to dwell upon as he opened his eyes this overcast morning. He dreamily let the dimensions of this other element slip about his mind, like a fine silk scarf drawn slowly over bare skin. It was the proximity of a certain someone who had maintained a hell of a good hold on his emotions: Kerri Lewis. Celine and Abby would fly in this morning from Old Lyme and they were bringing Kerri along. They had sent her a ticket to come out from California to join them. Everyone would enjoy a reunion for the holidays in the Alps.

At nine o'clock Roger rode to the airfield with Scartaino Scarpita to pick them up. Kerri was the first to come down the stairway, ahead of Celine and Abby. She wore a black body stocking, olive-drab military style parka, and Doc Marten boots. When she saw Roger, her eyes lit up like sparklers. She gave him a bear-hug that nearly broke his spine. He couldn't believe how good it made him feel. Under the padding of her clothing, her body felt as hard as chiseled marble. She kissed him, and he jumped as her sharp teeth nipped.

"You're bad!" he whispered in her ear.

She leaned back and hooded her eyes. "You think that was bad? We'll just see about that later, mister."

The next day he took her up to the warming hut. By late morning the sky was dark and a steady snow was falling. They stoked up the cast-iron stove and soon the hut was toasty. Kerri began stripping off her clothes. Roger sat grinning at the show. She dropped her shirt on the floor, then pulled him up and swiftly disrobed him as well.

"Boy, have I missed you," he whispered.

"Same here, and you're gonna find out how much right now."

They spent the next two hours ravishing each other, pausing only to throw a few more logs into the stove. The snow continued, and by the time they got dressed, the trail down the mountain had deep drifts all the way. Had Roger not been so familiar with the route, they could have easily become lost. They charged through the deep powder, letting themselves just fall down some of the steep sections. They played like children, cavorting all the way back to the house. Roger couldn't remember when he had laughed so hard. By the time they stumbled into the mudroom they looked like snowmen, covered from head to toe.

"Oh, goodness, there you two are!" Betty exclaimed. "We were getting worried about you, it's snowing so hard out there."

"Everything's fine, Betty," Kerri grinned, shaking off her parka. "I had a great local guide."

"Well I'll just bet you did." It was Emily, who looked up from some small squashes she was carving." Don't you wear her out now, Roger. She's just a young thing."

The two apes howled. Betty, all of her big yellow teeth garishly exposed, pointed her long finger at Emily, then lobbed a potato at her. She ducked, and the tuber struck a hanging pot, which rang like a gong. "Well, there's lots left over from lunch. The others finished awhile ago." Betty dabbed at her eyes with a tea towel. "You two hungry?"

"Oh my god, famished!" Kerri had peeled down to her tights. She tossed her boots and socks into a corner and padded over to Betty, giving her a big hug. Betty squeezed her for a second, then held her out at arm's length.

"Kerri child, you look positively radiant. Your cheeks are all rosy."

Kerri grabbed a wheat roll from the bowl on the table and began demolishing it.

"Why thank you, Betty," she said between mouthfuls. "Must be this mountain air, it agrees with me."

Betty lifted her chin sarcastically toward Kerri. "Oh, right, girl. It must be the air up here. Uh-huh." She turned toward Roger. "Celine and Abby are in the library, Roger. Celine asked me to tell you they'd like to see you when you got back from your walk."

He grabbed a quick sandwich, then dodged upstairs to his room and put on some dry clothes. He found the two elderly women sitting by the fireplace. Celine was reading and Abby was slumped to one side, snoring lustily. Celine smiled and put her finger to her lips as Roger came into the room. She kept her voice quite low.

"Sit down by me here, Roger. I had a fascinating conversation with Pongo this morning while you were out walking."

He pulled up an ottoman and hunkered beside Celine's chair.

She inclined her head toward him.

"Now, I understand from Pongo that something extraordinary is happening. He also told me that George had a talk with you about it right before I got here. Why didn't you mention it to me?"

Roger nodded, clasping his hands together. "Well, I wasn't sure it wasn't just dreaming. Are we talking about the same thing? The business about them being contacted by kindred beings, or something along those lines?"

"Of course. What else?"

"Right. Well, like I said, I didn't know how real it was. What do you make of it?"

"What I make of it, Roger, is that it is completely real, and I think you'd better get used to the idea. It might just get a lot more intense. These Orangs wouldn't play a mind game about something like this. Pongo went into great detail in describing it to Abby and me. Oh yes, it's the truth alright. He mentioned the warnings to you?"

"Actually, yes, he did." Roger was feeling a bit defensive, realizing that he might have fumbled the ball somewhat.

Celine sighed and leaned back a little. Abby snorted and jerked awake, groggily opening her eyes. She squinted at Roger, adjusting her eyeglasses.

"Ah, Roger!" she rattled. "I couldn't figure out what you were doing there for a moment." She looked questioningly at Celine. "Goodness. I must have dropped off, eh? Damn, I hate this getting old crap. No use for it at all. Okay, sorry. I'm up. What's going on?"

Celine jerked her thumb at Roger. "I was just asking him about the headaches."

Abby sat up straight. "Ah. Ah. Oh, yes. Very dangerous possibilities. You understand how it could be, Roger? Their retention of knowledge is phenomenal. They learn so easily and they seem to retain everything they learn. They're not like humans, even the smartest of us only use about four percent of our brains. God, they're brilliant, all of them. Can you believe the things they're all talking about now?"

Celine chuckled nervously. "They've read almost every book in my library here, and they can make direct quotes from all of them, and connect the information from different books to produce theory, for heaven's sakes." She glanced at Abby. "We feel like dumb bunnies half the time when we talk with them now. It floors me. George's computer is on line nearly all day, every day, hooked up to databases all over the world. He's sucking up information like a sponge."

"He asked me last night if he could get two new computers," Roger said. "Showed me the pictures in a catalog. I told him to ask you."

"Of course I told him he could. It's just fascinating. Abby and I traveled all over the world seeking this kind of enlightened beings, and now, well, here they are." She paused, staring into the fireplace. "What bothers me is that I'm almost ninety years old. Damn! I'm not afraid of dying, I just want to be around to see where all this is leading! This is the culmination of a lifelong search and I'm concerned my body might not get me the last few yards."

"Oh crap, Celine," Abby growled. "You don't look a day over eighty-five." They all laughed.

Then Abby became pensive. "But if their brains are getting too big for their skulls, that means pressure's building. And George wasn't wrong; if it goes on, they could have strokes, and they could die."

"How about Dr. Lewis?" Roger asked. "Maybe he could tell us if that's really what's happening."

Celine nodded "I already asked him. He's never dealt with anything even remotely resembling what's already happened with the Orangutans, so he can't rule out the 'over-grown brain' theory."

Strains of Mozart's "Cosi Fan Tutte" leaked into the room from down the hall. They could hear Betty singing along out in the kitchen.

Roger wanted to make sure he shared all his information. "George told me there was a plan, something they all wanted to accomplish together. Did Pongo mention some kind of plan they were working on? "

Celine reached forward and tossed another log on the fire. "Oh yes, he sure did. He says they'll tell us all about it tonight at dinner."

"Per pietà, ben mio, perdona all'error, d'un alma amante," sang Betty in flawless Italian, her voice flush with passion. "Svenerà quest'empia voglia l'ardir mio, la mia costanza!" She nailed the high notes perfectly.

Chapter 29

From his many years in the California Highway Patrol, Butch Turnbull had connections everywhere. People owed him a lot of favors. It just so happened there was a guy he knew at the airport. And as a matter of fact, the guy just so happened to be an aircraft mechanic at the ritzy private hangars where most of the big corporate jets were kept and serviced. Turnbull had been there many times, usually as part of a law-enforcement escort for various government swells who came to town.

After his chance meeting with Phil Holmbard at Jakes, Turnbull wasted no time. The same afternoon he drove to Execu-Air and found his friend working inside the main hangar.

"A big black jet? Sure I know about it," the man recalled. "There's only one all-black G-4 I've ever seen, here or anywhere else. Pretty impressive. I hear it belongs to a rich old lady from the east coast. Hasn't been here for awhile, though. Something up?"

Turnbull shrugged. He didn't think it was necessary to let the man know he was retired. After all, they weren't discussing anything too sensitive. "When was the last time you remember it being here?"

The man grinned. "That's easy. Early November, the first week. I had to stay late the night it left. I pulled it out to the flight-line. I remember 'cause it was a crazy scene."

"Crazy?" Turnbull acted nonchalant. "Like, something went wrong?"

"No, no. Nothing like that. Well, kind of. You know how it is around here, Sarge. Our clients want privacy. Rich people, famous people. All of us here know how to keep it cool. But that night the pilot of that black jet was acting weird. Kinda nervous-like. He said he needed the hangar completely cleared before his clients arrived, nobody could be anywhere around. The hangar doors had to be closed except just enough for a car. He asked us to wait in the back office and he'd call us on the squawk when he was ready for the tractor."

"Pretty high security. That's unusual."

"Yeah. That's what we thought, too, specially since we didn't see any of you guys or other guards. Anyway, what the hell. Me and the other guy on duty did what he asked. We took the hand radio and waited back there, watching TV, but the damn phone kept ringing up in the front office. I let it go for awhile, then I thought what if it's my boss and I don't pick up. I'll get in trouble. So I just went out there for a second to answer the phone. It was somebody calling about a fuel-up for the next morning, some bullshit. Anyway, thing is, I looked out through the window without thinking. I see an old car sitting by the jet, not even a limo. But I couldn't believe what else: a bunch of big-assed monkeys dressed up like people getting on the plane. Maybe half a dozen of 'em."

Turnbull squinted in exhilaration. "You're shitting me."

"Nope. I swear. Never seen that before. That was a new one. So I just kind of squatted low behind the counter for a minute and checked it out."

"Shit, I would have done the same. But, uh, you said *big monkeys*. How big?"

"Hell, real big, a couple of 'em." The guy held his hand out, demonstrating. "I don't know, they was far away, but maybe near five feet tall? And I mean, heavy, like gorillas, you know?

But I don't think that's what they was, because they weren't black. They all had red-colored hair."

"*Red* hair?" Turnbull strained to keep his voice low and even. "And wearing clothing, you say? Huh. So, anything else? Was that it?"

"No, no. 'Cause right then, see, this young guy, seemed like maybe he was with those monkeys, 'cause he had one by the hand, he and a little fat white-haired guy started really getting into it beside the steps. Hollerin' up in each other's face. Couldn't hear what it was about. Looked like they were about to start swingin' right there, though. The pilot had to push 'em apart."

Turnbull shook his head, acting innocently amazed. Had to have been Phil Holmbard, no wonder. Maybe there was more. He waited, then, "Well. You see a lot of crazy shit with rich people."

The aircraft mechanic chuckled. "Damn right. So, anyways, I went back to the rear office. Didn't want to get caught watching. Maybe a minute later we hear that car screech out of there, then the squawk call comes for the tractor. I went out and opened the doors, pulled 'em out to the line, they spooled up and took off. Last I saw of 'em."

"Shit. Hell of a story."

"Yeah, it is, huh? Funny you asked. I ain't told anybody else about it, but since you're investigating. So...something must be up with all that I guess?"

Turnbull smiled tightly, rubbing his palms. "Oh, I can't say. You know the drill. I appreciate you keeping this on the down low, okay?"

"Sure, Sarge, you got it."

"Hey, just one more thing. Any idea where they were going?"

The man shrugged. "Me? No. But you could find out real easy. Go over to the office and ask to look up their flight plan. They had to file one."

Turnbull folded his arms, looking out at the glare of the tarmac.

"Yeah. See, thing is, I'm trying to, like I said, keep this quiet. Unofficial. Suppose you could do it for me?"

Now the mechanic frowned. "Well...that'd be gettin' a little out of line for me. We usually don't have access to that. Suppose I could, though, if you really need it."

Turnbull discretely pulled out his billfold and palmed a couple of twenties, reaching out for a handshake. "You'd be doing me a favor."

The man pressed the money back. "You don't have to do that, Sarge. It's nothing. Just give me your number and I'll call you after the girl in the office goes for a cigarette break. I'll sneak in and look it up and nobody'll know."

Back at home an hour later, Turnbull got what he wanted. The black jet with its unusual passengers had set a course taking it all the way to Europe, landing at an airfield called Samedan, in south-central Switzerland. Confirmed arrived the next morning: 100% certain, the man told him. Turnbull thanked his friend, hung up the phone, then sat forward on his couch.

By nature he was a deliberate man and his mind was now running in high gear. He didn't have all the pieces, but he had a hell of a lot more than his department's detectives had come up with. This was something bigger than big, now he was sure of it. That creature that was driving the sports car that he'd clocked going 155 mph, that thing that had fought with him and kicked his ass and spoken to him, that thing was a *real ape*. Not a man in a monkey suit. He had his own experience to go on, but now also the anecdotal account given to him by his friend Phil Holmbard, an eyewitness, who was the attorney for the estate where the work invoice pointed his investigators as the probable location of the getaway car. And there wasn't just the one ape, there were several, "a bunch" as the airport mechanic (another eyewitness) recounted. "A victim of scientific experiments", that's what the big ape called himself during the fateful traffic stop. "Help me escape," he'd said. Add to all that the pictures found during the SWAT raid; pictures of red-haired monkeys dressed in human clothing. This was like something out of the movies except it wasn't the movies. Who could say how high up this might go? Military intelligence, C.I.A., top-secret scientific research? Some kind of genetic break-through? Or maybe espionage? Switzerland. That's where all the big spies hang out, right? All the big pharmaceutical companies were there as well. If this was what it seemed it might be, it was absolutely historic. And he, Butch Turnbull, knew about it.

He had a choice at this point. He could take his new findings to someone official and turn them over to the guys who still had badges. Basically, the same guys who had failed to find out any of this during the initial investigation. They might do better this time, or they might just bury it. He took it a step further: he'd stumbled onto something huge. With all this new information, what if they saw him as a threat to the secrecy of a highly classified project? *Maybe then they'd need to silence him permanently.* It wouldn't be the first time the government had done that. It even happened to presidents, like J.F.K., right? He was convinced of that.

His other option, he reasoned, was to pursue this matter all on his own, in secret, and get to the bottom of it without any official interference. If this was something evil, or just something incredible, and he brought it to light, he'd be instantly famous. A hero instead of an obscure retired cop.

He'd be in the newspapers, everywhere. They'd put him on the TV news. Might be a book deal. He didn't have to think about it very long. He was facing another lonely Christmas. He had no family and for the first time he wouldn't even have his work to distract him. Officially, he was now Mr. Nobody from Nowhere. Not a soul cared if he woke up dead in the morning.

He had a lot of money saved up, he had a passport, and something told him he hadn't even begun to unravel this thing. Time to get busy.

Chapter 30

At the dinner table, everyone enjoyed the hearty food and wines. The conversation touched on many subjects, but not "the plan". The humans occasionally glanced at each other, wondering if the Orangs had forgotten about it. But as everyone sat sipping coffee and cognac, Trent finally opened up.

"Don't you dear people think for one moment that we Mawas"—his hand swept around at the other apes as he addressed the humans—"have forgotten our lives before all our changes happened. No sir, we have not. In fact, we often think of those times with happiness and nostalgia. Really, that's true. Now, Celine, of course you know, I for one would never wish to return to that life. With my perspective now, I don't think I could go back." He held up his cognac snifter demonstrably, causing snickers among the other apes. "But those years in the forest were very peaceful and simple. Reading Emerson lately, I've realized that our self-reliance was a big factor underlying the peace we all felt then, before the logging crews came." He paused and sighed. "Look, I'm not saying we *focused* on the peacefulness, not in the way we can contemplate such a thing now, but it was there, pretty much every day, kind of like a warm blanket. Sure, we had our little daily tribulations, getting food and dealing with the weather, but that was rarely what you'd call stressful. I've been thinking about this, trying to connect what I've learned about human society. Once I became an adult away from my mother, if I got into a bad situation in the forest, if I fell and hurt myself or got sick or had a fight with a snake or an alligator, I was on my own. Nobody was going to come help me. If I was going to survive I'd have to deal with the problem myself. That sounds primitive and uncaring, but the end result is what we've all been thinking about. That's why we all want to learn everything we can, from philosophy to art to religion to politics to—everything. So we can depend on ourselves in this new world for us. Now, in politics, when a group gets together to accomplish something, they're called a caucus. Lately we've talked about certain things we want to do, working together, and so we've decided we're a caucus as well. We're going to call ourselves the "Simian Caucus"." He looked at Celine. "You like the sound of that?"

"Why, that's grand, Trent!" Celine laughed, clapping her hands. "The Simian Caucus. A toast, ladies and gentlemen, to the Simian Caucus. May you each and together achieve great and wonderful things."

They all rose, clinking their glasses, the apes' long arms easily reaching across the table to the others. But then there was the sound of a stifled sob.

Everyone turned to stare. It was Emily. She made a pitiful sight, standing with her glass still half lofted, shoulders jerking and her sweet face drawn into a contortion of attempted restraint. Further distressed by the focus of attention, she looked around desperately, then plopped down into her chair, seizing up her blue edelweiss-embroidered napkin and covering her face with it.

"Why, Emily," Abby exclaimed, "dear, whatever is the matter?" She shuffled around and placed her hands on heaving shoulders. The Orang sobbed for another moment.

"I'm so sorry, everyone" she wavered. "I'm sorry, I didn't mean to spoil this moment." She sniffled, wiping her sweet big nose with the dainty little napkin.

"Now, now. You haven't spoiled anything, dear girl, don't be silly" Abby soothed. "Now, please, won't you tell us what's wrong?"

With Abby massaging her shoulders, Emily began to compose herself, lowering her wrists to the table, twisting the napkin anxiously.

"I...it's just all this...change. So much has happened so fast, and, and, well...hearing Trent speak so well about it—it came over me all at once. We're so different from what we used to be, and so far from where we began." She looked down and dabbed at her eyes. "It's not that I hate what I've become, but now, well...now we're never going to be what we were before. We can't ever go back to that simple life again, not ever. There was a bird that called out, just before the sun came up, a sweet sound every day. That's always what I'd wake up to. The first leaves I'd eat in the morning always had a little cool dew on them. Even the rain was warm and soothing. And, well—I suppose I just miss those little things more than I had realized." Her lips quivered again, but then she caught herself, forcing a brave smile. Chloé leaned over and placed her head on her mother's shoulder, as Emily's voice fell to a whisper. "I'm sorry. I don't speak well like Trent, but I feel it so strongly. We're hardly even the same creatures now, the way we live is so different from before...before everything happened. I accept the new things, but, at the same time...I miss the forest, and my old life. I guess I'm just homesick, you know? But, even if I went back there now, it wouldn't be the same, because—*I'm not the same.*" Now her beautiful black eyes filled with tears again, and she covered her face with her hands.

Everyone there loved Emily beyond description. To see her so downhearted created a pall, and her recollection of the morning birdsongs seemed to go directly to the hearts of all the other Orangs. No one said anything for a long time.

"Oh my goodness," Celine finally uttered. "It's all my doing again, isn't it? I never thought about it this way before. I just assumed you were all happy in your new lives, I, I..." She looked at Abby beseechingly, but before the other woman could speak, Pongo Pygmaeus, all five feet two inches and three hundred pounds of him, slapped his huge hands down on the table. Glasses and silverware momentarily took flight, clattering noisily.

"Celine, please! Don't do that for even one more second. Everybody just stop, right there." His eyes flashed out from his broad face. "Let's get something straight. Celine, Abby, Roger, Kerri, none of you are to blame for anything. The things that happened to us just happened, plain and simple. Emily, it's understandable that you're homesick. It's natural, and you know we all feel that way from time to time. With the snow and cold weather here, maybe we feel it a little more keenly lately. But we shouldn't lose sight of the fact that we wouldn't be alive if it wasn't for what Celine did. So, Celine, let me say on behalf of everyone how much we are grateful to you for all you've done for us." The big animal's index finger pointed to the others. "Each of you know it's not easy being in our position. It's confusing sometimes. Hell, almost all of the time. I for one frequently have days at a time when I couldn't swear to just exactly what the heck I am, considering all the visions and intuitions that seem to be slamming me from every side. But, from what we've all read and discussed these last few weeks, it should be obvious to everyone that we're blessed to have been given our new abilities. I have no doubt that we have been chosen for this. Let's get rid of the sad feelings, let's remember our past with fondness, but let's go forward with courage. We have something of great

305

importance to accomplish, remember? Let's talk about our plan. George?"

The modest, smaller ape took over. He cleared his throat and held up a leather-bound book he'd had under his chair. "This is 'The Origin of Species', by Charles Darwin," he began deliberately. "I'd like to share some ideas I had while I was reading this. As Trent said, we can help ourselves, not just be helped." He studied a page closely for a moment, bending over it, then grunted with satisfaction. "I'm going to paraphrase what's here. Darwin says that organisms change in response to stimulus, usually with the issue of survival at stake. Let's say there's a threat to my survival. If I don't cope with it, then I die. I'm no longer around to mate, so I don't pass on my genes, right? But, if I do handle the challenge, then most likely my genes get passed on and there's a degree of probability that succeeding generations will continue to adapt along the path created by me—that is, correctly handling that particular threat or challenge which jeopardizes my species. We get to go on and grow; we develop and progress, because "we" didn't just end with "me". 'Natural Selection', Darwin calls it. It's Nature's way of seeing to it that things move forward. Whatever works is what gets to prevail. Darwin is clear about this. He writes, 'Natural Selection is daily and hourly scrutinizing, throughout the world, the slightest variations; rejecting those that are bad, preserving and adding up all that are good; silently and insensibly working, whenever and wherever the opportunity offers, at the improvement of each organic being in relation to its organic and inorganic conditions of life. We see nothing of these slow changes in progress, until the hand of time has marked the lapse of ages, and then so imperfect is our view into long-past geological ages, that we see only that the forms of life are now different from what they formerly were.'" George glanced up. "Now, he also talks about the efforts of man to change things in the world, like a kind of compressed emulation of Nature. Listen to his final sentences: 'How fleeting are the wishes and efforts of man! How short his time! And, consequently, how poor will be his results, compared with those accumulated by Nature during whole geological periods!'"

With a sigh, the ape scratched his nose, assessing his companions.

"So, Pongo made the point that we wouldn't be here if not for the merciful efforts of our friend, Celine. Very true. But go back with me to the original cause of our displacement. We were forced out of the jungle because men came and destroyed our habitat. And why? Because they *wanted something*. They wanted the trees we lived in because those trees were worth money. The cleared land could then be planted with palm-oil trees. More money. For people, having money works as a kind of 'instant evolution', because it provides the freedom to move about in the world, and access to the finer things. So. The men came, they took our trees, and we were forced out because we hadn't adapted to deal with that new challenge."

George closed the book. Leaning forward, he placed his knuckles gently on the table. A flickering glow from the table lamps made his eyes seem even more sunken and mysterious.

"We survived through the kindness of others, and we were taken to a safe place. Remarkable in itself. But then, something beyond remarkable. A spacecraft from a very distant planet crashed on top of our house...and some highly advanced biological processes were set in motion. We assumed capabilities that we never had before, and would never normally have. Our whole core elements of being, the very kind of creatures we were, changed radically. Something from that spacecraft, perhaps a concentrated intelligence plasma, if you will, settled on us and took up residence in us and now we are all seeing the very dramatic results from that. As Pongo just said, perhaps we have been chosen to have these gifts. Back when we were hounded from our forest, we couldn't do anything about it. We were helpless. Now, we are very capable of thinking about solutions to this kind of problem. It is too late to save our own forest, where we each lived. But we are all still Orangutans—Mawas. And at this moment many of our fellows are faced with the same horror that caused each of us such pain and confusion. The logging is going ahead down in Borneo and Sumatra. Not only are our fellow Mawas losing their homes and being killed, not only is our whole species headed for almost certain annihilation, but so is the entire rainforest!"

George was getting wound up, his voice filling with conviction.

"It is *horrible*" he intoned, "not just because our own species might vanish, but thousands of other species of plants and animals will go along with us. They'll go off into oblivion, all because a few greedy humans want to use those trees to saw up into lumber, or even worse, grind up to make pulp for paper." He closed his eyes, lowering his voice. "The ironic thing is, many of those plants can provide beneficial medicines for humans. Medical miracles are in those forests. Relatively few of those plants have ever been studied or catalogued. See what obtains here? Discovering those medicines would yield thousands of times more profit than logging. Cutting down the trees and destroying the rest of the ecosystem is like tearing down a skyscraper to sell the plumbing for scrap, when instead you could rent out space in the building for decades, making a fortune and giving thousands of people a way to make a living. It beggars the imagination."

He turned to a side table and retrieved a binder. Extracting four or five sheets, he spread them across the dining table.

Roger craned to look. Rows of figures, drawings and graphs. Also some sort of satellite photograph, but the location wasn't familiar. George waved his hands over the pages, like an invocation.

"Now. Ladies and Gentlemen. Humans want those trees for lumber and paper pulp. That is because money can be generated by doing this. Once that's done, they plant palm-oil plantations on the cleared land. So as long as that is the case, men will push roads deep into the most sacred and remote places, bring in huge machines, and mow down millions of trees until every last one is gone. The government won't stop this, because individual ministers and secretaries are getting rich from it. So the solution, as we've reasoned it out, is to remove the incentive *without removing the trees.* If we can make the trees monetarily worthless to the loggers and keep the palm-oil plantations from starting, then we will save the trees and the rest of the forest ecosystem as well." His eyes now took on a gleam as he tapped the papers spread before him. "Well, speaking for the Simian Caucus, I'm optimistic that we've come up with a way to do that very thing."

Chapter 31

Abby? Abby, are you awake?" Celine whispered across the aisle separating the twin beds in the shadowed master suite. It was Christmas morning, still about a half hour before dawn.

"I am now." Abby's hoarseness was muffled under the edge of a thick feather comforter. "What's the matter?"

"Nothing. I've just been awake for awhile, listening to the wind. I thought you might be awake, too. I had the most interesting dream."

Abby stirred, turning on her back. She cleared her throat noisily.

"All dreams are interesting. What was so catchy about this one?"

"Well, it was about Charles. Or...me and Charles."

"Really. It's been years since you've had one of those, right?"

"Yes. Years and years. But this was so real. I feel like I've just come from a visit with him. We were walking on a beach somewhere. Odd place, not much there. He was wearing white swim trunks. He was young, no older than when he died. But I was the way I am now. I knew that because he was holding my hand and the contrast was appalling. But he didn't seem to notice because he looked at me with exactly the same love in his eyes as he always had." Her voice broke a little. "He told me that he loved me and he kissed me."

The wind shouldered ferociously against the house, thrusting under the eaves. Deep within, the bones of the old place creaked and shifted, the pine and spruce timbers still pliant even after a century of punishment from alpine winter gusts.

"Abby. Do you think I made a mistake, not remarrying?"

"Did you feel very attracted to anyone else?"

Celine ran back through her memories.

"I liked a few other men—but very attracted...I'd have to say no. Not the way I was with Charles."

"Anyone you'd have compromised with? For companionship?"

"No. I guess not. I had my sister, and then you, dear girl. God bless you both."

"Well, there's your answer, sweetie. You didn't make a mistake. I wouldn't say I had a better life than you, just because I had a husband for forty nine years. Oh yes, he was nice—he was wonderful. But our lives come to us in phases. That was one phase, and when it was over, another one began; the one that we've shared." Abby considered for a moment, scratching her forehead. "We don't like to dwell on it, but there's not a huge amount of future for us. So the past becomes more important. You wonder if you made the best of it."

"I hope I have. I'm most grateful for my blessings." Celine noticed her breath was a cloud in the early light. "Damn, it's cold in here!" She shivered and slid deeper under the covers. "What about Roger and Kerri? They're trying to be discreet, but they're very much in love, wouldn't you agree?"

"Hell, yes."

"Kerri. That girl is just so amazing. I have to remind myself how young she is. So well-spoken and opinionated. Heavens. She has the most penetrating eyes I've ever seen. I'll bet Roger doesn't fully realize what he's got there. But he's quite a package himself. He holds a lot back, downplays his capabilities. I like that. Do you think they're right for each other?"

"They're perfect for each other, you know that as well as I do. They have a destiny. This has all happened for a reason."

"You know, he does remind me of my Charles. I didn't want to make an issue of that. It's just a coincidence, after all." She fell quiet again, and the now glowing windows revealed the new snow falling.

Abby changed the subject. "Celine. I must ask, because I've been delaying. But you know there's something very wrong with you, right, honey?"

Following a very long pause, Celine whispered "Oh, yes. I do."

"Then why aren't you doing something about it?"

"I suppose I've been afraid to hear...what comes next."

"I understand, dear. But you must do something about it. Will you, Celine?"

"Yes. Yes, I will. I promise."

"Soon?"

"Alright, Abby. I don't want you to worry. So. When we get home. It'll keep until then." Celine drew a gasp. "Oh my goodness, it's Christmas morning! I completely forgot. Good lord, what time is it? Merry Christmas, Abby!"

"Merry Christmas, darling." Abby chuckled as Celine swung out of bed, stepped into her slippers and began fussing with her heavy housecoat.

"We've got to get rolling, dear. So much to do. I do so want those hairy little darlings to have the most wonderful day ever. Can't wait to start baking those cookies and opening those packages!" She loped off toward the bathroom.

Everyone was down in the kitchen by seven-thirty, and Roger stoked up a Yule time bonfire in the hearth. Crackling and roaring, it drove away the chill. A champion breakfast was made. Mounds of waffles, hillocks of scrambled eggs, fresh biscuits, potatoes, bacon, ham, cheeses, fruit (including

Durians flown in as a surprise for the Orangs), gallons of coffee and teas—all were demolished with gusto. The glorious silver fir tree trimmed in the great hall was the next center of attention. Gaily-wrapped parcels surrounding it were the result of countless hours of thought and loving consideration. Celine had allowed the Orangs free use of her credit cards so that they might each have the pleasure of confidentially making their gift selections from catalogues. They had become experts in the art of phone-shopping. Roger and Kerri had been dispatched on buying missions, usually to St. Moritz, but once riding the train all the way in to Zurich, where they followed their shopping lists and scoured the fine shops along the Bahnhofstrasse. When the wrappings finally came off, there were oohs, ahhs, and squeals of delight. And no one was left out. Celine had flown Dr. Lewis over on the Concorde on Christmas Eve and so he was there, standing by the piano with all the others, belting out carols as Artod played the tunes. Happy, happy, happy.

A heavy snowfall insured that no one was coming or going, and two cases of champagne eased them toward the sumptuous meal planned for early evening. Three fine geese had been put in for roasting that morning. Alongside were creamed potatoes, spinach soufflé, candied carrots, hot elderberry jelly, turnips simmered in gin and caraway, sage-and-pear stuffing, and four or five different kinds of salads. And then the pies: pumpkin, mincemeat, coconut meringue—the Orang's favorite—a couple of each baked by Abby and Betty.

Nightfall wound the celebration down. Orangs and humans drew into smaller circles or even contentedly went off alone, reading new books, playing with toys, or just heading for bed.

Celine turned ninety on New Year's Day. She didn't want a party—not wanting to focus on the reality of her age—but at the insistence of all the others, a celebratory dinner was held. Each Orangutan stood and told a story of how Celine had touched them. She was visibly moved. They presented her with a gold ring set with an emerald. Inside the band were the words: "For Celine, So Loved, 1/1/90". She slipped it on the ring finger of her left hand, like a wedding band, and beamed.

During her visit Roger had noticed her looking progressively more tired. It seemed to him that she was losing weight. Once, while they were talking, she gave a sharp grunt and doubled over, clutching her abdomen.

"Are you alright, Mrs. Stertevant?" he asked, alarmed.

She waved him off. "It's nothing. I've been feeling a little ill lately but I'm just a little under the weather," she said. "All the holiday food. And I don't do well at altitude."

Dr. Lewis had returned to California two days before, getting back to his veterinary practice. He had examined the apes and reported they were all exhibiting symptoms of intracranial pressure. He confirmed George's earlier prediction. They were getting worse, and there wasn't much to be done. He left Roger a large supply of pain medication, and asked to be kept informed.

Since the moment George revealed the plan, it had been the buzz. Their health issues demanded that they waste no time accomplishing the goal, and extensive preparations had already begun. Supplies had been brought in from Zurich. George and a few others had been putting in long hours in a large closed-off parlor, working at tables crowded with chemicals and bits of electronics. The "Simian Caucus" would depart Switzerland within a week. First Celine and Abby would return to America, then the plane would make a quick turn-around to come back for the rest of the group.

Kerri asserted that she would stay with the group as they embarked on their mission. Everyone tried persuading her that finishing her final semester in high school would be the best thing, but she wasn't buying it. The plan might only take a few weeks to implement—if all went smoothly. She could make up the school work. And she was eighteen, she reminded them. She could legally make her own decisions. When would there ever again be another opportunity like this? She wanted to be with them at their finest hour. It was decided.

Mid-morning on the 4th, farewells were exchanged in the great front hall of Blauhimmelheim. The Orangs all hugged Celine and promised they'd keep her informed.

Scarpita arrived for the drive to the airport. This time the ladies had decided they would go to Glenwhylden. Celine had made her peace with old ghosts, she said. Now she wanted to spend more time there.

Roger and Kerri rode along to the airport.

"You still okay about all this, the plan and all?" Celine asked in the car. "It's not too late to back out. If you've got a bad feeling or something, we can always wait and think about it some more."

"No. I think it's going to work, actually. As long as we don't get caught doing it. I'll try my best, Mrs. Stertevant."

She nodded, sighing. "Alright then." She was pensive, gazing out at the passing snow-covered trees. "Oh, I wish I could go, too. It's hard to believe this is all happening so fast. I suppose it has to."

As they arrived at the tarmac, "Arjuna" was ready as usual; one engine already running and the cabin warmed.

Just before Chuck assisted them at the stairs, Celine turned to the young couple, taking their hands. For a moment they thought she would cry. "Godspeed, my dears," she said. "We'll be praying for you all."

Chapter 32

Samedan was like another planet to Butch Turnbull. He'd never been out of the U.S., so he arrived in Switzerland not knowing what to expect, only what he was looking for. The hotel where he'd spent New Year's Eve alone was basic but clean: a small inn near the middle of the village. It was among the cheapest he could find. But damn, it was still expensive. So was his tiny rental car. Everything in this country cost a freaking fortune. Gas (they called it petrol) $5.65 a gallon! Holy shit. He couldn't find a McDonalds or KFC. And this was supposed to be a civilized place? He'd gotten the local feel pretty fast though. The hotel provided a decent breakfast and dinner included with the room rate. Beyond that there was a nearby market where he could get his basic needs handled. The innkeeper did his laundry for a fee. Although he didn't know German or French, it was rare to encounter anyone who didn't speak at least decent English. And he didn't stand out, anyway; there were lots of foreign tourists, many of them Americans. He kept to himself.

What mattered most was tracking down that black jet, finding out whether it had come here only once, and so on. The normal details of an investigation and surveillance had to be followed. He knew the pattern and translating it to the environment of a foreign country wasn't such a big deal. Sometimes you didn't really have a plan, you just went to the place you thought would prove useful and started poking around. Hang out for awhile, observe the surroundings. Hope to catch a break. But it was slow going and he was getting frustrated.

At the airport's only charter office he posed as a wealthy retired businessman looking to hire a private jet to Rome. The stylish woman there was professional and friendly. She gave him some prices and only hesitated for a moment when he expressed admiration for a black Grumman G-4 he'd "seen here before".

"Oh, yes, I know it. Very deluxe. But that one is private, not for hire, sir. The owner has it here from time to time. I believe they have a house in the valley." She brought out another brochure, handing it to him. "If that is what you desire, we can get the same model airplane. If it's available it can be here early tomorrow, it must come from Zurich. Of course it is among the most costly."

He thanked her and promised to call when his travel plans were definite.

So. The jet had more than a passing connection to this place. Maybe there was a house here. But how the hell to find it? Sometimes luck has a hand in these things.

The next day was cold with a high overcast. He was in his car, planning a drive to the neighboring valley to look for anything that stood out. As he passed the airport, he couldn't believe it. Son of a bitch. Across the field, outside the charter hangar, there it was: a big black jet, stairs lowered and hot exhaust shimmering from a running engine. Had to be the one. Turnbull crunched his car to the shoulder and parked. Through his binoculars he saw a tall pilot in a dark suit and cap talking with a fuel truck driver. A small white van was there as well, painted with a smiling pig in a chef's hat. A woman in an apron was loading boxes. Caterers. That meant the plane was about to leave.

"Shit damn!" he cursed, eyed glued to the binos. The jet hadn't been there the evening before; he'd checked before supper. It must have arrived later that night and now it would soon be gone again. He frantically started thinking of a cover story so he could drive over there and chat up the crew. But just as he restarted his car he saw a limousine pulling up. Turnbull jammed the binoculars back to his face. Two frail elderly women, a young couple, and a driver got out. No monkeys. Luggage was quickly being put aboard. Couple and old ladies now talking at the steps, hugging. Then up the ladies went, waving from the door. The stairs retracted. Turnbull cursed again, freaking. No time to get over there. The plane immediately began taxiing out, and the others got back in the car.

Well, there was one thing he could do. He could follow the limo. In fact, that might be more valuable than anything else at this point. He spun his little toy car around and managed to get to the airport entrance just as the big sedan emerged. He fell behind it, trying to maintain a discreet distance, one or two cars separating them. As the limo got onto the highway leading out of town, Turnbull had a little trouble keeping up. The driver was going fast and the icy roads were treacherous for the skinny tires on his rental. He almost skidded out of control. Somehow he kept them in sight. Then, in what seemed to be the middle of nowhere, the limo slowed and put on a turn signal. It appeared to be going right into the dense forest. Were they making a U-turn? Had he been spotted? This is one of the hardest parts of tailing another car; deciding when you must keep going and possibly lose contact. If he pulled over and waited to see what they did, he'd be obvious. Turnbull figured he had no choice.

As he passed he saw they were, in fact, stopped at a gate set back from the road. The driver was out opening it. Turnbull made note of the spot and kept going. He watched the rearview as long as he could to make sure they didn't take off. A minute up the road he doubled back. Now the gate was closed again, the big sedan gone. There were, however, clear tire tracks in the fresh dusting of snow beyond the locked gate: tracks leading up a long forested road. "Bet your ass, the house," he muttered to himself. Why else would a limousine go up there? He sped back into town.

Within an hour he returned, fully prepared. In the village he'd bought snowshoes, a back pack for food and water, heavy gloves, and a parka. He'd also retrieved the Colt semi-auto .45 caliber pistol he'd secreted into the country disassembled and concealed in the false bottom of a suitcase. The odds favored him: he didn't look the type who needed to be searched by Customs. Sure enough, he and his luggage had cleared through unchallenged.

Leaving his car at a paved turn-off, he waited until no cars were in sight, then ran for the woods near the gate. Now his experience deer hunting in the high Sierra came in handy. Using the snowshoes he stayed well to the side of the narrow road the car had gone up, keeping his tracks off in the trees where they wouldn't be seen. It was hard work busting through the low branches and soft snow, but he doggedly kept going. He jumped a semi-frozen stream. Keeping an eye on the time, he knew he'd have only a few hours at most before he'd have to turn back. It would be dangerous to be stuck in this forest after it got dark. When he figured he'd gone nearly a mile, he began wondering just how far the road might actually go. But finally he saw a clearing up ahead. Reaching the edge, he gaped. A house alright, one worthy of someone with a jet like the one he'd just seen leave the airport. Dark golden against the pristine winterscape, the timbered mass of Blauhimmelheim glowed in the distance across a snowy meadow.

Turnbull had no idea if there was security here, whether there were cameras or guards or even remote motion sensors.

There could be dogs. With this kind of money it stood to reason there would be. He dug out his binoculars and checked out the house. Nothing obvious around the perimeter. No guard post, no people at all. No sign of the limo, either; maybe it was in a garage or had already left again. He maneuvered closer, still keeping back in the shadows of the trees bordering the open space. Now much closer, crouching behind a fallen tree, binos out again. From here he could actually see clearly through the expansive picture windows fronting the deep covered porch. He scanned across slowly. A few lamps on inside but still no people. He came to the last window on the right, a corner window seat, and almost dropped the binoculars. "Motherf..." he uttered before he caught himself to remain silent. Right inside the window, there "it" was: the large red ape, the very same one he'd fought with. That monstrous face. It was standing there, in a colorful knit sweater, gesturing and clearly conversing with two other red apes who were sitting in the window seat. They were dressed in human clothing also, all of them deep in discussion. The big one held up a small metallic box, describing something and pointing to what looked like wires hanging from it. Utterly transfixed, Turnbull watched, heart pounding. His heavy breathing was fogging his binoculars. And then, there! Movement to the right at the side of the house. He swung the lenses over. There in the snow, two more apes, smaller ones, wearing parkas, playing around, throwing snowballs at each other. He could actually hear their delighted laughter. One screamed out something in French. Holy shit.

He sat back for a moment, highly agitated. What to do, what to do? This was amazing luck, beyond anything he'd hoped for. He had the means to charge up to that house right at that moment and place them all at gunpoint. That was an option. He tried to reason it through. Then what? For one thing, that would be a serious criminal act. He wasn't a law enforcement officer anymore, and he wouldn't have any jurisdiction here even if he was. Beyond all that he knew nothing of who else might be at the house. It was huge. There must be security personnel, maybe military, others there, people with guns as well. Just because he hadn't seen any yet meant nothing. He might be shot on sight. Hey, maybe these talking apes had their own guns, why not? Anyway, nothing this monumental would be left just sitting around a country house unguarded. No, he had to be better organized when he made his move. Another swipe with the glasses. They were all still there. Rummaging in his pack, he realized that in his haste he had left behind the one thing that he needed most right now: his camera. Fuck, fuck, fuck! His ears were ringing so loud he could barely think.

As he willed himself to calm down, Turnbull began formulating a scheme. He'd just seen the plane leave, so these creatures probably weren't going anywhere soon. By the greatest stroke of luck, he now knew exactly where to find them. He'd approached to within 50 yards of the house undetected. Likely that was repeatable. He checked his watch: it would be dark in little more than an hour. With one last look he reluctantly started back toward the highway, assembling more details of his plan of action as he retraced his route.

First, he had to get proof of what he'd seen: video tape and photographs. He had to get the sound of them talking to make it irrefutable. Once he had that, he would go a step further: take at least one of them captive. He'd make sure it was one that could talk. It would be best if it was one that he already had on tape. Then he'd get it away from here, perhaps just to the nearest decent sized city. That's where he'd call the reporters and splash this thing far and wide. He didn't think it would be viewed as kidnapping; that would have to involve a human. No, the worst crime he could be charged with was theft. Not such a big deal. And after the world saw what he'd brought to light, that wouldn't matter much. Turnbull's mind was already flush with the vindication and respect he'd receive. He was a tenacious bulldog, not to be deterred, and he'd gone halfway around the world to track down and solve a mystery that everyone else had turned their backs on He'd show them, and good.

Finally, exhausted, just as the sky was growing dark he came to the main road and unstrapped the snowshoes. No cars coming. He ran across to the spot where he'd left his car. It was gone. What the fuck? He looked around in disbelief; he was certain this was where he'd left it. In the dirty slush there were lots of boot tracks and a larger set of tire tracks, like a truck. It was only then in the fading light that he noticed the sign standing not ten feet from where he'd parked over four hours ago. It had escaped his attention as he rushed into the woods. There was a large red circle crossed by a blue "X". "Kein Aufhalten" said the lettering below. He didn't speak German, but he could guess what that meant. "No stopping". His car had been towed.

Chapter 33

By the time he got back to his hotel it was nearly midnight. He'd walked a long way, trying hitchhiking, but there were few cars and for a quite awhile no one stopped. Finally a dairy delivery van driver gave him a ride, but by then he was only about two miles from town.

Turnbull was enraged; mostly at himself, once again. He had been sloppy, and that had caused a major screw-up that would waste precious time. He'd either have to deal with getting the car out of impound in the morning (that's if it hadn't been stolen) or else rent another one. His original plan had been to return to the big house early in the morning and have plenty of time to pick the best moment to snatch one of the apes. Now the temporary loss of his car would set him back. He couldn't find out anything right away, there was no one on duty at the hotel's front desk. The "Reception" closed at 10pm. He went to bed but barely slept.

At seven a.m. the clerk was at the desk; Turnbull was waiting. He explained about his car: he'd taken a hike to look at the scenery and it appeared to have been towed.

"Yes, of course, Mr. Turnbull," the young man was earnest as he brought out a small map. "I am apologize, this has happened before. Unfortunately it is the law in Graubünden." He circled a spot on the map "You must go to the polizei bureau, here. It is only about one and one half kilometers distance. They are begin at nine. I can call a taxi if you like. You must pay a fine there, then they will give you a paper to take to the storage where the car is kept. This is necessary to return your car."

"Not until nine?" Turnbull struggled to remain calm. "Can't I just rent another car right now and then go get the other one later? I have an appointment to get to."

"No, sir, I'm sorry. They must to have the fine paid first. This is the law here in Switzerland."

Turnbull didn't waste any more time talking. He decided to eat breakfast, then walk to the police station. A cab wouldn't save time and would be just more money wasted. The experience at the polizei bureau was formal and infuriating. The poker-faced sole officer on duty made a phone call and confirmed that the car had been towed. But because of the location, he said, it was the district police, not his office, which had the authority. Therefore Turnbull must go to the neighboring town, St. Moritz, where the car was being stored. It took everything Turnbull had to keep from exploding right there. But, he knew he would only call attention to himself if he gave way to his temper. Right now he was just a stupid tourist whose car had been towed; it happened a lot, apparently. How many parking/tow tickets had he himself written while he was in the CHP? Hundreds? For his entire career he'd been the one to call the shots, telling other people what to do. Now he was being made to dance at the end of someone else's string. It didn't sit well.

By the time it was all done, he'd spent over 400 U.S. dollars, including cab fare to St. Moritz, and it had taken nearly five hours to get his rinky little car back. It had been obstructing a snow-plow lane; that made the fine higher. The police in St. Moritz advised him "in future" to only park his car in lots marked "Parkplatz". Great, thanks. He sped back to his hotel in a state of barely contained fury. He picked up his gear and pistol, then stopped to buy a roll of heavy tape, some nylon rope and a large knife in a sheath. He made an improvised bludgeon by knotting a fist-sized wad of coins tightly into the end of a doubled sock. The final stop was at the "apothecary" for a bottle of maximum strength Benadryl liquid. It was now mid-afternoon.

Here was the new game plan: after leaving his car (this time in an approved lot down the road from the gate, he'd checked his map) he'd sneak back up to the house. The weather was better today, he'd make better time. He'd get as close as possible and wait for one of them, hopefully one of the smaller ones like he'd seen the day before, to come outside to play. After recording a short bit of video he'd rush up when its back was turned and knock it out with a blow to the head. He knew quite well how to do this, he was, after all, an expert. If he was lucky, no one would see this and it would be awhile before the ape was missed. He'd quickly drag it into the woods and bind its mouth, hands, and feet using the tape and rope. Before he gagged the mouth with tape he would force Benadryl down its throat. That would make it groggy, at the very least. The next part would be the hardest, but he knew he could do it. He'd carry/drag the animal out near the road, leave it tied up and concealed there, then go get his car and retrieve it. From there he'd drive straight to Zurich and go directly to the newspaper. As a CHP sergeant he'd dealt with lots of reporters, and he knew what the reaction would be to a story like this. Fame, fortune and vindication would be his. That simple.

Once he got rolling, all went well. Soon he was hidden in the bushes just a few yards away from the side garden where the two apes had been playing the day before. To his amazement there were still no apparent guards and no dogs. He did glimpse the young man and woman from the airport...they looked fit but not anything he couldn't handle if he had to. They had no obvious firearms. Almost giddy with anticipation, he watched through the windows as a few of the

325

animals walked by, sometimes talking. He shot some shaky video, but wondered if the sound would register. There seemed to be a lot of bustle going on inside the house: things were being shouted (he couldn't hear exactly what) and more than once he saw the humans and one or two of the apes carrying boxes. More than an hour passed this way, and none came outside. Just wait, Turnbull kept telling himself. Wait. This doesn't absolutely have to happen today. Better to have it go exactly right than to do something stupid out of impatience and blow your chances completely. At one point he heard noise coming from the front of the house: sounds of at least one vehicle, maybe two, crunching up the drive. But that was around the corner, out of his line of site. He briefly considered circling back around to check it out but then decided it was just normal activity. So a car was here, that wouldn't necessarily change his plan.

Then, finally, the door to the side terrace opened and a solitary ape ambled out. It was one of the smaller ones, wearing a dress and a pink cardigan sweater. Perfect.

All alone, Emily Forrestal walked out on the porch and wistfully looked up at the majestic mountains looming behind the house. This was her favorite time of day; the shadows began to creep across the meadow and the air became still as the evening came on. Usually she'd be in the middle of working in the kitchen, making dinner for the group. It was the time for everyone to gather, share their ideas, and have a nice meal. Often she'd walk down into the snowy garden for a minute or two to smoke a cigarette and take a break before going back to her chores at the stove. On this particular late afternoon she hesitated at the top of the steps, having neglected to put on her galoshes.

A mere thirty feet away Butch Turnbull was raising onto coiled haunches like a mountain lion, clutching his truncheon, seconds from launching out of his hiding place to club the unsuspecting ape into unconsciousness. It was ideal, no one else was around. "Just come on down the steps," he was thinking. "Come down those steps and you're mine."

"Goodbye, Switzerland," Emily whispered to the mountains and trees. Then, hearing her name called from inside, she abruptly turned and went back through the door, closing it.

Turnbull couldn't believe it. What the fuck? Adrenaline had him trembling, he had been so close. He seethed there in the bushes, wondering if he'd missed his only chance of the day. Then he reminded himself, patience. He held his position, carefully watching. There was still time, the same one or others could come back out. This was about the time he'd seen them playing the day before. If it got too dark he had a flashlight, he'd be able to get back to the road no matter what. Just relax. But then a few lights went out inside the house and for quite awhile he didn't see anyone moving. Odd; it was getting dark, why were they turning off lights? Growing anxious, he heard more noises coming from the front of the house. "Fuck it," he thought, "I gotta go see what's going on." Slowly, careful to stay hidden, he began working his way back through the darkening forest. The sound of engines starting made him quicken his pace. Just as the driveway came into view, he saw the limousine and a dark blue utility van, their lights on. The young male human was just climbing into the front passenger seat of the limo, closing the door. Both vehicles began to drive away. They receded around the meadow and disappeared down the road leading out to the gate.

Now Turnbull really had to restrain himself, sensing what had just happened. In disbelief, he waited a few more minutes, watching the house intently. There was nothing going on, no sound, not a soul moving inside. Most of the lights were out. "Holy shit", he started muttering. "Holy shit, holy fucking shit, damn it!" He'd reached his limit. No matter what happened next, by god he was going to take some action. Striding out onto the driveway in full view he went straight to the porch and bounded up the steps. He tried the doorknob. It was unlocked. With his pistol drawn he pushed the door open and charged into the house.

Chapter 34

Roger screamed out in horrendous pain and berserk terror. It seemed obvious he was experiencing the final few seconds of his life. On every side was ugly, brown, foaming, raging water. The speed of the current was phenomenal, a boggling, unstoppable force. Impenetrable topaz jungle whizzed by on each bank, a florescent, verdant blur above the muddy flood. The fragment of flotation material he clung to (the last remnant of a decimated raft) was pitching and slamming around wildly, out of control in the grip of the hellacious rapids. Huge rocks threatened every few yards. In disbelieving horror, he looked down at his right leg, the source of teeth-grinding pain. It wasn't there: missing, jaggedly torn away at a point just above the knee. His vision narrowed and dimmed...a fuzzy grey tunnel closing in. Right up ahead there was a massive, boiling head of mist rearing up menacingly from the thundering river. Now the current picked up even more, and a growing subsonic rumble left no doubt. He was about to be swept over a large waterfall.

With his last reserve of energy, he tried to force himself off the float, thinking that by some miracle he might be able to grab onto a rock or a branch or something. Dear God, please. Grab anything, anything at all. Do not go over the falls. But he couldn't. His limbs simply would not respond, his body felt heavy as ten men, as if he were weighed down ponderously by an invisible mass. Small matter that he couldn't move. He wouldn't have had time anyway. He was already within a few yards of the precipice, and the water was now sucking so hard it had become hissingly smooth. Then, in the next instant, patches of lighter color, daylight, from out in front of the falls. Here we go. Pitching out, beginning to free-fall. No, no, you can't even see the bottom. He screamed colossally, as if trying to make his person flee this body which was about to be rendered into shreds. The throttled scream, sounding more like a moan, was swallowed by the stupendous roaring of the cataract. There was an interminable hurtling down, and then oblivion.

"Dude. Dude! Come on. Hey, are you there? Easy, dude."

"I'm, I've gotta get. I, uh." Roger gurgled helplessly, looking up at something, a looming shape.

Someone was leaning over him in darkness. A woman. She was holding his arms, as if to restrain him. He shook his head. The surface underneath him pitched violently. He felt sensations of falling very sharply, then rising again. The rushing noise was still all around. Was he now on a boat? The woman spoke again, this time releasing her tight grip on his arm in order to stroke his face with her hand.

"Roger. You're just having a dream, lover. Come on, its me."

Thank holy God in heaven. He could absolutely not recall another moment in his life when he had experienced such relief. It was Kerri. In bed with him. He remembered now. They were on the jet, over the South Pacific, on the way to Malaysia. It was night, and Chuck Bartholdy had warned of bad weather along their route; a fairly weak tropical depression south of the Cook Islands. They were flying through the top of it, the big jet bouncing around on the updrafts from the thunderstorms. Roger sat up and held on to Kerri as hard as he could. The beds in Arjuna's sleeping compartment were narrow single berths, designed for two elderly women who were long past the time in their lives when they might want to sleep in the same bed with anyone.

But Roger and Kerri had not slept apart in several days since Celine and Abby had left Blauhimmelheim. On the plane, Kerri had innocently squeezed into Roger's berth when they retired, not wishing to see a good thing interrupted. This had necessitated her lying all but on top of him (she was a big girl) causing his leg to go to sleep. He struggled to move to the edge of the bed, but the leg was like rubber, and completely on fire now as he shifted his weight and blood began to flow in again. It stung like a billion needles.

"Holy shit."

"God, Roger, that must have been some dream. You were totally freaking."

Kerri was rubbing his glistening back now. He was in a cold sweat.

"Unreal. Un. Fucking. Real. I...hell, you should have been there." His voice was quavering. "I was, uh...on a, uh, piece of Styrofoam or something. Floating. Going over these gigantic rapids, this—a waterfall, huge. Huge. My leg was gone. Scared me shitless."

She hugged him from behind and put her lips close to his ear.

"Damn. Well, I guess so. I couldn't get you to come out of it. I was thinking I might have to pop you one."

He laughed, still quite shaken. "Thanks for sparing me. Man. I've never had a dream that real. Okay. I'm here. Damn." He exhaled heavily. "My leg fell asleep. It's killin' me." He massaged it for a minute or so, then lay back down. He could finally feel his heart rate retreating somewhat.

"Hey
Kerri ?" She was snuggling back in, pulling up the covers. "Give the leg a break, okay?"

She giggled, trying to shift her weight off him a bit, near impossible in the slender berth. He couldn't help himself, though. There was no way he was going to ask her to move to her own berth. If he had to be awake the rest of the night, he'd gladly do it, just to keep his arms around her. Always after they made love she fell asleep quickly, without a care in the world, her head on his chest, one arm and leg thrown across his body. He'd listen to her sweet breathing, while growing drowsy himself, feeling the warm pulses of her breath on his skin. It was heaven.

She dropped off again and he was left alone with his thoughts. For quite awhile he couldn't banish the horrific images of the dream; that and the pitching of the airplane kept his stomach in knots. But he breathed deeply and tried to relax, holding Kerri, and his mind shifted to the particulars of the Simian Caucus plan. He wondered if they could actually pull it off.

George explained that he had to find some way to make the trees useless to the logging companies, yet leave them effectively unchanged for the use of the animals and all other natural purposes. In Switzerland he worked with chemical compounds, finally hitting on a mixture that would cause a chemical chain-reaction within a tree's innermost structures. It would alter the tree's DNA. The substance had to be stored under pressure, existing in a heavy gaseous state. Once allowed contact with the air it instantly dispersed and precipitated. If George let a bit of the gas out into a room, for example, there would be a little purplish puff-cloud, then it would just disappear. It would next be seen as a fine, sticky residue covering everything nearby. Its effect on hardwood trees would be dramatic and fast-acting, George promised. The chemical would be absorbed through the leaves and upper branches, and within days all the wood in the entire tree would develop bright purple and mustard-yellow streaking. The original color of the wood would be irreversibly marred, every stick in the tree, although the color of the bark would not be affected. In addition, if the wood was cut, it would soon develop a powerful and exceedingly foul odor, like fart gas. The further the wood decomposed, the stronger the smell of rot would become. If the wood was burned, the stink of the smoke would be fearsome enough to cause gagging by anyone who got even a little whiff of it. One of the most ingenious characteristics of the compound was that the smell and color it induced could not be removed by any chemical or mechanical process. Even paper pulp made from this affected stock would not shed much of the lurid colors or obnoxious smell. George reasoned that any logs from trees the chemical contacted would be commercially useless. Therefore, once the condition became widespread throughout the logging areas, most tree harvesting would stop. One more thing: as the chemical made its way into the underlying soil, it would have a similar effect on palm-oil trees. Basically, George's miracle chemical left the land useful for only one purpose: a natural habitat as creation intended it.

The other problem to be overcome was the process by which the chemical would be dispersed over the vast areas of jungle which needed protection. George had evaluated many possible solutions and settled on a fairly simple strategy. Since the compound was a gas, it could be mixed with helium and used to inflate weather balloons. These could then be released from sites upwind of the targeted areas. The balloons would gain altitude and drift with the prevailing wind over the target area. Information on barometric pressure and wind speed aloft (from the satellite weather fax) in conjunction with a stopwatch would permit calculations plotting the track of the balloon in order to drop the load at the right time. Pongo had helped design a device made from a cheap transistor FM receiver coupled to a solenoid and a highway flare. Taped to the bottom of the balloon, it would burn a hole and rupture the balloon after receiving a coded radio signal. Ideally the chemical would be released into a mass of storm clouds, allowing the compound to be carried down to earth mixed in the raindrops. With multiple balloons working inside the storms, very large tracts of trees could be treated at one time. The chemical was super-concentrated, so a small amount could treat millions of trees. George projected that under ideal conditions a single balloon load could convert upwards of seventy five square miles of jungle.

As Roger continued to lie awake, riding the aircraft's climbs and drops, he weighed the risks. It was a pretty safe bet that if the authorities in Borneo or Sumatra were to catch someone in the act of destroying some of the biggest industries in the nation's economy, the criminal consequences would be grave.

Another concern was the seven Orangutans themselves. As an endangered species, they were contraband, especially in the part of the world where they were headed. It would be a challenge, keeping them safely sequestered during the time required to enact the plan. They considered having only Roger and Kerri go down to Borneo, with George giving instructions via satellite telephone. But as the plan matured it was obvious this would not do. The release of the balloons and chemical drops were complex operations, needing myriad calculations done both on the computer as well as in George's remarkable brain. No. George's presence on-site was not just an option, it was required. And Pongo would be needed to help, because he had extraordinary capabilities as well. The others would assemble over a hundred transmitters and receivers and help prepare each balloon for launch. It would take all of them to do this, Orangs and humans, and they'd have to work together as never before. If for some unforeseen reason the balloons failed in some places, individuals with backpacks might have to go deep into the jungle to shoot batches of the chemical skyward with a small rocket launcher. Who better to do this than the Orangs themselves?

And then, there was their health. Theirs, and his own. What a fine bunch we make, he thought. They'll probably go down with strokes and paralysis before long, and I'll be blind and deaf by next Christmas. This was something he had not yet shared with Kerri. But that day of revelation was coming too. It must. The one consolation in all of it was this mission, if it succeeded.

It had been decided that the safest and most effective way to launch the balloons would be from the deck of a chartered yacht, just offshore from the mountainous jungles that were the target zones. The yacht had been arranged: a two hundred and ten foot Feadship, the "Mori", out of Singapore, with an all-Chinese crew. "Mori" was one of the most modern and luxurious mega-yachts in the world. It belonged to a long-time friend of Celine's, Mrs. Chou Su Lin, habitué and part-time resident of Singapore, Paris, New York, St. Moritz and Montana.

The yacht was chartered as a "vessel to carry a scientific research party, making inquiries into meteorological phenomena around the coastal areas of Borneo and Sumatra." Her captain was being highly paid to be discreet and to make every effort to take his passengers wherever they deemed necessary. The vessel awaited them at Kalalusu, a tiny remote island among the Molucca chain. Kalalusu is one of dozens of near-anonymous atolls and islets that dot the Celebes Sea off the extreme northern tip of Sulawesi, Indonesia. The ship's first officer had assured Celine that he was quite familiar with Kalalusu, a desolate patch of sand and coral. It was the perfect out-of-the-mainstream rendezvous for the "Mori" and her intended passengers arriving on the jet. There was a seasonal fishing camp on the island, and more important, a long coral airstrip built during WWII. Comings and goings there were generally overlooked by the mainland Customs officials; it was too far out in the ocean to represent any kind of smuggling haven for coastal traffic. It was a fishing outpost, that's all, and during parts of the season it was totally uninhabited. Roger and his group were to land there, transfer their gear to the yacht, then be off for however long the job took.

The jet rose and plunged. Roger sighed, raising his wrist, squinting at the luminous dial on his watch. Four twenty-five a.m. He had pre-set the watch to the correct time zone when they stopped to re-fuel at the Marquesas. Because of the need to avoid strict Customs inspections along their route from Switzerland, their flight plan had been the "long way around", the southern route, rather than the more direct northern track. Their re-fuelling stops had been along the "back-alleys" of world air-traffic. Leaving Europe they had flown directly to Anguilla in the western Caribbean, from there onto the Marquesas, and then the final leg to the Moluccas. They were scheduled to arrive on Kalalusu island around six-thirty a.m. local time.

Kerri mumbled something sweetly under her breath, bringing her face closer to his. He touched his lips to her forehead, then finally drifted into an uneasy sleep.

They were startled awake as the jet's wheels abruptly grappled the compacted crushed-coral runway running the long axis of the fishing island. As they bumped along to a stop at the far end of the airstrip, Roger looked out the cabin window and got a peek at the flat atoll, just turning pink in the sunrise. It was essentially featureless, very few palm trees. The only real landmarks were man-made: a clump of weathered buildings which might be housing, a warehouse at the edge of the lagoon, and a dilapidated old hangar with a weary DC-3 squatting inside.

He roused Kerri and they both dressed hurriedly. Going forward he found the apes awake, peering out the windows on both sides of the plane. As they looked up he motioned them to stay put. The stairway was deployed and Roger went down, expecting to be met by someone from the yacht. There was no one. Even though the sun had barely cleared the horizon, to Roger—having just arrived from the high Alps—the heat and humidity already seemed shocking. The air was thick as chowder. He scuffed at the white powdered coral underfoot, looking over his shoulder as Chuck Bartholdy came down the stairs.

"What's the deal, Roger, nobody to meet us?"

"I guess not," he mumbled. He scratched his head and scanned the area, still feeling half asleep.

"They're here, though," said Chuck. "See? Over there. Behind that long shed there's a dock. The boat's tied up over there." He began rolling up his sleeves. "Man. Hot, isn't it? Hell, they gotta know we're here. It'd be impossible to miss the sound of this jet coming in on a little postage stamp like this."

Roger squinted over and could make out the white radio mast and satellite dome of the "Mori", looming over the low roof of the wharf shed. Out beyond the structures, the beach and lagoon were visible. Waves were thrashing along the shallow reef.

"Want to walk over there? Maybe we should...oh, wait, hey. Here comes somebody." Chuck nodded at a small truck pulling away from the distant wharf. It came straight across the airstrip toward them. A few moments later they were shaking hands with a trim middle-aged Chinese man in a crisp white uniform, sporting a nautical cap, Bermuda shorts and knee socks. He spoke excellent English, introducing himself as Herbert Chung, second-in-command of the "Mori".

"Mr. Caldwell. Mr. Bartholdy," he said, bowing. "We welcome you to Kalalusu and "Mori"."

Chung was aware that there were seven animals to be dealt with. Many of the details of this charter had been handled directly by Celine Stertevant and Abby, and they had been very specific about the arrangements. In addition to personal baggage, there were boxes in the plane's cargo hold containing the folded balloons, electronic components, laptop computers and scuba-type tanks filled with the initial batch of George's mixture. Also packed was sophisticated lab equipment and bulk chemicals. George would need to cook up more of the formula as they went along.

After a little shuttling back and forth, everything and everyone was aboard the yacht. Chuck would ferry the plane to Singapore and await word about retrieving his passengers.

A few minutes later "Mori" had cleared the channel through the outer reef, her graceful bow throwing a smart wake at twenty knots, heading southwest. Roger was up on the bridge deck, consulting with Captain Lau Jian Seng. The captain's English was a bit spotty, so Chung was aiding the process as they agreed upon their immediate itinerary. A deafening roar swept overhead. It was "Arjuna". Chuck rolled the wings slightly as he raced out ahead of the yacht, skimming low over the ocean, then climbed steeply, banking and vanishing into one of the puffy clouds that shaded the horizon.

Captain Lau smiled at Roger. "Beautiful," he said in English.

Their route would head them for the Straits of Macassar, skirting the southern coastline of Borneo. There would be some stops in that area, and then from there they would proceed to the Java Sea, en route to Sumatra. At their normal rate of speed, the first landfall they would make would be some twenty-four to twenty-eight hours ahead. Roger was grateful. This would give them all some time to rest up and relax, and George would have an opportunity to get the equipment set up so he could commence monitoring the weather.

Roger made his way aft and went down the main staircase, proceeding toward the staterooms. He and Kerri had set up camp in the master stateroom. The Orangs were in the guest suites one deck below.

He looked around for Kerri. Her bag was on the floor, opened, and clothing casually distributed in the near vicinity. Her boots, which in complete opposition to the forces of Nature she had worn as little as possible in the freezing Swiss Alps, were discarded in a corner. Now on the enclosed rear sundeck, she was sprawled out on a chaise longue, nearly naked, sleeping in the warm tropical sun. He was tired himself, and the other chaise beside Kerri beckoned. He found his bag and prepared to undress, but then had the thought that he should check on the apes before napping.

No response after he knocked at the room where George, Pongo, Artod, and Trent were bunked. He cracked the door and saw all the curtains drawn, the animals lying on their berths with their travel clothing still on. Getting settled only a half hour before, they claimed not to be tired. Their suite also had a satellite TV set-up, and they had been scanning through the channels, their old favorite pastime. Now, the television was off and the room was silent.

"Hey, guys." Roger spoke softly. He went over to George. "You guys okay? Takin' a nap?"

George turned over slowly and raised his head a little to look at Roger.

"Roger. We've all got headaches." His voice sounded alarmingly weak, barely above a whisper. "Bad. Do you have anything stronger than this Tylenol? We've already taken four apiece and it doesn't seem to be working in the least bit."

"Wow. This just happened, huh? You guys were fine just awhile ago. Did you eat something or drink something?"

"No. Nothing. I don't feel like talking right now. Could you take care of us? My head's killing me and the others are the same. Could you, Roger?" He spoke with eyes closed, sounding desperate.

Roger felt a jab of panic. This was the worst he'd ever seen them. "Sure. Sure I will, George. I'll go get the kit right now." He looked in on the females. Same situation.

He located the medicine box in his cabin. Mark Lewis had sent it to him before the group left Switzerland, and it contained syringes and vials of the painkiller, Demerol. There was also morphine, if things got that bad. Roger had been given a basic course in administering injections. Returning back downstairs, he touched George on the shoulder.

"Any better?"

"No better. Did you get us something?"

"Yeah. There's Demerol. I can give you guys injections. I don't know exactly how long it lasts, but at least three or four hours. Mark says it'll kill just about any kind of pain. That okay?"

George lowered his head back to the pillow. "Yes, please. Go ahead."

One by one, Roger prepared the syringes. He did the males, then went into the females' cabin. When he was done he went back to the suites' shared sitting room and began re-packing the kit. He was still doing that when George and Pongo strolled out and nonchalantly sat on the couch opposite Roger.

Roger looked at them expectantly. "You feel better?"

"Oh, yes. Much better, thank you so much," George said. His speech was soft-edged from the narcotic. But his face had relaxed noticeably. Slumping into the cushions, he allowed his head to rest against the seat-back but kept his eyes open. He turned to Pongo for a moment, and the other ape gave him a bleary glance.

It seemed to Roger that they were communicating non-verbally. "So. Do you have any idea why this happened so suddenly?" he asked softly.

"Probably the air pressure change in the plane's cabin made it worse. This time. But I really don't think we've got a lot of time left." George said this without apparent fear. "The thing that most concerns us is to get this job of protecting the forests completed before our physical problems become overwhelming. Get it done while we can still function. I don't like to dwell on it, but if our brains keep swelling, along with strokes we might have seizures or even go insane before it kills us. We don't want you or Kerri to have to deal with a problem like that. Pongo and I talked about this on the plane while we were coming down here. We decided that if that sort of thing were really to happen, we would want you to kill us, Roger. Just give us an overdose."

Roger couldn't believe what he'd just heard. He felt his whole body stiffen and his mouth go dry.

"Damn it, George! Don't even talk like that. Nothing like that is going to happen, for God's sake. We'll find a way to take care of this, I know we will. Just put that crap out of your minds."

They all just sat there then, looking away from each other. The subtle vibration of the ship's engines pulsed up through the floor, and Roger's attention was drawn to a little bronze sculpture of a whale which sat on the coffee table by the couch. It rattled against the glass top very slightly with each new wave of vibration. At that point, it created a welcome diversion, and he rose and went over to it, slipping a piece of paper beneath it to silence the rattle. He turned and stared at the two Orangutans, feeling quite upset by what George had just said.

"Okay, listen." Roger stopped and crossed his arms, trying not to let his voice shake. "I understand this is a serious problem. But we'll find a way to deal with it. I'll do anything it takes. We're not going to lose anybody. Okay? So, do me a favor." Now his voice rose. "Never say anything again about having me kill you. Got it?"

The apes looked up, surprised by his intensity.

"Okay, Roger. We won't," Pongo promised in a sobered voice.

"Good." Roger sighed and walked over to one of the curtained windows. He pulled the drapery back and gazed out at the placid tropical sea sliding by. "Now, I don't know if you guys are going to feel up to it later, but if you do, come upstairs and get me. Kerri and I can help set up your equipment. George, we'll do whatever else you need. The captain just told me that we'd be underway for nearly a whole day before we get to our first target zone in Borneo. That'll give everybody time to unwind." He turned back around and walked over to the two apes. They hadn't moved at all, and now they both had their eyes closed. Roger reached down and touched George's arm.

"Are you awake?"

George's eyes flickered. "Oh, sorry, Roger," he murmured. "Really sleepy now. I think I'll take a nap for awhile." He smiled up dreamily. "My headache's all gone, thank you very much." He closed his eyes again, not moving. Roger mounted the stairs back up to the master suite.

With the arrival of the dinner hour, Roger called up to the purser and asked that the evening meal be served in their quarters. He requested that foods for the Orangutans also be brought to the master suite. The animals were accustomed to eating with their owners, he explained. The food was brought in and the serving staff withdrew. The apes revived enough to come up for dinner, and as they did it was apparent that their headaches were still vanquished. They went right for the bar. Pongo's sense of humor had returned as well. He loved black humor, and after a few cocktails he got up and did one of his enormously amusing Jack Nicholson imitations, this one a scene from "The Shining".

"You believe his health might be at stake," he sneered, posturing. He glowered and thrust his huge, jowly face right up to Kerri's. "You are concerned about him." She giggled, assuming the role of the quivering Mrs. Torrance, using a rolled-up magazine as her baseball bat, swatting at him while shrinking away. Pongo chased her over the back of the couch. "Gimme the bat, Wendy. I'm not gonna hurt yuh. I'm just gonna bash your brains in!" The others fell on the floor.

Dinner was delicious and the mood convivial. The yacht proved to have a very impressive wine cellar. Afterward they all sat out on the rear deck watching the moon rise over the shimmering wake. Charts were brought out to pinpoint their initial target areas. They discussed the weather. George planned to set up his equipment the next morning to get satellite pictures of cloud formations and barometric pressure bars in their destination area. Nothing would be better than a storm.

No more mention of the earlier headaches was made, but Roger could not help stealing looks at them throughout the evening. He felt curious and concerned. Beyond pain medication, he hadn't the slightest idea what to do. The party broke up early; they all knew the next day would be a long one. Their first anchorage off Borneo would be made in mid-afternoon.

Before bed Roger and Kerri went up to the bow deck, standing with their arms around each other, feeling the warm, humid wind rushing past them. The sky was the darkest purple imaginable, with stars like hundred-watt bulbs scattered in boggling profusion. The bow rose and fell gently as the powerful yacht muscled through the ocean swells.

"Hey." Roger whispered in Kerri's ear. "You miss Santa Barbara?"

She put her lips against his ear. "No." Then, after a moment, "You?"

"No." He buried his face in her hair, smelling sandalwood oil and flowers.

Her voice took on an edge of concern. "The Orangs and all the headache stuff. It's really scaring me. Is it going to be okay?"

He waited a long time before answering. "I don't know, honey. I just don't know."

Chapter 35

"We're in luck, Roger," George remarked. "Take a look at this. There's a good strong low pressure trough moving in here, and we're almost certain to get some rain over the mountains out of it."

It was around seven-thirty in the morning and Roger had just walked into the Orang's suite. Pongo was lounging on the couch, attired in a pair of Hawaiian-print bathing trunks and a Rolling Stones t-shirt; his attention focused on the television screen where CNN World Report was in progress. George, swaddled in a white terry-cloth bathrobe with "Mori" embroidered on the breast pocket, handed Roger a sheet he had just ripped from his weather fax. He had highlighted the satellite photograph with a red felt tip pen, and a line of encroaching cloud cover was clearly visible, striping diagonally, approaching the dotted outline of the northeastern Bornean coastline.

"I guess that explains why it started getting a little rough here last night." Roger gestured out the window at a substantial running sea. Sometime around midnight the "Mori" had begun to pitch against her ground tackle.

For two days they had been lying at anchor, tucked away in a remote cove along the desolate coast near the village of Tanahmerah, Borneo. They were at four degrees north latitude, less than a half-day's travel from the equator. It had been sunny, humid and stultifying hot when they had arrived. Directly inland from them was a vast swampy delta, one of the most bio diverse areas on the entire planet. The thousands of insects which converged around their lights at night were

345

unfamiliar and often bizarre, unlike anything Roger and Kerri had ever seen. The ship's crew had warned them about which ones would bite or sting; this seemed to be nearly all of them. The clear skies were expected to change; George was tracking a low pressure front that had been sweeping directly toward their anchorage. The original weather projections stipulated that Tanahmerah would be the ideal spot from which to launch their initial barrage of balloons. Now, however, it seemed that the brunt of the developing weather would move slightly north and east, necessitating a change of position.

"Okay." Roger turned the image around in his hands, finding the proper orientation. "Yeah, that looks good, George, I guess. I mean, it's all heading in the right direction, right?" He looked at the Orangutan with a quizzical expression—it was clear who was the expert here.

George took the image back in hand and ran his finger along a section of it.

"See here? These are the places that will get the most wind and rain. The coastal lowlands and the mountainous regions along the Brassey, Witti and Walker ranges. Prime territory for us, Roger. Exactly where we want to get wide coverage. That's the heart of Central Sabah, and with help from the wind, we'll also get sporadic coverage clear down into the forests of northern Sarawak. We need to be dead upwind from the target zones. But we won't be if we stay here...we'll miss the best wind channel. It's changing, because the front is moving more westerly from the Celebes Sea and that means we would do much better to be up here." He gestured at a spot on the chart. "The Turtle Islands, off from Kuala Kinabatangan. That's where we'll get the best results from our balloon releases. Could we ask the captain to run us up the coast to the Turtle Islands right away? It's only a hundred seventy-four nautical miles."

Roger spread his arms, palms up. "Hey, it's our call. He takes us where we want to go. The Turtle Islands it is."

Within minutes the anchor was aboard and "Mori" was underway, heading for the pristine, isolated clumps of land which jut from the sea to the east of Sabah. According to the charts on the ship's bridge, there were good anchorages throughout the area, and although Captain Lau was not personally familiar with these islands, he saw nothing that would prevent them from navigating and finding safe holding-ground in that area. The run up the coast was exciting, with a strong header sea building in intensity as they neared their destination. By two in the afternoon, "Mori" was maneuvering bow-on into a burly twenty five knot wind, directly to the lee of a tiny islet. The small bit of rock and vegetation was nonetheless rather tall, and it afforded an excellent deep-water anchorage while blocking most of the prevailing wind and swell. Snugging the big Feadship close into the sheltering lee, the crew set the ground tackle uneventfully.

George was intent, down in his suite. He was watching his own instruments and checking the satellite weather update every fifteen minutes or so. The others, on standby, sat around on the couches, zoning on U.S.A. satellite television and waiting for George to give them the word. Abruptly, he did.

"Okay. This is it, everybody. It's time. Let's get up to the deck and get a couple of balloons set, please. We'll start with two and see how we make out. I'll help you fill them."

Everyone jumped up and began getting the pressure tanks and balloons ready. There was no rain as yet, but the wind was puffing from fifteen to thirty knots. The skies to the east were dark and the temperature had fallen at least ten degrees. They brought the tanks and balloons up onto the large deck aft of the master suites. The wind in the area directly to the lee of the island was far less than was evident only a few hundred yards out to either side of the large yacht. Roger and Kerri held the neck of one of the balloons to the pressure nozzle on one of the helium tanks. George had assembled a special valve which mixed the active chemical compound into the helium flow. The wind was a problem as they inflated the first balloon; the big gas bag bounced around, nearly slipping their grasp several times. As it finished filling, Roger twisted the stem and doubled it over, then tied it off with nylon line as they had rehearsed. Then Kerri strapped the electronics package onto the base, using lots of duct tape. All in all, the whole thing went smoothly. George stepped in and studied the assemblage. He turned to Kerri, raising his voice over the wind.

"The batteries were in the receiver when you attached it? And you turned it on?"

"Yep. Made sure."

"And the flare side of the box is against the balloon?"

"Totally."

George noted the time on his watch. "Let it go."

It was astonishing how fast the yellow orb took off. It shot up into the blackening sky, and when it reached about one hundred feet of altitude, it was no longer blocked from the sweeping wind by the land mass of the island. It hit the wind stream up there and began to disappear downrange, constantly gaining altitude.

"Okay, looks good," George said, squinting up at the fleeting balloon. "Let's get the other one set right away, we'll need to have them both go off in the same place."

By the time they had the second balloon ready to go, the rain had become ferocious and they were all soaked. The wind was whipping now, and it took a huge effort to prevent the slippery balloon from being torn away as they were preparing it. Pongo gripped the base of the big pneumatic rubber bag, using his powerful hands and bulky body to anchor the thing as it strained to escape. Again, George checked it over. When it was released, this second balloon vanished within seconds, obscured by the heavy sheets of rain. They all went inside to dry off and monitor conditions, calculating when to send the radio signal that would trigger the drop.

George slumped in his chair, a towel over his head and shoulders. He was fixated on a stop watch, computer screens, anemometer readings, and weather fax updates. On the table in front of him was an FM transmitter, a common "business-band" type transceiver which he had modified to have far greater than normal output power. When he pushed a button, it would transmit a series of tones on the frequency to which the now airborne receivers were tuned.

"Well, it looks like we're going to do quite well here," George murmured to no one in particular, while studying the satellite image. "The wind is going exactly where we need it to and I think we'll be able to send the drop signal in about thirty to forty-five minutes."

While Betty, Emily, Chloé, and Artod worked at assembling another set of receiver devices with flares, Roger, Kerri, Pongo and Trent played a game of Rummy at the corner table. Above the rain lashing the windows, Kerri caught part of what George said.

"You're gonna send the signal, George?"

He cleared his throat and spoke louder. "No, no. Not for about forty-five minutes. It's looking good, though."

"Something I've been wondering about, George," Roger said gingerly, looking up from his cards. "How are you gonna know for sure if those balloons actually rupture? What if the device fails, or the radio signal doesn't get through? We don't have 'em on radar or anything, do we?"

The small red ape turned in his chair. With a white towel framing his primitive features, he had the appearance of a monk. "No, they're not on radar. But they'll rupture, don't worry. I know, for sure." He paused, then pulled back his big lips in a huge grin. This infected the others with giddiness and they all laughed, pointing at him.

About an hour later George still hadn't sent the signal. He was hovering over his computers, watching the displays. Between hands of Rummy (Pongo was winning big) Roger kept glancing over, apprehensive that the button had not been pushed. He was on the point of asking if something was wrong, when the Orangutan's finger flicked out and touched the switch. There was nothing else to show that anything at all had happened. No light, no bell, nothing. George said nothing and continued to look at the weather satellite display on a video screen. Roger gestured to the others and now they all fixed their attention on George.

"You did it?" Roger asked.

George half turned, nodding. "Yes. That was it."

Kerri got up and went over to stand behind George's chair. She leaned over his shoulder and studied the monitors. "Where, George? Can you show me on the screen?"

He pointed to a spot where the satellite depiction of cloud cover seemed quite dense. "That's almost exactly where the balloons are now—or, where they were, until just a moment ago. Right now, the chemical agent is getting spread all over in the sky above this region," he circled his finger across the screen, "and the rain and upper level winds are going to really distribute it. We're lucky, actually. We did better on the first try than I expected."

Roger now crossed the room to look. "Wow, look at all those cloud echoes. Must be raining pretty hard up in the mountains, huh? And you popped 'em up there. But, George, come on. Tell me, just for the hell of it. How can you know, for sure, that they did rupture? How do you know that one of 'em or even both of 'em didn't get caught in a downdraft somewhere and just went into a mountainside or something? How do you know they didn't get struck by lightning? I'm just really curious." George had pulled the towel off his head and was scratching his scalp. He started typing something on one of his lap-tops, distracted, seemingly not having heard Roger's question. Then he stopped to look out the window at the water sluicing down.

"Well, Roger," he said very softly, "every little thing is connected. Connected and re-connected." He turned to the two humans standing behind his chair. "I knew we were going to Switzerland, didn't I?" And for the second time that day, he produced a huge grin.

The weather continued foul for the next three days and George insured that they made full use of the opportunity. They filled and released balloons at various times of the day and even a couple of times in the middle of the night, all the while directing Captain Lau and his crew to move the yacht to this place or that, up and down the entire upper-eastern coast of Borneo. The wind would change, or a barometric pressure bar would shift, and they would weigh anchor and decamp to the next optimum location, simple as that. George would come up with a new point on the charts and Roger would relate this to Mr. Chung. Each time he went to the bridge to request a move, Roger mused about what the crew was making of all this arbitrary chasing around. It was fortunate that on a pricey charter like the "Mori", no explanations were needed. Celine's money did all the talking.

The apes and humans were now on a very irregular schedule. They ate and slept only when convenient. The work took priority. They had almost entirely isolated themselves from the yacht's crew, who had been told not to come aft into the guest quarters without first obtaining permission. Food was brought in only when requested, with Roger and Kerri carrying the dirty dishes back up to the galley. Each time balloons were sent up, the follow-through was the same: George hunching at his computers, the rest of them soldering and assembling the next batch of radio relay devices and flare boxes. Then the button would eventually be pushed and they would move on and do it again. It was a methodical carpet bombing of some of the most awe inspiring rainforests and mountainous jungles on the planet. Only these bombs were raining life, not death; preservation and salvation, not destruction. By the time the first storm had run its course, they had been at twelve different anchorages and released a total of seventy-nine balloons.

Chapter 36

It was now Sunday, the fourteenth of January, 1990. The weather had begun clearing the previous evening and they had sent up the last balloon of this series around seven p.m. George announced there was no additional weather on the horizon within the next forty-eight to seventy-two hours. This meant that they could all unwind for awhile, get some sleep and take regular meals. While they were exhilarated that their mission was going as planned, they were all bone-tired. The idea of a few days to relax sounded good.

They had a little party to celebrate their progress. After dinner Artod got up and performed a song and dance from "Westside Story". With the sound-track on the stereo, he sang along with Natalie Wood. His hips wrapped in a towel to make a skirt, he raised his growly voice to a lilting falsetto. Prancing around, jumping on the furniture, he pouted and smoldered. Betty, Emily, and Chloé were the chorus. "I feel pretty, oh so pretty..." Halfway through the song Kerri was hysterical—paralyzed on the floor in a fetal position, unable to breathe. She waved her hand for mercy, but Artod rushed over and smooched her with his floppy lips, crooning "Pretty, so pretty, and gay!"

The next morning, Roger asked Chung if he could recommend an attractive island nearby where they could anchor up and enjoy the sunshine. They wanted to snorkel, play with the ship's jet ski and Avon skiff, maybe do a little beachcombing and exploring. "Maratua", the officer responded immediately. Not far from the coastal town of Tanjungbatu, it was an uninhabited atoll with extensive coral reefs. This was the ideal spot, he assured Roger, and it would further work well since the ship was in need of some fresh fruit and other perishable provisions, which would quite likely be available at Tanjungbatu. Roger approved.

After briefly idling just off Tanjungbatu while a shore party made the necessary purchases, "Mori" again made out to sea, now headed for Maratua atoll. Within two hours they were setting tackle again, with the beautiful little island as a backdrop.

For the next three days the weather was idyllic. Cloudless skies, light breeze, temperatures in the low nineties. The ocean grew calm; royal blue, sparkling and mirthful. Roger and Kerri swam and sunned, buzzed around on the jet ski, snorkeled along the colorful reefs, and spent relaxing hours strolling on the atoll's sugar white beaches. They took the Orangs exploring through the island's central coconut tree groves and had picnics in the cool shade there. The apes spent some time climbing in the trees, something they missed in their new lives. They also got rides on the jet ski.

Once, Roger spotted one of the crew members standing at the rail near the bridge, snapping photos of him and Pongo on the jet-ski as they raced under the bow. This was precisely the sort of thing he worried about. Although the apes were not seen talking or otherwise engaging in any pointedly non-ape-like behavior, they were nonetheless being recorded on film, riding around on a jet-ski, and there was just something threatening about this. He considered whether he should take up the matter with Mr. Chung; perhaps this would only serve to draw even more unwanted attention to the subject. After that he kept the jet-ski and the Avon well away from the yacht.

On the "Mori" Roger and Kerri had been drawing closer. Of course, they were sleeping together. The sex just seemed to get better each time. And it would be hard not to feel pretty giddy, being aboard one of the world's premier yachts. It was a perfect place to be romantic. But now, the relationship was getting to be a full blown thing, and Roger was growing uneasy. He knew what lay ahead for him and he hadn't been upfront about it with Kerri. She was affectionate and easygoing. That let him muse that she could be casual about their attachment, but he knew that wasn't true.

On the morning of their third and last day at Maratua atoll, all of them were at breakfast on the master suite sundeck. Roger assumed that they would all do pretty much the same thing as the day before: pack a lunch and take the jet ski and the Avon into the lagoon. They would swim and play and spend the afternoon napping in the shade of the coconut trees.

"Can you guys be ready to go in about fifteen? I think the cook should have our lunch just about packed." Roger lifted his chin expectantly at the group.

Pongo wiped his mouth, not seeming in any hurry. His eyes flicked over at George, who was distracted by the television. It was tuned to CNN World News, something the Orangs relished at the beginning of each day.

"I think we'll stay here today, Roger. You and Kerri go on over without us, why don't you."

Roger sat up and looked closely at Pongo. "Really? Why? Don't you all want to go? You don't have another headache, do you?"

The headaches had returned in the last week. Once, a few of the apes needed injections.

George shifted his attention from the news report.

"Oh, no. Nothing like that, Roger." His face was blank, pleasant. "We just want to stay out of the sun today, that's all. It's going to be quite hot."

"You and Kerri please just go ahead and have a good time," Emily added, spooning up some papaya. "We want to read and watch the television. We'll be okay, honey-pie."

George got up. "And I have a little work to do on the computer. Actually, before you go, could you come downstairs and help me with something for a moment? I'd appreciate it."

Roger rose from the table and followed the lumbering Orangutan as he swayed down the circular staircase, heading for the lower suite. When they were inside, with the door closed, George turned and eyed Roger.

"There's nothing to help me with, Roger. I made that up so I could speak with you privately."

"I see. Well, that's okay, George, nothing wrong with that." Roger then stood and looked at him, but George said nothing. He just looked back at Roger pleasantly, as if they were about nothing more than discussing the weather outside church after the Sunday service. Roger finally said "So?"

"All of us want you and Kerri to have the day to yourselves today, that's what I wanted to tell you. We've all been together so much, maybe it would be nice for you two to be on the island alone today." He paused and smiled, conveying a sense of mystery. "Are you going snorkeling? The water is so clear, isn't it? Yes. Have a good time with Kerri, Roger. The rest of us will be fine here today." George reached out and took Roger's elbow, squeezing it a little. This all seemed so odd that Roger giggled nervously. He suspected the apes had planned some kind of elaborate practical joke.

He half-leered at George, hoping to get some sense of what was up. The Orang gave up nothing, however, just fixed his usual mild expression.

"Well. Alright then, George. If you're...sure you don't want to go. We'll go on over."

Back up in the master suite, Roger and Kerri packed the few items they'd need for a day of leisure. Roger described George's behavior. Kerri was stuffing her mask and flippers into a mesh bag, shaking her head and grinning.

"You think they're gonna ace us somehow, huh?"

"I don't know, what do you think?"

Kerri looked out the window at the island, shimmering in the morning glare.

"Pongo didn't let on about anything after you guys left, but then...those little devils."

They both traded a look.

"Well, shit." Kerri threw the bag over her shoulder. "Let's not get all defensive here. I mean, so a bucket of cold oatmeal falls out of the palm tree or something like that. After all, how much could they do?

Roger raised his eyebrows. "Oh, quite a lot."

The beauty of their surroundings that day was almost overwhelming. The skies were preternaturally blue, with cloud billows camping right along the horizon, their towers reflected in the placid slick of the ocean. A nominal breeze stirred, just enough to rustle the tops of the coconut trees and cool the skin. They snorkeled on the reef, hand-feeding the colorful schools of parrot fish. A perfect little lunch: smoked salmon on baguettes, a fruit salad, some cheese, and a bottle of iced Montrachet. They took a nap after lunch, and after about an hour Roger decided to hop in the lagoon and wake up a bit. Kerri was still sleeping, so he got up quietly and walked down the slope of the beach, slipping his mask over his face as he entered the gin-clear water. He swam along lazily, floating, looking down at the coral and fish like he was in a dream. He noticed something: the same patterns of light that had occurred in the Tornquist's pool back in Montecito, these same hypnotic lines were crossing the sandy bottom of the lagoon. It was because of the calm conditions, he realized. Normally the surface of the lagoon would be too choppy to allow these lines to be so clear. He entered his favorite meditative state, floating with his head down, uninterrupted due to the snorkel.

There was the blurry form of manta-ray stirring the sand on the bottom about seven or eight feet directly beneath his position. He hovered, keeping very still, enjoying the languorous wanderings of the ray as it fluffed the sand, looking for a morsel. There was a sparkle then, a glinting. Roger looked closely. The ray moved on and the sparkling thing was still there, although near completely concealed by the ruffled sand. When the ray was well off, Roger took a gulp of air and dove, carefully brushing the sand away with his fingers. He was amazed as he plucked the item off the bottom. Even without his glasses, he could see that it was a ring, a gold ring, with what seemed to be a sizeable diamond set in its band. He returned to the surface and pulled his mask back, gripping the ring firmly as he treaded water. He examined it more closely. Yep, no doubt about it. It was an engagement ring, very valuable if the stone was genuine. The marquis diamond was easily over two carats. He marveled at the thing, glittering in the sunlight. It had to have been lost there recently, he reasoned. Some wealthy woman would be most upset. He scrutinized the inside of the band, looking for markings or an inscription. And there was something, but he couldn't focus enough to read it. Roger was excited and he turned back toward the beach, intent on showing Kerri his remarkable prize.

He had found the ring about seventy yards offshore, a distance he could easily cover in about three or four minutes, steadily kicking his flippers. But in that short time a powerful feeling came over him. This freak discovery was a sign, he decided. It was a tipping point, giving him the courage to do something he should have done a long time ago. He must tell Kerri, right here on this perfect little island, that he was losing his sight and hearing. He must explain how extravagantly he loved her, but he must have the integrity to give her the sad facts and release her to go on to find someone with whom she could truly be happy. He had been selfish and dishonest, he would confess, and now it was time to come clean. She deserved that much and more, and the ring was a present he could give her to soften the pain she would feel.

In the shallows he paused, leaning down to take off his flippers. Up by the trees Kerri was doing yoga, or her own version of it. On her towel she was entirely naked except for the strings of shells, beads and beach trinkets that she had recently added to her adornments. The mid-afternoon sunlight was coming through the palms behind, illuminating her in a most ethereal manner. She was dark as teakwood from the equatorial sun, and her hair (which she'd grown out a bit) had become more blond than chestnut. Roger tried not to succumb to her physical magnificence, especially not at this troubling moment. He got closer and he could see her most strikingly beautiful, wild face. Her eyes were closed as she lay prone, arching her upper body up from the ground. He began to move faster, reaching the dry sand, trotting now. This must be done, this full accounting, even though it would ruin this idyllic moment. He made a vain try to stop himself; to turn around and go back into the water. But it was as if he was on rails. He sank heavily to his knees about three feet from Kerri's towel. A few drops of water flew off as he came down; they splashed her. She looked up and smiled, shading her eyes.

"Hey lover. How's the water?" Her voice was soothing and cool. She sounded thoroughly relaxed. Good, Roger thought.

For his part, he felt a searing sensation between his eyes, like the flame of a blowtorch on his forehead.

"The water? Oh, wonderful, wonderful." He looked off down the beach for an instant. "Hey, uh...listen, Kerri. Have you got a minute?"

"What?"

"Oh, yeah." He rolled his eyes with a strained laugh as he realized how idiotic the question had been. "Well, okay, listen. I've been thinking about things a lot. Quite a bit, actually. About you, Kerri. And I wanted to tell you that I think you're just, incredible..." he now stumbled, "as a, uh, a person, I mean. You're incredible." He felt a band of apprehension constricting his throat and he stalled, composing his next sentence. He had the ring balled firmly in his fist and that hand began to tremor.

Kerri sat up and squinted at him now, baffled. "Okay."

"What I mean to...what I'm saying, Kerri, is that, it's been great being here with you. But I think you should know the truth about how things are."

Her face hardened. "Wait a minute, Roger. You're not, like, sending me home or something like that, are you?" Her mood had changed in an instant and she was glaring now.

"Oh, no." He shook his head, throwing more water. This wasn't going well. "I wish that's all it was. But the thing is, there's something way worse." He exhaled deeply. "Kerri, I don't think we should stay together."

Before he could say another word her hand was around his throat and she clamped down hard. "Shut up. You shut up, Roger." Her words were hard as steel, and a menacing look came into her eyes that he'd never seen before. Damn, she was strong, and he couldn't breathe.

Her voice became the low snarl of an animal. "If you're trying to break up with me, I'll thrash you right here, I mean it."

Her other hand came up. He felt more than a touch of panic. If he actually had to fight this girl to get her hands off his neck he wasn't at all sure who would win. He waved furiously shaking his head. "Let...me...finish," he gurgled.

She relaxed her grip, but just a bit. "Don't even go there," she warned.

He talked fast, words gushing out. "No, Kerri, listen, listen. It's not that. I'm...see, I've got something called Usher's Syndrome. It's a nerve disease. There's no cure for it. I got it before I met you. My father had it, and like I told you before, he killed himself. That's why. It'll make me blind and deaf, maybe in only a year. I was going to kill myself, at Glenwhylden. But right before I could do it I met the apes."

She kept her hands at his throat, her eyes clouding with suspicion. "That's bullshit."

He gently took hold of her forearms. "No, honey. I only wish it was. You know the thick glasses I have to wear? And the way I can't hear you half the time? You get pissed off having to repeat things to me. Well, pretty soon I won't be able to see or hear at all. Kerri, honey it's true, it really is, and I'm sorry. And what I'm getting at...is that I won't be any good for you. How could I be, all messed up like this?"

Now her eyes filled with tears. "You're not lying, are you? You better not be lying, Roger."

"No. I should have told you. But I put it off. That was wrong, but I...it was too wonderful being with you."

She launched forward and held him as tight as the death grip she'd had on his throat. "Oh god, Roger," she cried. "Is that all it is? That's it? You're going deaf and blind, and that's what this is all about?"

At this he pushed her away, frowning with his own anger. "Well, yeah, Kerri. Deaf and blind, yeah, that's all. Excuse me, but it seems like kind of a big fucking deal to me."

"Roger, no, it's totally a big deal, I know that, that's not what I meant." She looked down, her voice shrinking. "I just thought...I thought you were gonna tell me you didn't love me."

He shook his head in befuddlement. "Kerri. Of course I love you. I love you beyond anyone else, ever. How could you doubt that? That's why I'm telling you this now, so I don't string you along. Who wants a guy who's blind and deaf?"

She fixed him with blazing eyes and put her hands on either side of his face. "Listen here, Roger. You pay attention. I want you. You get it? I want you. I don't care if you're blind and deaf. I'll be there for you. I'll do the seeing, I'll do the hearing. Whenever you reach your hand out I'll be right there to take it. You understand? We're together, and I'm going stay with you however you are. It's final, you're stuck with me, got that?"

He felt tears on his cheeks. How could anyone be so lucky?

"You're so young. You'll change your mind," he murmured.

"You ever say that again and I'll slug you good." She hugged him once more and held him tight for a long time. Finally her eyes fell to the towel and she spotted the ring he'd dropped there when she grabbed his throat.

She picked it up. "What's this?"

"Oh, crap. I was about to show you that before you went after me. It's a gold ring. I just found it, out there on the reef while I was snorkeling."

She was examining it, growing excited. "You found it? My god, it's beautiful." Then, "You're full of shit, you expect me to believe that?"

He spread his palms. "I'm completely serious. I was looking at the bottom, I saw this manta ray move, and then that ring was sparkling in the sand where the ray had been. Somebody must have lost it."

She squinted at him. "Somebody? Roger, this is Celine's engagement ring. She's shown it to me before. I remember the diamond and this inscription inside the band, 'Forever Dear Heart, 1921.' And the diamond is set into these little gold acorns."

"What?"

"Here..." she rummaged in their bag and handed him his glasses. "See for yourself." Roger stared dumbly at the details. "No. I don't get it. How'd it end up out there on the reef?"

They looked at each other, then both said at the same time, "George."

He smiled at the realization. "Celine must have given it to him. That's why he wanted me to let him swim off the jet ski yesterday. He made me stop out there. And that's why he sent us over here alone today. Jeez, you ever feel like we're nothing but puppets? But how the hell could he ever expect me to find that thing?"

She moved over to his lap and held her hand up, sliding the ring onto her finger. "I don't know, and right now I don't care. How about we make this official?"

He happily gave up. It was a done deal. They lingered on Maratua almost into the evening, watching the pre-sunset colors sift into the clouds and reflect off the lagoon. They talked for a long time about how much their lives had changed—how all this excitement might be a hard act to follow later when things became more mundane back at home. Finally, when the sun was just about to kiss the horizon, they started the jet-ski and headed back to the "Mori", first making a leisurely loop around the lagoon, taking a long look at what now would forever be "their" island.

All the Orangs acted surprised and delighted when given an account of the day's events. George remained opaque, claiming ignorance.

"Honey," Emily said as she encircled Kerri with her huge arms. "You beat me to it. I was thinking I'd marry Roger."

Chapter 37

After dinner George showed them the latest computer models. New unstable air masses were forming east of Sumatra and they might turn these to their advantage. However, a substantial distance would have to be covered in order to reach their next position of opportunity. George suggested that part of the run be made overnight. Time was short if they were to intercept this new storm. The call to the bridge was made, and Chung said "Mori" would soon be underway on the prescribed southerly course, later turning west to skirt along the lower coast of Belitung. Then they would anchor near Bangka island, off the southeast tip of Sumatra. Chung cautioned that the weather where they were headed would make conditions onboard uncomfortable. Nothing that would threaten the yacht, but still bouncy and wet.

By early morning much rougher seas were marching under a sky veiled by a high cloud deck. There was no land in sight as Roger sat up in bed and looked out of the window. He decided to let Kerri sleep and went into the other room to call Celine and the others. He wanted to give them the good news about the engagement. The phone at Glenwhylden rang only once before Polk's familiar voice came on the line.

"Whitney. It's Roger. How you doing?"

"Oh, Roger. Ah'm so glad you called." For some reason Polk sounded down. "How is everything on that boat way out there?"

"Fine, Whitney. Really good, actually. I hope everybody's doing fine there? We have a bit of wonderful news to share with everyone."

"Well, uh...Mrs. Stertevant and Mrs. Horvath aren't here right now. Matter of fact they're both over to the hospital. They've been there all last night."

Roger drew a breath, readying himself for what he might hear next.

"They're at the hospital, you said? What's the matter, Whitney—is Mrs. Stertevant still sick?"

"Yes...yes." There was a long pause on the line, and static, then haltingly, "There's some terrible bad news. We didn't even get the word about this ourselves until yesterday evening. It's so sad, surely is. I guess Mrs. Stertevant has got cancer."

Roger straightened and pressed the receiver tightly to his ear.

"Whitney, wait a minute. What did you just say? Celine has cancer?"

"Yes, Roger, she does." The butler's voice was quite low, barely audible.

"Oh, man. No."

"Yes. It's terrible. Bless her heart. We're all prayin' for her, every minute. But I think she's pretty bad. Mrs. Horvath tells me that's what the doctors say. Stage four, they call it. She got pancreatic cancer. She'd been gettin' worse the last week or two, havin' a fever and all. Just feelin' sick all the time since she got back here from Switzerland. We didn't know what it was. Thing is, she didn't tell nobody about this for a long time. She kept it to herself and so she didn't get to the doctor early on. Everybody's real sad around here right now. I guess Mrs. Horvath was going to call you this morning."

"No, Whitney. I can't believe it. I just...I don't know what to say. I feel terrible." Desolate, he sank down onto the couch, looking out at the pitching, steel-blue ocean. His empty stomach was churning.

"Yes. The staff's just all down in the dumps, you know."

"Well, sure. Sure." Roger floundered, trying to think of what to ask next. "Whitney, have you been told, or...can she be treated? Are they going to start her on chemotherapy or something?"

"Don't know, Roger. They're doing some things for her at the hospital. Mrs. Horvath and me drove her over yesterday afternoon because she fainted, you understand, when she get up to go to the bathroom. I was real concerned. She's lost a lot of weight. And Mrs. Horvath has been over there with her all night."

"Oh my God. She looked bad in Switzerland but I didn't have a clue it was this."

Roger finished his sad conversation with Polk, asking that the butler please have Abby call him just as soon as possible. He had completely forgotten to mention his and Kerri's engagement. It now seemed all but insignificant. He went out on the rear sundeck, just to get some air. Standing out in the whipping gusts, he stared at the foaming wake of the yacht and allowed himself to cry.

Back inside the steward was quietly setting the dining table for breakfast. Roger nodded as he came in. The crew on the "Mori" had been just wonderful to all of them. Service in the guest living quarters had been a paradigm of politeness, propriety and respect for privacy. Not once had anyone entered the Orangutans' rooms without first checking with Roger. Everything was always done just right, with amazing attention to detail.

Roger slumped on the couch just as another steward arrived with the hot food cart. Roger glanced at his watch: seven-twenty, right on time. There was a standing arrangement for breakfast, and the Orangs knew that it was alright to mount the steps to join Roger and Kerri in the master suite after seven-thirty. Roger thanked the men as they left, then went into the bedroom to see if Kerri was up yet. The tousled bed was vacant; he sat on its edge, waiting for her to come out of the bathroom. Presently she did, still working her wet hair with a towel. Seeing Roger there with a doleful expression, she knew something was wrong. She crossed the room and sat beside him.

"You don't look so good. What's the matter?"

"Yeah. I don't feel so good." He put his arm around her and rested his head on her shoulder momentarily. "I'm sorry, sweetheart, but I just got some bad news on the phone."

Kerri dropped the towel to her lap. "What is it? My grandpa?"

"No, no. It's Celine. She's in the hospital in Santa Barbara. She's got pancreatic cancer. Stage four."

For a moment she just stared at him, disbelieving. Then she crumpled and turned to lay face down on the bed, saying nothing. She grabbed a pillow and held it tightly to her face. Roger put his hand on her back to comfort her and could feel her heaving. After a few minutes she sat up and threw her arms around him, sobbing on his shoulder.

"She's dying?"

"Could be. I talked with Polk. Abby's supposed to calls us back."

The day only grew worse. Roger and Kerri sat glumly waiting for the Orangs to come up for breakfast and by eight-fifteen, they had not yet appeared. Roger went below and found them all still in bed: incapacitated with severe headaches again. They were in agony and there was nothing else to do but give them Demerol again. There were only nine vials of the solution left in the first-aid box. It usually took two vials to treat all the animals. Would nine vials be enough for the rest of their journey? He did his duty, and within ten minutes they were getting up and fumbling through the morning's showers and tooth brushings. With Roger bringing up the rear in case someone should stumble, the Orangutans swayed up the stairs for breakfast and encountered a wan-looking Kerri curled up in a chair, vacantly staring out the window. She turned as they entered and offered a brave smile. They picked at some fruit and toast and sipped coffee. There was silence while they were at the table. Kerri flipped through the television channels; Roger sat with the Orangs and nursed a cup of coffee.

When they had finished eating, he gave them the bad news about Celine's cancer.

"She might not have long."

Pongo opened his eyes and squinted at Roger foggily. "Her, as well? Oh, my. This whole thing is getting very complicated." His speech was mushy and slow. George nodded his agreement.

"There's something else, Pongo?"

The ape sighed and rubbed his temples slowly. "Yes. Obviously, we're getting these headaches almost all the time now," he said, barely above a whisper. "We all know why it's happening, there's really no longer any doubt. Last night we had a long connection to our kindred beings. They are very familiar with us now, cognizant of what is happening to us. It seems that we ourselves don't have very much longer."

For Kerri, this statement, coming on the heels of the morning's other bad tidings, was too much. She jumped up and ran over to Pongo, kneeling beside his chair and throwing her arms around his neck. She buried her face in his bushy red side-locks and wept uncontrollably. He seemed startled by this, holding her and putting his head against hers.

George began sketching on a notepad. He made a few strokes, then dangled the crude drawing.

"See this? This is our cerebrum." He tapped the page with his fingertip. "This is the cerebral cortex. Here are the frontal lobes. These are the principal areas of accelerated growth."

He was thick-tongued, speaking through the haze of pain medication.

"Our brains are being stimulated into abnormal growth by all of the incoming information, which we retain completely. The intelligence entities that migrated into us are doing it. It's something like Celine's cancer. Cancer cells multiply and mutate. With us, no mutation, just too many cells. Our bodies weren't designed for this. We can't stop thinking or gathering information, so the cell-growth won't stop either. And time is running out." George tossed the drawing on the table, then made a slow sweeping gesture with his hand, out and up. "We can only count on another few weeks," he stated dryly. "Stronger headaches, loss of motor skills. In the final stage, we'll become comatose."

With tears streaming, Kerri rose and crossed the room, closing the bedroom door softly behind her. Roger sat stunned. Inevitably, the Orangs would all die. In what amounted to only a handful of days, all of these brilliant creatures, so amazing and inspiring, these miraculous beings who were now his dear friends, would be gone forever.

"There might be something of a solution for us, Roger," Pongo finally said, hesitantly. "It's only a possibility, but it's better than nothing. That's the good part. The bad part is that we must leave in order to engage in it."

Roger inclined his head. "Leave? Leave how? What, you have to physically die first?"

"Oh, no, Roger. Not at all." The ape roused himself from his slump and kneaded his forehead. "This is going to sound totally crazy, so get ready. The kindred beings will come here and take us. They can transfer intelligence from one host to another." He clasped his hands and leaned forward. "Whatever the substance was that changed us can also be used to fix us."

Roger was squinting at Pongo and his eyes were watering. He realized he probably hadn't blinked for minutes. He felt like a kite with no tail, whipping and spinning in a gusty wind. The whole morning had been a non-stop action-packed nightmare; a buffeting of charged emotions and unmanageable information. It hit him—his once boring dead-end life had been transformed into a campy science-fiction movie.

He burst out laughing at the absurdity. The Orangs seemed unfazed, solemnly waiting for him to compose himself.

An electronic trilling sounded from the end table beside the couch and they swiveled their heads toward the telephone. Wiping his eyes, Roger lifted the receiver.

"Roger? That you, dear? It's Abby." Her gravelly voice was muted. "Polk said you called. He gave you the news, did he?"

"Yes, Abby. We're just sick. I don't know...sitting here talking about things. Boy. A number of things. How is Celine?"

"Well, she's very ill, Roger. It's bad. Now, before I go on, please understand that I'm calling from a public telephone, all right, dear?" She was reminding him that their line was not secure. "So. At any rate, I've just come from her room. They've got her on pain medication, but she's awake, more or less. Her doctor from Connecticut just arrived and he's with her right now, so I stepped down the hall for a moment to make some calls. She has pancreatic cancer. It's metastasized into her lungs and kidneys."

"Oh, no." Roger briefly squeezed his eyes closed. "Poor Celine." He groped for words. "Is it...can anything be done?"

"It doesn't look good." She paused, the static on the line crackling. And then she broke into sobs.

"Oh, please, Abby..."

After a moment, her voice breaking, she wavered "I'm sorry. I saw something and I didn't push hard enough. I should have taken charge."

"Abby, now you can't blame yourself. She does what she wants, we know that. You're the best friend Celine could ever have."

"I don't feel like it right now." She sniffled a little more, struggling. "Look, Roger. They told her to put her affairs in order. You're down there doing what you're doing and you need to hear the truth. We must all pray for her but we have to be realistic. Things could...come quickly."

The "Mori" was rolling. Loose objects in the room had fallen off tables or shelves and were now peregrinating around on the floor. Roger glanced briefly at Pongo and George. Both had their eyes riveted on him.

"It's that bad?" He struggled just to think. "Well, hate to say it, but something very similar is happening here. Should we just stop what we're doing right away and come home?"

"Oh, no, absolutely not," she declared. "That's not why I'm telling you all this. No, you must carry on. Celine said to make sure you continued with your work, regardless. So. Is it working out?"

"Well, the work is going great. That part's amazing. But the headaches are much worse. And there's a lot more than that."

"The worst as well?"

"Yes. We were talking when you called. But there's a new wrinkle, to say the least. When can we get a private line?"

"My God, what a day this has been. Okay...let's say about two hours from now. I'll be back at the house waiting."

"Right, Abby. Call you then." He brightened momentarily. "Uhm, hey Abby? Before we get off here, there's something else. Maybe this'll cheer up Celine a bit. Yesterday I found a ring in a lagoon, and Kerri and I got engaged."

Now Abby gave a delighted snort. "Engaged? My heavens, oh, that's just the best! I can't wait to run back and tell Celine. Congratulations! And you say you found a ring?"

"Yes. I went into the water snorkeling. There was a manta ray on the bottom. It kicked up some sand and there was a sparkle. There was a ring lying there! An antique gold engagement ring with a big diamond! Isn't that insane? Anyway, I brought it to show Kerri, and one thing kind of led to another. But an even crazier part is that Kerri swears it's Celine's ring. She's sure."

"Celine's ring, you say? " Abby's voice now took on the quality of Miss Marple pursuing a clue. "Does it have any special markings?"

"There's an inscription. Let's see, I'm trying to remember exactly. Oh yeah, 'Forever Dear Heart, 1921'. I'd call that an antique, wouldn't you?"

"Little vines growing around the band, acorns, leaves, engraved in the gold? Marquis diamond, about two carats?"

"Yes!" Roger was flabbergasted. "No way. How could that possibly be?"

"I promised to keep mum, but, oh, hell. Celine gave that ring to George, right before we left Switzerland. She had a feeling about you and Kerri. The South Seas are magical. So she thought George should have it to give to Kerri as a present from her if something happened."

373

"But...but—how could she have had a feeling when I didn't even have a feeling?" Roger sputtered. "It wasn't planned at all."

"Oh, you had it written all over you, Roger."

"But...the fish, swimming over it to move the sand. What explains that?"

"Ask George. When something is supposed to happen, it will happen. No matter what gets in the way."

Roger looked over at George, who was now studying a computer screen. He raised his voice so the Orang wouldn't miss what he said. "Believe me, I will ask George about the ring." He left the line promising to call the house in exactly two hours. After he told the two Orangs the latest about Celine, he looked pointedly at George.

"So, George. You know a little something extra about that ring I found in the lagoon yesterday?"

George shrugged sloppily, looking drunk in his anesthetized state. "I only dropped it where time told me to."

"Where time told you?"

"Absolutely."

"So, that is Celine's ring?"

"Of course."

"How in the hell did you think I would ever find it out there? How?"

George wrote something down, then began folding the slip of paper. "You didn't find it, Roger, it found you." He looked up. "You and Kerri have things to do together. Remember what I said on the mountain? You'll help each other. You're both here doing something important right now, aren't you?" He held up a paper airplane. Rocking his wrist he propelled it lazily across the cabin. It climbed, then slowed at the top of its arc, making a graceful descent toward the bedroom door. At that instant Kerri re-emerged, red-eyed from crying. The glider completed its journey right at her waist and she deftly caught it. In spite of everything, she had to smile at this neat little trick.

"Hey. What is this, a note?" She looked around at the others, then pulled the folds apart. She read the brief message aloud. "Timing is everything."

Chapter 38

Over the following six days, more balloons rose off the afterdeck of the "Mori" in an inexorable sequence. Everyone worked feverishly, making the most of the inclement weather conditions. "Mori" shuttled around just about non-stop, charging from one position to the next, all subject to George's directions. They were sending up balloons at all hours of the day and night. The drill was always the same: fill the balloon, seal it off, attach the gear package, final inspection, release, then go inside to await the proper moment when the 'drop' button would be pushed.

The group ate and slept whenever they could, since the main focus was the task of deploying the balloons. An unpredictable and demanding schedule coupled with the persistent pounding the yacht was taking from the storms resulted in all of them becoming fatigued; in addition, as expected, the Orang's physical problems began to noticeably worsen. More intense headaches, blurring vision, mild intermittent tremors, and unusual moodiness. Under such conditions there were bound to be some mishaps—they lost two balloons; the shrieking wind tore them from their grasp before they were fully prepared for launch. Kerri sprained her ankle when a huge rogue wave broke over the yacht's stern rail, nearly washing her overboard and pinning her against a stanchion. This happened in the middle of the night; if she had actually gone over the side, the chances of finding her in the raging ocean would have been virtually nil. After that, they all took to wearing safety lines secured around their waists at night or whenever conditions were extreme.

All that aside, their success was nothing short of astonishing. George had a computer model, which he updated daily, showing the theoretically probable (and according to him, highly accurate) areas of coverage they had achieved. The maps of Borneo and Sumatra had ever-swelling blotches of red spreading across the lowland swamps and mountain rainforests.

The Orang's contacts with their "kindred beings" was becoming routine and the transformation curve this escalating contact was evincing in them was pronounced. The way the Orangs moved and spoke was palpably altered. Each day they grew more brilliant, saying things that would stop Roger or Kerri in their tracks. Kerri told Roger that sometimes she felt she hardly knew George anymore.

Pongo's earlier suggestion that the Orangs' might be saved by the kindred beings was given an agenda: they would be taken away and their problems corrected in a place where the equipment and knowledge existed to accomplish this. And this was only a few days off.

The phone calls escalated, back and forth between the yacht and Glenwhylden. Celine's doctors advised that she be made as comfortable as possible at home and only treated with pain medication. Staying in the hospital would be pointless and traumatic; better that she live out her remaining days in the serene surroundings of Glenwhylden or Marsh Meadows House. It wouldn't be long.

On the phone she sounded frighteningly weak; nothing like the dear familiar Celine they had last seen getting into the jet in Switzerland. She tried her best to be upbeat and bright, especially about Roger and Kerri's engagement, but her once strong and commanding voice was now wan and hoarse.

So many wrenching goodbyes. Celine would pass away and the Orangs were to be taken as well, likely never to return.

Abby confided to Roger that for the first time in her life, she was slipping into depression. She couldn't imagine spending each day without her dearest friend. Kerri was often long-faced; Roger found her off by herself weeping more than once. The Orangs were her family; they had raised her and instilled her fierce values. Her loss would be enormous.

They tried to put aside the strain of the impending sadness, mostly by fanatic dedication to the work. The final few days were intense, yet all continued to go smoothly. The balloons rose and met their targets, one after another.

The final balloon was released toward the close of a blustery Thursday afternoon, January 25, 1990. They were in the straits of Selat Bangka, just off the northeast coast of Sumatra. Black clouds boiled in a low deck, scudding over the quarreling seas. "Mori" was underway, poking along on an easterly course. The storm was clearing, with the sun peeking out of the glowering cover. Pongo held the readied balloon, and at George's signal, he freed it for its purposeful flight. The orb shimmied and bulged, then bounded enthusiastically skyward.

Half an hour later, it had drifted up and over the vast primeval swamps and lowland forests of the Banyuasin river delta. It popped right on cue, in the middle of a thunderhead at fourteen thousand feet. The affected ground area was over a 65 square kilometers, completing a program of treatment for the entire region.

George declared that success had exceeded even his best expectations. Just that morning, the "Mori" had made a supply stop at Duma, Sumatra. They anchored about a quarter mile offshore and lowered the crew launch for a grocery run. Among the items brought back were current copies of an English-language newspaper from Singapore. Prominent on the front page was the first article they had seen actually addressing the issue of an inexplicable new disease afflicting epidemic numbers of old-growth hardwood trees. The symptoms of the blight described in the article matched those predicted by George.

"Officials in the timber industry have expressed concern that the mystery disease must be controlled soon, as it appears capable of threatening the entire exotic hardwoods logging industry."

There was a celebration in the master suite as he jubilantly read the article aloud for the others. The apes and Kerri all high-fived each other. It was the first truly happy moment in the last six or seven days, and they reveled in it. There it was: independent confirmation that their goal was being achieved. Roger quoted the last paragraph, which included some hair-raising figures on just exactly how much timber was actually felled in the rainforest regions each year. He grinned as he spoke the last lines, then held the paper up like a trophy.

"Everybody! Let me just say for the record, right here and now, that you, George, are a genius, and you deserve every drop of the credit for this." He shook the paper. "I'm sure millions of trees and billions of animals thank you for your inspired idea. And, George, ol' buddy—I, uh, never doubted you for a moment."

The others roared at this. George was grinning, shy in the warmth of adulation.

"Well..." he began, then halted, thinking for a moment.

A modest victory speech would have been expected, but instead he dropped a new bombshell.

"Things have gone our way, haven't they? We can all feel good about it, and the credit belongs to everyone, but especially Celine. We couldn't have made any of this happen without her." He paused and coughed softly. "We all love her so much, and it's been very stressful for all of us, knowing that she is so ill. All of us have given this a lot of thought. We quite naturally wished there was something we could do to help her, as she has done so very much to help all of us. She saved our old lives and made it possible for us to have new ones. He paused, as if uncertain about going on, but then: "So we want to try something. We want Celine and Abby to come here, now. We want them to be with us when the time comes. We'll all surround them and hold their hands. Maybe they'll go with us."

Kerri gasped. "That's incredible, George!"

"Do you think it will work?" Roger asked, stunned.

"We can only hope. All we get from the kindred beings is love, constantly, for us and all living beings. We believe they will know why Celine and Abby are there. If it doesn't work, we've lost nothing. Celine will die anyway, and if it means we don't go as well, we've decided that's what we want. We're all agreed. We stay with Celine and Abby. We'd feel selfish going without them."

Kerri went to George and hugged him. "I always suspected you were an angel, George. It'll work. I have a feeling."

"We all do too," said Emily, wiping her eyes. "It's the only way."

"Yes. But we must act quickly," George warned. "If they agree, then the airplane must bring them right away. Time is very short. Will you call them, Roger?"

A call was placed and Roger explained this newest and final plan.

"At least we'll go down swinging," Celine said with no hesitation. "Sitting here waiting for the inevitable would be far worse. Tell them all we're coming right away."

Finished with the need for bad weather, the group on the yacht gratefully retreated to the east, directing Mr. Chung to set "Mori's" course for the northeastern coast of Borneo and then on up into the Celebes sea. Hot sunshine and calm seas returned. They proceeded to Kalalusu island. There they would meet "Arjuna", which would bring Celine and Abby. "Mori" would then depart for another isolated island. The group would be delivered there, and left alone. The kindred beings would handle the rest, whatever that meant.

Chapter 39

Sunday morning, January 28, 1990. The heat bearing down on Kalalusu island was ferocious and unrelenting. Not a cloud in sight. Not even so much as a puff of wind. The entire world seemed to be holding stock still—everything on this parched little speck of land was roasting in the mid-morning scorch.

"Arjuna" dropped out of the sky right on schedule, almost to the minute, at 10:03. The glistening black fuselage hunkered shockingly dark atop the bone-white coral runway. Fuming clouds of bleachy dust reared up behind the screaming engines as she re-traced the length of the airstrip and taxied up to the waiting truck. Bartholdy waved jauntily from the cockpit, brought the craft to a smooth halt. Moments later the stairs were unfolding. Roger climbed up and entered the cabin, mentally preparing as he went aft and knocked.

"Yes?" he heard Abby call out.

"It's Roger, Abby. Should I wait?"

"Oh, Roger! No, no, we're ready. Please come in, dear."

He swung the door open and saw Abby sitting on her bed, looking natty in a white blazer, peach blouse, long peach colored skirt and white shoes. Celine was reclining on her own berth, also dressed and ready to go. Roger got a good look at her as he entered. She was almost unrecognizable. He had to mask his alarm at how much weight she had lost. Her hands, gnarled, almost skeletal, were folded primly on the lap of her lapiz blue pants-suit. Her face, though affixed with a brave smile, was emaciated—the eyes sunken, cheekbones prominent. She was breathing with some difficulty. There was an oxygen tank and mask beside her. A wheelchair sat waiting at the foot of the bed. Unnerved by her frailty, Roger compensated by forcing his voice to be bright and upbeat.

"Well! There she is! We're so glad you're here, Celine," he sang. He had a ludicrous grin on his face. "How was your flight?" He hated this. Hell, they all hated it, Celine most of all. This was the most distasteful kind of necessary behavior when in the presence of a gravely ill person. He leaned down and took her trembling hand.

"Roger. So good to see you, dear boy," she croaked. "You look wonderful. So tan."

"Yes, well, you know, the sun down here..." he bobbed his head. "It's great."

She said nothing more, just nodded minimally and smiled.

God, thought Roger. He turned to smile at Abby. The strain of all this was showing in her features as well. She and Roger had grown closer in the last week or so, with all the phone calls and decisions they'd had to make together.

"So, how's it going, Roger? Everything sublime?" Abby smiled at him stoically. Using his handshake grip as an assist, she hauled herself up from the bed and adjusted her clothing, then set about maneuvering the empty wheelchair into position.

"Oh yes. It'll be great to have the whole group back together again."

Abby took a few stiff steps and looked down at the still reclining Celine. "Alright, dear. All set? Let's us go for a little boat ride, how 'bout it?"

Celine and Abby made sure to bid Chuck Bartholdy a formal farewell, not letting on that he would not be seeing them ever again. They'd all traveled many thousands of miles together. He'd been an important player in most of their big adventures, just as he was on this one. With Abby holding her hand, Celine wept as they were driven to the yacht. Roger realized that she had endured many such farewells in the last few days. She would never see her beloved Marsh Meadows House again. She would never see Glenwhylden, nor any of the devoted people that were part of her life in those places. The reunion with the apes on board ship was the only thing that seemed to lift her spirits.

Thirty minutes later the crew cast off the dock lines. George now disclosed exactly where they were headed: Lipang Island, 3.56 N. latitude, 125.23 E. longitude. A mere dot on the charts in the Kepulauan Sangir. Remote, not really near anywhere else, yet only about a half-day's cruise from Kalalusu. George asked Roger to instruct Captain Lau that the yacht be moored just off the west side of Lipang. That's where they'd wait. The departure party would be taken to a beach on the island. They would be left to "camp-out" overnight. By the next morning, they'd know the outcome.

Arrangements on board "Mori" were shuffled: Roger and Kerri vacated the master suite in favor of Celine and Abby. Roger moved onto the couch in the anteroom of Pongo and George's suite, and Trent and Artod occupied a smaller cabin on the starboard lower deck. Kerri, for the first time since Switzerland, separated from Roger and moved in with the female Orangs.

The transit to Lipang took about four hours, with calm seas all the way. They dropped ground-tackle at about two-thirty in the afternoon. The island, visible in the distance, was essentially a nothing—just a half-acre dry spot surrounded by the vast ocean.

Supper in the master suite was subdued. Celine presided from her wheelchair at the head of the candlelit table. The gentle flickers softened the startling ravages the illness had wrought on her elegant features. Having rested all afternoon, she seemed a bit perked up, her voice a little stronger.

"My goodness. This has been such a whirl. I've just been thinking all evening—about how grateful I am to be here with all of you." She smiled with affection at all the faces around the table. "I only wish this could go on forever." Everyone murmured sympathetically, and she struggled on. "There are things I must say right now. First, I want to congratulate you all on the success of your mission. It's a stunning accomplishment. I can only marvel at what you've done." She raised her glass, and they drank a toast. "And then, of course, I couldn't be happier Roger and Kerri are engaged. You're going to be good for each other, I'm certain." She gestured. "That ring looks smashing on you, darling." Kerri rose and gave the elderly woman a tender hug and kiss. The others all applauded. "Thank you, my dears. Now, I don't know when you two plan to tie the knot. But I want you to have a few things to help you get started. It's all taken care of and there will be scads of papers for you to sign later. So, then. Glenwhylden will be your house, my dears, as my legacy to you. And I only wish that you will live there and enjoy it as Charles and I would have done. That would make me very, very happy." She pointedly looked at Roger. "You see? You really did have a connection to the house. Now it will be yours and Kerri's. Raise your children there. Light it up with love." Roger's eyes filled at these words. "I also give you Marsh Meadows house and Blauhimmelheim. I only ask that you keep my staff on. They're all wonderful, top rate. As a matter of fact, I just gave them all a raise two days ago. And you'll need them, take my word for it." She raised her hand as if in testament.

Abby grinned. "You most certainly will."

"Now, don't worry," Celine continued with a tone of amusement. "I wouldn't dream of leaving you all this property and employees without providing you some way to maintain the lot." She gave her head a bemused shake. "I am giving you both a substantial portion of my estate. After all is said and done, this will amount to something in the neighborhood of two and a half billion dollars." Kerri gasped, raising her hands to her mouth. Celine nodded with emphasis. "A lot of money, isn't it? Oh, yes. It never failed to amaze me each year when my advisors would tell me my approximate net worth. It's far more than anyone could ever spend—or more than I could, that's for sure. I give away millions every year, tens of millions. But even with that it just keeps growing."

She leaned forward. "You are both going to have to be extremely careful. It might seem that you're being dropped into the lap of luxury, but I pray that you won't see it that way. Having billions of dollars can ruin you. Someone once told me that it was an obscene amount of money. She would have been right, had I not truly done my best to apply it correctly. There's only one way to prevent the wealth from being obscene. You have to use it for the good. Stick together and work together. I want you to find extraordinarily worthy projects to pursue together, much like the one you have just done so well with here. You've proven yourselves. Use the power of money to accomplish great things. Conservation, medicine, education, art—I don't know just what they will be. That will be up to you. You'll put your stamp on the world. Your lives will change, and you'll change the lives of others. I'm lucky to have helped so many, but I've received so much more in return."

Then she fixed the couple with a purposeful gaze. "You're strong, Roger and Kerri. I'm passing the baton. Do these things in your names, not mine. I've had my go at this, now it's your turn." Her hands, birdlike, had been fluttering as she spoke. She lowered them to the table. "I have a great sense of peace," she declared, nodding. "Life is adventure, and not knowing is part of it. You begin with the unknown, and you end with it."

She looked at George, who had been sagely witnessing all of this with a face as placid as the moon. "My wise friend insists that we will all go together, wherever that is. I am most grateful and so thankful that I will not be going alone."

"And, Roger and Kerri, it will be alright no matter what," said Abby, taking Celine's hand. "We've all decided that if we're all still there in the morning, or if it's just us old girls left behind, then...we're going to just take a little swim."

As the meaning of this registered, no one spoke. The bet was placed and they were all in. A divide had been crossed. It was the end of one time, and the beginning of another.

"Celine," Roger finally said, "You saved me just as much as you saved our friends. And I promise you that Kerri and I will do everything—"

But then suddenly Kerri came up out of her chair.

"Roger, wait. I just realized that I can't even think of getting married to you..."

He felt a spire of ice shoot up his spine.

"...without all of our friends being with us. Can you?"

She was brilliant. "No. No, of course not."

"Right. So. Tomorrow morning, then? First thing. Sunrise. Anybody for a wedding? Can't the captain do that?"

Roger picked up the phone and dialed Herbert Chung's extension. He explained that he and Kerri had decided to tie the knot the next morning. Would Captain Lau officiate? Chung called back to say the Captain had enthusiastically accepted.

Betty thought of something important. "Kerri, do you have anything to wear at your wedding?"

"Well, okay. I've got a pair of white cut-off jeans. They're kinda falling apart." she shrugged. "Oh, yeah, and a white tank top. That'll do, right? Let's see. I guess I don't really have to wear shoes, you think?"

Everyone laughed uproariously at this.

"Oh, hell. Does it matter?" She shot a look at her groom. "You're not marrying me for my clothes, are you, Roger?"

"Of course not. I'm marrying you for your money."

Later when everyone else had retired, Roger and Pongo sat on the edge of George's bed. George complained of a severe headache after dinner and now he was groggy from the injection. But he'd opened a large chart-book, the "Guide to the Night Skies of the Southern Hemisphere."

"This is where to look. See?" A lengthy digit tapped the page. "Right in this spot, to the left of the tail of Scorpio. This is where we'll be."

Roger pulled the book closer, staring at the constellation. "And you know that? Wow." He shook his head. "It's so hard to believe. I mean, Orangutans from the rainforest. And not very long ago, either. Incredible. And now you're gonna be trillions of miles out there, beyond that tiny dot. Light years away." He was seized with incredulity. "George, how can they do it? How can they get you there fast enough to head this thing off?"

"We're not sure they have to get us there to do it. But, since you asked, there are ways of getting things across great distances far faster than the speed of light, Roger. The kindred beings know how. They use shortcuts. You pop through a gravity hole in your part of the universe and end up in another part. And, when you can move around so rapidly, it makes the cosmos a fairly small place." George's eyes were twinkling. "You see, Roger? We really won't be that far away. So, if you and Kerri stand out on the lawn at Glenwhylden some evening and you find the right spot in the sky, you can point it out to her and say, 'That's where they all are. Right over there.'" George was trying to be comforting to his dear friend. Technically, there was nothing to be sad about.

Pongo was nodding at all this, supportive. Roger looked at him.

"Well, Pongo, it looks like you're getting your wish."

The ape hesitated, confused. "What do you mean?"

Roger raised his brows, ironic. "Go faster."

No one is ever very far away from anyone or anything else. But while they wouldn't be "gone" as in "dead", they would still be out of reach and out of touch. No amount of technical explanation would remove the emptiness of his friends' absence. Roger had struggled to avoid it, but now a wave of sadness and loneliness engulfed him. He had come to love these Orangutans with all his soul. They were his family as well. Now their conversations and constant amazements were about to end. He would miss them profoundly. He looked at the chart, as if to study it again, but felt his chest tighten.

At that instant, he flashed back to the dream he'd had in Old Lyme when he'd first gone to meet Celine. He had completely forgotten it until now. He remembered the scene: he was with someone in a darkened room. A hairy little man with a round face, dark eyes and a red beard. Of course, he had known nothing of the Orangs at that time. Together they had been looking at a dark blue page with white dots. He recalled feeling intensely sad, and wanting to cry, his whole body seizing. The dream had foretold this moment.

For the first time, Roger hugged George and Pongo and kissed their foreheads. "I love you both so much," he cried. "I can't tell you how much you mean to me, and how much I'll miss you!" Tears were streaming down his cheeks. "I love you all, and you'll all be a part of me forever. Always, no matter where you are."

George closed the book. "Roger, because we love you so much as well, we want to try to give something to you. We hope it will make your suffering a little less."

Roger smiled through his tears, curious. "My suffering?"

George exchanged a glance with Pongo. "We know about your illness. That you will be blind and deaf."

Roger lowered his head. "Oh, that. Did Kerri tell you? I didn't want you to worry."

"No, she didn't tell us. We've known about it almost since we first met you. We can see it sometimes, like a cloud around you. You even wanted to kill yourself, didn't you?"

He bit his lip. "Yes. Yes, and meeting you was what saved me. But sometimes I think I still should."

In the dim light George shook his head. "No, Roger. You just think that because you're frightened. But don't be. There is another way to see and hear."

Roger peered at the Orang. "How? What other way?"

George stood up and took the young man's head in a gentle grip. "Relax. Close your eyes." Roger then also felt Pongo's enormous hands saddling his shoulders.

A powerful light sprang up in his mind, searing and disorienting. Then he was swept off, plunged into a sea of shooting stars, swirling through a harmonic river. He felt heat, and wind, and a wash of bubbling raindrops distilled from prismatic colors. He was huge and tiny at the same moment. His body was gone and the deepest sense of peace filled his spirit.

"Open your eyes now, Roger," he heard George's voice calling in the distance. "Come back."

They were all still there. Nothing in the room had changed, and yet everything was different. Roger knew immediately what was altered. His overwhelming fear of loss was gone.

George and Pongo took their hands off him.

"We don't know if your eyes or ears will be any better, Roger," Pongo said, "but now you'll be able to know what's there, maybe just as good. Some little bit of what the kindred beings gave to us, we have now given to you. It's kind of like personal radar. It'll come to you a little at a time, if you want it."

Later Roger lay awake in the darkness. His former life in Santa Barbara was only a movie he'd seen once, the details receding into the past. He knew he'd be back home soon, but one thing was sure: life would never remotely again be the same.

Sitting up he fumbled for his glasses, then looked out the window of the cabin. He listened to his own breathing, marking time, and regarded the moonless indigo sky, teeming with unfathomable multitudes of stars. He picked one out, a lonely one that seemed to have more space around it than the others.

"Right over there." he said softly. "Just right over there."

Chapter 40

Captain Lau, resplendent in his dress white uniform, stood stiffly on the bridge deck, listening intently as Abigail Horvath confidently briefed him in Mandarin. It was five-forty seven a.m. The eastern sky was growing rosy and within the next few minutes the captain would be performing his first wedding at sea. Chung was also on the bridge, but it seemed that his translating services were not needed. Abby's command of Chinese was creditable since she and Celine had spent many months traveling within Chinese speaking countries. Another twist: the captain was a Methodist. He had a Seaman's Book of Common Prayer, albeit in his own language. Would it be alright if he married the couple in Chinese? Abby figured she could prompt Roger and Kerri when to answer.

Now they all gathered on the sundeck aft of the master suite. The Orangs were bunched on deck chairs, reluctantly silent of course. Abby was up front and Roger (in jeans and a white long-sleeved shirt) stood at the taffrail alongside Captain Lau. Celine's wheelchair was drawn up at the grand piano, with the big windows opened wide to allow the music to waft out.

As the sun peeked over the horizon, Celine began to play Chopin's nocturne, opus two, number nine. She had apologized for not knowing the Wedding March.

The door to the cabin opened, and as everyone swiveled around, Kerri emerged. When he caught sight of her Roger felt his knees losing resolution. She was breathtaking. Emily, Betty, Chloé, Celine and Abby had all made a group effort before going to bed the previous evening. They had taken one of the white linen sheets from the yacht and had torn it into strips, knotting and twisting the various pieces together to form a kind of way-out Hellenistic toga. She wasn't what anyone could have called well-covered—the outfit showed a lot of skin—but she was the very image of a goddess. The white fabric contrasted with her bronzed body. She wore all of her handmade shell jewelry, and strands of scavenged ribbon were woven into her blond-streaked hair. A dramatically opulent gold and emerald choker (yet another gift from Celine, no doubt) graced her neck. And she was, astonishingly, wearing eye make-up. Herbert Chung had been drafted to give the bride away, and he stood at the ready, offering his arm as she advanced from the bedroom. Standing alongside the five foot, three inch Chung, Kerri seemed even more statuesque than usual. They walked slowly forward, Kerri smiling radiantly, holding a garland of white miniature lilies from the yacht's refrigerated store.

The actual ceremony went by fast; a good thing, too, as Roger and Kerri had a hard time keeping straight faces during Captain Lau's Chinese recitations. He'd bury his nose in the little dog-eared prayer book, plugging away in a monotone; then raise his face to peer expectantly at either Roger or Kerri. Abby would prompt, in a stage whisper, whatever should be said. Finally they heard the translation: "man and wife."

Afterward Captain Lau seemed most proud of himself. He grinned at everyone, even the Orangutans. He bowed to anyone who looked his way, his cheeks showing the rosy flush of satisfaction.

But like the chrome-happy front grillwork of a '57 Chevy succumbing to the maw of a junkyard crushing machine, Captain Lau's expression collapsed when, after only one official champagne toast had been mounted, Abby shuffled over, thanked him in Chinese, then tactfully requested that, now that the actual ceremony was over, the guests might be allowed to once more enjoy the privacy of their quarters. He gaped at Abby over a few unbelieving seconds (perhaps hoping that her Chinese had, somehow, finally been remiss?) but with trained professional composure, he bowed politely, and he and Chung withdrew.

This of course, meant that the real party could now begin. All of the profoundly frustrated Orangutans began to act normally, jumping from their chairs and mobbing Roger and Kerri. Everyone was jabbering at once, and only Trent had the presence of mind to begin the vital chore of uncorking the next bottle of champagne; a 1976 magnum of Ayala Blanc de Blancs. They had a sumptuous buffet breakfast, and everyone—even Celine—passed the rest of the morning in the master suite chatting, laughing, listening to good music, and generally having a wonderful time.

Toward midday, Roger and Kerri met alone with Celine and Abby, discussing and signing numerous legal documents transferring Celine's many properties. Faxes had been sent the night before, and the arrangements had been processed by her New York attorneys. The co-signed and witnessed copies of these transfers—the ones just executed on the yacht—were Roger and Kerri's independent absolute proof of their newly assumed ownership. Just to make doubly sure, Celine had recorded a ten minute videotape—also supplied to all parties concerned—in which she categorically reiterated her intentions and wishes. In this tape, Celine explained that, having disposed of all her earthly possessions, it was now her intention to withdraw to an unspecified place of seclusion, that she might spend her "few remaining days in peace and tranquility, and in a spiritual frame of mind". She would not return, either alive or deceased, and that there was to be no burial, funeral, or memorial service for her.

The day, which had begun with cloudless skies and hot sun, slowly made an early afternoon transition to overcast with just a hint of an easterly breeze.

About two o'clock, George went looking for Roger and found him sitting on the sundeck alone, intently reading some documents. The Orang told him in a soft voice that, as expected, the departure group would be leaving the next night. A clear message had come to him: the group should all be on the island by sunset tomorrow, and the entire area should remain cleared until sunrise the next day. Roger went around telling the others. Since the assumption was that there wouldn't be any belongings taken with them, there wasn't much to do in the way of getting ready.

Celine and Abby called the captain and Chung into a meeting.

"We will need the launch tomorrow evening," Celine began. "Mrs. Horvath and I will be taking our pets for a night of camping out. I wish the yacht to withdraw to some distance and leave us alone. Further, gentlemen, we shall not be coming back, at all."

Chung frowned. "Not coming back? Excuse me, Mrs. Stertevant, but where will you go? We are far from anywhere."

"My dear man, that is our affair." She smiled patiently. "As you've likely noticed, I am quite ill. Dying, in fact. I have arranged for another party to pick us up. We'll go to a place where we can be at peace until...well, until things resolve. Now, Mrs. Horvath and I wish this matter to be kept completely confidential. Roger and Kerri, that is, Mr. and Mrs. Caldwell, are my heirs." She handed the astonished officers a packet. "Here are all the documents making it official and detailing my intentions. Everything is there. We will bid you goodbye tomorrow evening. I assure you this is entirely my idea and I expect full respect for my final wishes."

Chung shook his head disbelievingly. "Oh madam, please. I do not recommend this. Leaving you and Mrs. Horvath alone with the seven large animals?"

"Why, Mr. Chung," Abby interjected, "they are better behaved than most humans. Haven't you noticed?"

Chung's eyes widened. "Now that you mention it, Mrs. Horvath, I have. We all have. In fact, more than once I have expected them to just start talking."

Celine and Abby could not help smiling slightly.

"Yes," said Celine. "Odd, isn't it? But there you go. You see, we'll be more than fine with them."

Chung still wasn't persuaded. "But are you not too physically ill to be outdoors overnight, Madam? I must say, this does not seem right at all." He said a few words to the by now puzzled captain, whose face then also registered his own great alarm. They conversed for a moment, then Chung turned back. "Mrs. Stertevant, with all due respect, Captain Lau asks if the "Mori" could not take you to where you wish to go? This would be far safer. Please, madam, we are most concerned for you."

"Thank you, Chung, I appreciate that," she replied, patting his arm. "But as the captain will understand, then it wouldn't be a secret, would it? We'll be safe, I'm certain," she placated. "This is what I've decided and its final. Who we are meeting and where we are going will remain private."

Chung was deferential but unconvinced. He looked down, shaking his head slowly.

"Really," Celine added, "there's nothing out there but sand and we'll have warm clothing and rain gear. We'll be in good hands. Nothing can hurt us."

Chapter 41

If there was a perfect example of a vessel that represented everything the "Mori" was not, "Bajau Kee" would be a prime candidate. The 56 foot diesel crabbing trawler was butt-ugly and splotched with rust; it was also noisy, slow, and supremely uncomfortable. She rolled like a cork on all but the calmest of seas. Below decks dank, airless cabins and passageways stenched of rotting crab and human sewage. The Malaysian crew, while able to understand and speak some English, preferred not to. To a man, a criminal background was a given. And, as far as the cook was concerned, if it didn't come out of a can, he wasn't going to bother with it.

Flying by the seat of his pants, on a limited budget and totally unfamiliar with this part of the world, Butch Turbull's options were limited. The "Bajau Kee" was the only sea-going vessel he had been able to charter on short notice out of the tiny port of Kota Kinabalu, Malaysia. It was the off-season, the boat wasn't crabbing and the elderly captain was willing to cut a deal. Turnbull's cover story was that he was a bail-bond agent pursuing an extremely high dollar subject on a fancy yacht. The captain shrugged at this and recruited a mechanic, an alcoholic deckhand and a putative cook. Together they had set off around the northern tip of Malaysia, bound toward Kalalusu, just over three days away.

But they had not caught up with the "Mori" at Kalalusu or anywhere else, and now the five men had been aboard this tossing hell-hole for nearly two weeks. Turnbull's remaining sanity receded with each fresh onslaught of sea-sickness. To be fair, he couldn't be sure that this was the cause of his incessant retching; the slop that came out of the galley could just as easily have been to blame. But the rest of the crew didn't seem to have the problem. He wondered if they were poisoning him.

Turnbull had left Switzerland supremely frustrated but far from empty-handed. In their hurried departure from Blauhimmelheim, the Orangs and their humans had left behind a rich treasure-trove of information. Scarpita would soon return to clean everything up, but during the half-hour or so that Turnbull had to search the deserted house, he found notes, maps, drawings, schedules, almost everything. The name and coordinates of the island where the jet would be taking them to meet a chartered yacht. The name of the vessel itself. Partial elements of "The Plan" were even sketched out in some of the paperwork. Weather balloons, chemicals, radio-controlled incendiary detonators. They were clearly up to something fiendish.

Turnbull felt fringes of madness as he pored over the stuff once he was safely back in his hotel room that evening. Good god, they were going all the way to the South Pacific. Borneo. Malaysia. All of the notes about chemicals and high-altitude detonations made little sense to him but reinforced his perception that great evil was at work here. He was right to be pursuing this group. Yet, since all he really intended to do was capture one or more of the talking apes and expose them to the world, the rest of it was secondary. He wanted to clear his name and finally best that thing that had bested him. It would be icing on the cake if he also stopped some dastardly plot. Once again the ex-cop had gotten a solid lead about where to chase his quarry next, if that's what he wanted to do. Well, that's what he wanted to do. He was on a mission now, and nothing, nothing would deter him. He would pursue them to the ends of the earth and that seemed to be just about where they were going.

But again, his biggest problem after getting underway on the trawler was actually locating the "Mori". The yacht had several days lead on him and there had been nothing in the purloined notes and maps about exactly where it would go once it left Kalalusu. It could now be anywhere in a region with hundreds of islands and isolated ports. He only knew they meant to do something involving coastal Borneo and Sumatra. Undeterred, Turnbull took an old street cop's approach to solving this challenge. He asked around the neighborhood. As the trawler rounded the top of the main island and headed south, he bribed the captain to poll his contacts in the fishing community via radio-fax for information. Surely a vessel as prominent as "Mori" would be noticed by other fishermen in the region. From its description it would have to stick out much as did the black jet, wherever it went. This time-tested strategy worked. Within a short time there were reports coming back: the "Mori" was spotted sitting at anchor near Tanahmerah, Borneo. The "Bajau Kee" headed that way but the weather grew worse, and before they could even reach the Borneo coast the captain got another tip that "Mori" was underway again, this time heading north.

An extended game of cat and mouse followed, as each time the luxury yacht was sighted somewhere it would quickly take off for somewhere else. Making matters worse for Turnbull, the whole chase seemed to be following any and all bad weather, as if that was exactly what the party aboard "Mori" wanted. This seemed to make no sense. While at least seaworthy, the "Bajau Kee" was no match for the "Mori's" powerful engines and advanced technology. The trawler did have a capable radar unit (vital for any ship in these waters) but no satellite telephone/TV link. "Bajau Kee's" only auxiliary craft was a small Avon used for freeing snagged trap lines. Her twin diesels could make about sixteen knots in calm seas as opposed to "Mori's" top speed of nearly thirty. So Turnbull and his motley crew were always a step behind. This began to wear thin and Turnbull was forced to up his charter rate to keep the game going. The crew began to think he was crazy.

The big break came as the weather cleared. Turnbull had the "Bajau Kee" aimlessly scouting off the central east coast of Borneo. For two days they'd heard nothing. Then the captain got a radio call from a friend on a coastal fishing sampan. The mega-yacht, "Mori", was newly anchored off southern Pulau Lipang Island. "Bajau Kee" had just taken on fuel at Semporna, and when the news came Turnbull ordered a full speed charge toward Lipang. It was now or never; he was running out of everything: time, the crew's patience, money.

They would need a day and a half to make the crossing. The sea was calm and as Turnbull entered the wheelhouse before sunup the second morning, his captain was excited. He pointed at the radar. "They come at us!" he jabbered.

"What's coming at us?"

"Mori." See? Is on radar, Tarnball. Look it." He tapped the monitor.

Turnbull squinted at the screen. A large green blip pulsed south of the outline of Lipang. "So you mean they're moving again? Fuck!"

"No fuck! Is moving but come at us. Get closer right at us! Only about 20 kilometer now."

Turnbull slammed his hands on the chart table. "Intercept them! Where are they headed?"

The captain shrugged. "If they go land, only place close is Sangihe." He showed him on the map. "Just to north and west."

"Keep 'em on radar and go straight at them! Understand?"

Turnbull stayed glued to the screen, finally feeling his luck had turned. The big yacht seemed to be at full speed, coming right at his nose. As dawn came up the looming mass of Sangihe could be seen out to their right. And less than an hour later, through the binoculars, holy shit, the lights of the "Mori." Finally.

Turnbull didn't know how, but he was going to get aboard that yacht. He was all in. When they were within a mile, the captain spoke up again. "They stop now. They stop." The radar blip had ceased moving.

"Okay. Slow down, but keep heading toward them." Turnbull raised the binoculars. "Mori" was majestic in the early mists, now halted and holding in deep waters just off the coast of the island. All of her floodlights were blazing. Then he spotted something that got his heart beating faster than at any time since he was crouched ready to spring at the ape on the porch in Switzerland. "Mori" was lowering a boat. Two people, looking to be the same young couple he'd seen before, were going down the ladder, followed by the large red ape. There he was, sure as hell! He was carrying some kind of large bundle and they were all now getting onboard the dinghy. Turnbull spun toward the captain. "Get the Avon ready to launch, right now."

Chapter 42

Roger couldn't sleep, although he'd been in bed for hours. It was the final night the group would spend together on the "Mori." By sunset of the coming day all the farewells would be done and he and Kerri would be left alone to go on with their lives.

He tossed and turned, profoundly uneasy. Everything seemed so outlandish, considering it all as he was in the middle of the night. "Kindred Beings" coming to get the Orangs, Celine and Abby. Take them away, "fix" them. He felt for his watch on the bedside table, squinting at the luminous dial. 4:40 a.m. Damn. He exhaled deeply, punched the pillow, and turned on his side, clamping his eyes shut.

Then he heard the door click. He sat up in the darkness. "Kerri? I couldn't sleep either. That you?"

The light snapped on. It was Pongo.

"I'm sorry, Roger," he said in a shaking, utterly uncharacteristic voice. "I'm so sorry."

"Pongo? What's the matter?"

"Please come with me right now."

Roger followed him to the male apes' bedroom cabin. He was surprised to find all of them there, the females as well, in their pajamas, silently clustering around George's bed. They turned as he came in.

It was Emily who spoke first. "Oh Roger, honey. Our dear little George is dead. He's really gone."

Roger froze for a moment, looking down at the still form against white sheets. "Oh, no." Then all the breath went out of him. He fell toward the bed and began sobbing, clutching

402

George's lifeless hand. For awhile that was all he could do. The others began a low moaning, raw grief. Roger felt his heart would finally break in two.

Finally he was able to ask, "What happened? Does anyone know?"

"He woke me up about fifteen minutes ago," Pongo choked, shaking. "He called over to me from his bed and said he wasn't going to make it. I got up and turned on the light. He was convulsing. He looked up at me and told me to put him in a tree, that's all he said. 'Put me in a tree.' Then he said 'Goodbye, Pongo,' and he just stopped breathing. Before I could do anything. I didn't even have time to say anything back to him."

Over the next half-hour Roger struggled to think clearly. His greatest fear was that the news would be too much for Celine. He decided to wait to tell her until a bit later, when she awakened. He got Kerri up and brought her down to the Orangs room where she dissolved into shock. Then he called up to Chung and asked that they immediately get underway at full speed. They must go to the nearest forested land with large trees. He didn't explain why but by now the crew was used to such things from these passengers. The closest place like that was Sangihe, Chung blearily related. About four hours due south. As was typical, in mere minutes the crew raised anchor and a boiling wake trailed "Mori" as they dropped the hammer to the ship's twin screws.

Pongo asserted he would go ashore at Sangihe. He would carry George's body into the forest and place him in the branches of the canopy, as had been his dying request.

There was no time to spare. In order to get there and back in time to meet the deadline for the pick-up that night, they would have to hurry greatly.

Celine and Abby were given the news about seven-thirty. Celine placed her head in her hands. "So that's why we're underway."

"Oh, he was the best of us all," Abby whispered. "It's not fair."

The run down to Sangihe was in complete numbness, no one saying much. Celine found a beautiful white silk kimono in the closet, woven with gold and silver threads. They carefully wrapped George in this and held a vigil by his bed.

Arriving off Sangihe it was foggy and misting but calm. A hundred yards away they could make out a long deserted beach and a thick green curtain just at its inner edge.

"Stand by here," Roger told Chung, still providing no reason. "We won't be long." The Avon was lowered and Roger, Kerri, and Pongo took their pitiful bundle and went in.

"I'm going to find a really beautiful tree," Pongo said on the sand as he removed his human clothing. Tenderly, he gathered up George's swaddled body. "He deserves a special tree. There should be one close by. I'll be back soon." With that he vanished like a ghost into the gloom of the jungle, bearing his best friend, the little brother ape who had called himself "the gardener". With all they had on their minds, none of them had paid any attention to a tired old trawler a half a mile away, loitering in the waters close to shore. Such craft were common everywhere in this region. No one saw the vessel launch its own dinghy, with a solitary man turning it urgently toward the beach.

Chapter 43

Down low the tangle of vines was dense as cargo netting but Pongo wasn't slowed by this as he carried George aloft. Climbing upward it all came back to him as if it had been just yesterday: the smells, the way the branches gave and flexed as he grasped with one hand and his feet, then released and swung to the next. Intuitively he sensed just how much weight each one would hold. Moving through the mid-canopy his mind was a cloud of bereavement, spilling over with feelings he'd never before experienced. In his earlier life, in a simple way, he'd grieved when others died, but it always passed quickly. One must always move on with the daily business of survival. But the lifeless body he now cradled meant so much more to him than any being ever had before. What was this strange, encompassing thing of human emotions? Were they entirely human, or a mixture of his old and new intelligences as well?

The search didn't take long. Rearing out of the mists, there it was: a magnificent, soaring teak tree, over 150 feet tall and at least 1400 years old. It towered above all the others around it: an elder, a survivor, an ancestor tree of the greatest veneration. As one of earth's oldest living souls, its welcoming highest branches would be fitting final guardians for George's remains: a bridge between the earth and the sky. Pongo quickly reached the top of the giant and began making a traditional Orangutan sleeping nest, interweaving branches and leaves. He had done this a thousand times, making his bed for the night high above the rainforest floor. This time the bed would be not for him but for his dearest friend. He carefully made a leaf cover to keep off the rain. As he laid him tenderly to rest, Pongo plucked fragrant flowers from nearby vines and placed them all around George's still form. He carefully opened the silk fabric and gazed upon the solemn face one last time.

And then a pitiful keening came out of him: primal, desolate. The plangent sound of his unfathomable grief. It mounted from his chest and throat, swelling, carrying across the treetops for all other beings nearby to bear witness. Those that heard this froze in their activities and wondered. It was profoundly mournful, freighted with emptiness. Finally he spoke aloud in a trembling voice: "I will never forget you, George. Goodbye, brother."

For a few more minutes he wavered, reluctant to leave his friend. Perhaps he should stay here and let nature take its course as it had with George. Maybe he could even will it to happen. But a sense of duty prevailed. He must be with the others and he must go back to Roger and Kerri. They were waiting. With one last look he began climbing down, getting closer to the forest floor where he could move his massive weight through the larger lower branches more reliably.

"Stop right there, asshole. I'll blow your head off."

It came from below, a human voice, speaking American accented English. Pongo froze. Looking beneath him he saw the crazed, upturned face of Butch Turnbull, the Highway Patrolman. He held a pistol high, aiming right at Pongo. So astonished was the ape that he blurted out "I don't understand."

The man cackled with glee. "I knew it was you, fuckhead. Heard you moaning and talking up there. You really are a monkey, aren't you?"

"An ape. I told you before."

"And you can talk!"

"Obviously."

Turnbull carefully held his aim. "Well, you're gonna get to do a lot more talking, ape. I chased you halfway around the world and now I got you. Get down here." Still confused at the sudden appearance of this man in this most improbable place, Pongo nonetheless managed to consider for a moment. He could start down but then shift around the trunk, shielding himself, and move off far faster than the human could follow on the ground.

Turnbull, having rehearsed just such a showdown in his mind a hundred times and with a clear shot, took this hesitation as a cue to open fire. He squeezed off one round. Pongo felt the bullet tear through his upper arm, and the shock and searing pain made him lose his grip. He crashed through the branches, ending at Turnbull's feet. Immediately the gun barrel was jammed into his temple.

"Stand up and don't even think about trying anything else," Turnbull snarled, grabbing the hair on Pongo's neck with his other hand. "I ain't losing you again, monkey man. I'll kill you first. Start walking toward the beach. We're going to my boat."

Chapter 44

Half an hour had gone by. Roger and Kerri grew concerned. Then another half-hour. It had been too long. Much more delay and they wouldn't get back to Lipang in time for the appointment.

"I wonder if the "kindred beings" will give them another chance if they miss this one?" Roger fretted.

Kerri bit her lip. "Maybe we should go look for him."

"Bang!" A sharp crack reverberated from deep in the jungle. Unmistakable: a gunshot. A congregate of birds startled from the trees, alarmed into flight.

"What the hell was that?" Kerri exclaimed, jumping up from the inflatable boat. "Sounded like shooting!"

"A hunter? Oh, damn it! Not now."

Kerri scanned the forest wall anxiously. "Now we gotta go find him."

They beached the boat higher and began tying it to a log. Then there was a second shot, sounding closer, echoing.

Both of them sprinted up the wide beach toward the tangle of vines and trees. Just as they got to the edge they nearly collided with Pongo, who came stumbling out, his arm and head bleeding.

Shrieking, Kerri grabbed him. "Oh my god, what happened?"

The ape was panting. "That man. That same policeman again, from Santa Barbara. He's back there in the jungle. I don't know how...I couldn't believe it. He shot me. But I got away."

"A Santa Barbara cop?" Roger gaped.

"Is this where you're shot?" Gently, Kerri took Pongo's huge arm in her hands.

Pongo gestured. "My shoulder. It's not bad, I don't think it went in."

"Let me look." Kerri examined his wound, tearing off her shirt to wipe around it, then applied pressure.

"Thank god, you're right. It grazed you, it's not deep. Here, hold this against his wound, Roger." Her voice shook with rage. "Where is he? I'm gonna go kill that fucker."

Pongo sank down on the sand, heaving. "Wait, Kerri, no. I choked him out. He's unconscious." He stopped, catching his breath. "When I came down the tree he was right there below me, aiming. He shot me before I could do anything. I dropped and he put the gun at my head. Said he was taking me back to his boat."

At this the others jerked their eyes over to the trawler, still hugging the beach. A man on the foredeck was watching them with binoculars.

"That boat over there..." said Roger, beginning to realize how this could have happened.

"I started in front of him but then I let a big branch snap back in his face. I jumped on him and his gun went off again. I got my other arm around his neck and choked him. He'll stay down for awhile."

"Your head's bleeding too." Kerri said, parting his hair, looking for the wound.

"It's nothing, I just bumped it when I was getting away. I'll be okay." He turned to Roger. "What time is it?"

Chapter 45

The "Mori's" engines were glowing when they once again caught sight of Lipang's low form. They had pushed the yacht to its limits, both throttles wide open all the way. It was late afternoon.

During the run Pongo's wounds had been cleaned and bandaged and there was a discussion about the harrowing incident in the jungle.

"That's astounding," Celine gasped. "You're sure it was the same officer you fought with back in Santa Barbara?"

"No doubt about it," Pongo replied. "I recognized him. And he told me he'd chased me halfway around the world."

Celine spread her hands. "I don't get it. What for? As far as my attorneys have told me, the investigation was closed. Why would that man still be after Pongo, months later and thousands of miles from home?"

"Good question," responded Roger. "But if he followed him this far and somehow he found him way down here in the middle of nowhere, then he's not gonna stop back there at Sangihe. Something else that we don't know about has got to be going on. This is just totally crazy." They all looked at each other.

"Maybe he's crazy. Why didn't you kill him?" Kerri demanded of Pongo. "He would have killed you."

Pongo looked down. "No, Kerri. I don't want to kill anyone or anything. I just want us all to get away. Even if it's too late for George."

"Okay, look," Roger asserted. "Even if he's still coming, we're way ahead of him. That trawler he was probably on can't go nearly as fast as we can. So we've bought a little time. Plus, he's gonna be looking for this huge yacht. Once we get you all to shore on Lipang, we'll take off with the "Mori" and be a decoy. He might find us but he won't find all of you."

Kerri smacked her fist into her palm. "I'll be looking forward to meeting him."

The sun was closing on the horizon when the crew launch was lowered from its davits. It bobbed in the swell, tied alongside the amidships gangway. Roger checked that basic supplies were aboard: blankets, flashlights, packages of food, water bottles, some ponchos, a few folding chairs.

He jogged back up to the master suite. Everyone was waiting, uneasily sitting on the couches. The shock of all the day's events had changed what should have been optimism into fear and anxiety. Celine was in her wheelchair, wrapped in a long tan raincoat and slouch hat. For all the bravery she possessed, she now wore an apprehensive expression on her withered face. Everyone looked up as Roger came through the door.

"The boat's ready."

The brief trip over to the island was restively silent. Even though something monumental was about to transpire, their minds were on George and the bizarre man likely still chasing them.

They made an uneventful landing, approaching a sandy bar on the low tide and running directly up on it. There was a hasty unloading process. Roger carried Celine and then Abby over the shallow water between the boat and dry sand. Kerri lunged back and forth, helping to haul all the supplies. The Orangs fended for themselves, leaping the gunwales to wade ashore.

Then they were all there, minus their quiet little hero. The setting sun filtered through ominous clouds and Roger looked around despairingly at the group huddled in the half-light. Timely and momentous things should be said, he was thinking, but the words didn't come.

This was it.

Kerri came unglued, tears rolling down her cheeks. She went around hugging each of the apes, sobbing goodbyes. She tenderly held Celine for a long time, then embraced Abby last of all. Roger followed her and it was a moment of tremendous sadness.

They lingered on for another minute, artificially finding things to do, helping to set up a few of the chairs and distribute some flashlights. But the daylight was failing rapidly and Pongo motioned to Roger that it was time to go.

"Are you sure this is going to be alright?" Roger could not help asking Celine one last time. "I mean, I'm just getting more and more concerned about just leaving you all alone. Especially with that guy out there. Shouldn't we, maybe—"

"You should just get back on the boat now." Celine smiled firmly from under the brim of her hat. "Remember? The decoy? We all love you both, my dears. We'll never forget you. So, please, go on now, you two. We'll be fine. Be happy for us. Goodbye, Roger. Goodbye, Kerri. Take good care of each other." She reached her hands out, one for each of them, and they held on to her for a last brief moment.

Warm water swirled around their legs as they waded to climb aboard the launch. Backing away from the sand bar, Roger began to turn the boat around in deeper water. He had brought along his little camera and somehow had the presence of mind to snap a couple of pictures as final keepsakes. Kerri was holding onto him with one hand, blinking through her tears at the group on the beach, waving farewell.

Then the launch gathered speed, bouncing off toward the shimmering white palace at anchor three quarters of a mile away. Roger and Kerri kept turning to look back until they finally rounded the tip of the island and the far beach slipped from their sight. The last thing they saw was a poignant vignette: everyone waving, some of them turning on their flashlights, distant points of light like fireflies dancing amid the indigo gloom of dusk.

It all seemed to have gone by in seconds. Roger was left feeling absolutely empty. He imagined beforehand that there would be enough time to say all the things that he'd thought about, but there had been none.

Back at the "Mori" they glumly climbed aboard and made their way aft. The launch was swung up and the big yacht got underway. At their stand-off position about ten minutes later the sky was dark and Lipang had receded out of sight.

The newlyweds were bone-tired. Neither had succeeded in getting any sleep the previous night. Now all they could think about was the brave little group huddled on the beach, awaiting their fateful rendezvous. Roger tried to tell a funny story or two, about things the apes had said or done, but realized this was only deepening the sense of loss. They went out on the afterdeck to lie on the chaises. Perhaps they might see something: a light in the sky, a glow or a streak. Exhausted as they were, they couldn't just go off to bed.

"What if the beings don't show up?" Roger worried aloud.

"Celine made Chung promise not to go check on them."

Roger sighed. "Well, she didn't make us promise." He looked off in the direction of the invisible island. "First light, we'll go check."

The "Mori's" engines murmured peacefully as the craft held position, hove-to in waters too deep for an anchor. They tried their best to stay awake, chatting about this and that. They saw nothing. Sometime after one a.m. fatigue overcame them and the vigil was defeated.

The sound of the buzzing intercom snapped Roger awake. He stumbled up and grabbed the handset on the bulkhead. It was Chung.

"Sorry to wake you, sir. The watch says a fishing trawler has approached nearby, on radar. They've stopped and their lights are off. You asked me to inform you of any such thing."

Roger's gut clenched. "Right, Chung. Hang on a second." His attention was drawn to the faint sound of an outboard motor. With his diminished hearing, for a moment he thought he'd imagined it. No, there it was again. A small boat with an outboard motor, nearby. He leapt to the rail, peering into the blackness. They had intentionally left floodlights on to draw in the trawler if it appeared. Now reflective strips on an Avon about a quarter mile away flickered, showing it was bouncing through the swell.

"Wake up, Kerri!" he yelled. "Somebody's out there."

Now they both watched the little boat as it slowed for a moment in the darkness, seeming to turn their way.

"Figure it's him?"

"Gotta be. Let's get ready."

"Don't forget he's got a gun."

Just then a searing beam issued from the bridge deck, illuminating Butch Turnbull alone on his dinghy. The crew had put him in a spotlight.

Roger was about to order Chung to make way toward the little craft, maybe try to swamp it, but just then it took off again, heading toward nearby Lipang, its outboard motor screaming.

Chapter 46

It is a little-known fact that most police dogs (K-9s) have much in common with a bullet as it is fired. They cannot be called back. There are rare exceptions, but when released by the handler and chasing a suspect, K-9s enter a mental state known as "drive mode". The animal has but one focus: to pursue, catch and kill the subject. Most people believe that a trained K-9, once it has caught the subject, can then be called off by a verbal command from the handler. But in the dog's mind, catching (biting) the suspect isn't enough. The animal hasn't "won" yet. So, in almost every case of K-9 deployment, the handler must physically choke-out the dog, using a special collar, in order to force it to release its bite-hold on the suspect.

For retired CHP sergeant Butch Turnbull, the sequence of events was a bit different from a K-9 pursuit but the result was much the same. After being choked unconscious by Pongo in the Sangihe rainforest, Turnbull was lost to himself. He'd once been a controlled, logical officer of the law, sworn to protect and serve. But after coming to under the vines and realizing that he had again lost a physical contest to this otherworldly thing, this talking ape, this nemesis, he'd lost all reserve and become a different being. His immersion in the hunt for this hairy beast and the others like him, the perceived arrogance of these mysterious people with their mansions and jets and yachts, their devious conspiracies; the defeats, frustrations and delays—all had combined to utterly take him over. He was in "drive mode".

Of course, he ordered "Bajau Kee's" captain to immediately pursue the "Mori".

"What is this all, Tarnball?" the captain probed, uneasily. "I look at people on the beach after I hear you shoot."

"So?"

"They have a big Mawas with them, is ape, with blood. Is illegal, you shoot this animal, much trouble in this country. Why you do that?"

Turnbull spun on the captain. "None of your goddamn business. I pay you to follow that boat, so just shut up and get moving. We're losing time." To emphasize his point, he drew his shirt back to reveal the .45 automatic tucked in his waistband.

Tracking with radar, they followed and finally drew near "Mori" in the wee hours. Turnbull instructed the captain to douse all lights and close to within a half mile, then lower the Avon. "Wait here until you see me fire the flare gun," he barked. "Then come get me."

On the inflatable Turnbull made straight for the coruscating lights of the "Mori", intending to board by force if necessary. He didn't really have a plan. But as he got closer, a blinding beam was trained on him. He slowed, then something clicked, his hunter's instinct. He was lit up, so the crew aboard "Mori" knew he was here. Two people were visible at the rail, watching him. And yet the big yacht hadn't moved. There wasn't any commotion, no one had guns out, they hadn't fired any warning shots. If they wanted to, they could put it in gear and leave him far behind, just like they had back at Sangihe. Why hadn't they? Because whatever they were protecting wasn't onboard that yacht, that's why. This was a head-fake. The prize was on the little island nearby. He just knew it. He opened his throttle and wheeled around.

"He's heading for Lipang!" Roger exclaimed.

There was no time for discussion. Charging down the ladder to the davits they lowered their own inflatable and sped away into the darkness. Again, they had the faster boat, but Turnbull had a slight head-start.

"Come up behind him," Roger yelled. With spray hitting them in the face, he gave Kerri the wheel. "I'll jump over and tackle him."

"What if he starts shooting?"

Roger grabbed the hand-held spotlight. "Put the beam in his face. Blind him!" Now over the sound of their own motor they could make out the whine of the other boat's outboard, very close in front of them. Roger flicked on the spotlight and there was Turnbull, only about fifty feet off, going hell for leather. He was wearing some kind of vest, possibly body-armor. He looked over his shoulder for a split second but didn't slow down.

Just then both boats rounded the point of the island and to Roger's horror he could clearly see twinkling lights on the little beach, right where they had left the group. They were all still there. The two small boats raced directly toward them.

Less than a hundred yards from the beach Kerri had the nose of their craft right at the stern of Turnbull's dinghy. Roger made the leap and grappled with Turnbull. It wasn't even close. The trained fighter hooked a couple of sharp punches into Roger's gut, knocking the air out of him. Then he shoved him overboard. Both boats side-by-side now, still pounding at full speed, and Kerri tried slamming Turnbull's boat with hers. To no avail. She made a last desperate try, abandoning her boat to jump over to Turnbull's.

"Fuck you!" she screamed, jerking him backward and landing a solid punch to his kidney. Strangely, it had no effect; it felt like punching a sand bag. The body armor. This fight lasted a few more seconds than had Roger's and she got in a good elbow shot to his head, but even Kerri was no match for the hulking martial-arts expert. A few quick blows from hammer-like fists and a knee to the crotch and she was down on the thwarts of the dinghy, gasping, nearly unconscious in pain.

In helplessness the group watched the brief battle-in-motion unfolding offshore. At first they had only heard the boats coming but were unable to see who it was. Then as the jousting craft drew closer and the spotlight came on, horror seized them.

"Oh my God, that's Roger and Kerri," Celine gasped.

"And that's the man, in the other boat," said Pongo, voice shaking. "That's him."

Seconds later Turnbull's boat ran up on the sand and he jumped out, drawing his pistol. Its laser aiming-beam and bright barrel light illuminated the six Orangutans and two old women clutching their little flashlights, sitting ducks, only a few feet away.

There hadn't been anything they could do from the beach, they were unarmed. But as Turnbull came ashore, Pongo started toward him.

"No, Pongo, don't!" yelled Emily, but it was too late. A flash burst from Turnbull's gun muzzle and Pongo doubled over sharply, collapsing to the sand.

"Any more of you freaks want to get shot?" Turnbull bellowed. Then he began rasping out commands: "Don't fucking move. Let me see your hands. Don't move or you will be shot."

"How dare you? This is an outrage! I demand that you leave us alone immediately!" Celine's voice rang out, sounding stronger than it ever had before.

"Shut-up, you old bitch," he snapped, placing the laser point right on her chest. "All of you, keep your yaps shut. Hear me? I got you now and I'll tell you what to do."

Pongo made piteous moaning sounds, gurgling, clearly struggling to breathe.

"At least let us help him!" Emily pleaded. "Please sir, he's dying."

Turnbull was right up on them now, a shaved-headed monster in black clothing, his face smeared with camouflage paint. "That's his own fault. Shut your pie-hole. Don't you move." With his free hand he pulled a bunch of nylon tie strips from his vest, tossing them at Abby's feet. "Start tying everyone's hands behind their backs. The monkeys first. Do it now."

Abby raised her chin. "Go to hell. I'll do nothing of the kind."

"The fuck you won't, bitch," Turnbull snarled, taking a step that way.

"Stop it! Please sir, you don't know what you're doing," came Roger's voice from the shallows. He had managed to swim in and was hobbling ashore.

Turnbull whipped around and fired a warning shot over his head.

"Stay there!" he screamed. "One last time, stop resisting, all of you. Don't move. The next shot goes in your face!"

"Oh, no, no," Kerri sobbed, sitting up in the boat. "Pongo!" she called out.

But Pongo was now motionless, crumpled.

Turnbull did indeed have them. It was over. He reached into his vest and pulled out a flare gun. Fumbling with it, one handed, he raised it over his head.

At that precise moment came the snow. It didn't start slowly. It dumped like a dam breaking: all at once, snowfall so thick and intense that it was instantly impossible to see more than a few inches. Snow, real snow falling, seemingly from nowhere, on a night-shrouded tropical beach where the temperature was in the low 80's. There was no wind and it cascaded straight down, coating all of them in seconds, a suffocating curtain. Along with it descended the cold, beyond polar, a freezing plummet below zero. "What the fuck?" came Turnbull's muffled curse. His flare gun did not fire.

A few yards away Roger had made it to the side of the boat where Kerri was huddling. He grabbed her arm. There wasn't even time for words.

A blue-white radiance burst from within the spot where Turnbull stood with the group. A silent explosion, piercing the snow curtain, painful in its intensity. It was a like a snow globe with a nuclear warhead detonating inside. Blinded, Roger and Kerri had to look away. There was no sound at all, none. From there maybe it took two more seconds, possibly three.

The light disappeared, the snow ceased, the cold vanished. Warm, humid air rushed back in. Roger and Kerri, both thickly covered with snow, gaped toward the darkened beach. Still no sound. Kerri reached for the boat's spotlight and flicked the switch. There was the shoreline, pristine white under a fresh snowfall, and absolutely nothing and no one else. All of them, Butch Turnbull included, were gone.

Chapter 47

Later that morning Roger and Kerri sat holding hands on the large couch in "Mori's" master suite. The yacht's two senior officers sat stiffly in the facing chairs.

Lau and Chung had at first bowed politely but now stared at the two Americans for a moment. They turned toward each other and initiated a hushed conversation in Chinese. This went on for about a minute, during which the mechanical blankness of the two men's facial expressions revealed nothing. Neither man gestured with his hands or even slightly raised his voice during the exchange. Finally they fell silent and turned back to the young couple.

"Mr. Caldwell, do you yourself know where Mrs. Stertevant and Mrs. Horvath have gone to?" Chung asked.

"No, sir. I'm afraid I do not."

"And you, Mrs. Caldwell? Do you know?" He looked at Kerri. Her eyes were puffy from crying.

"No, Herbert. She really didn't want anybody to know."

Captain Lau said something in Chinese and Chung translated: "Who was the man you followed last night in the Avon?"

Roger cleared his throat. "He...turned out to be nobody."

"Nobody? With all due respect, sir, you seemed quite anxious to pursue him."

"Oh, that. Well, we just wanted to make sure he wasn't someone who might disturb Mrs. Stertevant and her party before they were picked up. That's all. But, as I said, he was nobody."

"I see." Chung sighed, stymied. He nodded to the captain and said a few words. The two stood up, keeping their caps tucked under their arms. Roger rose along with them. Chung addressed him in a respectfully formal tone.

"Mr. Caldwell, you must understand that nothing like this has ever happened to either Captain Lau or myself at any time during our careers in maritime service. There is much about all this that appears to be irregular. Now, if Mrs. Stertevant and Mrs. Horvath had simply disappeared without explaining to us and leaving the documentation, we would be required by law to conduct a search for them and notify the local authorities to assist us. There would be an inquest by the maritime board in Jakarta. However, because of the meeting they had with us and the documentation provided, we must conclude that there has been no foul play. We apologize if we have inconvenienced you."

"No need, Chung. We understand."

"But now, we must raise another matter. Mrs. Stertevant was the charterer of record for this vessel. As her heirs, do you wish to continue the charter, sir, and if so, how do you wish us to proceed?"

Roger had an answer ready. "Actually, gentlemen, my wife and I would like to go home," he said in a soft voice. "Our airplane is waiting in Singapore."

From a half mile away the crew of the "Bajau Kee" watched "Mori" depart the area. The trawler's captain then made for Lipang to investigate why Turnbull had not returned. By now all traces of the snow had vanished. The crew retrieved their Avon from the beach and conducted a brief, halfhearted search of the area. Nothing. Combing through Turnbull's cabin, they found $17,000 in U.S. currency and some ammunition in his duffle bag. There was no passport or other documents. Having hated the man from the beginning, and having suffered daily from his insults and scolding, their decision was simple. As far as the captain knew, Turnbull had contacted no one while he was aboard the trawler. The captain knew of no one to notify about his disappearance. Turnbull had told them nothing of his plans when he had left the trawler the previous night. He could have been taken away onboard the "Mori". Who could say?

"Bajau Kee" got underway for her home port, with the captain making plans to purchase new equipment for the upcoming crabbing season.

Chapter 48

When Roger and Kerri arrived back at Glenwhylden, they were in a whole new reality. No longer mere employee or visitor, they were now the owners of this remarkable place. Left standing together on a glaringly lit-up stage, all eyes were expectantly fixed on them.

A state of shock still lingered from all that had happened in the hours before they left Lipang. There had been George's death, of course. Then they had witnessed Pongo being shot, perhaps fatally, and an apparently deranged man commandeering their loved ones. It had been nothing whatsoever like the peaceful departure they expected.

And had it, in fact, been a departure at all? Given what they saw that fateful night, could the entire group have been vaporized on the spot? There wasn't so much as a lawn chair remaining. Perhaps the "kindred beings" had merely eliminated some troublesome remnants of an earlier accident. But, if that was the case, why were Roger and Kerri left behind? There were no answers to these questions, nor did it appear that there ever would be.

The staff at Glenwhylden received the news that Celine, Abby, and the apes would never return with understandable surprise and anxiety.

"This is what she wanted," Roger assured them at an initial meeting. "We really can't say more, but as far as we know they're in a place where they want to be and they're safe. He looked around at all the alarmed faces. "Please don't anyone worry. Everyone who wants to stay will keep their jobs."

"Since we're married now, we'll live here and raise a family," Kerri added, holding Roger's hand. "Celine wanted that, too. You're all needed, just as much as before."

But after only about a week, it became clear to both Roger and Kerri that things should not and could not be as they had been before all the changes had come to Glenwhylden.

They were sitting at the breakfast table. "Even with a family eventually, this house is way too big for us, isn't it, Roger?" she said out of the clear blue.

He smiled. "I'd been thinking the same thing."

"Well, Celine said we should do whatever we thought was best, remember? We should decide. It's our house now. So isn't there something better we could do with this huge place?"

It didn't take long for them to come up with their own "plan". This was the way forward from the sadness over the loss of their friends. Celine had been absolutely right: they should put their mark on the world and help others. And just as Celine had admonished "Not in my name", Roger and Kerri decided, not in their names either.

The "Simian Caucus Foundation" took shape rapidly. The gates of Glenwhylden were thrown open and several schools were established on this grand campus. Chancellor Whitney Polk, Jr. was placed in charge of the day-to-day operations. Tasteful new buildings were constructed, with faculty and additional staff hired. The "George Villafranco Institute for Botanical Research" was founded and soon had some brilliant minds at work looking for new medicines derived from rainforest plants. Students came from around the world to study amid the inspiring surroundings of Glenwhylden.

Down in Borneo and Sumatra, Roger and Kerri endowed the "Pongo Pygmaeus Technology Fund," dedicated to engendering high-tech and modern agricultural industries to help replace the jobs lost when the old logging industry was greatly reduced. They partnered with local entrepreneurs who themselves had ideas, and turned these into jobs and a better standard of living for countless people. The fund also bought large areas of wilderness land to keep as perpetual forest preserves for the Mawas and several rescue facilities ceased to have money problems.

Kerri started a line of eco-friendly clothing, simply called "Betty". Designs for the original line utilized some of Betty's old sketches. These were soon selling like hotcakes, with all of the proceeds going to other charities. A cookbook with her recipes also caught on.

There were other legacies to be honored: Artod's collection of elegiac poems about the rainforest was published and an annual prize for excellence in poetry established in his name. The "Chloé Poe Project", headquartered in the former Marsh Meadows house, guided inner-city children toward the pleasures of studying contemporary music. And the "Emily Forrestal Charitable Trust" supported research and services for caring for the aging at numerous hospitals and universities. Her name also graced a new art museum in Santa Barbara. Some of her original watercolors competed favorably among Celine's collection of masterpieces by famous artists.

In a vast, renovated former factory in downtown Cleveland, Ohio, the "Trent Alanadale Center for Performing Arts" was commissioned, with theaters and a school.

Blauhimmelheim was converted into a "Conference Center for the Promotion of International Peace." It served as a refuge for high-level government types who needed a quiet, neutral place to work things out.

And Chuck and "Arjuna" were given a new mission as well: flying critically ill children and their families to hospitals and care centers around the world. He was in the air nearly every day, and never happier. Hwang Shu studied for his R.N. certificate and became a fixture on these mercy flights.

After giving over much of Glenwhylden's main house and other buildings to the activities of the schools and foundations, Roger and Kerri moved into the top floor of the house. It had all they needed: two bedrooms, a library, kitchen, bath.

Their youth and the mystery of their ascent to power were endlessly speculated about. Kerri's resistance to fashionable dress spawned fads. They became Santa Barbara's most watched power couple. They were deemed interesting, charming and quirky. Roger kept the Porsche, though he could no longer use it. Whenever he and Kerri went out she usually drove them in her grandfather's old Dodge pickup. In his dotage, "Doc", as everyone called him, had taken up residence in the forest cottage where Roger once lived.

Kerri went on with her education; first an equivalency exam for her high school diploma, then a B.S. in zoology which she pulled off in just over two years of study.

In August of 1993, she gave birth to their first child, a girl christened Emily. With all the staff and students competing for doting privileges, for awhile the child was in peril of being spoiled. The arrival of her brother, George, in early December of '94, evened the course of Emily's sweet corruption.

Roger's sight and hearing had not completely gone. He could still make out shapes and the newest hearing aids gave him at least some ability to hear. What helped most of all was George and Pongo's gift, the "other way" of perceiving. It had become like a sixth sense, and to most observers Roger could appear normal.

On a windy autumn night, he awakened in the wee hours and lay with eyes open, unable to regain sleep. The Santa Ana winds were cranked up, shrieking and tearing at the windows. He listened in awe, gently stroking Kerri's head as she peacefully slumbered next to him. He always worried when the winds roared like this, concerned for the estate's marvelous old trees. He decided to get out of bed and take a stroll—get a sense of how things were holding up.

He pulled on a robe and padded into the hall. At the children's room he listened in; both indisputably in dreamland. He wandered downstairs, passing darkened classrooms and laboratories.

Battering gusts lunged and swirled but Glenwhylden stood unmoved, with nothing so much as a tiny creak in response. Roger ambled into the main salon, now a student lunch room, and approached the expansive bank of windows. He knew the inky sky would be bell clear—always the case when the Santa Anas blow. He pushed his hands deeper into the pockets of his robe and used his extra-vision to project up through the panes, envisioning the magnified jangling stars. Absently lingering on a familiar outline, suddenly he realized what it was. Scorpio. He smiled a little and located the tail, then shifted his focus just to the left, as George had instructed on their last night together. There. Concentrating his awareness hard at the miniscule point of luminance, he got an urge. He raised his right hand to give a jaunty little wave. "Hi guys. Miss you."

On the trek back to his bed, he passed by the open door of the upstairs library. A faint grinding noise coming from the shelf of the credenza caught his attention and he paused. His fax machine was muttering, probably a tedious missive from a distant banker or an administrator of one of the foundations. This was quite common—he often woke to find a whole pile of overnight faxes waiting for him, which his secretary would then help him wade through. Anyone with extensive overseas business becomes accustomed to the twenty-four hour workday. Roger hesitated, sighed, then walked into the room. Snapping on a couple of lamps enabled him to see at least a little better. He sat down behind the desk for a moment, waiting for the fax to complete printing. On the opposite wall hung a pair of gold-leafed frames. These encased his most treasured possessions. In the top frame were two letters, matted side by side. The one on the left began: "Dear Mrs. Stertevant, My name is Roger Caldwell." The companion letter opened with: "Dear Roger Caldwell, Thank you for writing and expressing your interest in Glenwhylden." The second frame, directly below, displayed a photograph. The Orangs are grouped on a sunset-mauve tropical beach, with Celine Stertevant in her wheelchair and Abigail Horvath standing just behind. It was the last photo Roger snapped as the launch pulled away that final evening on Lipang.

The grinding noise behind him ceased. He turned, wondering what the fax might say. As good as his "vision" had become, he still couldn't use it to read words on a page. This one was different though. It was handwritten, not typed; that much he could make out. He took it into the bedroom to wake Kerri.

"What is it, Roger?" She rubbed her eyes as he turned on a reading lamp. "Is it the baby?"

"No, no. He's asleep. I'm sorry. It's probably nothing, and if it is you can punch me. I was just up, you know, and I heard the fax machine. It seemed like something unusual. I don't know why."

She sighed. "What time is it?"

"Oh, about three, I guess." He handed her the paper.

"Roger," her voice was mildly annoyed. "You get faxes all the time."

"Please? Just this once."

She rolled over and groaned. "This better be good, mister."

She held it under the lamp for inspection and a fierce bolt surged through her body. The scribbled note had an unmistakably childish, yet determined caster. No one else she had ever known produced such distinctive handwriting. Roger heard her gasp "Oh my God!"

He sat on the bed beside her. "Uh, oh. What is it?" The paper rustled, then he heard her begin crying. "Oh, crap, don't keep me hanging. What the hell is it, Kerri?"

She put her arm around him. "Roger. Listen to this."

****

Dear Roger,

We're all waving back to you. Not supposed to do this, but everybody wanted to. We're all fine, wonderful. George is here. He didn't die like we thought. Even the man who chased us is here, but he's our good friend now. Wish we could be there to play with the children. Don't know if we'll ever be back, but we'll see you again. That's for sure. We all miss you and Kerri very much.

Love, Pongo

****

Made in the USA
San Bernardino, CA
16 February 2020